RULE OF THREE

BARANOVA BRATVA

MISTI WILDS

Rule of Three

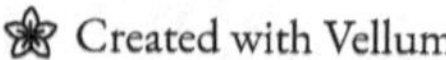 Created with Vellum

To my Angel.
This book wouldn't exist without you. 🖤

CONTENTS

Author's Note — 1
1. Valentina — 2
2. Valentina — 8
3. Andrei — 18
4. Valentina — 28
5. Ezra — 36
6. Valentina — 44
7. Valentina — 53
8. Mikhail — 63
9. Valentina — 76
10. Valentina — 89
11. Andrei — 103
12. Ezra — 113
13. Andrei — 125
14. Valentina — 140
15. Valentina — 153
16. Valentina — 164
17. Mikhail — 177
18. Valentina — 184
19. Valentina — 198
20. Andrei — 211
21. Valentina — 218
22. Valentina — 231
23. Andrei — 237
24. Valentina — 243
25. Valentina — 257
26. Ezra — 268
27. Valentina — 280
28. Valentina — 290
29. Valentina — 307
30. Valentina — 320

31. Valentina   326
32. Andrei   333

Russian Terminology   341
Acknowledgments   343
About the Author   345
Also by Misti Wilds   347

Author's Note

Rule of Three is a smut-stuffed, Russian mafia, why choose, dark romance that ends on one hell of a cliffhanger (that's absolutely fucking delicious).

For content warnings, please check my website: MistiWilds.com

CHAPTER 1

VALENTINA

Five Years Earlier

THE THIN PARCHMENT in my hand slips from my fingers and flutters to the ground. I press my palm to my chest and shut my eyes, willing the room to stop spinning.

It can't be true.

But I'd recognize my mother's handwriting anywhere. There's no mistaking it; she wrote the letter. The only thing I don't understand is *why*.

Why would she leave the life she spent decades building?

Carefully, I remove the white veil from my head and set it down on the ottoman by my feet. Piece by piece, I remove every glittering ornament from my body, starting with the dazzling diamond earrings that sparkle every time I turn my head. The golden bracelet comes next, then the set of rings on my fingers. None of it matters. Not the satin gown hugging my hips. Not the hundreds of people waiting in the chapel. Not the promise I made to the man I love.

In the end, there's only the truth.

Before she died, my mother wanted to leave this life behind. She wanted *me* to leave with her.

If there's one thing I am, it's a good daughter.

And good daughters always follow their mother's wishes.

~

Present Day

The rules for being a mafia princess aren't written in ink.

They're written in blood. The kind that flows from one generation to the next, passed down from generations of good daughters who become perfect wives, until finally, they become mothers raising their own good daughters.

As one of those daughters raised within the mafia, I can recite the rules blindfolded with my hands tied behind my back. Knelt by my bedside in nightly prayer, or in front of whichever man decides I look better on my knees.

It's something every good mafia daughter can do, no matter the circumstances. We're taught to follow the rules. Keep our heads down. Smile pretty. Spread our legs.

After eighteen years of preparation, it should have been easy for me to follow my mother's teachings and step into the role I was born to fill.

All I ever wanted was to make my mother proud. To be just like her — radiant as a summer sun every hour of the day. She was regal like that, undaunted no matter the storm rumbling on the horizon.

I thought following in my mother's footsteps would make her happy. Prove that not only am I a good daughter, but a perfect mafia princess, too.

Even after she died, I thought marrying the man she and my father chose for me was what she would have wanted. I'd be a wife, then a mother, just like she was.

I thought I knew what she would have wanted for me.

But for the first time in my life, I was wrong.

Following the rules should have been easy.

Breaking them should have been impossible.

A mafia princess doesn't suddenly decide to run away on her wedding day. . .

Unless, of course, her mother tells her to.

I take a deep breath and shake my head, hoping to dislodge the recurring thoughts from my mind. They aren't helpful anymore; they're distracting. The minute I stepped past city lines and entered Baranova territory, I haven't been able to get images from my wedding day out of my head.

It's the last time I was here. Decked out in white and gold from head to toe. Putting on my prettiest smile. Ready to sell my soul to make my parents proud.

What a load of *bullshit.*

If the past five years have taught me anything, it's that living your life for others' gratification is stupid.

Now, I'm living for my own.

My fists clench as I stare down the latest obstacle to my desires.

A road block. *Literally.*

The wrought iron gates to the Baranova estate are always closed. Night or day. Rain or shine. I can't think of a time I've seen them open.

Today is no exception.

They're locked up tight. No one is getting in or out without proper authorization, including their long lost mafia princess.

After five years out of the city, you'd think I would have a plan for breaking into my childhood home. A team assembled for this kind of thing. Security, or backup, or at least a friggin' grappling hook or something.

Instead, I've got a pair of worn combat boots, a skirt I snagged from the thrift store a few blocks away, the plainest, gray sweater in existence, and a whole lot of courage.

My father is not a forgiving man.

The minute he sees me, he'll condemn me to whatever punishment he sees fit for my crimes. Abandonment. Breaking a vow. Being a bad daughter. The possibilities are endless for both the sentencing and what reparations follow.

But I'm not here to *stay*. I'm not planning on coming back into the fold of the Bratva. I'm here for one thing and one thing only.

Answers.

A girl shouldn't lose her mother without warning, and she sure as shit shouldn't still be left wondering what happened to her, five years later.

My breath catches as the trees overhead rustle in the breeze, dropping crisp brown leaves on my head. Movement out of the corner of my eye makes my heart beat double-time.

I haven't been invited back home. I'm trespassing on dangerous ground by coming here unannounced. *Especially* after undoubtably pissing off not only my father for taking his only heir away from him, but my fiancée for walking out on him.

My punishment will be severe.

Standing here being nervous about it won't solve my problems, though.

Climbing this damned fence *will*.

I hike my skirt up a little higher and plant my boot on the first rung of iron. My pulse races as I pull myself up off the ground and start climbing. Autumn leaves fall like rain around me, and I pray that it's enough camouflage to keep me hidden from any wandering eyes. My father always kept tight security on the grounds, probably to keep my mother and me *in* rather than keep anything *out.*

I reach the top of the fence and breathlessly peer down the other side. The drop looks more intimidating from above than it did from the ground. I throw my right leg over the side and notch the toe of my boot against one of the bars, securing my weight as I swing my other leg—

My left boot tightens painfully around my foot as I try to swing my remaining leg over, the laces caught on something.

Lovely.

As I try to wriggle my boot free, panic sets in with each passing second.

If my father catches me, he might wrap his iron fist around my throat and *squeeze.* But if one of his guards sees me perched atop their precious fence, they might shoot first and ask questions later.

If I can't free my boot from this *godforsaken fence*, I might have to gnaw off my own ankle and crawl to the back door of my father's house, the shame from my botched break-in killing me before the blood loss ever could.

I grimace at all those outcomes.

None of them get me even remotely close to why I came here.

Which means, none of those outcomes are acceptable.

When frantic leg tugging and toe wriggling doesn't work, I start rotating my ankle and trying, desperately, to will my foot to shrink by two sizes to squeeze it out of the chokehold knot my laces have tied themselves into.

All of a sudden, something in my boot shifts and it works. My foot slides free, I swing my leg over, and I can finally call this nightmare of a climb—

Riiiiiip

The next swift breeze blows more than just the leaves free —it blows my skirt right off my ass.

I watch in horror as the fabric slides gracefully off my thighs and catches in a nearby tree limb, the black fabric fluttering in the wind like a flag announcing my presence to the entire freaking world.

Hey, look up here to find the freak on the fence!

I should have worn pants to this little B&E attempt, but the laundromat ate my only pair last night, leaving the mini skirt I found on clearance as my sole option.

Just another sign that karma's out to get me for my transgressions, and she's one mean bitch.

My only saving grace in this *fine* hour of need is that my ass is *fat*. If one of the guards sees my pretty peach hanging in the air, maybe they'll be so distracted that they won't shoot me, after all.

I cling to that hope as I barrel down the other side of the fence, moving as fast as I dare with only one boot, until I slip and fall the remaining two feet to the ground.

I hit the grass *hard*, yelping in my surprise. Thankfully, there's not a soul in sight. Not a single guard patrols the grounds. No glimpse of my father strolling through the gardens.

No sign of my fiancée out here, either, thank god.

I'm not sure I could take coming face-to-face with my ex when I'm in an oversized gray sweater and the plainest gray panties in existence.

Not that I care what kind of panties he sees me in.

He shouldn't see me in *any* panties. Period.

I chew the inside of my cheek as I mull over which section of the house to infiltrate. Preferably one with a bedroom, now that my cheeks are on display.

First, find pants.

Next, find my father.

And finally, get answers about what *really* happened to Mom.

Chapter 2

Valentina

After an uneventful sprint across the lawn, I enter the estate with total ease. The back door opens with a simple push. It's not even locked.

At first, I'm eternally grateful. *Giddy,* even, like I'm a master thief who's just broken into the richest vault in the city.

As soon as my eyes adjust to the shadows inside, however, a violent shiver runs down my spine and I regret *everything*.

I've walked straight into a morgue.

Gleaming silver tables, long enough to hold a body, neatly line one wall, with floor-to-ceiling freezers making up the wall behind them. Of all the medical instruments and machines in the room, only one stands out—the one splattered red.

Carefully, I step toward the odd one out to find dark red liquid pooled across the far end, with bloodied bandages and giant tweezers and a scalpel and a bowl with little metal bits scattered around inside and—

I swallow hard and turn away, *noping* right out of there.

I'm not here to investigate or snoop around in the underbelly of the mansion. I'm here to see my father.

From where I'm standing in the middle of the room, there are two doors out of this place. My sense of direction is shit, so I pick one on a whim. Carefully turning the knob, I open the door and peer inside the room. Slivers of sunlight peek in around thick curtains, casting enough light for me to know that this is, in fact, a bedroom.

Bingo.

A smart woman might turn on the light, but a *stealthy* one moves in the dark. I tiptoe toward one of the shadowed pieces of furniture against the wall and start feeling around for a clothes drawer. As I pull open the topmost one, I rattle whatever sits on top of the dresser, knocking invisible objects over. One such thing rolls to the edge and *thumps* to the floor.

To be honest, I don't care about a few broken baubles as long as I find some freaking pants. Goosebumps race down my bare thighs as a chill settles over my skin, and I paw around in the drawer for the first scrap of clothing I can find.

Except, there's only knickknacks and cold glass *somethings* in here. I close the drawer and move on to the next, rattling the shit on top of the dresser again as I push the first drawer shut and pull open the second.

This drawer proves more promising as my fingers snag on fabric, *thank god*. Snatching a handful of garments from the drawer, I turn around and head toward the window to see what treasure I've found.

Please be pants. Preferably a size 18.

On my way over, I kick whatever object fell from the dresser, and it *clanks* against something else in the dark. I freeze in place, waiting to hear footsteps from above or shouting from the next room to indicate I've been caught.

Nothing happens. I can breathe again.

Once beside the curtains, I draw them back one small inch for some sunlight, silently cheering once I realize I've grabbed not just one pair of pants, but *two*. Thick, black denim with a million shiny, silver zippers—the kind of pants that give off emo vibes.

I don't care as long as they fit.

I've got one leg in the air when I catch movement in my peripheral, and my head snaps to the side just in time to see a glowering mountain of a man barreling toward me.

We collide, the sheer wall of muscle body-checking me into the window. A large, calloused hand wraps around my throat, squeezing tight enough to cut off most of my air supply.

As my fight-or-flight responses kick in, my hands sink into the curtain and rip it down. The rod clatters to the ground noisily, alerting everyone in earshot of my presence.

So much for being stealthy.

Warm sunlight floods into the room, and I finally get a glimpse of my soon-to-be murderer. Panic and adrenaline mix, giving me a sudden rush of anticipation as I imagine the same handsome face I grew to love five years ago.

My eyes focus, and instead of finding my ex glowering at me, I see someone else. Dark hair thrown haphazardly over midnight eyes. A scar cutting down the corner of his lips and over the curve of his clenched jaw. .

It's not my ex-fiancée. It's my ex-*bodyguard.*

Relief washes over me as I expect him to let me go. Out of all the men from my past, Ezra's the one who would never hurt me. He vowed to always protect me — and all men within the Bratva take their vows seriously.

My relief is short-lived as his grip *tightens,* cutting off my air supply completely. He swallows hard and pins me under his heavy gaze. A rumble reverberates through his chest as he damn near growls out my name in thickly accented English.

"Valentina Baranova."

Heat floods my system all the way from my head down to my toes. I know that voice, and the man behind it, *very* well.

Ezra Reinoff wasn't just any bodyguard, he was *mine*. My *personal* bodyguard for years, up until the day I left.

A heated shiver runs down my spine as he repeats my name, the low rumble reverberating through my bones. All members of the Bratva make a point to learn American English, but Ezra always struggled to kick his Russian accent the most. It gives his voice a harsher tone — one I never minded. In fact, I begged him to teach me a few Russian phrases just so I could hear him speak.

I may have been engaged to Andrei, but I had a one-sided love affair with Ezra's voice.

He mutters something under his breath, and a traitorous *trill* sends goosebumps rolling down my arms.

Time hasn't changed *that* little detail one bit.

I try to say his name, but my lips part and no sound comes out.

Oh yeah, probably because I'm dying.

His dark eyes narrow and take a slow drag down my body, and I try, in vain, not to get all hot and bothered about it.

He was off limits five years ago. But now?

We're making the rules up as we go.

"Why are you here?" Ezra asks, his grip on my throat loosening just enough so that I can breathe.

Blood rushes to my head, and I nearly pass out. My knees buckle, and Ezra immediately pins my body against the cool glass window. The contrast between the warmth of his touch and the cold glass is like fire and ice — both burning, but in completely different ways.

I've never been man-handled like this before. . . but I think I like it.

A crimson blush blooms across my skin as heat rushes between my thighs. Ezra's body is warm, and not only that, but he's *shirtless*. Tattoos snake across his skin in intricate patterns, more than I can count, and I get lost in how beautiful they are. My fingertips graze his ribs, and he flinches, his dark eyes flashing dangerously.

"*Valentina*," he growls, making my toes curl, "what do you think you're doing?"

I have no fucking clue. I'm probably dying.

Finally, I manage to intake enough air to speak. "Your tattoos are beautiful."

His expression hardens like iron. I must have said the wrong thing.

"Ezra—"

"*Shut up.*"

In all the years I've known him, I've never seen his temper. Around me, he's always been stoic. Passive. *Professional.*

But now, his armor is off. A myriad of emotions flicker across his face, too fast for me to keep up. It's dizzying to try, and I lean my head back against the window. The room spins behind his head. A groan slips past my lips.

Ezra releases me without warning and my knees buckle, dropping me to the hardwood with a heavy *thud*. The next thing I know, he's crossed the room and flicked on the lights, a scowl settling across his features as he looks down at me. His nostrils flare, but I hardly notice over the fact that I now have a full-bodied glimpse of him.

And *fuck*, he's gorgeous.

I always knew he was ripped, but his muscles were hidden under a bulletproof vest and thick pants. Now, the only thing keeping him decent is a pair of black boxers hugging his thighs.

And what thighs they are. Toned muscle, smooth as the finest marble, covers the man head to toe. The tattoos I spotted earlier start at his neck and trail down his chest, disappearing beneath his underwear only to reappear on his thick thighs. I've never seen so much ink on one person.

Or so much cock.

A prominent bulge at his front catches my attention, and I can't look away. It has to be at least nine inches. Maybe *ten*.

He grunts, distracting me from my measurements. "Get up."

My heart hammers as I obey. My gaze flickers towards the bed beside us. This must be his bedroom. The sheets are rumpled, the comforter thrown to the floor.

I must have woken him up from a nap. . . or some *alone* time.

I bite my bottom lip as I imagine how soft his sheets would be against my skin. How warm his body would be over mine.

Forbidden thoughts. *Dangerous* ones.

I have no business sleeping with the enemy, and I'm pretty sure this isn't a happy reunion for him.

When I look back at him, he's stiff as a board in *multiple* places. With a jerk of his head, he gestures towards one of the pairs of pants I dropped when he grabbed me. "Get dressed."

Oh, right. I don't have pants on, either. I rub my thighs together and catch Ezra staring.

"Yes, sir."

His eyes snap to mine, and this time there's no mistaking the desire burning in their depths.

I take my time getting dressed, making sure he gets an eyeful of *ass* when I bend down to unlace my remaining boot and pull the pants up over my thighs. I might not be able to see his face, but I can feel the heat of his gaze on my body.

It was always his job to watch over me. To keep me safe and make sure I was okay at all times. Because of that, I'm used to him staring at me at all hours of the day.

But not like *this*.

Not like a man who wants to devour me whole.

I shimmy the last bit of fabric over my hips with a delicate sigh. When I look back up at Ezra, he's thrown on a black muscle tee and pants that match mine.

It's not meant to be cute that we're matching, but it is anyway.

"Favorite pants, huh?" I tease. He must be one of those guys with multiple pairs of his favorite outfits.

With the way those pants hug his ass, I can't say I mind.

Now that we're both clothed, some of the tension in his shoulders relaxes. He rolls his neck, cracking the joints loudly.

I straighten my spine and pin him under my gaze. Despite the rocky start, I'm here on business. I need to see my father. I make a point to clear my throat. "Ezra. I need to see—" The words *my father* turn to ash in my mouth. Familial ties don't mean as much as rank to the Bratva, so I know a better word to use than father. "—your *pakhan*." Lifting my chin, I meet Ezra's onyx eyes. "Take me to him."

Ezra's jaw clenches. I imagine he's weighing all his options for what to do with me. It's unorthodox to interrupt a *pakhan's* schedule without warning—in fact, I'm sure men have died for it.

With how angry my father undoubtedly is after my sudden departure, I might not survive the encounter, either.

I *really* should have brought backup.

"You want to see the *pakhan*," Ezra repeats, his eyes narrowing. "Why?"

"That's— that's none of your business." Some of my bravado fades, but I keep my head held high. In truth, seeing my father makes me nervous. I'm not expecting him to give me any answers willingly. I'll probably have to trade him something of equal value to get what I want.

A shiver runs down my spine. All I have is my name, my body, and my bloodline.

Three things that I *should* own. But that's not how life works when you're a mafia princess — you're rarely in charge of your own life. Someone else claims it for themselves, turns you into a marionette, and pulls your strings however they please.

It's the life I thought I was destined for.

I clench my fists by my sides. But that won't be the life I accept anymore. "I need to see him. It's the only reason I came back."

Ezra's scowl deepens. After a long moment, he gestures towards the exit. "Then go find your *pakhan*."

I swallow hard. The thought of facing my father alone. . . Icy dread snakes through my veins. The last thing I want is to be alone in a room with him. "Take me to him," I order Ezra, lifting my chin. I resist the urge to say *please*, but only just.

We stare at each other as the seconds tick by. Finally, he moves to the door and holds it open, his face an impassive mask as he slips back into the role of protector.

I roll my shoulders back as I step past him. At least some things haven't changed—

A hand on my wrist yanks me back into the room, and all of a sudden I'm tossed face-first onto the bed. Before I can react, Ezra presses the full weight of his body over mine and wrenches both my hands behind my back, cinching them together tightly.

"Ezra!"

"Quiet."

"What are you—"

He snarls in my ear, and a shudder wracks my entire body.

Fuck me.

"You do not get to call shots." Coarse rope wraps around my wrists, tying them in place at my back, Ezra's breath hot across my neck. His scent envelops me from all sides, hinting of metal and smoke and *danger*.

After five years away from the blood and ruin of the Bratva, I forgot what that tasted like.

"You do not get to do *anything*."

"Ezra, *please*—"

"You *left*, Valentina."

My blood runs cold at the venom in his voice. He must blame me for all kinds of hell he endured once my father realized I was missing.

I can only imagine what tortures my father inflicted upon the man in charge of my protection. . . or keeping me inside a gilded cage.

Part of me has always known the truth, but I never wanted to look too closely. Having an armed guard at all hours of the day is a blessing, I've been reminded all my life. I'm so *lucky* that my family loves me enough to spare no expense at keeping me safe.

My breath catches as the knotted rope secures behind my back. Tears pool in my eyes. Ezra was always kind to me, but now. . .

I doubt there's any trace of my protector left in him, and that reality *hurts*.

If he was ever really my protector at all.

Ezra reaches over me to snag one of his pillows, pulls the pillowcase off, and twists it into a thin rope. Shoving it between my teeth, he ties the ends into a knot behind my head.

I try to speak, but the gag makes it impossible. I don't even know what I'm trying to say.

I'm sorry for leaving?

I'm not.

I made a mistake?

I sure as shit did, coming back here.

Forgive me?

There shouldn't be anything to forgive.

Ezra lifts me by my bound wrists, shooting sharp pains through my arms and shoulders. Spinning me around, he shoves me in front of him toward the door. I stumble, but he catches my bindings and tugs me back upright. More pain rips through my muscles, and a single tear falls free.

I won't let him see me cry. I won't let anyone *see me cry.*

Still, my vision blurs, and it's a constant battle to keep my emotions in check.

"We move," Ezra grunts, "or I drag you."

Shame fills my chest as I take small, uncertain steps out of Ezra's room and into the creepy morgue. How was I even remotely attracted to him, past or present? What is *wrong* with me?

When I move too slowly, Ezra pushes me forward, his hand burning into my back.

"You know where to go," he growls, "don't you, *lisichka?*"

The pet name stings, the comfort it used to bring me twisting into something darker. But I keep moving, taking larger, more confident steps the more familiar the terrain becomes.

I *do* know where I'm going. . . but I have no clue what awaits me.

The doting father or the cruel *pakhan?*

CHAPTER 3

ANDREI

Five years.

Time passed in a whirlwind of anger and *hurt*, hurt so deep that it surprised me.

I always liked being around Valentina. She gave me those *innocent eyes*, full of shy glances and rosy cheeks that let me know her attention was all on me. There were no other men in her life—by design, I'm sure, so that she was amicable toward our betrothal and subsequent marriage. But the machinations behind our union didn't bother me. They're just another part of Bratva life that you either get used to, or you swallow bitterly with your morning coffee.

No, I didn't mind as long as Valentina was mine.

Some men would have found her insufferable. They don't fuck with blushing virgins, preferring a more direct approach to physical affection.

But me?

I was as enamored with her as she was with me.

Or so I thought.

Standing at the altar awaiting your soon-to-be bride,

subjected to the rising whispers and anxieties of the crowd wafting through the air like smoke, until finally your best man returns to whisper in your ear that *she's gone* . . . will do things to a man.

Very dark, very *bitter* things.

I've spent the past five years chasing a ghost . . . but now she's returned.

Mikhail studies my face as he gauges my reaction to the video footage he's brought me. "She's in the house, Andrei. She's come to you, just like you said she would." There's a hint of respect in his voice, but he should have known just as well as me that the moment she stepped into the city, she was always coming here.

The only question is—*why?*

What is she after?

My heart clenches at the thought that she's here for *me*, but I wall off the feeling as quickly as possible. By the time I'm taking my next breath, I've recovered.

She won't receive a single shred of my feelings for her. I'm locking those up tight.

All that's left for her is retribution.

Two pairs of footsteps gather toward the door, and I focus my gaze in their direction. My pulse quickens, but I steel my body and mind to keep my reaction passive.

She doesn't deserve *anything* from me.

The handle turns down, the heavy, wooden door swings open, and there she is. Valentina Baranova.

The woman who *ran*.

Full lips, fuller figure, and eyes that flicker from false bravado to uncertainty in an instant. When Ezra rips the gag from her mouth, she throws a glare in his direction.

"Where's my father?"

No. Her focus should be on me. I clench my fist behind my back to avoid gritting my teeth. My eyes catch on shiny silver zippers crisscrossing her thighs, ones that match Ezra's exactly, and blood roars in my ears.

What the *fuck* is she wearing?

Ezra raises a brow, his attention wrongfully focused on her. "You said *pakhan*. He is here."

"My father is *pakhan,* asshole. I want to see him."

Ah, she doesn't know. A hint of satisfaction curls in my chest. We have the upper hand in more ways than one.

"Your father is dead," I say, interrupting them. "*I* am head of the Baranova Bratva, Valentina. You answer to me."

As you always should have.

Her gaze whips in my direction, her dark hair tumbling across her shoulders. "You're lying. Ezra only brought me here so you could fulfill some sick revenge fantasy."

Ignoring her comment, I take in her appearance from head to toe, my lips twitching at the edges upon seeing those pants again.

Ezra grunts noncommittally, seeing the question in my eyes. "She was missing pants."

"If she arrived naked, she should *be* naked."

Valentina's jaw unhinges, a flicker of fury in her emerald eyes – fury she has no right to.

I take a calculated step forward, and her fury wanes in the presence of my own.

I'm not sure where my anger stems from. Maybe it's the humiliation I've been harboring for five years. Maybe it's seeing another man's clothing on her skin. Maybe it's the way she waltzes into *my* city and *my* home like it's *hers.*

She owns *nothing.*

"Take them off."

As I continue advancing, she retreats until her back hits the wall and a picture frame clatters to the floor, glass shattering at her feet. She gasps and breaks our gaze to jump away from the debris.

Mistake.

I close in on her, glass shards snapping under the soles of my shoes, and lift her chin. The touch makes me crave more, but I squeeze my fingers along her jaw to keep my hand from wandering. "I gave you an order."

Our eyes meet, and *fuck*, I'm transported back in time to when she yearned for my attention, when she craved the simplest of touches.

Her body betrays her now, a pretty pink flush spreading down her neck. Maybe she's remembering it too.

"I don't take orders from *you.*"

I click my tongue. "You will learn obedience. How much it hurts—" with my free hand, I snag the waistline of *Ezra's* pants and snap the button free, "—is up to you."

She starts to struggle, but there's not much she can do with her hands tied behind her back. Still, I appreciate the effort.

It shows me what she looks like when she tries to fight, and it's *delicious.*

I shove my forearm against her collarbone to keep her immobile as I unzip her. "Careful, Valentina. You're going to hurt yourself."

"S-screw you," she says, her voice wavering with her fear.

I pause, my hand hovering over her hip. Fear and . . . something else? Moving slower than before, I lower my face to her neck and blow gently. Her entire body starts to tremble. I brush my lips across her pebbled skin, eager to taste what I've been denied all these years. I press a gentle kiss to her skin and bite back a groan as she instinctually tilts her neck to grant me access. She's scared, but also. . . *tempted.*

It's fucking *delicious.*

"W-what are you doing?" Her voice shakes, her shallow breaths uneven.

A question. Not asking me to stop. Not telling me to continue.

She doesn't know what she wants.

"Undressing you," I answer, removing my arm from her torso to lower both hands to her hips. I pull the fabric over her plump ass, my knuckles skimming over her skin. As I reach her thighs, she sighs, the sound going straight to my cock.

"Step out, Valentina."

She obeys, sliding her feet out of each pant leg, and I sweep the broken glass away from her feet with my arm.

Dropping Ezra's *fucking* pants to the ground, I graze my palms up her calves, then her outer thighs, and hook onto her hips as I stand at my full height.

The flush on her cheeks has darkened, her pupils dilating as our connection *zings*.

I've always wanted her, body and soul. I've remained patient for as long as she's been promised to me, confident that my time with her would come due. . . and even though this isn't *quite* like I imagined it, perhaps that time has come.

Perhaps she's finally going to submit to me completely.

My cock twitches in response to how pliable she's proving, but I pay it no mind. This demonstration isn't for me. It's for her to learn the rules.

I take a step back, and her gray sweater falls lower, covering the swell of her hips and kissing the tops of her thighs. "Move to the desk."

Her gaze flicks to the furniture behind me and she licks her lips, desire making her less cautious. Then, in the next second, she catches herself and flinches away from me. "No. Screw you. I'm leaving. I'm here to see my father, not you." She glances at the ground and picks the safest path toward the door, stepping carefully to avoid injury.

Ezra catches her as she tries to flee, snagging her arm and tossing her toward the center of the room. She stumbles and hits the desk hard, bending at the waist as she slams into the wood, unable to catch herself without use of her hands. Pens clatter to the floor, papers go flying, useless office supplies scatter across the wood.

I don't give a fuck about any of that.

I fill the space behind her before she has a chance to stand. With one hand on her lower back, I press her body harder against the wood. I use my foot to nudge her own apart, to brace her stance for what's about to come.

"What are you doing?" she shrieks, fighting against me. It's no use. I'm stronger than her, and holding her down is easy. Mikhail walks to the other side of my desk and grins down at her, clearly enjoying the show.

"You never told me she was this pretty," he sing-songs, leaning down to peer at Valentina's face. Whatever he finds there turns his grin *wicked*. "I think she likes what you're doing to her."

"Fuck off," Valentina snaps.

That only makes Mikhail laugh. He straightens, pats her head, and leans back to watch. "I like her. Can we keep her?"

Of course, we're keeping her. That isn't even a question.

Valentina walked back into our lives *willingly*.

I'm not letting her leave *ever* again.

Mikhail's question, however, makes Valentina freeze beneath me. I can practically taste her fear.

"What are you going to do with me?" she asks, her voice softer, quieter now. It's reminiscent of the old Valentina, the one wrapped around my finger. The shy young woman I *thought* was meant to be my wife.

But the woman who walked back in here? Half-naked and demanding an audience with the leader of a Russian crime syndicate?

That woman isn't shy.

"Speak up." I spread her legs farther apart, keeping my

knee between them. She gasps, and images of her body convulsing as I grind my knee against her clit flash white hot in my mind.

Another time, perhaps.

When she doesn't answer, I smack her plump ass, leaving a red handprint on her skin.

"I said, *speak up.*"

"Fuck you!" Valentina arches her back as she tries to glare at me over her shoulder. Little does she know, this only presents her even better for spanking.

Going for the other side, I smack her again.

She hisses, then *finally* repeats her question. "What are you going to do with me?" There's nothing quiet about it this time. She's angry. Probably humiliated.

It's exactly what I want from her. That feeling? I've been living with it for the past five years.

She can endure five minutes.

I consider my answer to her question, combing through the possibilities in my mind. To be honest, or to string her along on false hopes of freedom?

Which would be sweeter to taste?

"If you'll recall, Valentina, we made very important plans together."

I refuse to let memories of our botched wedding ceremony creep up. The past is dead. But a promise is a promise, and I think I'm owed something quite valuable . . .

"Plans that *you* ruined. I think it's only fitting that you're the one to set them right again."

"What the hell does that mean?" She starts fighting me again, but I grab her ass harshly, digging my nails into her flesh.

She yelps and freezes, likely still feeling the burn from her spanking.

Ezra mutters something behind me, something in Russian, and the words send blood roaring through my veins.

She's dripping wet.

I don't dare look. I don't trust myself to witness her desire and *not* act upon it.

For five years, I've imagined what her traitorous cunt tasted like. What it would feel like wrapped around my cock as I fucked all of my anger at her betrayal into her body. As I *bred* her, rutting ruthlessly, filling her up with so much cum that she leaked all over the sheets.

I don't dare look.

But that doesn't keep my hand from sliding lower, daring to brush against the dampness between her thighs and feel how soaked her panties are.

She gasps, but her thighs spread *wider*.

I curse all the gods in both Heaven and Hell for their cruelty. My innocent little fiancée is not so innocent anymore.

Five years ago, I thought she was perfect as she was, but I was wrong. The little spitfire in front of me is more fitted to the role of mafia wife, and perhaps *that's* what true perfection means.

Aligning my jagged, broken pieces with hers and finding that they fit together perfectly.

Perhaps she and I were meant to break five years ago so that we would find each other again, just like this.

I draw a deep breath and refocus on the task at hand. "You swore your heart to me, Valentina, and I plan to collect."

"Like hell you're getting anything from me!"

I chuckle and shake my head. "Fine, don't give me your heart. I have little use for it, anyway."

She stiffens, but I continue before she can retort. "But your name? *That* will be mine. And *this*—" I thrust my cock against her ass, letting her feel the weight of me, and bite back a groan.

God, that's going to be addictive.

She writhes against me and, gods above, makes things worse. I grab her hips to keep her steady and *fuck*, that hot little cunt of hers aligns perfectly with my cock. We both freeze, and I clench my jaw. "*This*," I hiss, thrusting against her panties, her whine making my head spin, "will be mine to ruin."

She moans and I wedge myself against her lips. There's too much fabric between us to make good on my word, but *soon*, she'll be writhing beneath me as I pump inside her.

"You ruined us," I snarl, grinding against her roughly and digging my fingers into her hips. "So I will ruin *you*. Get ready, Valentina Baranova, because I am a ruthless fucking man when something is taken from me. Do you understand?" I pull her hips back and mime the dance we'll be doing *very* soon, my control slipping. A snarl catches in my throat. "Do you understand what you stole from me?"

Five years. Five *bitter* years, alone, watching her father waste away and being unable to claim his kingdom because *she* was missing. The heir to the Baranova Bratva, *my fiancée*, left me here to rot in her father's dying kingdom.

She will *pay* for every second of happiness she stole from me.

With a hiss, I release her and step back. I'm too angry. I can't think straight. She *does something* to me.

I've worked hard to control this city *without* my bride, and one woman won't take that power from me.

Running a hand down my face, I shut my eyes and take a deep breath. "Take her to her room," I command, knowing both of my men will follow orders. "She's not allowed out without an armed escort. See it done."

I leave immediately, storming through the halls until I reach my quarters. Slamming the doors shut, I pace back and forth, unable to get the feel of Valentina's body out of my mind. Haste makes me careless as I throw my clothes to the floor and palm my naked cock, groaning as I imagine Valentina writhing naked beneath me, hate in her eyes as I fuck her raw. Hate and *desire*, so wicked hot that it burns us both.

I come violently, coating my hand and painting the bedsheets. It feels like a waste, and I quickly vow not to come again until it's inside Valentina.

She *will* bend to my will. Marry me. Fuck me. Birth my heirs.

Love doesn't have to be part of the equation.

Hate, however, might be my new favorite flavor.

CHAPTER 4

VALENTINA

HUMILIATION KEEPS me silent as both Ezra and the other guy drag me through the halls. I'm pantsless—again—which is only made more mortifying by the fact that their boss just dry humped the shit out of me . . . and they all stood by to watch.

As I moaned. Beneath my enemy.

My face flames red as evidence of my desire drips down my thighs.

I'm a horny bitch. I can admit that.

But why did I have to be a horny bitch *today?*

Ezra grunts and pulls me to a stop by my bound wrists while the other guy opens a set of double doors. I expect to find my old bedroom, but the room inside is larger and more elegant than anything I've ever had. "Whose room is this?" I ask, eying everything skeptically. "Is this where Andrei keeps his whores?"

The man with the wicked gleam in his rich brown eyes smiles coldly, like this is all a game to him. "Is that what you want to be, *malyshka*? A whore?"

I bare my teeth at him, and he cackles gleefully.

"Do not antagonize her," Ezra grunts. "She will be boss soon."

The other man rolls his eyes. "As if she'll ever tell us what to do." He turns his attention back to me. "She might like to think she's in control, but I'll bet she becomes Andrei's little puppet the minute she takes his cock in her mouth for the first time."

Oh, how I *long* to punch that fucking smirk off his face. I've never punched anyone before, but I'm a quick study. Give me a chance to swing, and I'll take a motherfucker down.

He must recognize my silent fury, because his grin slides back into place. "Oooh, she's a feisty one. I *like* her."

"You already said that." Ezra starts patting me down, and I swivel around and lift my knee to his crotch. I miss, jabbing his thigh instead, and he exhales sharply, black eyes flashing in annoyance.

"Try that again, and I will leave you tied up for entire night."

"As if you were ever going to let me go!"

He raises an eyebrow at me. "Untying you and letting you go are two different things, hm? I could let you go and keep your wrists tied while you ran. Would make for more interesting chase."

I shiver at the thought of being chased through the cold dark by my former bodyguard. I doubt he would be kind when he catches me.

I open my mouth to tell him to *fuck off* when my boobs start to vibrate. I bite my lip and pray that Ezra doesn't notice, but either his ears are sharp or he's just that fucking perceptive, because his eyes drift down to my breasts.

I'd completely forgotten that, in lieu of pants with pockets, I shoved my cell phone into the depths of my bra for safekeeping. A girl never knows when she'll need to dial 911.

"Mikhail," Ezra grunts, "hold her still."

An arm immediately circles around my waist, the other one gripping my shoulder tightly. "With pleasure," Mikhail purrs in my ear.

God. I must have done something horrible in a past life to deserve this kind of treatment in my own home. "Get your hands off me!" I jerk my shoulder, and his nails dig through my sweater and bite into my skin.

Everything about this situation is new. It's nerve-wracking and infuriating and... *kind of hot.*

I've only ever been with gentlemen. They're sweet and careful and gentle, as in the name. That's what I should want, right? Someone who's kind and wants what's best for me.

These men *take*, and they have no problem claiming you for themselves.

I shouldn't be so damned excited about that.

I bite my lip as Ezra lifts my shirt, and his eyes track the movement. I stare at his jawline as it jumps and hold my breath as, finally, my shirt lifts over my breasts. He lets it drop to my chest once it's cleared the threshold, and his gaze zeroes in on the vibrating block wedged beneath my left boob.

His next movements are methodical and quick. A man on a mission. He lifts my boob from its bra cup with one hand and grabs the phone with the other. Scanning the screen for a moment, he frowns, then turns the phone around for me to see who's calling.

Liam. My boss slash ex-boyfriend. With a picture of the two of us from last year's Christmas party as his contact photo. I internally cringe. I really need to change that photo.

Ezra raises an eyebrow as the call goes to voicemail. "Who is he?"

"My—" *Boss* doesn't sound threatening enough, and ex-boyfriend means he's a part of my past. So I lie instead, hoping for some leverage. "Boyfriend. I was supposed to meet him for lunch today. I forgot."

"You forgot about your boyfriend?" Ezra narrows his eyes, trying to spot the lie.

My face flushes, and I start to ramble in a desperate attempt to be convincing. "Yeah, I was so hell-bent on coming here." I laugh a little. At least *that* part is true. "I totally forgot to tell him I wouldn't make lunch. Just a . . . spaz. I'm a spaz. I forgot."

Ezra hums in the back of his throat. "Call him with apology."

My smile freezes on my lips. "What?"

Ezra nods to Mikhail, and my bindings come free. Blood rushes to my hands, and my shoulders scream as I pull my arms back to the front.

The first order of business is pulling my shirt down. While I cover myself as quickly as possible, Mikhail *laughs*, like it's the funniest thing in the world.

"Call him," Ezra repeats, placing the phone in my palm. "*Now.*"

Fuck me.

I grasp the phone tightly in my fist and consider my options.

I could beat Ezra with my cell phone. Maybe he'd be so surprised that I could spring free and make a mad dash for the exit.

But then there's Mikhail, and there's no way I could outmaneuver *two* men.

I could call my grandmother. She'd know what to do. When I walked out of the chapel, her car was waiting for me. It's like she knew what decision I'd make before I did. Ever since, she's been in my corner and supporting me every step of the way. She's the reason I found a job with Liam in the first place, and she's been letting me live with her all this time.

If there's anyone I owe an explanation to, it's her. Not my boss slash ex.

But Ezra is watching me like a hawk, and he'll know if I dial a different number.

I swallow and open my missed calls. Clicking on Liam's name, I hold my breath as it starts to ring.

Ezra grabs the phone and puts the call on speaker, holding it up for all of us to hear.

"Valentina!" The relief in Liam's voice makes my heart clench tightly in my chest. "I was starting to worry. Where are you? Are you okay?"

I'm being held hostage in my father's estate a few states over, what's new with you?

"I'm fine. I got caught up with this thing . . . with my dad."

Liam and I have known each other for over four years now, and he knows that I *never* talk about my father. It's Forbidden with a capital F, because I don't like to tell people that I was raised by a mafia king, and my grandmother insists we remain as hidden as possible in the event that we're ever found by my father's men.

I send a silent prayer to my grandmother, asking for forgiveness and hoping she'll hear it.

"Oh," Liam replies, clearly taken aback. "I didn't think you were on speaking terms with him."

"I'm . . . trying to fix that. I should have told you I left. I'm sorry."

There's a pause.

"I would have come with you, you know."

I can practically see Liam standing there in his office, a hand fisting his honey-blonde hair as he looks out the window. He's always been protective of me, even before we ever started dating, back when we were just friends. I'm sure if I'd asked him to join me in confronting my past, he would have come with me in a heartbeat.

I squeeze my eyes shut. "I know. I couldn't ask that of

you."

Literally. My grandmother would kill me if I told an outsider about our ties to the Russian mafia.

Liam sighs through the receiver. "Are you alone? Traveling can be dangerous if you're not careful. Why don't I meet up with you? How far away are you?"

Ezra's midnight eyes pierce into mine like daggers.

"I'm— I'm sorry, I have to go!"

"Valentina?"

The arm around my waist suddenly cinches tighter. "Tell him you love him," Mikhail murmurs in my ear. "Unless he's *not* your boyfriend, after all."

Shit. I must not have been convincing enough.

"I'll be home soon," I say, rushing through the words. "Bye!" I jab my finger on the *end call* button as fast as possible.

"You didn't tell him you love him," Mikhail sighs, almost like he's . . . pouting? Is he upset that I didn't confess my undying love for Liam over the phone?

"It is good she did not tell him. It would have been a lie." Ezra frowns at my phone before pocketing it. "He does not have tracker on you, does he?"

I sputter aloud. "I'm sorry? Do most boyfriends put trackers on their partners' phones?"

"The smart ones," Ezra answers, his lips curving into a small smile. "Yes."

Mikhail's fingers start tracing my exposed hip bone, and I'm instantly reminded that *I have no pants* and *I'm in a bedroom with a man I don't know.*

Ezra, I know. Even if he's become a heartless bastard, at least I can say that I more or less know the guy and may or may not have had a crush on him once.

Mikhail, on the other hand, I *really* don't know.

I smack his hand and he chuckles, letting me go and backing away with both hands up in front of him like *he's* the one defending himself. "Can't help it after your little display earlier. You're *divine*, you know. That rosy blush on your cheeks as Andrei rubbed his cock against you. The way your eyes drifted out of focus." He licks his lips. "Delicious, *malyshka*. I'd love an encore performance."

My face burns, and he laughs harder.

Ezra glares at Mikhail, and the man at least has the wherewithal to shut up, even if he can't stop grinning.

"You will stay here, Baranova. You will not try to run. You will not try to hurt yourself. Do you understand?" Ezra crosses his arms over his chest, and I'm reminded just how *large* he is compared to normal men. Mikhail's stature is lean, Andrei's is broad-shouldered and fit, but Ezra's is *massive*.

With a huff, I mirror his posture and cross my arms over my chest. I'll have to come up with an escape plan once they're gone. "*Yes*, I understand. Now get the hell out of my room."

Mikhail walks backwards out of the room, watching me the entire time, that same wicked gleam and goddamned smirk on his fucking face. Ezra doesn't bother looking at me, and I can't say I blame him.

I've had enough of him for one day, too. Of all of them.

"Can I at least have some fucking pants?" I yell, throwing my hands in the air. "What is *with* you guys?"

Howling laughter echoes down the hall, and I stomp over to the door and lock it up tight. I bet one of them has a key, if not all of them, and I scan the room for something to jam under the doorknob.

The dresser's too heavy. The desk is on the other side of the room . . . but the chair. That, I can move.

It feels flimsy shoved up against the double doors, but it's better than nothing. A ripple of fear at Ezra's strength makes me nervous. He could probably shove the doors open with his bare hands, locks and makeshift barricade be damned.

I search the entire room, but there's not much here.

Empty dresser. Empty closet. Empty bathroom, save some spare towels and a bathmat. The bedroom's bare, save the furniture and twin lamps on the nightstands, each one with golden vines spiraling up the base, splitting into equally golden leaves. Glass lampshades in the shape of roses give the finishing touch, and I sigh as I click one on.

There's no way I'm sleeping in the dark, if I manage to sleep at all.

The second lamp, the one closest to the door . . .

Well, a girl's gonna need a weapon if one of those monsters comes creeping in the middle of the night.

I hug my knees to my chest and shut my eyes, drawing the comforter up around me. It smells of cinnamon and vanilla, and I curl up as best I can and try my hardest not to let my thoughts spiral.

It's a futile effort. My thoughts swirl around Andrei, Ezra, the new guy Mikhail, until finally, I think of my mom.

It's impossible not to when everything around me screams her name. Golden roses, vanilla creme, silken sheets . . . all of her favorite things in one place.

A tear slides down my cheek and a sob breaks free.

I shouldn't have to stay in my mother's old bedroom, haunted by her ghost. It might be the cruelest thing anyone's ever done to me.

CHAPTER 5

EZRA

THE LAST THING I expected to wake me up in the middle of the afternoon was a ghost from my past.

Mikhail shrieking about the latest problem with one of his businesses? Sure. Men rushing into the clinic, needing immediate medical attention? That's just another fucking day at the office.

But *Valentina?* The girl who *left?*

No fucking way.

Yet there she was.

Bathed in sunlight, just like the day she left. Holding something in her hands, staring out the window like a lost girl. Like a ghost.

The curtain fell across her shoulder like a veil, and I thought I was dreaming about her again. Imagining she was really here, like I have a thousand times.

But then I heard her. Stomping about. Ruffling the curtain. Saw her holding my pants, as though she'd stumbled upon some kind of treasure.

And then she was naked.

Not completely, but more than enough for me to get an eyeful.

Running a hand down my face, I groan.

Valentina has haunted my dreams, and now she's haunting my life—again.

It's one thing to know you'll never have her. To watch as she marries another man. To be sworn to protect her, always.

It's another thing to watch her betrothed nearly hate fuck her into his desk, to see how turned on she was by it. By *him*.

The woman who slipped through my fingers. The one I was never meant to have.

The one I still want.

I stew on that thought for what feels like eternity. She was out of reach for years. Dead. A ghost.

My heart seizes in my chest, and I curse it for its stupidity. I hate her for leaving, but part of me will always . . .

I clench and unclench my fists by my sides. This is stupid. She belongs to Andrei, as she always has, and nothing about that will change.

With a scowl, I walk down the hall in silence, Mikhail's constant humming at my side the biggest fucking nuisance in the world.

"Stop," I grumble, shutting my eyes. "You give me headache."

"Valentina gives you a headache," he clarifies, chuckling to himself. "She makes everything more complicated, doesn't she?"

"It does not matter what she does. It does not change situation."

Mikhail hums once more in the back of his throat before ceasing like I'd asked him to. "I can see why you're both enamored by her. Andrei fucking hates her, and you can't decide if you want to fuck her or kill her." His grin is so wide that it nearly splits his face. "But in the end, she'll choose me."

I snort, loudly, at how ridiculous the idea is. "She, love *you*? It is Andrei she loves."

"It's Andrei she will *marry*," Mikhail corrects, lifting his finger like he's rattling off a list. "She can fuck you, too, for all I care. But she'll *choose* me. She'll *love* me."

"You cannot force a woman to love you."

Especially not Valentina.

Mikhail shrugs, not deterred in the slightest. "Believe what you will. But you'll see. You'll *both* see. She'll choose me first."

Rolling my eyes, I push open the door to Andrei's office. It's already back to its pristine condition, all the papers and pens and miscellaneous objects from his desk back in perfect order. The shattered glass on the floor is gone, the only remnants of its existence the new scratch on the hardwood and the broken frame in the trash.

"That took longer than expected," Andrei muses, watching us from his desk chair. "Did she fight you?"

Mikhail licks his lips. "Wish she fought harder. Pretty little thing when she gets all worked up."

I shoot Mikhail a glare, and he snickers like it's the funniest thing in the world.

I hate the man sometimes.

"She got phone call." Fishing her phone from my pocket, I unlock it and hand it to Andrei. "Says it is her boyfriend. I do not believe her."

"She doesn't love him," Mikhail supplies helpfully. "Or so Ezra says."

"She does not." I cross my arms. "That is clear."

If anything is clear from Valentina's conversation with this Liam, it's that he's not her boyfriend, and she's a fucking liar.

I hate liars.

Even if they're Valentina. *Especially* if they're Valentina.

Andrei starts searching her phone, pretending to look

bored, but I know him. He'll devour every scrap of content in its system before he sleeps tonight.

"Find out what you can about this man. His name, location, job title. See if you can connect him to Katya or find her location. She has many things to answer for."

The day Valentina disappeared, so did Katya Baranova, Valentina's grandmother on her mother's side. We've always suspected the two were connected and that Katya has been keeping Valentina's whereabouts a secret from us all these years.

The woman is a snake in the grass. I've longed to cut off her head.

"Tolkotsky should have killed her long ago."

Andrei glances up at me. "She's well-loved in the Bratva. She still has support in certain circles."

In other words, *be careful what you say about her.*

I cross to the window and stare out at the afternoon sun, weariness stinging my eyes. I didn't get enough sleep, and now I doubt I'll get much more. A sigh passes my lips. "She will come looking for Valentina." I can see Andrei's reflection nod through the glass.

"Yes. She will arrive just in time to witness her granddaughter's wedding."

Mikhail tilts his head. "We don't have time to plan a wedding. The city's in shambles. I'm barely keeping a hold on our properties as it is. I can't go to parties and dinners and all that nonsense." He waves his hand in front of him, like he's brushing away the idea of playing socialite.

"You're the best for it," Andrei tells him seriously. "You clean up better than most, and as the largest shareholder for most of the city, you'll be expected to be there." He addresses both of us next, and I brace myself for what's to come.

Valentina is *definitely* complicating things.

"All three of us need to be available to solidify Valentina's return to the Bratva. There are many who will need to be convinced." Andrei pulls up a list on his laptop and spins it around for us to see. I leave the window and stand beside Mikhail, both of us scanning the names.

Many, *many* big names in the city. Both young and old, some within our fold, some not. "You intend to invite them to wedding." I scratch my stubble with a grimace. "You want us to schmooze them."

"Take Valentina," Andrei says, smiling as her name leaves his lips. "She'll need to be reintroduced to our world. Learn our ways. Our names. If she's to rule, she must look the part."

"Some will be loyal to her," I say cautiously, studying Andrei's expression, "not to you."

"I'm aware." The man's shoulders tense. "But Tolkotsky left this Bratva to me. He left his *daughter* to me. They'll come around."

Mikhail nods along, but I'm not sure he's really listening. He's always beat to his own conceited drum.

I shake my head. "This plan of yours is crazy. We should kill her. They think she is dead, anyway."

I can feel my heart pumping blood through my veins, but it feels heavy, leaden, like poison.

I've imagined Valentina's face a thousand times, and the press of her cold, dead lips or the chill of her pale, lifeless skin always haunt me the most. I don't want her dead. But it would make things *much* easier for me.

Maybe then I'd finally get a good night's sleep.

I run a tired hand down my face, willing the headache looming behind my eyes to disappear. "I will find information on fake boyfriend. Then we will see about party planning."

"The wedding will be soon. We can't afford to wait too long."

"Why wait at all?" Mikhail asks. "Marry her tomorrow.

Announce her as your wife and corral the straggling loyalists to your side."

"They will know she has been forced, and they will side with her. They may plan to overthrow us, if it means seeing Valentina on the throne alone." Andrei taps his fingertips across his desk, drumming them in a quick rhythm. "We can't allow that to happen."

"Then, what do you suggest?"

"We need to win her over." Andrei's lips curve into a smile that I know all too well. *He's plotting something.* "And I need both of your help with that."

Mikhail perks up immediately, his eyes widening with keen interest.

"I will secure the Baranova bloodline and bring Valentina into the fold through marriage. But in order for this to work, she needs to believe she's needed. Show her our world. Convince her she is a part of it. Give her the duties of a queen, and she will stay for her people. Additionally, I have tasks specific for each of you."

Mikhail is practically bouncing up and down in eager anticipation. I scowl at what he thinks Andrei is asking of him.

The bastard will probably twist Andrei's order to suit his own wants.

"I will marry her. I will fuck her." Andrei's eyes narrow as he stares off in the distance. "But I will not *love* her. I won't even pretend. She will know her place at my side." He grins with a menacing flash of white teeth. "Or in my lap. Either way, I need both of you to convince her to stay."

Unease sits in my stomach. I don't like where he's going with this, and Mikhail's intensity makes it worse. "I will give her projects," I offer, already thinking of a few she may take to and actually enjoy. The gardens. The orphans. The wives' club. "She will find place and purpose."

Andrei's eyes cut to me, through me, and I know what he's plotting.

He wants her to fall in love. With our way of life. With one of us.

"I don't care who she chooses," he says slowly, studying me closely. "But she *will* choose, and she will feel loved, whether or not it *is* love. I don't care which of you claims her." He waves his hand dismissively. "Share her, for all I care. But make her feel wanted. Make her feel loved. And she will stay."

His eyes grow distant, and I almost pity the man. I know the look. He's thinking of the past again, like he's pulling apart all the threads, searching for where he went wrong.

Why she left the first time.

I grit my teeth and refuse to let my mind wander. The past doesn't matter. Not anymore.

"And if she doesn't fall in love?" I take a deep breath. "If she doesn't want to stay?"

"She has no choice."

"Convince her to stay so that she looks the part of Bratva bride," Mikhail mutters, piecing together whatever demented plan he's got brewing in his head. "Show that she's with you willingly, and they'll accept your marriage. They won't take her side over yours. There's only *one* side." He grins like a cat cornering its prey. "Don't worry, *pakhan*, I'll win her heart and give her a reason to stay." His gaze slides over to me, and even though he's not laughing, I can see the glee in his eyes. "I'll make sure she chooses *me*."

I roll my eyes. "This is not competition."

"Not to *you*. Not until you see her looking at *me* the way you always wanted her to look at *you*." He must see the murder in my eyes, because he laughs and sidesteps out of reach. "Don't worry, I won't tell her how much you've pined after her all these years. Your secret's safe with me." He winks, and I think of all the ways I could gouge his eyes out right here and now.

Andrei turns his laptop back around and starts typing rapidly, seemingly disinterested in what just transpired. "I'll set up her introductions. Be ready at any moment. We must also keep an eye on Katya's whereabouts. If she's involved like we suspect, she will not sit quietly once she realizes we have Valentina."

We're dismissed, and as Mikhail drifts off to god knows where, I retreat back to my room. The light's still on, and the mess Valentina left in her wake remains. Rustled bedsheets. A missing pillowcase. My watch and other miscellaneous baubles strewn across the floor. Her scent in the air.

I dive headfirst into the sheets, shut my eyes, and will the clock to rewind.

Before I met her.

Before I *wanted* her.

Before she came tearing back into my life, finally close enough for me to touch.

No longer forbidden . . . and no less wanted.

Fuck.

CHAPTER 6

———

VALENTINA

THE *CLICK* of the door lock makes me jump out of my skin.

How long have I been sitting here? An hour? Two? My heart rate ratchets up to dangerous levels, and I quickly grab the lamp by my side, poised to strike the moment someone walks through those double doors. I slink closer to the door-frame and hold my breath, lamp held high overhead.

The door handles turn down, and both doors swing open in one broad sweep. The chair I'd placed as a barrier earlier today clatters uselessly to the floor as the intruder pushes inside the room. "I've brought you gifts—" The man pauses, glances down at the fallen chair, and *laughs.*

Mikhail.

I can't see his face from behind the door, but I can already picture his ear-splitting, shit-eating grin.

"Do you like games, Valentina?" He takes a step into the room, drops the shopping bags he's holding like they're dead weight, and holds up both his hands. "See, I love games. I'm *really* good at winning." He takes a careful step forward as his eyes sweep the room. "How about we play a little game?"

I catch his reflection in the window and try to shrink into

his shadow, praying he won't see me hiding behind him. I've never been hunted before, but this feels like the start of a very dangerous game where I'm the helpless prey and he's the seasoned predator.

The lamp in my hands grows heavier by the second, and my resolve wavers.

Will hitting him with a heavy, blunt object kill him? I grip the metal neck tighter, my palms starting to sweat.

Do I care if it does?

"If I find you," he murmurs low, "I get . . ." He slides his tongue over his teeth as he contemplates his prize. "Five minutes with you all to myself."

That's a weird request, but I can't dwell on it now.

"But if you manage to get past me and into the hallway, I'll give *you* five minutes."

The last thing I want is to spend five minutes with this creep. Is he crazy?

"What do you say? Do you accept?"

I want to yell *fuck no*, but this is part of Mikhail's little game. He wants me to say something so that I'll reveal myself.

He hovers near the door, and my confidence in my attack plan wavers. But beyond that flickering confidence is fear that grips my heart in a vice. I choke on panic and adrenaline as my flight-or-fight response kicks in, and I pull my arms back to chuck the lamp at Mikhail.

The cord snags and drags against the nightstand, unplugging from the wall. The long, black, *traitorous* electrical cord reveals my location the moment it slides across the floor toward me.

As Mikhail spins around to face me, the wicked gleam in his eye gives way to shock.

It's too late.

The lamp smashes against his head, and I *run*.

Shoving past the dazed man, I trip over the half dozen

paper bags on the floor. Expensive bags. Designer labels embossed in metallic golds and silvers gleam up at me as I stomp all over them in my frantic retreat.

"*Valentina,*" Mikhail fucking *growls,* "that wasn't very nice." A hand wraps around my wrist and pulls, and all of a sudden, the ground slides out from under me.

Two of the bags vault into the air as they slide out from under my feet, and as clothes start raining from the sky, I break free from Mikhail's grasp and tumble out of the room and into the hallway.

I slam into the wall before I can catch myself. At my feet are a handful of clothes I must have dragged from the room in my haste, so I grab the closest one that looks like pants and start running.

"*Valentina!*" Mikhail roars from the bedroom.

I double-time it.

I wasn't made to be an athlete. Big-boned girls like me don't try out for track. It's intentional—our boobs hurt when we run, and wearing two bras just to keep the girls stable is ridiculous.

But today, I don't give a flying fuck about any of that. I run like my ass is on fire. Like I've got a psycho criminal on my tail. Like gravity's not about to rip my fucking tits off.

The world rushes past me in blurs of color. Most of the estate is built from dark wood imported from some mountain climate where the oxygen levels do something to the wood to make it stronger. All this does is make it harder to distinguish where I am as I barrel through the halls, praying I don't smash my face against thousand-dollar wood stain.

My father would kill me for smudging the walls.

The air rushes from my lungs, and I nearly trip.

My father.

If he knew what his men were doing to me, he'd be outraged. No one touches his only daughter. That's why Ezra was assigned as my bodyguard in the first place—to make sure that everyone kept their hands to themselves.

Nothing Andrei, Ezra, or Mikhail have done follows protocol for how to treat a mafia princess. *Their* mafia princess.

My dad will be livid.

Breathing hard, I duck into the library to catch my breath. No one ever comes here, because all the knowledge in the world is at our fingertips these days. *Thanks, internet.* But for a lonely girl without much freedom to roam, the library has always been my solace.

I stumble around the shelves, trying to find a place to hide. Not much has changed since I was here last, and I'm eternally grateful as I travel familiar territory.

If Mikhail follows me in here, I can outmaneuver him.

No one comes in here but me.

My teeth ache as I try to calm my breathing, but my heart won't stop pounding. I realize I've got a death grip on something soft—the pants I snagged from the hallway—and pull them on as fast as possible. Smooth fabric hugs my thighs, and I gasp at how perfect they are. Not too tight around the waist, not skimming the floor, and made from some kind of pristine white fabric that kisses my skin.

I'm still marveling at the luxury wrapped around my calves when I catch deep, dark laughter echoing through the room.

The high, vaulted ceilings have always made this room more acoustic than a library should ever be, but when I was younger, I liked it. I could sing to fill the empty spaces left after my mother passed.

"Your five minutes are up," Mikhail taunts. He steps into the library, and the cold marble at his feet clicks with each step he takes.

I listen for where he moves and slowly step in the other

direction, careful to avoid his line of sight as we dance through the shelves.

"I think it's about time I earned *mine.*"

There's a possessive growl attached to the word *mine,* and I gasp as heat floods my body. Nothing about this situation should be hot. I'm terrified. My adrenaline's running on high, and my heart feels like it could beat right out of my chest.

I'm being hunted.

By a maniac.

Probably a killer.

A *very hot* murderer. Why is it that the villains are *always* sexy and delicious?

Little drops of red paint the white marble floor in swaying lines, and as I follow the trail with my eyes, I realize that it's blood . . . and it's not mine.

There's only one other person in this room, and he's stalking me. *Bleeding.*

If someone hit me like that, I'd run the other way, probably screaming my lungs out the entire time. But these men are made differently than most, and a little blood doesn't scare them.

It might even excite them.

"Are you scared, *malyshka?*"

Shit, he's closer than I thought. I got distracted and let myself slow down.

"Can you feel your heart pounding?"

My heart skips a beat, and I have to bite back a scared little whine in my throat.

"Your pulse racing?"

I draw as deep a breath as I dare and start walking faster toward the exit. My socks give me relative stealth, and I walk as quickly as possible.

"I won't hurt you," Mikhail murmurs, so soft that I

wouldn't hear him if it weren't for the echo. "If that's what you're so afraid of, I promise, I'll never hurt you."

Forgive me if I don't believe that from someone I just mained with a fucking *lamp*.

"But I think . . ." His voice echoes from all sides.

I whip my head around to try and catch him walking toward me, but it's impossible to know where he's coming from. The blood on the floor is splattered all around now, impossible to track as we walk in circles around each other.

"...I think that you're scared of something else." He steps into view at the end of my aisle, the grin on his face pure triumph. Blood drips down a gouge in his forehead, covering his cheek and staining his crisp blue button-down, before *drip-dropping* on the marble. "Any idea what that could be?"

I lift my chin high and stare Mikhail down. My knees are shaking, and I think the adrenaline is making me woozy, but if he enjoys the hunt, I won't give him the satisfaction of chasing me down.

I'll come to him.

I take careful steps forward, running my hand along the shelf to my right to keep me steady. He stands completely still as I approach, his eyes alight with mischievous joy as I stop in front of him.

But I'm not here to play his little game.

"I want to see my father." I cross my arms over my chest and press my lips together tightly. "*Now.*"

Mikhail tilts his head to the side as he studies me. "And what do I get for taking you to him?"

My confidence wavers. What if my father already knows I'm here? Is he avoiding seeing me? Is he allowing his men to toy with me?

Is he really dead like Andrei says he is?

Mikhail's hand cups my cheek, his expression softening.

"Don't look so sad, *malyshka*. These are the rules of the game. You need to learn them to survive."

"I don't want to play your stupid games."

He tuts softly. "Not *my* game. *The* game."

"What?"

His lips curve into a smile. "You were born to play this one."

I still don't follow, and he laughs at me. "Don't worry. I'll teach you everything you need to know to win. But for now, I'll take you to see your father, free of charge." He winks. "It will be my second kindness for the day."

The man is *crazy*. "You call stalking me across the house kind?"

He takes a step closer to me and I retreat. Two more steps, and I'm backed against the bookshelf with nowhere to turn. I can taste the metallic scent in the air near him, but the bleeding has lessened to a slow trickle.

Mikhail's palm on my cheek slides down to my jaw and holds on tight. He wrenches my face up to meet his eyes.

"I bring you gifts," he murmurs, his voice rumbling like thunder, "and you not only make me bleed, but you *run* from me. That's a double insult. Then you walk over to me, and instead of apologizing, you start making demands." He leans closer, his warm amber eyes half-lidded, and I almost expect him to kiss me.

My eyes widen and my breath hitches in anticipation, my heart stuttering in my chest.

This is all kinds of fucked up. Everything about today. Everything about this man. Everything that he makes me *feel*.

Breathless. From fear and desire and my own kind of crazy.

Turning my head roughly to the side, he crowds in closer and brushes his lips against my pulse point. A shiver rolls through him, and he kisses the sensitive spot like a lover.

"You're trembling, yet you're brave enough to let me get close. To make *demands* of me." His chuckle rumbles deep in his chest, and my toes curl without my consent.

"I'm not apologizing," I say, forcing my voice to remain steady.

"I don't want you to." Mikhail stands back up and brushes the pad of his thumb against my lips. "A queen never apologizes."

His eyes linger on my lips for a moment longer before he lets me go and gestures toward the exit, his expression turning serious. "I'll take you to see your father, Valentina."

I bite the inside of my cheek and watch Mikhail for signs of crazy or betrayal. "Just like that?"

He raises an eyebrow. "Would you rather me drag you kicking and screaming back to your room?"

My defenses flare. "No, but . . . you're injured." My eyes flicker up to the deep cut on his forehead. "Shouldn't you get that checked out first?"

With a short shake of his head, he plants his hand on my lower back and steers me out of the library. "Not important."

I fail to see how a head wound isn't important, and guilt eats at me the longer we walk through the house. I *injured* him. He's right. He brought me clothes in all those designer bags, and the first thing I do is throw a lamp at him. Then I ran away. Now, he's taking me to see my father—the one reason I came to this fucking place to begin with—and isn't demanding anything in return.

I don't know what kind of game Mikhail is playing at with these strange acts of kindness, especially after everything I just put him through. I should feel good about it, right? I'm getting what I wanted, apparently free of charge.

The whole reason I came here was to get answers from my father, and now it's finally happening.

And yet. . .

I have a feeling that Mikhail's the one calling the shots after all.

Chapter 7

Valentina

My father's gravestone looks nothing like I imagined. I'm not sure *what* I imagined, but this isn't it. Plain, gray stone, its edges hard and sharp, juts into the sky like a monolith. Singular. Striking.

Lonely.

There are no words of wisdom etched on its face. No titles, such as *loving father* or *fearless leader*. Just his name, Mikolov Tolkotsky, and his birth and death dates.

Two years. He's been gone almost half the time I was away, and no one told me. I find it hard to believe that my grandmother didn't catch wind of the news; she's got friends in high places within the city. I doubt she went *completely* dark after we left.

She may not have held much love for her son-in-law, but she loves *me*.

I should have known he was gone long before now.

But would knowing have changed anything?

I stare at the gravesite in silence. If I'd known he was dead, I could have stayed away from the city. Andrei wouldn't have found me, and I would have been free to do whatever I wanted with my life. *Truly* free.

Sighing, I press my fingertips to the back of my eyelids. My grandmother must not have known, or she would have brought us back sooner. Maybe we could have stopped hiding in fear that he'd find us.

Maybe Andrei wouldn't be so bitter.

An ache blooms deep inside my chest as I think about my ex-fiancee. If there's one thing I regret, it's whatever turned the man I once loved into something cruel. Was it me? Is it my fault he's like this?

With a grimace, I open my eyes. What happened while I was gone can't be my fault. I wasn't even here.

I'm sure Andrei blames me anyway.

I focus on my surroundings to dull the ache inside my heart. The area around my father's grave is barren, with dying grasses and dark earth peeking through the blades. No one is buried near him, and I glance around the Baranova family cemetery to count the stones.

We're some of the founding members of the city. Ancient, unmarked graves sprinkle the landscape in mismatched rows. Beyond that, once documentation became more legitimate, you begin to see names and dates carved into the stones. Organization and structure begin when you reach the 1700s, although the number of graves decreases with each century.

The family cemetery stretches on for at least half a mile in all directions.

My father's grave is in the center of it all, like he claims power over his ancestors, even in death.

"What happened to you?" My words are little more than whispers, but in the end, it doesn't matter.

The dead can't listen.

I came here for nothing. Drawing a breath, I let reality sink in. I gave up my freedom, and for what? The chance to talk to a corpse?

My eyes burn, and I rub them with the back of my hands. *Stupid Valentina.* Getting carried away again. Caught up in a fool's errand.

"You wouldn't have answered me, even if you were here," I find myself saying. "You never talked to me, anyway."

Memories of my life pierce my skin like shards of glass, each one sharper than the last. My father was known for his cruelty, and that cruelty extended even to his daughter. Cold, clipped words. A pat on the shoulder when I kept silent and smiled prettily. Gifts that reminded me I was meant to be a doll, kept on the shelf to be admired, but never anything more than that.

I'm not sure how my mother could stand living next to someone as unaffected as he.

It's probably why she left . . . and why she died.

I swallow the lump in my throat, but my eyes won't stop burning.

I never got to say goodbye to my mother. One moment, she was combing my hair and telling me how beautiful and strong I was. The next, she was gone. Vanished in the middle of the night, like she never existed at all.

Sick, my father said once. Then he never mentioned her again.

I didn't get to say goodbye to my mother, but I *chose* not to say goodbye to my father when I left.

My fists clench at my sides.

"What secrets are you keeping?" My knees hit the earth, and I stare at the grass covering his grave, picturing him lying below the surface like he's sleeping in silk. Dressed in a suit, like always. Out of reach, like always.

His secrets buried with him.

My mother's secrets too.

Maeve Baranova-Tolkotsky knew her place within the Bratva. She kept her nose out of trouble, taught her daughter to stay silent, and played the role of the perfect wife.

To me, she looked like a queen. Perfectly curled hair pinned around her face. Yellow diamonds lying across her neck, matching ones clasped around her wrists.

They might as well have been made of iron, because a Baranova woman is a woman shackled. To her duty. To her husband. To the *Bratva*.

I picture myself on my wedding day, wearing my mother's yellow diamonds, my hair pinned in neat curls on my head, my smile as perfect as my mother's.

By following in her footsteps, I believed I would become closer to her. Catch glimpses of her beyond the veil. See her when I looked at my own reflection.

When the letter arrived—unmarked like it, too, was a secret—it took me by surprise. I'm not sure where it came from, or how it got into my dressing room, or why it had been hidden for so long.

The curved script was familiar the instant I saw it.

She deserves a life full of love. A life without violence and death around every corner. One where she will be cherished. Where her husband will do anything for her happiness.

I close my eyes and picture the words I've long since memorized.

You should want what's best for our daughter.

Although my mother never accused my father of anything, I could read the subtext in every line.

I'm giving our daughter the life I never had.

A tear falls down my cheek.

I ruined my mother's sacrifice the moment I stepped back within the city limits. Back into my father's territory.

Only, it wasn't my father who was waiting for me.

It was my ex-fiancé.

The man groomed to be just like him.

Andrei Leonov.

I sit in silence on my father's grave as I search the pieces of my life for answers. When my mother died six years ago, was I too blind to see anything? Any hint of what happened to her?

A Baranova funeral is a grand event, and people from all corners of the city came to bear witness to my mother's. People I'd never met—some even traveling from as far as Russia—gathered around to listen to my father give her eulogy. He said pretty things about his pretty wife, but I can't remember a single word.

Her empty casket spoke volumes. For a man so powerful, even he couldn't find his missing wife.

But that's not right. Narrowing my eyes, I look deeper. *He told me she was sick. A sick person's body doesn't just wander off.*

There were pieces missing from my father's story. Pieces he'd intentionally left out.

Like a secret letter saying she was leaving him and taking me with her.

Mikhail stands behind me in silent observance, giving me space to absorb this moment. I'm grateful for it. Out of the three men holding me captive, I would have expected him to be the loudest. The one snickering in the background as he counts my tears.

I stand from the dirt and brush what I can from my new pants, frowning at the stains already setting in. "I ruined your pants," I say simply, glancing up at Mikhail. The shoes, too, judging by the dirty streaks clinging to the white leather.

He shrugs one shoulder. "I'll buy you another pair if you like them so much." A twinkle enters his eye, like he enjoys the idea of buying me things . . . or of me enjoying his gifts.

I sigh and shake my head. He's still covered in blood, though it's mostly dry, the red streaks muddying his otherwise handsome complexion. Stubble lines his cheeks, and rich brown waves curl around his ears. His stylist must be proud; the man clearly cares about his looks and takes his hair care routine seriously.

He stares right back, a small, confident smile playing on his lips. He knows he's gorgeous, and he enjoys the attention it brings him.

I turn away from him to find my mother's grave. Because there was no body to bury upon her death, my father delayed creating a marker for her. I remember asking him about it, finding it strange that there was no memory of her in the house. No pictures of her or our family, none of her favorite paintings hung on the walls, and not a single of her favorite roses filling the vases scattered around the property.

It's like she never existed at all.

"Where's my mother's grave?" I ask Mikhail, meeting his eyes. In the year after my mother's passing, I waited for my father to make good on his word of finding the perfect spot to bury my mother's empty casket.

I waited. And waited. *And waited.*

Until, finally, I left. But surely, in his remaining years before he died, he found the time to memorialize his wife.

Mikhail's expression flickers like he's in pain. He reaches

for my hand and tugs me closer to him. "Valentina . . ." He draws a breath and brings his other hand to my face, tenderly brushing a loose strand of hair behind my ear.

I wait for him to lead me in the direction of her grave. I'd like to pay my respects. Tell my mother hello, even though she's not really there. Shed a tear or two for the time we lost.

I wait . . . but Mikhail doesn't move.

My breath catches. "No." I shake my head, not willing to believe what his silence is telling me. "No, that can't be." I try to turn my head to survey the entire family cemetery, but Mikhail's hand dives into my hair and cradles the back of my head.

"*Shh.* It's okay."

He tries to capture my attention, but I'm frantic, battering my hands against his chest. "No. *No.* Nonono." I strain my neck against Mikhail's hold, but he pulls me into his arms and locks me against his body. Like statues, we stand together, the cool autumn air surrounding us.

Suffocating us.

I try to breathe, but it comes out ragged. "How dare he. *How dare he.*" A sob racks my chest, but I rein it in, choking on my sudden, overwhelming sorrow.

It doesn't make sense. They were married for twenty years! How could he not fulfill his promise and give me something to remember her by. How could *he* not want anything?

A chill creeps up my spine as I think of my mother's secret letter.

"No." I push against Mikhail, but he holds me tight, rigid in his embrace. "Let me go, Mikhail. *Let me go.*"

"I won't let you hurt yourself."

I snap my head up to meet his eyes. "I'm not going to hurt myself," I hiss, glaring at him. "I'm gonna . . ." I struggle to find the words. What *am* I going to do?

It doesn't matter. I just need to *do* something. "Just let me go, okay!"

He exhales slowly, his amber eyes intense as he studies me. "If you run, I'll catch you."

I almost laugh. Where does he expect me to go?

Slowly, hesitantly, he releases his hold on me. I can tell he doesn't want to; he grimaces like it's a horrible mistake and stays close enough to grab me if I fall or flee.

I do neither. Instead, I turn back to my father's grave and glare daggers at the dead bastard's buried corpse. "You didn't even bury her!" I yell, stomping on his *stupid* plot. "All this space out here! A fucking *casket*, Dad! You bought the most glamorous casket I've ever seen, and for what? To put on a show?" I clench my fists. I want to punch something. Throw something fragile and hear it break. Strangle my stupid, arrogant, lying bastard of a father.

He wasn't looking for the perfect spot to bury his perfect wife. He was never going to bury her.

"What is *wrong* with him?" My frown feels permanent as I stomp over his corpse and plant the heel of my foot on the gravestone. I push, extending my leg as far as I can, but it doesn't budge.

Of course, it doesn't.

My rage grows. What else did he lie to me about? What else did he hide from me?

Mikhail's arms lock onto my own, and he hauls me back, forcing me away from my father's tombstone. "You're going to hurt yourself," he murmurs gently.

"I want to hurt *him*," I snarl, still glaring at my father's *stupid* tomb. "This is all his fault!"

Mikhail hums in the back of his throat as he drags me out of the cemetery. I don't have the energy to fight this time, so I let him half-carry me across the lawn. We move in silence until Mikhail starts veering in the opposite direction of the house, toward a long, unbroken line of wrought-iron fencing on the far side of the property.

"I want to show you something." His eyes sparkle like he's got a secret, but I'm *done* with secrets.

"Tell me what it is, or I'm not going." I plant my feet and shrug out of Mikhail's grasp, crossing my arms over my chest. "I can't deal with any more secrets today."

He places his palm on a scanner I didn't notice, and the gate slides open enough for a single person to pass through. "No secrets, then." Taking my hand, he leads me through the gate, and it closes automatically behind us. "Not between us."

"That sounds like a promise."

Smiling, he squeezes my hand as we step through a thin patch of trees and immediately onto a sidewalk. The contrast from expansive lawn to shining cityscape is jarring, and I stumble as he leads me away from the Baranova estate.

"There's a place I like to go," he says slowly, looking off into the distance. The sunlight pours over him like liquid gold, revealing auburn highlights in his hair I didn't notice before. "When things in my head get too loud, it helps drown out all the noise."

The sound of waves crashing along the shore reaches my ears, the caw of seagulls joining in the moment we clear the last row of seaside boutiques. An endless expanse of rich white sand stretches in front of us, cut off only by the waves lapping at its heels.

I had no idea a beach even *existed* so close to home. Part of that truth hurts, because it means I was kept so cloistered that I didn't notice . . . or I willingly missed the hint of salt in the air any time I stepped past the estate's walls.

Which is it? Willful or forced ignorance?

Mikhail pauses at the sand's edge and looks back at me. The light shifts as the sun begins to set, casting shadows behind palm trees and reflecting orange off cresting ocean waves. Each passing minute alters our scope of reality as day gives way to dusk, the world shifting before our very eyes.

I'm drawn into Mikhail's gaze and, for the second time today, close the distance between us willingly.

His smile is brighter than the setting sun.

Lifting my hand to his lips, he presses a kiss to my open palm and takes a single step backward, silently urging me to follow him.

Like a tiny moth, enticed by the forbidden flicker and heat of a deadly fire, I choose temptation over safety.

I follow the light and let it burn away everything that hurts.

CHAPTER 8

MIKHAIL

THICK, salt air brushes against my skin as a breeze kicks up across the long stretch of white sand. I have to brush my hair from my eyes to catch a glimpse of Valentina's dazzling smile as the wind whips around her.

She's with me.

Willingly.

I never expected her to follow me off Baranova grounds. By all accounts, she should have run from me the moment she had an opening. Whether while walking across the lawn or the moment she bypassed the gate, she should have run screaming.

I chased her through the house.

I brought her to her father's *grave* without reminding her beforehand that Daddy Dearest was dead and gone, six feet under, years ago.

If that wasn't enough, I've made it no secret that I harbor a malicious sense of glee when she squirms. *Especially* when she squirms.

And yet, here she is, with me.

Perhaps we both lack the skills to make proper, sane judgment calls. Because as much as she should be running from me, *I* should be running from *her*.

Andrei says he doesn't care who Valentina chooses between the three of us, as long as she chooses to stay. Yet the man was practically foaming at the mouth the minute I showed him security footage of his runaway bride poorly scaling one of our fences. He's spent years searching for her, even after Tolkotsky was too sick and feeble to give the order.

Even after Tolkotsky *died*.

Ezra pretends to be flippant about her sudden return to his life, but the man could drop a bagel and find reason to brood about it. Valentina waltzing into his bedroom unannounced?

The man will brood for *weeks*.

As cool and unaffected as he pretends to be, even Ezra wallowed in sorrow, pity, and self-hatred for *so long* after Valentina disappeared.

Both men can claim they aren't interested in her, but anyone with half a brain knows how shit-faced of a lie that is.

I'm playing a dangerous game by claiming Valentina for myself. By teasing her and stealing her away from right under their noses.

But what's life without a little chaos thrown into the mix?

As we wander closer to the sound of crashing ocean waves, I can't keep the grin off my face. I'm going to have *so much fun* toying with *my* girl.

She catches me staring at her and has the decency to blush pretty pink all for me.

My new favorite color.

Valentina brushes dark curls over her shoulder and attempts to braid them. She avoids my gaze, her cheeks still faintly flushed, and busies herself with her hands. "You're staring again."

I watch her fingers' nimble movements with mute fascination. She's not even paying attention to what she's doing; it's automatic. The braid comes out perfect, despite the tumultuous sea breeze attempting to thwart her efforts.

How many hidden talents does she have?

Which ones involve those dexterous fingers?

"I'm allowed to stare," I say simply. She couldn't stop me from staring if she tried.

"It's indecent." Her lips purse ever so slightly, like she's tasted something sour. "You look like a madman."

My tongue slides out across my upper lip, and her eyes catch the movement. She blushes harder.

Will she tell me I taste like a madman too?

The urge to steal a kiss from her while she's distracted pumps like lead through my veins, powerful and demanding. I bet catching her by surprise would be even more delectable than the kiss itself.

I draw a deep breath, imagining the wide-eyed shock rendering her completely still in my arms. Her body warm against mine. Her lips soft, pliant.

Tempting, but it'll have to wait.

Instead of feeding my inner demons, I pull off my Oxfords and socks and set them aside. "At least I'm not about to walk the beach in my shoes." I stare pointedly at her feet.

A rush of pride rolls through me at seeing the shoes I bought her hugging her soles. White leather looks good on her skin. I'll have to buy more for her.

With a huff, she kicks off her shoes and haphazardly sets them beside mine. Before I can snag her arm, she starts walking away from me and down the short boardwalk to the beach. I take my time following her, enjoying the way the sun plays on her dark hair and highlights the tiniest slips of skin on display.

Namely, her neck.

The gray sweater she has on does little for her figure, and I think back to all the gifts I brought her this afternoon. If she'd put any number of them on, she'd look even more ravishing right now than she already does.

She curves her spine to glance over her shoulder at me and quickly turns back around when she realizes that, *yes*, I'm still staring.

She'll learn soon enough that I'm always going to be watching.

When she reaches the edges of the waves and the rolling water touches her toes, she shrieks and jumps back. "It's freezing!"

I'm not sure what she expected. It's nearly winter.

She turns to look at me again, and the way her mouth opens in a shocked little *o* makes mine water. Eyebrows raised, cheeks flushed, sunset playing in her eyes . . .

Desire curls low in my loins, and I bare my teeth at her, raking my eyes across the curve of her neck, the swell of her plush breasts, down the arch of her back.

She's too distracted to resist, so I close the distance between us in one graceful swoop. Laying my arm across her waist, I drag her away from the rising tide kissing at her heels. "Careful, *malyshka*, or you might get pulled in."

Pursing her full lips and crinkling her nose at me, she makes a sour face but doesn't pull away, and *that* is the first of many small victories I intend to collect.

"By what, the Loch Ness monster?" She scoffs.

"Maybe." My lips curve into a small smile as I lower them to her ear. "I'm sure there are plenty of monsters vying to keep you."

A chill runs down her arms, spreading goosebumps in its wake. I chuckle and blow across her sensitive neck, making her gasp.

The sound is just as delicious as the rest of her. I hold her tighter to my side and ignore the way my cock twitches impatiently in my pants.

It can wait.

"You can't be serious," she murmurs, the incredulity in her tone raking against my nerves. I joke about a lot of things, but about how desirable Valentina is?

Never.

"I'm *very* serious."

She tilts her head back to glance up at me. "*Please.* There's no such thing as monsters."

Oh, malyshka.

Our breath mingles as we hover close enough to kiss.

On impulse, I brush my knuckles against her rosy cheek. I want to kiss her. *Badly.* Almost bad enough to say *fuck the consequences* and go for it, even if she screams. A shiver runs down my spine.

Especially if she screams.

Her words come floating back to me as if in slow motion, their meaning taking far too long to register in my brain.

There's no such thing as monsters.

What a tempting challenge she's all but dropped in my lap. To prove monsters exist. It would be so *easy.*

Her body tenses as she realizes how fucking close we're standing. She turns her face away from mine and laughs, but it's forced. I hate the way her voice flatlines.

"What happened to my armed escort?" she asks suddenly, sidestepping out from under my arm and cleverly disguising it as jumping over a puddle of saltwater. "I thought I was supposed to have a guard at all times."

The air instantly cools with Valentina so far away, and my lips twitch into a heavy scowl. "Cute." I try not to roll my eyes and *barely* succeed.

Not only do I carry a semi-auto pistol at all times, but I've got a knife strapped to my thigh and plenty of hidden weapons caches around the city. We won't be wanting for weapons anywhere within reach.

I'm all the protection she needs.

"What?" She flashes a fiery glare in my direction before she catches the look on my face. Her eyes widen, and she nearly trips over some seaweed. "You're armed?"

What kind of a question is that?

"Of course, I'm armed." I raise an eyebrow at her. "Who did you think you were with, Prince Charming?" I nearly laugh at the thought. Prince Charming couldn't protect his princess, even if her life depended on it.

He *definitely* couldn't press a gun to her lips and order her to suck it like a good fucking girl, either.

My cock stirs at the thought of Valentina stroking my handgun with her tongue. Maybe I'll test her limits very, *very* soon.

While I'm imagining her lips wrapped around my piece, her eyes latch on to the side of my face, and it takes me a second to realize why. I've still got dried blood on my cheek from when she threw a lamp at my head. A nasty gouge in my forehead, too, if memory serves.

Judging by the look on Valentina's face, she forgot about it too, and now she knows I'm armed *and* dangerous. Her eyes nearly bulge from their sockets as she sucks in a deep breath and holds it.

She looks like a goddamned puffer fish about to pop, and it's probably the most ridiculous thing I've ever seen. I'm not going to hurt her over a mishap with a fucking lamp.

"Of course not" she snips, her surprise quickly morphing into sass the longer I stare at her. "You're nothing like Prince Charming." She whips her braid over her shoulder as she turns on her heel and walks away.

The temptation to snatch her up and devour that smart

mouth of hers is like poison in my veins. She's right — I'm not Prince Charming.

I'm something much, *much* worse.

Every time she whips her head around like that and turns away from me, she's one step closer to realizing just how real monsters are.

Close. But not there yet.

I press my palm to the rod of iron in my pants, hissing through my teeth at the discomfort. It's too soon. I want to savor that fiery temper she has a little longer before I shove my cock down her throat. I bet she'll glare at me while she sucks it, too.

My eyes roll back. *Fuck*, that's gonna be a pretty sight.

I follow Valentina down the shoreline, ignoring the wet sand clumping between our toes and on our ankles the longer we walk. The cool twilight air helps lessen my throbbing need for her, so I allow her to take her time and enjoy the moment. Soon enough, we'll have to turn around and head back to the estate. Andrei is expecting her, and he can be a mean bastard when left waiting too long.

We walk in silence for another mile, those quick, little birds trotting across the sand our only company. She keeps her distance from me, which is fine, so long as she's within grabbing distance.

I haven't put it past her to run yet, even barefoot.

"Why did you bring me here?"

I barely hear her over the crashing waves and cawing gulls, so I use it as an excuse to stand closer. Brushing our shoulders together, I dip my head lower. "Come again?"

She sucks in her cheeks, and I quickly commit the stubborn defiance in her emerald eyes to memory.

Fucking delicious.

"You heard me."

I did, and she called me out on it. I can't keep the smile off my face. Not everyone's so brazen, especially to a made man. My smile quickly fades, however, as we come to the answer of her question.

"This place . . ." I run a hand through my hair and gaze out at the horizon, watching the fading sunlight disappear like sand slipping through an hourglass.

I've never brought anyone here before. It's a public beach, so it's not like it's mine. I don't *own* the beach. Still, despite the dozens of properties I keep across the city, this place is my favorite out of every single one.

As I ponder my answer, Valentina watches me. A warm sensation rolls down my spine. I *like* how it feels to be watched by the very woman I've been staring at every possible second. A small smile flickers across my face for the briefest moment.

And then, once again, it dies. "When things get tough, or there are too many thoughts rattling around my skull, I come here."

The sun finally bids farewell and dips beneath the ocean surface. The temperature instantly drops, and any remaining beachgoers start moving with haste to retreat indoors to safety and warmth.

But things like safety and warmth aren't guaranteed, no matter where you are. Not at home. Not at work. Not in the arms of a lover.

Safety is a feeling, a false sense of security.

This place brings me as close to *safety* as I can get.

Valentina waits patiently for me to continue. I'm not sure I have anything more to say. But I did promise to teach her the rules of the game, and while I have her attention, perhaps it's best she learns something, after all.

I draw a deep breath and decide to jump straight to the heart of Valentina's pain — the reason we're here at the beach in the first place. "Do you know why your mother doesn't have a grave?"

Valentina visibly jumps, like a crab just pinched her toes. It's cute, but if I smile now, she'll hate me for it.

She bundles up as best she can in her sweater, closing in on herself in an instant. I know she's cold, but she's not *that* cold.

"Because my father was a cruel man," she murmurs softly, her eyes flicking up from where her ankles are sinking in the sand to latch on to something more solid and permanent. Like me.

Her eyes search mine for answers, like she wants me to tell her that he wasn't a cruel bastard.

Too bad. He was fucking vindictive.

I nod. "He was. But that's not why he refused to bury your mother."

Valentina sinks deeper into the sand, and I watch the last rays of sunlight flicker out. I don't like talking about what comes next. It enters personal territory, and that's a place I keep out of reach, even for myself.

I don't like to go there. Ever.

For the first time in a long time, I feel my mouth curve *down*, and I already hate it. But the beautiful woman by my side asked a question, and although I could deflect or tell a lie, I made a promise.

No secrets. Not between us.

I take a breath to stall for time. I'm tempted to pull Valentina's face to mine and bury our problems beneath that kiss I keep thinking about. I bet it would be mind-blowing to get my lips on hers. To soothe our aches with each other's bodies and pretend our battered bruises and scars don't exist.

If we get lost in each other, we won't have to dig up the past. We won't have to have this conversation, or any others like it.

But Valentina's eyes pull me in, the confusion and pain etched within making part of me bleed with her.

That's new. I usually don't give a fuck about others' pain.

But Valentina's . . . makes me uncomfortable.

I draw another breath and try to detangle the chaos that is Tolkotsky in bite-sized pieces for her to understand. "You may have known Tolkotsky as a father figure, but I knew him as a *pakhan*. He was ruthless when it mattered most, especially when it came to how he ran the Bratva. Every *pakhan* demands loyalty, but your father had a . . . flair about it." I clench and unclench my jaw as memories rise to the surface. *Bad* ones. But if Valentina is going to understand what happened to her mother, she needs to know what happened to *my* father.

"I knew this guy, once. Best in his sector. A leader that everyone looked up to. Your father respected him enough to make him head of our properties division. It's a high-ranking position that requires a lot of knowledge about the city and its districts. *And* how much they're worth." I pause to make sure Valentina is paying attention. When she meets my eyes, I continue. "Well one day, he decided he'd had enough of Bratva life. But the thing is, once you're in, there's only one way out."

"Death," Valentina murmurs.

I nod. "So this guy, he wants out, right? He has access to hundreds of properties within the city and all their stats. Property values, equity, market rates, maintenance reports, everything. He gets the bright idea to sell some not just the info, but the properties themselves to a rival family. This would have given him quick cash to get out of the city while also undermining Tolkotsky's influence within his own territory. If he acted fast enough, the money would have helped him escape. The trick is, he had to be *really* fast." I turn my gaze toward the sea, letting a shiver roll down my spine.

In the end, my father wasn't smart enough, or quick enough, to pull off his grand plan.

"Anyone trying to undermine or overthrow Tolkotsky was sentenced to die one way or another. If not a swift death, then a painful one. This man's fate was much the same as all the others who tried before him."

I remember the night vividly. The look of relief on my father's face when he saw it was me who came for him. How he tried to coax me into leaving with him. Said he did it for our family, to give us a better life.

Please. He was ready to bolt while my mother and sister sat in the other room, completely unaware of his plan and the half-packed suitcase full of his belongings.

When Andrei seemingly materialized from the shadows behind me, however, my father turned white as a ghost. Started stuttering apologies. How he didn't know who the buyers were or what their plans were for the properties or the city. Claiming that he wanted to turn a profit for the Bratva, of course, nothing more.

The lies were pitiful, falling from his lips like shards of glass, each one cutting deeper than the last.

When his words failed to move Andrei, my father turned back to me, red-faced and spitting mad. *You brought him here, didn't you, brought him here to watch me die and carry the news back to that bastard!*

Tolkotsky was a cruel man, yes. But my father was a cowardly piece of shit, when it came down to it.

I'd rather he have faced death with dignity, instead of cowering like a scared animal.

Shooting him in the back of the head was a mercy he didn't deserve.

"What does that have to do with my mother's burial?" Valentina asks, crossing her arms.

It's simpler than she realizes, and she's not going to like it.

"That man was labeled a traitor, Valentina. Not only was he killed for it, but he was never buried."

Whether someone is a traitor doesn't matter. It sets a precedent for others.

Don't fuck over the Bratva.

Don't fuck over your *true* family.

Valentina may not realize it, but leaving Andrei at the altar and ditching the Bratva brought her dangerously close to *traitor* territory. It's only by the grace of her bloodline and Andrei's interception that Valentina's father, and our Bratva, didn't disown her for it.

She needs to learn this lesson if she's going to survive. She won't get a second chance if she tries to leave again.

Valentina purses her lips like she doesn't believe me. Or, more likely, she's too stubborn to accept the truth.

"My mother didn't betray anyone."

"So you say."

"She *didn't*."

"How do you know?" I fix Valentina with a pointed stare. "She disappeared, Valentina. The only reasons people disappear within the Bratva are bad ones."

I don't actually know the details surrounding Maeve Baranova's disappearance. Rumors from outside Bratva lines say that she ran away, but anyone within our ranks knows that she'd never escape her husband's wrath if she so much as tried such a thing. His fury had no bounds. No matter which corner of the earth she ran to, he'd find her, and he'd make her pay for the insult.

No, Maeve Baranova didn't run away. She's dead. Named a traitor, most likely, and paid the ultimate price for it.

Just like my father.

Just like all the men who came before him and proved their disloyalty.

If Maeve had an affair, said the wrong thing in public, or tried to leave, Tolkotsky would have enough reason to kill her.

That doesn't mean I agree with it, but we don't have to agree with all the rules of the Bratva. We just have to follow them.

Valentina huffs defiantly and walks away from me, toward the boardwalk. I have to jog to keep up with her. "Valentina —" I grab her wrist as she takes her first step on the wooden walkway, and she snaps her head around to glare at me.

"Don't *touch* me," she hisses, wrenching her arm free from my grasp. "You think this little walk was *fun?* You just told me that my dad probably killed my mom in cold blood. That's not fun, Mikhail. That's the opposite of fun."

"The truth isn't always sunshine and rainbows, *malyshka.*"

"I don't need sunshine!" She shoves my chest and pushes me back a step. "I just need my world not to crumble in one fucking day! Jesus. It's like you guys get off on giving me bad news!" She throws her hands up. "First, my father's dead. Then, my ex is the new leader of the fucking Bratva. And *now,* my mother's not only unmemorialized, but my dad might have killed her. How could this day get any worse?"

I part my lips to tell her what's next on the agenda, but she clamps her hand over my mouth. "*Please,* no more. Just take me back already."

She glances over my shoulder at the darkened beach, a hollow look in her eyes. "This day couldn't get any worse."

I curl my fingers around hers and press a kiss to her palm. It's not her lips, but she still manages to blush for me. A flash of heat burns deep in my loins, and I'm smiling as I pull her hand away and give it a squeeze.

"Okay, *malyshka.* No more from me tonight."

She nods, relief clear on her face.

I *could* warn her about what's waiting for her back home .. . but that would be more bad news, and, well, I'm nothing if not a man of my word.

Besides, the look on her face when she realizes Andrei expects her to join him for dinner tonight will be *priceless.*

Chapter 9

Valentina

Mikhail and I walk in silence as we return to the estate, through the secret gate and across the lawn. The warm glow of porch lights guides me home. I never thought I'd say it, but I'm grateful to return to Baranova grounds and, hopefully, to a warm bed.

Anything to erase the past three hours of my life would be *great*.

Does Mikhail get off on delivering bad news, or is he *that* out of touch with humanity?

I ignore him as best I can the entire walk back. I can feel his eyes on me the whole way, digging into the back of my skull. If he wants to know what I'm thinking, *tough shit*. I'm not talking.

To think I was actually *grateful* that he took me to my father's grave at first. Ha! How things have changed!

I hug my arms to my chest and hop up the three short steps onto the back porch. Still, he says he took me to the beach to help me drown out all the noise . . . and I guess, in a way, that's sweet. But my heart has no business melting a little because of it. Stalker men with guns, no matter how rich and handsome, are still dangerous.

He chased me through the house. I hit him with a lamp.

Nothing about that screams romance.

And yet. My heart skips a beat as I resist the urge to sneak another peek at him. He didn't have to do any of those things for me today. He could have kept me locked up in my room and forced me to play dress up while he sat there and told me to spin around for him to get the full picture.

My heart flutters in my chest. If I played along and tried on all those outfits for him, would he like what he sees?

As I reach the door, I'm lost in thought about how praise might sound on Mikhail's lips. I don't notice a figure emerging from the shadows until he speaks.

"Did you enjoy your evening, Valentina?"

I scream.

Andrei folds his arms over his chest and frowns at me, like a disappointed parent catching their teenager sneaking out of the house. It gets worse as his eyes graze my body and he spots the stains on my pants. Particularly, the two circular ones hovering right over my kneecaps. "Why are you covered in dirt?" His eyes narrow before flicking up to Mikhail. "What did you make her do?"

"Nothing," Mikhail replies breezily. Even without facing him, I can picture the smirk plastered across his face. "She asked me for something, and I delivered. She was so grateful for it too. Isn't that right, *malyshka?*"

The innuendo sends a rush of desire rolling through my veins. If I'd gotten on my knees for him, would he have called me a good girl? I suck in a breath and channel all the horny energy into something else: annoyance. I can't let these men get to me so easily.

"Don't call me that." I don't know what *malyshka* means,

and I'm suddenly *very* agitated about it. "He took me to my father's grave," I snap, glaring at Andrei like this is all his fault.

It kind of is, since he's the one who decided to keep me here in the first place. If he had let me go, maybe I wouldn't be having all these fantasies about dark and delicious Russian men. I could be normal again, fantasizing about a cute barista writing his phone number on my to-go cup or the handsome mailman bringing me a *special* delivery.

Instead, I'm left wondering how Ezra's tattoos feel under my palms, how Mikhail's praise might taste against my lips, and how rough Andrei might fuck me now that he hates me.

Desire burns through me just as hot as my anger. Maybe hotter. I have to fight to stay focused.

Andrei stares at the dirt stains over my knees. "I would have taken you to see him."

My nostrils flare. "I don't want to be anywhere near you." I storm past Andrei and into the house, both men following me inside.

"Valentina—"

"I'm going to my room."

Goodbye, bitches.

As I turn a corner, annoyingly, I find that both of them are still following me. "Alone," I huff. "I'm going to my room *alone.* Neither of you are invited. Go away, now."

One second I'm walking down the hallway, and the next I've got my back to the wall with an *angry* mafia man holding me there. His hands on my hips burn white hot. "You don't get to give orders. You take them."

This is the moment all mafia princesses are trained to avoid, or in instances like this when it's too late, when we beg for forgiveness. We're supposed to look down at our feet. Apologize for our error. Maybe offer to suck a cock as penitence. But *fuck* that. I'm not their princess anymore.

I won't take orders from anyone.

"Get off of me, Andrei. I mean it."

He exhales across my face. "Go change and meet me in the dining room."

I sputter. "I'm sorry?"

"Go change," he repeats, his grip on my hips tightening, "before I come undress you myself."

"You get off on that, don't you?" I can't help but egg him on now that I've got a backbone. I have no doubt it'll get me in trouble, but my heart hammers in my chest, pumping adrenaline through my veins. This is *new*. This is *exciting*.

I'm not the same girl I was five years ago. I'm not afraid to break the rules if they don't serve me. And the rule about doing what you're told is *stupid*.

I won't be Andrei's plaything.

Still, my body betrays me as I remember how he helped me step out of my pants in his office earlier this afternoon. The way his hands grazed my thighs. How he threw me onto his desk and held me down, pinning me beneath his hips . . . and damn near shoved his cock inside me.

My core clenches at the memory, and part of me hates myself for it. I shouldn't like his behavior, but it's another thing that's new.

Five years ago, he wouldn't have dared touch me that way.

But now?

All bets are off. The man in front of me is changed. *I'm* changed.

And as dangerous as that may be . . . it's also thrilling.

Andrei hooks his hand under my chin and leans in close. My breath catches as I picture him kissing me. We've done this part a thousand times, stealing kisses when we thought no one was looking.

Innocent kisses, but kisses nonetheless.

The way his blue eyes smolder over mine is anything but innocent, and another wave of desire rolls through me.

I might hate him, but *fuck* is he hot.

Our lips brush, and our eyes lock. Not a kiss, but not *not* a kiss.

"Defy me again and find out."

He releases me, and I try not to melt in a puddle on the floor. Mikhail's laughter mocks me as I promptly lift my chin, roll my shoulders back, and march down the hall to my bedroom. Thankfully, this time, neither of them follow.

As I close the double doors and test the lock, I run a hand through my hair, my fingers snagging on my braid. Frustrated, I start pulling it loose as I trudge into the bathroom. Someone's been here while I've been gone, filling the counter with various hair and skin care products, a wide array of makeup options, and even a jewelry stand tucked into the corner. Jewels of all sizes and colors twinkle up at me, and I resist the urge to throw them on the white marble floor.

None of this will buy my heart or my loyalty.

Then again, Andrei told me he didn't *need* my heart.

Just my name . . . and my body.

I stare at my reflection as I peel off my clothes. One by one, I drop each luxurious piece of fabric to the floor until I'm completely naked.

I'm more than a body. I'm more than a name.

If Andrei wants those, he's going to have to take all the rest, too.

The shower is fully stocked when I step inside and turn on the hot water. I scrub my entire body from head to toe, removing all traces of the beach from my skin. I comb my fingers through my hair and use a generous amount of conditioner to fix my curls. How would Andrei react if I walked out of here naked? Sat across from him at the dining table, dripping water all over his fancy chairs and shining silverware?

Would he bend me over the table and spank me for it?

Once I've rubbed my skin raw, I turn the shower off, twist my hair in a towel, and move on to the bedroom.

Everything that was once in disarray is now organized again, from the furniture to the clothes Mikhail and I scattered across the floor during our *misunderstanding* earlier. Every piece of clothing lays in neat stacks across the bed. Dresses and blouses more fit for spring or summer than winter, then woolen sweaters bunched up in various shades of forest green or royal blue, and an array of pants, skirts, and stockings that I have little hope of ever wearing this time of year.

Someone went well out of their way to provide these for me. Each and every item still has the tag attached, a golden *CM* brand logo glinting up at me. I've never heard of *CM*, but as I rub a blouse between my fingertips, I know I'll never forget them. Everything screams luxury. No expense was spared with these clothes.

A tented card sits on the nightstand where the lamp used to be, and I drop the blouse to flick open the card and see what it says.

Keep what you want and burn the rest. —M

I roll my eyes and set the card down.

Seems that Mikhail has a flair for the dramatic. Who would've guessed? But at least things will stay interesting around here.

As I choose my outfit and decide to go without makeup, I keep looking over my shoulder, expecting one of the three men to appear out of thing air. I'm used to Ezra being a silent sentinel just outside my door, or on the balcony overlooking the lawn, but now I keep picturing Andrei sitting at the edge of my bed watching me get ready, or Mikhail grinning at me from the doorway as he imagines all kinds of twisted ways to agitate me.

It's as annoying as it is nice not to feel alone, even if they are dangerous for me to be around.

I sigh as I toss a pair of black flats into the closet. I don't have any slippers, so I guess I'm going barefoot. My stomach growls, reminding me that I haven't eaten since breakfast.

If Andrei makes me beg for food, I'd rather starve.

With one last, deep breath, I unlock the bedroom doors and pad down the hall to the dining room. It doesn't take long to get there; it's the center of the house and used for all manner of events — parties, conferences, everyday meals. The biggest room in the house, by design.

The doors are open when I arrive, and I'm surprised to find Andrei sitting alone at the head of the table. The room feels spacious without dozens of guests socializing within, filling the room with their gossip and banter. The last time I stood in this room, it was for a bridal shower, and I wore a white lace tea dress meant to remind everyone who the lucky bride was.

Not like anyone could forget. It was supposed to be the wedding of the century.

And now, I'm alone with the groom I left at the altar.

Our eyes meet, and he inclines his head in greeting. "I see you chose something casual."

The sweater is the softest one I found, a pale blue that reminds me of a spring sky. The pants are loose, with white fabric flowing around my ankles every time I take a step. Comfortable more than stylish, but this isn't exactly a night out on the town.

My stomach growls again, louder this time, and I grimace. "Sit."

Two gleaming silver cloches lay in front of the only two

chairs in the room: mine and Andrei's. I'm surprised when he stands and pulls out my chair for me, the one seated directly to his left.

"Where are Ezra and Mikhail?"

Andrei pushes my chair in now that I'm seated. "I thought we might have a moment alone to discuss our engagement."

"We're not engaged."

He lifts the cloche over my plate, and steam wafts into the air. A perfectly-seared steak, grilled asparagus, and mashed potatoes. A tiny gravy boat accompanies the plate, reminding me of all the meals I've had just like this one in the past. Some fancier, some not. My mother made a point for me to try as many dishes as our chef could make, so that I would be well versed in schooling my expression if something didn't agree with my palate.

"It's rude not to finish a meal," she used to tell me. "You must try everything on your plate and always give compliments to the chef."

I wonder if Andrei kept the same kitchen staff, or if that's changed, too.

"I never rescinded my offer of marriage. To my knowledge, you have not, either." Andrei uncorks a bottle of red wine and pours us each a glass. He holds one out for me to take. "That makes us very much engaged, Valentina."

I don't accept the wine, so he sets it down in front of me. "You'd think one public rejection was enough." My hands shake as I pick up my dinner fork and a knife. I clutch them as tight as possible to keep my hands steady. "Leaving you at the altar should have made my intent clear. I don't want to marry you, Andrei."

It's the first time I've said the words aloud, and my body trembles. I thought I'd feel confident saying that to his face, but I want to hide, instead. There's nowhere for me to go unless I crawl under the table, so I remain seated and start cutting into my steak.

I can feel Andrei's eyes cutting into *me*, and I try not to look nervous.

He hums in the back of his throat. "Fortunately, what you want doesn't matter."

My knife screeches against the porcelain plate.

I look up at my ex to find him smirking at me over his wine glass.

"I won't marry you." I set my knife and fork down and ignore the way my stomach drops. "You can't make me."

"That's where you're wrong." He sets down his wine and leans back in his chair. "You were promised to me, Valentina. *You* made a promise. Publicly. Many times."

I wince at the reminder of how long our engagement was. We attended dozens of private parties and public events within the city, wrapped in each other's arms, smiling like two lovesick fools for all to see.

Our engagement was *very* public.

"This Bratva is built on the vows we make. The vows we *keep*. As its heir, you can't break your vows, Valentina."

I summon all the courage I have and push my chair out to stand. Andrei doesn't make a move, but his jaw visibly tics. "Watch me." I make it halfway to the door before Andrei calls out.

"I wouldn't do that if I were you."

Sighing, I glance at him over my shoulder. "Why? Because you'll punish me for it?"

He cuts into his steak like this is the most casual conversation in the world. Lifting a piece to his lips, he takes it into his mouth and makes me watch him swallow. My stomach clenches painfully. I'm tempted to march back over there and take my plate to-go, even if it *does* piss him off.

"I'm thinking of paying your grandmother a visit. I'm sure she'd love to see me after all these years."

Ice splinters inside my heart. My grandmother is all the family I have left. She made a point to stay far, far away from the Bratva after we left.

I thought it was to keep my father's men from finding me, but now that Mikhail has so graciously informed me that people who try to leave, die trying . . .

Maybe she was saving her neck as much as mine.

"You don't know where she is." I clench my fists to keep them from shaking. "You won't find her."

"We will, soon enough." Andrei's confidence radiates from his entire body, his presence filling the room from floor to ceiling. I used to find his strength alluring.

Now, it's suffocating.

He stands from his seat and rounds the edge of the table. "When I see her again, will I have good news, Valentina? Or bad?" I'm frozen to the spot as he closes the distance between us. I forget how to breathe.

This is fucked up. This is *seriously* fucked up.

I've always known that my father cavorted with unkind people. But I held a belief that he, himself, remained good. He didn't steal. He didn't murder. He stayed above the law as best he could, given the nature of Bratva business.

My world view is crumbling before my eyes, and the truth is pitch black.

Andrei stands in front of me. He doesn't touch me. But the way he looks at me is complete possession, like I'm already his.

Like I always have been.

"What will it be, Valentina? Good news, or bad?"

My mother's face flashes to mind, the golden crown I used to admire now heavy over her head. Did she have to make these decisions, too? Was her life, or mine, or her mother's, threatened if she didn't obey?

But Andrei won't kill *me*. He needs me. He's said so himself.

And, my grandmother is a tough, old Russian woman. If Andrei's men find her, she won't go down without a fight.

That makes my decision easy. After this particular display of cruelty, I take my metaphorical knife and not only stab Andrei in the heart, but I twist it, too. I place my palm over his chest and feel the steady beat of his heart.

He may have spent the past five years bleeding, but he can withstand a little more pain.

"I'd rather die than marry you."

Anger flashes like lightning in his sapphire eyes. "You are *mine*." His hand wraps around my throat, warm and solid, as he drags my chest against his. I fight his grasp, clawing at his fingers, but it's no use. I might as well be a rag doll with how easily he throws me around.

"Your life, your death, your soul. All of it is *mine*." He squeezes my throat tightly, panic ripping through me as he cuts off my air. My heart beats frantically in my chest, begging for life.

"You *will* marry me, Valentina Baranova, because I won't settle for less." There's a hunger in his eyes, and then his mouth descends, crashing over mine with such force that my body succumbs. My knees buckle, and he groans as I fall into his arms.

Black spots dance in my vision. Not only is he choking me, but he's not giving me any room to breathe, even if I could. A whimper catches in my throat, and he drags me to the dining room table. Sitting me down on top of it, he looms over me, holding me upright.

The moment he releases my throat, I gasp for air, each breath burning in my lungs. As I inhale deep, he descends again, groaning as he steals more from me. His fist tangles in my hair and holds me in place.

Somehow, I muster the strength to grab his cheek and *push*, digging my nails into his skin. He hisses into my mouth but doesn't relent, molding his lips to mine with such fervor that I drown.

No kiss has ever been like this.

I can feel darkness taking over, like a poison pulling me under. I'm swept away by it, powerless as I'm dragged further away from life and closer to death.

Andrei tastes like whatever waits on the other side. A promise of power and possession, wrapped around me like satin ribbons. Soft at first, tempting me into submission, until he grasps the ends and *pulls*, cinching them so tight that I bleed.

The longer the kiss lasts, the more I succumb. One kiss turns into many, and I lose myself in them. They become familiar. They become *wanted*.

A kiss will never be the same again.

When he finally pulls back, he breathes just as heavily as me. My nails left half-moon indents across his cheek, one of them pricking with blood. He licks his lips and takes a step back, admiring the sight of me disheveled, lips swollen, throat red, gasping for air.

He stretches his fingers in front of him. Like the past few minutes never happened, he starts talking business. "You will spend the next few weeks reacclimating to life within these walls. Additionally, I will be taking you out into the city for various social events. Mikhail and Ezra will be doing the same. I'm sure you remember the duties of a *pakhan's* wife?"

My brain struggles to keep up. I stare at Andrei, the man I once loved, and barely recognize him. Maybe the man I loved was never real, after all. Maybe *this* cruel version of him is the truth.

A single tear rolls down my cheek. Maybe this is exactly what my mother was trying to save me from before she died.

Andrei lifts his finger and claims the teardrop before it falls. "By the time our wedding comes around, you will have reclaimed some of your old duties and taken up new ones. We will rekindle relationships with prominent families within the city, and everyone will be reminded of our strength. There will be no room for doubt." He cups my cheek. "Will there, *moya zhena?*"

My heart clenches as the familiar Russian phrase passes his lips. I used to love the way he called me his wife.

Now, however, I'm not so sure.

I don't respond, to which he sighs. "Come, now, Valentina. I asked you a question."

This is part of the role I'm meant to fill. Speak when spoken to. Say *yes, sir.* Follow orders.

It's tempting to slip into the role. It would be much easier for me to submit. Less painful than if I fight.

But I didn't spend five years away to come crawling back to him. I've learned a few things while I'm gone. One of them being malicious compliance.

If he wants a queen, I'll give him a queen worth remembering.

"I understand."

He takes my hand and leads me back to our seats, seemingly placated by my acceptance of my fate.

But as we dine together and he rattles off plans for the next few weeks, I make my own. A queen, after all, has power and influence just as much as her king does.

If there's one thing I learned from my mother, it's how to command respect within a crowd. To gain power by means other than fear.

I'll give Andrei his queen, but he may regret choosing me when our vows are made in blood.

CHAPTER 10

VALENTINA

My first week in the estate is spent monitoring its schedule. The staff moves as one cohesive unit, each person having their purpose within the well-oiled machine. It's nothing new, since the estate has always been professionally run. My mother used to manage the household, and my grandmother before her.

Now, it's my turn.

Many faces recognize me, though few seem thrilled with my return. Most are passive and polite. I'm not sure how Andrei has been running things in my absence, but the lack of warm fuzzies within the staff leaves much to be desired.

I find our head chef Louis elbow-deep in planning a weekly menu. "Thank you for the steak last night," I tell him quickly, not wanting to take up too much of his time. "It was delicious."

"When I heard you were back, I knew it was the perfect welcome." He winks at me. "You've always been a meat and potatoes girl."

Warmth fills my heart. At least someone remembers me fondly. I thank him again and leave him to his work. A few more minutes is all I need to familiarize myself with all the new names and faces in the kitchen and introduce myself to every single one.

A few are grateful, but most are surprised.

I doubt Andrei took the time to learn their names.

When my tour of the house and its mechanics is finished, I find myself wandering the gardens. Endless rows of seasonal flora greet me, and I wish I had a sketchbook to note their arrangement. Someone must have a guide or blueprint. I make a mental note to ask for the head landscaper to give me a guided tour soon.

I want to know every square inch of this property, down to the last root and stem. The best way to claim power is to take it right from under my fiancé's nose, one sliver at a time.

I'll show him what it means to rule a Bratva. You can't solely focus on the business and forget about the people whose backbones it was built on.

As I avoid the rose garden and its labyrinth of thorny walls, I catch someone spying on me from the back porch. "Back to our old routines, are we?" I raise an eyebrow at Ezra. "I thought you might have grown out of the whole bodyguard thing. Haven't you been promoted yet?"

Ezra grunts, but doesn't take the bait. I'll have to riddle out his official job title on my own, or with the help of the staff. They always know more than they let on.

He crosses his arms and leans against a cement statue of two lovers dancing together. It's always been one of my favorites within the gardens. "What have you been doing past five years?" he asks.

I shrug. "Not much. Working. Dating."

His eyes narrow. "How long have you and Liam been together?"

"That's none of your business."

He stares at me, so I cross my arms and stare right back.

When I don't elaborate, he moves on. "Your work. What did you do?"

I don't mind answering this question. "I worked in real estate. We bought properties, repurposed them, and sold them for a profit. Kind of like flipping houses, but commercially." I don't know the logistics of how it all worked, but between milling about the office and perusing files left out at Liam's apartment, I saw enough reports to get an idea of the company's resources and profits. "We're a big company. Multi-million dollars worth."

"What is company name?"

I press my lips into a thin line. "I hardly see how that's important. You asked what I did for work, and I've told you." Now he's just digging for secrets to blackmail me.

My eyes widen. Or, more likely, he's trying to find my grandmother. I promptly shut the fuck up and go back to wandering the grounds.

Over the next few days, I catch glimpses of all three men. Ezra keeps an eye on me from a distance, Mikhail is on the phone a lot, and Andrei stays holed up in his office most of the time. I eat dinner with Andrei every night, as he promised, and he tells me about what events he's lined up for us.

"The mayor's birthday is this weekend," he tells me one such evening. "I expect you to join me."

"He won't know who I am."

"He will," Andrei assures me. "Everyone will, and they'll all be clamoring for an invite to our wedding." He swirls the wine in his glass with a small, twisted smile. "It'll be even grander than the last."

I clear my throat and smooth my napkin in my lap. "I'd like to help with the planning."

Tilting his head, Andrei studies me. "You were barely interested in planning our first wedding."

Damn, I was hoping he'd forgotten about that. "I'm

older now. I know what I want." I pop a cherry tomato into my mouth. "If you pick a hideous color scheme, that's all anyone will remember. Andrei and Valentina, married by clowns." I pull a face. "That's not how I want people to remember me."

He continues to watch me as I swipe my dinner roll across my plate. "Be up and ready by nine. We'll meet with our coordinator in the morning."

After dinner, I'm excused, and we go our separate ways. He doesn't try to kiss me again.

I almost wish he would. My heart races every time he comes close to touching me . . . and then I'm left aching for something I shouldn't want.

The last few days have been torture of a different kind. I expected him to beat me. Curse me. Rage over and over again. But he's been decidedly calm, when I'm expecting the wrath of a storm.

Has my submission pleased him that much?

Or is he waiting to strike when I least expect it?

The anticipation is its own kind of high, and it leads me down dangerous paths. More than once, I lie awake at night, shoving my fingers inside my drenched pussy as deep as they can go, all because of that *fucking* kiss.

It was earth-shattering. Mind-breaking. And my body wants more. So how can I get what I want?

If I go to him, straddle his thighs at his desk or, more likely, at the dinner table, he'll pride himself on making me want him. It'll be proof of his claim over me. Of his *power* over me.

That's not what I want.

So instead of going to him, I start trying to lure him out.

The library is the first place I desecrate. If we had a chapel on the grounds, I might have picked it first. There's something inherently deviant about feeding your sexual demons on holy ground, but since that's not an option, I pick the next best thing.

Hunkering down in my favorite reading nook, with my back against the cool, stone wall and my leg propped up on the window seat, I spread my thighs wide.

To passerby outside, it might look like I'm taking a cat nap in the silver moonlight.

But to anyone within earshot, there's only *one* plausible explanation.

I bite my lip as I knead my breast through my nightgown. My other hand travels lower, ghosting over my panties. I'm already soaking wet, amped up by yet another sexually-charged dinner. I made sure to lick my spoon graciously, sucking on the tip as I listened to Andrei prattle on about seating arrangements and guest lists for the wedding.

I might be laying it on thick, but at this point, I don't care. I want him to cave before me, and I'll use any trick in the book to make it happen.

My back arches as I slide my fingertips into my panties and swirl them over my clit. A cry catches on my lips, and I shut my eyes as I imagine Andrei standing over me, hooded eyes burning like liquid sapphires, as I touch myself.

He kisses my neck and groans in my ear, pressing the heavy weight of his rock hard cock against my thigh. As I plunge a finger inside my molten core, he grinds against my leg and pants in my ear. When he speaks, it's not Andrei's voice growling in my ear, but Mikhail's, low and deep and filthy as he tells me what he's going to do to me the next time he gets me on my knees.

I whimper and grind my clit against the heel of my palm. It's not enough. It's never enough. Heat rushes through me as desire coils deep in my belly. My fingers aren't thick enough. My reach isn't deep enough. My voice is whiny and shrill as it echoes through the library, not deep and sensuous.

In my delirium, I imagine Mikhail's mischievous chuckle vibrating across my skin, the word *malyshka* turning into a low moan in the back of his throat.

Even *Mikhail* is starting to get to me.

Fuck.

I cry out as I come, my body trembling. White stars fill my vision, and I pull deep lungfuls of air. Sweat slicks my skin and makes my nightgown cling to my curves.

I'm not usually like this. Even with Liam, nothing was ever this intense. When we were together, I didn't feel the need to rub myself raw in the middle of the night. In the middle of a *library.*

Shame tries to douse my inner fire, but it's nowhere near strong enough to succeed. I'm a woman on a mission. I'll claim my gilded crown and enjoy all the cock that comes with it.

A faint echo through the rafters sets my heart racing.

"Malyshka."

A deep laugh, then footsteps coming closer. "Someone's being a naughty girl."

I catch a silhouette at the end of an aisle before he disappears behind a bookshelf. His footsteps tap lightly as he wanders the library. I wonder if he's coming closer or circling the room to build anticipation before he reveals himself.

Slick desire drips down my thighs from my release. A touch of fear makes everything more intense, from the chill in the night air to the ache in my back from lying on a bench for so long. Goosebumps trail down my arms, my nipples hardening beneath the thin fabric of my gown. I hold my breath as I wait for something to happen.

You're engaged, the voice of reason in my head reminds me. *You shouldn't bait the devil with your body.*

But isn't that what I've been doing all along? Trying to lure a devil out of his hiding place and into my bed?

I caught one, but it's not the devil I intended.

Still.

I can't deny my attraction to any one of the men holding me captive. Not just Andrei, but Ezra and Mikhail too. All three of them are driving me mad without even trying. Glimpses of them in the hallways are like little teases, making me crave more attention from each of them.

Mikhail chuckles once more, the sound reverberating through the air and dancing across my skin. I'm already in the deep end and treading water. I might as well dive under and give in to temptation.

I hold my breath and swirl my fingertips over my clit in one steady, slow motion. A moan catches in my throat, deep and needy, my eyes fluttering shut.

So what if Mikhail watches?

Maybe I want him to.

I prop my leg up higher on the window seat and pull my panties down my thighs. Cool air on my sensitive parts makes me shiver and my nipples even harder. I lick my lips and slide a single finger inside my heat.

It's not enough to get me off, but knowing that Mikhail might be watching makes my core clench greedily. My finger slides deeper, sucked in easily, then a second joins the first. My breathing shallows as I pick up the pace, moving between rubbing my clit and fingering myself, my skin flushed, my desire building.

I hear Mikhail groan nearby.

A wave of pleasure rolls through my body from head to toe.

"What's going on in that pretty little head of yours?" His voice rumbles close by, making me gasp. "Who are you imagining, Valentina? Is it Andrei bending you over his desk as he pounds deep and hard? Or is it Ezra you imagine walking in on your filthy display and licking your dripping cunt clean?"

I moan as both of those fantasies flicker through my mind. Either one would be *amazing*. I want both.

Warmth covers my breast as Mikhail lays his hand on my chest and squeezes, fitting my taut nipple between his fingers. Pleasure zips down my spine, and I gasp, my eyes snapping open.

Mikhail grins down at me, the copper glimmer in his eyes wicked and sinful. He kneads my breast and rolls my nipple between his knuckles. "Such a naughty girl, wanting more than one man." His eyes travel down my body and lock onto my bare pussy as I curl two fingers inside my heat. "You're soaking wet," he groans, massaging my breast harder. "You've been waiting for someone to catch you, haven't you?"

My body twitches, burning red hot, as he says the truth out loud. It sounds much more vulgar in the open than it did in my head.

"Yes." The admission feels dirty, but I can't hide from it. That's exactly what I've been waiting for.

And now, I've been caught.

Mikhail reaches for the hand caught between my thighs and pulls it away from my body. He holds it up and inspects my fingers, looking serious as he twists my wrist in the moonlight. "You've been at it so long, your fingers have pruned." Our eyes meet as he holds my fingers to his lips and slides one inside his mouth. His eyes roll back as he tastes me, swirling his tongue around my finger before adding the second one and doing the same.

My jaw drops. No one's ever sucked my fingers before, especially after I just came all over them. His tongue flicks against me, and *god*, I'm so close to coming again.

"*Mmm.* You taste divine, *malyshka.*"

A whimper catches in my throat. More desire drips from my aching core. I shouldn't enjoy this so much when I wanted Andrei to find me first. But, if he happens to catch me and Mikhail in here together . . . I bite my bottom lip as I tilt my head to the side and come face to face with evidence of Mikhail's arousal. He hasn't made a move to free himself from his pants, but *fuck*, I can see the outline of his dick.

I reach for his belt buckle, but he drops my hand and takes a step back.

"Ah-ah. What would Andrei think if he found you sucking my cock all of a sudden?" Mikhail clicks his tongue mockingly. "Of course, we could *invite* him." Reaching into his pocket, he pulls out a cell phone. "What do you say? Should we call Andrei and tell him that you want my big, fat cock buried in that sweet pussy of yours?" He takes a step closer and unlocks the screen. "Would you beg for permission first, or for forgiveness after?"

Oh, god. I don't know. What kind of a question is that? I swallow hard and try to think through the lust fogging my brain.

I *did* say that I'd claim my crown . . . and cock.

Could I really have *multiple* cocks? Multiple men?

I'm not into one night stands. I want to be with someone who cares about me for more than my body. Andrei used to love me. Part of him still might, if his possessiveness is anything to judge by. Ezra has always looked out for me and protected me, and even though he's upset that I left five years ago, I know that our history can't be erased.

Mikhail is the one I'm unsure about.

I bite my lip as indecision clouds my judgement.

My hesitation doesn't go unnoticed.

Mikhail's eyes narrow. "Oh, so you want my cock, but without anyone knowing about it, is that it?" He closes the short distance between us and kneels on the bench, lifting my thighs so that he can wedge himself between the wall and my pussy. He bends my knees and plants my feet on either side of of his hips, the soles of my feet pressed flat against the cold marble wall.

His cock strains against his slacks, thick as a steel rod. As he lowers it over my pussy, he clenches his jaw iron-tight. The weight of him settles over me, his package fitting perfectly over my exposed entrance. He rotates his hips, drenching his pants as he grinds against me.

Pleasure floods my system as he applies pressure exactly where I need it, rubbing his cock directly over my clit.

"You're a filthy fucking girl," he growls, gripping my thighs and spreading them farther apart. "You want to be seen shoving your fingers down your pussy, but not by *me*." He bares his teeth as he chokes on jealousy. "I promise you, *malyshka*, I can make you come so hard that you scream. You'll forget all about Andrei and Ezra while my cock is driving you mad." He thrusts, sliding his length between my lips as the tip rubs my clit. "I can fit better than your fingers ever could. I can make you cream all over my cock. Over, and over, and over again." My tits bounce with each thrust of his hips as he drags his cock through my slick folds, staining his slacks with my arousal.

This is obscene.

This is *wrong*.

But *holy fucking shit*, do I *love* it.

I reach for Mikhail's phone and pull it from his pocket. He continues grinding while I struggle with the lock screen.

"Two, six, two, five." Mikhail grins, the mischievous glint in his eye returning. "That spells *cock*, in case you're wondering."

My laugh is rich, echoing through the room. A weight on my heart lifts, just enough for me to notice it was ever there at all. I can't remember the last time I laughed. It feels heavenly.

"He's under favorites."

I click to the *favorites* tab and scan the names. There are only four of them. *Pakhan.* Muscle. Stylist. Someone named with only the letter *M*. "Your stylist is in your favorites?" I can't help but giggle. "You must call them a lot."

Mikhail's smile sharpens. "Call your fiancé or give the phone back, Valentina."

My mind sobers at the threat laced through his words.

It's then I realize—I have a cell phone in my hands.

I could call for help. I could be *free.*

Mikhail realizes the same thing at the same exact moment I do. He shifts his weight and quickly climbs on top of me, knocking the phone from my hand as soon as he's within reach. It clatters to the floor and skids down an aisle.

With a glare, he realigns his cock to my center and *thrusts*, but the pressure hurts. I whine as pain mixes with pleasure.

"Say you want me." He fists my hair and wrenches my head to the side, forcing me to look out the window. The courtyard is empty. My breath fogs the glass. I don't know what I'm supposed to be looking at.

"See how your body aches for mine."

I allow my eyes to unfocus, and *then* I see us reflected in the window. Cramped in the alcove, barely able to fit, our bodies locking together like puzzle pieces. He's on his knees, with my thighs pressed firmly to his as he damn near bends me in half, our hips aligned perfectly as he thrusts, hard and heavy, on top of me. One of my arms wraps around his shoulder, while the other is crushed between our chests, my fist clenching the collar of his shirt. I've ripped the first two buttons open. I hadn't even noticed.

"You want me," Mikhail seethes, his lips ghosting the shell of my ear. "Or you wouldn't come for me like a dirty fucking whore."

"*Ah*," I moan, the insult running hot through my veins. An ache settles deep inside my core. I crave more than Mikhail is giving me, *much more*. I dig my nails into his shoulder as he continues torturing my clit.

He groans and drags his lips against my cheek. "I bet you'd love for me to shove my dick inside your tight little hole." When I gasp, he laughs. "Maybe we'll have to ask Andrei for forgiveness, after all. What do you say? Want me to fuck you, Valentina?" He lowers his voice to a whisper. *"Right here, right now."*

I whimper, but can't form any words. Pressure builds deep in my belly, signaling my coming demise.

"I bet he can hear how wet you are for me all the way in his office. This room amplifies sound, and you're fucking *drenched*." Mikhail turns my face back towards him and brushes our lips together. "But don't worry, I'll cover your mouth when you scream."

Panic laces with anticipation as he reaches between us.

He's going to fuck me. He's going to rip down his zipper, pull out his cock, and shove it inside me, all because I couldn't say no.

Because I didn't *want* to say no.

His lifts his hips to create space between us, and I shut my eyes to prepare for the hottest, most indecent fuck of my life.

Something thick glides inside my pussy, stretching out my walls, before retreating again. I choke on a moan as I realize it's not Mikhail's cock—but his *fingers*. He slides two of them inside me, only to drag them back out nice and slow, the surge of arousal coursing through my veins making me gush around his thick fingers.

"*Fuck*, yes," he groans, repeating the motion. There's no mistaking the slick, wet sound filling the air, and I tremble as pleasure builds rapidly.

Oh, god. He was right. He *does* fit better than my fingers ever could. I cry out as my orgasm crests *hard* and washes over me like a tidal wave.

True to his word, the moment I tip over the edge, Mikhail's mouth is on mine, swallowing my scream as I writhe on the bench beneath him. He doesn't stop plunging inside me as I come—he drags out my pleasure one wicked finger curl at a time.

Only when I'm a whimpering mess does he relent, pulling his fingers from my sticky center.

His tongue swipes against my lips as he continues kissing me, molding our mouths together like he's content to stay there forever. His hand travels up my curves, trailing my sticky desire across my skin and marking me with it.

My body trembles as I wrestle with what just happened. I let another man touch me—and I *liked* it. There's no telling how Andrei will react. Will he kill Mikhail for touching me, or will he kill me for enjoying it?

Only once Mikhail is satisfied does he let me go, breaking the kiss with a satisfied hum. He brushes a lock of hair from my face and stares into my eyes like he's trying to capture my soul.

My heart skips a beat when he smiles, his expression softening as he gazes down at me.

"Good girl," he praises, kissing me again. "You come so well for me. It's a shame we didn't have an audience."

Boneless, I watch as he detangles our limbs and stands. Silver moonlight streaks through the window, outlining his dick print with excruciating detail. He squeezes his package with a groan. "I'm gonna come so hard thinking about you, *malyshka*." He cups my jaw and swipes his thumb against my bottom lip. "It's a shame you won't get to wrap those pretty lips around me."

I couldn't agree more.

He grins down at me when I bite my lip. "Hold on, stay still." Picking up his cell phone, he quickly snaps a picture before I realize what he's doing. "That'll be my new wallpaper. Maybe I'll send it to the guys so we can share."

My cheeks burn as I sit up. "You wouldn't."

"Oh, there's a lot of things I'd do to you, Valentina. Sending a picture of your creamy pussy and tits out is just the beginning." He winks. "Be a good girl, now, and go to bed. It's past your bed time."

I listen to the click of his shoes as he exits the library. It takes a long time for my breathing to return to normal, but my heart rate stays elevated long after he's gone.

Someone could have heard us. Someone likely *did.*

I sit up, biting my lip as I rub numbness from my pretzeled limbs. In truth, someone hearing us isn't what troubles me.

The fact that I *want* someone to have heard us, does.

CHAPTER 11

ANDREI

A LIGHT *PING* on my cell phone catches my attention. Not that there was much keeping it to begin with; ever since Valentina arrived, she's all I can think about. To make matters worse, she's taken to roaming the house and speaking with anyone and everyone within reach—meaning that not only am I thinking about her constantly, but I'm getting visual and audible reminders of her existence consistently throughout each day.

Not only is she haunting my daylight hours, but she's haunting my midnight ones, too.

That part isn't new. I've been having nightmares about Valentina ever since the day she left me standing alone at the altar. But the dreams have taken on new life, morphing into sexually charged fantasies that pump desire through my veins all hours of the night.

I've awoken with a swollen cock, aching to fuck my bride's brains out, more times than I can count.

Tonight is no different. I'm not even sure I've slept at all. She won't get out of my head.

The wedding planning doesn't help, either. My imagination runs wild, conjuring up images of her in lacy white thongs and a matching veil, with nothing else keeping her modest.

The elastic waistbands in my pants will be worn out by the time our wedding comes around. They've been fighting to keep my cock under control nearly all damned day this week.

With a groan, I roll onto my side and ignore the monster between my legs to reach for my phone.

The moment I open the group chat between Mikhail, Ezra, and I, a curse flies past my lips and a jet of cum soils my sheets.

Someone's sent a sexy-as-fuck picture of *my* wife.

Valentina's *fuck me* eyes are on full display, but so are her gorgeous tits. My gaze drifts lower, and a growl catches in my throat at what I find.

Her bare fucking snatch, glistening in the moonlight, like she came all over herself seconds before the picture was taken.

A new message from Mikhail bumps the picture higher in the chat.

> Someone's been a naughty girl.

My mouth curves into a deep scowl as I fire back a text.

> Did you fuck her?

I didn't set any rules about fucking Valentina. In fact, I distinctly remember saying that Mikhail and Ezra *could* claim her, heart and body, as long as one of us convinces her to stay in the Bratva for good.

That doesn't mean I wasn't looking forward to being the first man to claim her, though. Anger surges through me as I imagine Mikhail impaling her with his cock and holding his hand over her mouth so that I don't hear them fucking in the library.

Are they in there now? Is he balls deep this *fucking* second?

> Not yet. But you need to get in there, fast. She's gonna ruin that fucking bench if she keeps this up.

How long has she been in there? How often? I toss my phone to the mattress and throw my legs over the side. Fuck sitting here. I need to know more about what my wife's been up to.

I throw on the first pair of pants that I find and leave my bedroom. The hallways are empty save for the few guards on patrol. I ignore them as I make my way to the library.

The door is wide open, and I step across the threshold and into the cold night air. The library is one of the oldest rooms in the house, and the tallest. The rafters reach higher than other sections of the house, allowing for picturesque windows to reach high up above and filter natural light inside.

The walls and floor are covered in marble, making the room colder than the rest of the house. A lack of insulation on the outside wall doesn't help matters.

Why Valentina likes it here, I'll never understand.

I ignore the icy floor and make my way to the back where all the window seats reside. Every single bench is empty, and I check the image on my cell phone to find the one Valentina sat in. I didn't ask Mikhail when the picture was taken, but as my eyes sweep the wood, I realize I don't have to.

Running my fingers along the seat, I touch a damp spot and groan. I lift my fingers to my face and inhale, catching a whiff of Valentina's arousal.

This is the exact spot where she exposed herself and played

with her pussy until she made *such* a pretty little mess of herself.

My cock twitches in my pants, impatient for release.

"You think you can come without us finding out, *zhena*?" I grit my teeth as I undo my pants and allow my cock to spring free. Gripping my shaft, I pump slow and steady, picturing Valentina lying naked on the bench in front of me. "We see *everything* you do. One of us is always watching, always listening."

Even if we weren't keeping constant tabs on her, there are security cameras recording footage all over the house, *including* Valentina's bedroom, but I've yet to check them. I have no doubt Ezra has been keeping tabs on her, though, as part of his job. He monitors all of the security footage across the estate, or instructs his team to do so. The bedrooms, however, I know he monitors himself.

If she's been masturbating at night, he'll know about it.

I glance up at the camera secured to the corner of this room. I wonder if he'll replay the footage of whatever happened in here, too.

I'll have to get him to send me a copy.

Pleasure zips up my spine as I stroke myself faster, imagining Valentina panting as she watches me, her lips parted in a pretty little *o*. Her fingers slide inside her dripping wet cunt, and she gasps like it's a surprise that it feels fucking amazing.

"Just wait until I get my cock inside you," I growl, my movements growing frantic as my balls tighten. I haven't come since she first arrived a few days ago. I vowed to save it for her, but *fuck*, I can't wait any longer or I'll drown her in cum. "You'll turn into my perfect little slut, won't you, *zhena*? Begging for it every single day."

I hiss as I explode in my fist, ropes of my seed painting the bench white. I squeeze my shaft and pull every last drop from my cock, adding to the depraved display.

Mikhail would call this a masterpiece, the sick fuck.

On a whim, I snap a picture and send it to the group.

> She's next.

Three pulsing dots signify someone's incoming reply.

> Are you going first?

I consider the question as I tuck my cock inside my pants and zip up. All of my men defer to me as their *pakhan*, and as their leader, it's my right to take what I want, when I want.

I know I'll fuck her. It's not a matter of if, but *when*. I'm sure that's what Mikhail is asking—am I going to waltz into her bedroom and claim what's mine *first*, before either he or Ezra gets a taste, or is she fair game for round one?

I share many things with Ezra and Mikhail. My power, my home, my life, my secrets. I'm not used to sharing women, though. It's never come up before Valentina. But I'm nothing if not a man of my word, and I told both of them that not only could they have her, but that we need *her* to choose someone to love between the three of us so that she has a reason to stay in the Bratva.

Or, she could choose *all* of us instead of only one.

I imagine Valentina kneeled before me as I come all over her face. Then it's not *just* me standing there—it's Mikhail and Ezra, too, all three of us covering her face and tits with our cum at the same time.

My cock swells at the thought.

But will she want all three of us, or only one? A rush of curiosity mixes with my desire for her. I want *her* to decide who she wants.

Whether that's one of us, or *all* of us.

Valentina can decide.

Mikhail's reply is immediate.

Wanna make bets?

I check the read receipt to see if Ezra's keeping up with the conversation. He's seen all of the messages, but he hasn't replied. I open our private messages and send him a quick text.

What do you think?

Ezra is my longest friend and confidante. We ended up at the orphanage together when we were teenagers, and we've been inseparable ever since. Some believe we truly *are* brothers, but we are only in title, if not by blood. Not that that matters within the Bratva.

He takes a few minutes to reply. I'm already in bed by then.

I do not make bets.

Ezra takes calculated risks when the outcomes are in his favor. He doesn't gamble. Mikhail, on the other hand, likes the unpredictability of luck and gambles more than any of us, just so he can see the outcome.

Valentina adds another factor to the mix that neither of them can predict well enough yet.

In time, perhaps. But not yet.

I won't get much more out of Ezra through text messages, and he's preoccupied with the latest task I gave him. It will take time to complete, and I can't afford for him to be distracted. Still, I want him in the loop as far as Valentina is concerned.

He needs to be just as invested as Mikhail and me if the three of us are going to control her.

The voice in my head laughs. *Is that really what you want? Another puppet to master?*

I scrub my hand across my face and stare up at the ceiling. Having Mikhail and Ezra as partners has worked wonderfully. It pays to have people you can trust.

Can I trust Valentina?

My heart aches deep in my chest, and I apply pressure to try and soothe it, like I always do. It never works. I rub the muscle anyway, pretending it does, and close my eyes.

Once, I thought I could trust her. I thought there was no risk involved. I'd calculated all the outcomes, and every single one had her standing by my side, if not as a queen, then as a lover and companion, at least.

She proved me wrong when she left. I can't trust her like I can Ezra and Mikhail. They are dependable and solid.

She's more like water—fluid and soft.

I can control something solid. I can hold it in my palm and mold it however I wish.

But water slips through my fingers. It flows on its own, no matter how much pressure or power I apply, and ultimately slips away. *Unless*, it's kept in a container and locked up tight. Then I can hold it. Then I can *keep* it.

Which do I want? A woman I can keep in a cage and have at my beck and call for pleasure, or someone who can handle not only my cock, but the weight of the crown and all its demands?

Which do I *need*?

My phone *pings* again, and I blindly reach for it. Another text has come through, this time from Ezra.

She is pretty in blue.

I pull up the photo of her in the library and zoom in. Her

nightgown is the palest shade of blue imaginable, thin and see-through and hanging off her shoulders, her rosy nipples on full display. But her panties are a deeper shade of blue, caught around her ankle like an after-thought.

An outfit like that isn't an accident.

My cock swells at the thought of Valentina naked in her bedroom, meticulously planning her outfit for her late-night solo session. She wanted to be seen. She wanted to get caught.

A moan catches in my throat as I grab the base of my shaft. I imagine all three of us are stroking ourselves now, imagining that we're coming all over Valentina's pretty face and tits instead of our hands.

But if she wants me, or Ezra, or Mikhail, she's going to have to act on it first. She's going to have to submit of her own free will.

I fire off a quick message to the group.

> Don't approach her or talk to her about what happened tonight. Don't try to fuck her. If she wants us, she will come to us.

> You want us to wait?

Mikhail's always been impatient.

> You should have seen her, Andrei. All flushed and moaning our names. She wants us.

> She will make the first move, or you won't touch her.

A thread of satisfaction curls in my chest. If it's about making the first move, I'll be the victor. I'll be first. I'm spending the most time with her, after all. If she'll pick anyone, it'll be me, if not because she wants me the most, then because I'm the most available.

It doesn't matter how I win, as long as I'm first.

> If I showed up at her door, do you think
> she'd let me in?

I picture Mikhail knocking on Valentina's bedroom door, a wicked grin on his face as she appears in her little blue nightgown. I try to erase the image from my mind as quickly as possible, knowing that it likely leads to him fucking her in her bed, and I don't want to picture that while I've still got my aching cock in my hand.

Ezra's reply is perfect.

> No.

I toss my phone to the bed and fist my cock. I won't sleep until I come again. My movements are rough and frantic as I imagine Valentina riding me, creaming all over my cock as she bounces up and down, her head thrown back and a cry on her lips as she clamps down around me and comes.

With a growl, I shoot my load, bucking my hips and wishing I was inside her. Painting her white. Filling her past capacity, watching my cum leak out of her tight little cunt.

Soon, I'll have her body. She will submit to me.

I roll onto my side and try to picture the moment she walks up to me and asks for it, but I get caught up in the details. Blue panties turn white and lacy. Her lips painted deep red to match the bouquet in her hands. A veil frames her face as her eyelashes flutter and her cheeks blush bright pink.

My heart *hurts*, stealing the breath from my lungs.

I want her body, but in the end, I want so, *so* much more

than that . . . and I will have it all, whether she gives it to me or not.

The clock is ticking, Valentina. Make your move, or I will make mine.

CHAPTER 12

EZRA

AFTER MY TRANSFER from Russia to the US sector, I burned through two *pakhans* and three states before I ended up in Harlin Heights. There wasn't a placement for me immediately, so I lived in the orphanage as they decided what to do with the Russian transfer with more scars than he had sense.

I met Andrei, and we roamed the streets on our own after dark, picking fights with anyone who needed a reminder of who ran the city. It wasn't us back then, but we liked to think we were setting an example, even at a young age.

People noticed. *Tolkotsky* noticed, the *pakhan* himself, appearing at our doorstep before we'd even turned sixteen. Every child the Baranova Bratva claims as their own is given a choice once they come of age: pledge themselves to a life of service within the family or accept a lump sum to try their luck elsewhere.

I haven't known a single soul to turn down their *pakhan*'s offer of a forever family.

When Tolkotsky formally gave us a choice, my answer was immediate. So was Andrei's. Both of us were men committed for life, no matter what was asked of us. No matter the years it shaved off our lives or the dangers it pitted us against.

For the first time in our lives, we were given a purpose. We were given a home.

To this day, I never say no to a job. It's how I transitioned from a simple errand boy to bodyguard within a few years. It's how Andrei moved up from gun running to tactical negotiations, and eventually, up to the top. He brought me with him the entire way up the ladder, making room for me where others turned their noses up at two orphan boys playing at becoming something bigger.

Tolkotsky recognized something in each of us, and for that vote of confidence, I owe him my life.

By extension, now that Tolkotsky is gone, I owe *Valentina* my life.

I scowl at Valentina's phone in my hand. If Andrei wasn't so obsessed with her, I wouldn't be here right now, playing errand boy for the first time in years. She'd be gone, a distant memory of a woman fleeing the scene in a wedding gown, nothing more than a blip on our radars.

Women come and go. Andrei could have easily replaced her.

But the man's been obsessed for all these years, and his obsession knows no bounds.

I check Valentina's phone again, the address for *work* in her maps app clear as day. I'm standing right here, inside Valentina's workplace. An office of sorts, as far as I can tell from its architecture.

But the building is empty. Whatever used to be here has been packed up, and quickly, if the scuff marks on the faux wood floor are anything to go by. Not a single rolling chair remains. No partitions. Cubicles. Brochures. Not a single scrap of paper that might hint at the business name or type.

Closing my eyes, I fight an oncoming headache. I left as

soon as Andrei gave the order, going on a measly five hours of sleep over the past thirty-six hours.

I'm tired, but I never turn down a job, especially not one involving Valentina.

I walk the building, checking every nook and cranny for any scrap of evidence. The building's large enough to hold at least one hundred employees, probably double that. Triple, if you count the warehouse adjacent to the office.

Making my way around the perimeter of both buildings, I scan for anything I might be able to bring back. Security cameras. Trash. Buried treasure.

I end up with nothing, other than the biggest fucking headache in existence.

Pulling up a second address on Valentina's phone, the one labeled *home*, I hop on my bike and drive the short eight miles to my destination. The house is dark. No cars in the driveway. No porch light on. A single-story ranch home can't hold too many secrets, but I keep my wits about me as I pad up the front steps and try the front door.

Locked, but that's no surprise.

I check the windows, then the creaking screen door out back, and pick the best point of entry. Wrapping my fist in my jacket, I punch through a pane of glass on the back door and flip the latch to let myself in.

Any smart homeowner would have an alarm system or a guard dog, but Valentina has none. A nerve in my neck twitches at how stupid that is. Does she *want* to get killed by some rando?

I drag a hand down my face and listen for any signs of life, but a quick sweep of the kitchen and living room proves that Valentina doesn't have roommates, or if she does, they're immaculate and like funny little crocheted doilies on end tables.

This can't be Valentina's house.

I check the address again, and just like with her workplace, I feel like something's *off.* This is the right place. It doesn't feel like a twenty-something's home, though.

I pick through the home, room by room, and though it has all of the typical objects and furniture one might expect, it lacks personality. A single, half-gone bottle of vodka is the only indication that someone of taste actually lives here.

I grab the bottle and unstop it, take a quick sniff, and swallow a few mouthfuls. The burn sends welcome heat through my chest and into my gut, and I end up carrying the bottle with me from room to room.

The master bedroom is just as pristine and perfect as the rest of the house, with little in the way of personal effects. No picture frames. No jewelry. It's almost like a staged home. Even the linens are all folded and put away. I can't find a single lost sock or dust bunny anywhere, and a sinking feeling hits me the longer I stay in the house.

The office was gutted by a professional, and the house was staged much the same way—professionally.

It's something *we* might do to throw casuals off our scent. Make things look boring. Scrub every scrap of DNA off every surface imaginable.

Clear the scene.

Annoyance ripples through my body, reverberating in my bones with each step I take. I've been sent on a wild goose chase, and we're being played as fools. There's no other explanation.

Someone is keeping secrets, and they're hiding them *well.*

I pull out my own cell phone and check for messages from Andrei. He's busy today—something about dragging Valentina to the mayor's birthday party—but he'll want to know about this.

I just hate coming up empty when I was given *one* task.

My phone settles like dead weight in my pocket as I decide

not to tell my boss anything just yet. I pick through the master bedroom, tearing its immaculacy apart as my frustration grows. Bedsheets torn from the mattress. Books ruffled and thrown to the floor. Furniture overturned. Silly knickknacks broken.

It's a pointless endeavor, and I storm through the bathroom and closet like a whirlwind. Still, I find nothing.

It's when I come to the *next* room that I move a little slower. This bedroom shows a different style, a flair for bohemian macrame and various shades of green in the upholstery and accent rugs. Still kept to perfection, with not a single thing out of place, but different than the rest of the house.

Art lines the walls, various hand-drawn sketches of dark ivy crawling up brick walls and muscled men with undrawn heads and hips. Numerous sketches of hands in all different poses, both masculine and feminine in shape and form, sometimes drawn apart, sometimes with fingers intertwined.

Valentina used to keep sketches on her bedroom wall at the estate.

I pick through what little pieces of personality exist within the room, not finding much of note. If Valentina lives here, she definitely doesn't stay here often. Or it's been made to look that way.

Mikhail looked up the property before I left, and the owner came back as a man who's been dead ten years. No known family. No landlord keeping the place tenanted. It was purchased five years ago, a few months before Valentina and Andrei's wedding.

Could be a coincidence . . . but most likely not.

One other person went missing the same day Valentina did—Katya Baranova, Valentina's grandmother.

We've always suspected that she had something to do with Valentina's sudden departure, if not *everything* to do with it.

Kidnapping people is just another day in the life of the Russian mafia.

But if Valentina didn't want to leave, she could have alerted me or Andrei or any one of our men that she was in danger, and we would have killed the threat instantly.

So, Valentina must have left willingly.

Her grandmother likely spirited her away in secret and kept her hidden from view, somewhere outside the Bratva's reach.

There isn't much we can't find without enough leverage and money. Valentina's disappearance, therefore, was infuriating for all parties involved.

There's no way Valentina stayed hidden of her own accord. Her grandmother, however, has connections linking back to her old Bratva family, the Dolohovs. If she were desperate enough, she could have leaned on old ties to start a new life.

I pinch the bridge of my nose and screw my eyes shut. This is too much for five hours of sleep. I'll leave the conjecture to Andrei and stick to my task, which, *oh yeah*, I'm failing miserably.

I have little hope that the rest of the house isn't staged, so I drop this lead and pick up the next. There's one more location of interest on Valentina's phone. As I stare at the screen, one word screams up at me.

Liam.

If Valentina's boyfriend is real, and he sounded real enough on the phone, he should have a well-lived-in place. Valentina's personal effects should be there, too, if they're close enough. And if not, I can always wait for him to come home and spring a little impromptu interrogation.

The address is real. The man exists, even if he's not Valentina's boyfriend. They *know* each other.

I think back to the phone conversation, my lips curving

into a frown. It was one thing to watch her with Andrei, but to know she's been with someone else?

A thread of jealousy curls in my chest like smoke, expanding in my lungs with each breath I take. She's not *mine*, but that doesn't mean she should be anyone else's, either.

Andrei's the exception, as she was always his. That hasn't changed. I don't expect it to.

But someone outside the Bratva claiming our woman?

My fists clench by my sides. *Unacceptable.*

Despite how much I want to meet the bastard who potentially fucked our girl and got away with it, I'm forced to be careful as I exit Valentina's home. I keep an eye out for any stalkers or people armed with either weapons or cameras. Someone will likely be casing each of these addresses, since they've been professionally detailed.

Would Katya have gone to such lengths to hide her whereabouts? Is she paranoid that we'll drag her back to Harlin Heights if we find her? Or is she trying to protect Valentina?

I wouldn't put it past the woman to cover her own tracks where she lives, but to move an entire business just because Valentina worked there? It doesn't add up.

Unless the business was already moving, and you just happened to come by afterward. But there was no sign of a recent move, and that's a bad business practice for anyone trying to keep their clientele.

I hang on to the hope that Liam's address will put more pieces of the puzzle together.

If I return home without concrete details about Valentina's whereabouts and activities these past five years, Andrei will be livid.

The GPS brings up an apartment complex, and as luck would have it, the bastard lives on the top floor. It's six flights of stairs to his number, and I jog halfway up to get my cardio going. I might be tired from not getting enough sleep, but there's no way I'm getting beat down in a fight, if it comes to that.

Unlike Valentina's workplace or home, *this* building has security, and a key card is required to access any of the floors from the stairwell. I pull up the app we recently had developed for these kinds of inconveniences, and after a few seconds, the lock clicks open with a *beep*.

If only we had these when I was kid.

I don't have the physical key to Liam's apartment, but a quick, hard twist to the doorknob breaks the lock and lets me inside. Floor-to-ceiling windows give a perfect view of the city below—not as large as my home city of Harlin Heights, but large enough to feel familiar. I recognize a camera in the corner of each room and make a mental note to check for its receiver. If the man's smart, it's connected to his personal devices, but it won't hurt to check for the security system setup in the closet.

I go through the mail, send Andrei and Mikhail a quick text of Liam's full name, and start casing the property.

My blood chills as I start finding empty rooms. Empty closets. Empty bathrooms.

The master suite has a made bed with two matching nightstands on either side. I cross to the framed photograph sitting out and recognize Valentina's smile in a heartbeat. Picking up the frame, I stare at her picture. There's no one with her, just Valentina posing alone in front of a Christmas tree. I pry open the back and find neat handwriting dating the picture as last year, with the words *moya zhena* tagged beneath the date.

My wife in Russian.

I snap a picture of the front and back and send them to the group text with Mikhail and Andrei. Neither of them has seen any of my messages. Andrei has an excuse, but Mikhail doesn't. What the fuck is he doing? Someone who knows *Russian* took this picture of Valentina and had the sick fucking humor to call her *his wife*.

My skin crawls, and I have the need to cut into someone's flesh, preferably Valentina's "boyfriend's."

I pocket the photograph and flip the mattress over, pulling all the blankets off before overturning the nightstands. Other than a red wine stain on the comforter, nothing else stands out, and the nightstands are empty.

The closet is my next target.

I pull open the door and flick on the light.

Against the back wall are dozens of printed photographs, some curled at the edges, like they've been there a while, others crisp and bright and new. I scan the closet for traps, then check behind me and do one more sweep of the entire apartment.

Every room is empty, except for this one.

My phone vibrates against my thigh as I receive a text, likely from one of the guys, and I dig it out to take a video. "The place is fucking empty. They are *all* empty," I growl, practically running back to the master bedroom closet. "Except one. Look here." I hold the phone up to the wall of photographs, my blood boiling.

This sick display was left for us to find.

Valentina is the centerpiece of each photograph, some with her looking at the camera, others taken without her realizing. There are pictures of her at lunch, in the bookstore, in the green bohemian bedroom at the other house. She sits at her desk, a pencil in hand as she sketches one of the drawings I saw pinned to her bedroom wall.

One of the newest photographs catches my attention, and I pluck it from the rest. The white bedspread has a distinct wine stain on it, the empty glass lying on its side nearby. Valentina's dark curls lay spread across the plush pillow as she sleeps, and in the glass picture frame hanging over the bed, I can see the silhouette of the person taking the picture.

A man's figure, but that's all I can see. Holding up a cell phone. Taking a picture of our girl.

I pocket the photo before I can tear the thing to shreds.

Either Valentina has kept a big fucking secret about marrying some Russian bastard, or she has a stalker who she *thinks* she can trust.

Who's probably been lying to her for the past five years.

I end the video and quickly send it to the boys. Mikhail has texted back while I've been filming.

> Liam West doesn't exist. Fake name.

My curse comes out as a scream.

Gathering all the photographs from the wall and the few pieces of mail I spotted on the kitchen counter, I shove them into a pillowcase and carry my haul into the living room. I send a message to one of my men and tell them to bring a crew. We're taking the cameras, the wine-stained comforter, everything.

Andrei still hasn't seen our messages, and I have half a mind to call the man. Instead, I type a quick text.

> Where is Valentina?

> With the boss. Saw the video. That's fucked up.

Yeah, it is. I stare at the camera overhead and bare my teeth at it. "You think this funny, *suka*?" I throw my evidence to the ground and crack my knuckles. I'd rather be cracking the man's skull, but it'll have to wait. "I am going to find you, and I will rip out your teeth, one by one."

It's one thing if Mikhail wants to be a pervert and take pictures of Valentina while she sleeps. I don't give a damn about what that man does or what fantasies go through his head. He might spook her a little, but he won't hurt her.

He won't *lie* to her.

I hate liars with every fiber of my being.

And this fucker has been lying to Valentina for *years.*

My mind shifts to Katya, and my rage doubles. What lies has Katya been spreading? Has she been feeding Valentina lies this entire time? With bullshit like—

Splitting pain ricochets around my skull, and I groan as my stress levels rise to unhealthy levels.

My head spins. I can't think straight. Blood roars white hot in my ears and pulses hard through my veins with each beat of my heart.

I pace the room as I wait for my men to arrive. We're two states over from Harlin Heights, but I brought a few men with me. They should arrive here within minutes.

I look out at the cityscape, take in its gleaming rooftops and shining glass windows in the daylight, and have the violent urge to burn it all to the ground.

No one fucks with Valentina and gets away with it. I'll make sure everyone involved meets the violent, bloody end they all fucking deserve.

Then, while their blood hasn't even cooled on the concrete yet, I'll make Valentina finally say *thank you.*

A rush of adrenaline floods my system as I imagine Valentina's pretty emerald eyes looking up at me with gratitude.

Thank you, Ezra, for saving my life.

She wraps her arms around my chest and holds me tight, finally letting me fold my battered, broken wings around her, shielding her from all the daggers held at her back.

I used to be her guardian angel. She told me that once.

A strangled laugh cracks in my throat.

Angels don't do the kinds of things I do. But you keep on believing, Valentina, and maybe someday, I'll become the man you think I am.

CHAPTER 13

ANDREI

THE MAYOR'S birthday is always one of the biggest events of the year. People from the highest levels of society show up just to make an appearance, have their photo taken, order a two-hundred-dollar cocktail, and slip out the back door.

A few actually take the time to network or talk business, but most stick to their usual groups to spread gossip.

It's the perfect place to show Valentina off and reintroduce her to society. She should know a few of the bigger names, but some things have changed in the last five years. With my rise in the Bratva, we've had to make a few changes to key positions within the city. Not everyone supported my succession as *pakhan* without Valentina's Baranova blood behind me. They quickly made their objections known . . . and just as quickly disappeared from view.

Tolkotsky promised me his throne, and instead of it gracefully falling into my lap upon his death, I had to take it from his cold, dead grasp.

Without Valentina's help.

A seed of anger pulses in my heart.

She was supposed to stay by my side through everything—all the challenges, all the strife, all the bloodshed. But she ran.

I'm not sure I'll ever forgive her.

But in the end, forgiveness isn't necessary for marriage. I can crave her, claim her, ruin her, but I don't have to forgive her.

Still, she will need to be respected among society, regardless of how anyone feels about her departure. This party is a good place to start reminding everyone exactly where they belong—at our feet, whether kneeled in front or beneath them.

The party is as extravagant as expected, and Valentina captures attention from every single person in the room, from the servers carrying trays across the room to the most prominent members of society.

I've been coming alone to the mayor's parties for years. There's only one woman I'll ever entertain by my side. This is known far and wide, because I've put a personal stake in finding her. The entire city knows this, so they know who Valentina is the moment she steps into the room, regardless of if they've met her before.

Our Bratva heir has returned, and she's more radiant than ever.

Valentina clings to my arm with a vice grip every time we come into contact with someone from our past she doesn't like, and there are several. I start veering us in their direction for the sport of it. We'll have to reintroduce ourselves to everyone in time, so it doesn't matter who we go to first.

I just like the way she feels wrapped around my arm *extra* tight.

When she's forced to play along and laugh at whatever joke someone's attempted to pull, she digs her nails into my arm and flashes those emerald eyes my way, as if to say *you'll pay for every second of this, jackass.*

I cling to her just as hard, squeezing her hip with enough force that I've no doubt, when she peels away her dress later this evening, there will be a heavy bruise for each of my fingertips, if not the entire palm. Similarly, I'm expecting tiny half-moon pricks up my entire forearm.

It's almost like a game, seeing who can mark the other the most.

I like to think it's because we're claiming each other's territory, but I know the truth.

She doesn't realize that she was born to play this part. She wouldn't hate it as much if she leaned into it more. The guests drink up her smiles and laughter like addicts. It makes me proud.

The photographer comes around without warning and takes photos of every attendee, sometimes trying to be clandestine in the background, other times getting right in people's faces to land a candid, if not annoying, shot.

When the photographer rounds on Valentina, he steps on her dress and makes her trip. I've got her, so she's not in any danger of falling, but the man should be more careful. His camera *clicks* as Valentina's skirt rustles around her legs, and his eyes quickly jump up from my wife's ankles to his next target.

I whip in his direction so fast that he flinches. My smile hides the malice I feel thrumming beneath the surface. "Excuse me. You stepped on my wife's dress." The man looks confused, and my jaw clenches as I fight the urge to punch him. "Apologize," I command, pulling Valentina closer to my side.

She digs her nails into my arm, but her voice is smooth as velvet when she speaks. "Darling, don't scare the poor man. He didn't mean anything by it."

I bend at the waist to be closer to the cowering man's

height. "So, I imagined his camera dipping low enough to peer under your skirt, did I?"

The man's eyes bug out, and a layer of sweat breaks out across his brow. "I swear, I didn't see anything."

My smile could crack diamonds. "But you tried to, didn't you?"

"Let him go," Valentina murmurs harshly, trying to pull me away from the fucking scum standing before us. "You're causing a scene."

"This man deserves to rot," I say loudly, enjoying the way the photographer squirms.

"What's the meaning of this? Mr. Leonov?" The mayor of Harlin Heights appears to my right, a balding, fat, jovial man whose pockets I line quite generously. "Is something wrong?"

"Your photographer." I nod toward the man in question. "I believe he's been peering up ladies' skirts all evening. If I may, I'd like for my wife to check his footage. Is that all right, Mayor?"

The mayor blusters but nods all the same. "Yes, yes, of course."

"Thank you." I snatch the camera from around the scumbag's neck and hand it to my wife. "Check the images, darling. Perhaps I'm wrong, and this is all a misunderstanding."

I'm not.

Valentina's face pales as she clicks through the photographs. "Oh. *Oh.* Um. How do I delete these?" She bites her lip and looks to me for help.

My heart soars at the small gesture.

I show her the *delete* button as the gathering crowd starts to spread news of what's transpired. Angry murmurs rise around us, and I let the chaos fuel me.

"What's your name?" I step closer to the photographer, allowing Valentina's arm to fall from mine for the first time all night.

"T-Travis," the man stutters.

"Travis Jacobs," the mayor finishes, red-faced with either embarrassment or tipsy anger. "I gave you this job as a favor to your mother. I *paid* you—"

"That's all right, Mayor. I'll handle this." I clamp my hand on Travis's shoulder and steer him toward the elevator. "We'll be right back, everyone."

Valentina is still absorbed in the photographs, but when she notices me walking away, her eyes widen with panic. She doesn't want to be left alone with the other guests. Handing the camera to the woman closest to her, she patters behind me just in time to enter the elevator before the doors close. We start to descend, and Valentina stands back, nervously shifting from foot to foot.

She doesn't know what I'm going to do, but she came, anyway. Part of me celebrates the fact that she didn't run away the first chance she got.

But I can't celebrate for long. I tighten my grip on Travis, and he whimpers. Once we're out of earshot from the rest of the party, I slam the man's face into the metal wall.

Blood starts to trickle from his nose, and I hope it's broken.

"Travis Jacobs. This is the last time you'll ever hold a camera." I dig into his pocket and pull out his cell phone, throw it to the ground, and smash it under my heel. The screen cracks with a satisfying *crunch*. "I have eyes everywhere in this city. They will be watching you. Do *not* test my patience."

He whimpers and the sour scent of ammonia hits the air as he pisses himself. *Pathetic.*

"When this elevator hits the ground floor, you will walk out of here and throw out every single camera you own. I don't care how expensive they are. You will also delete any photos you've taken without consent of the parties within. I'll have someone come by to check your progress within an hour."

The elevator dings as we descend another floor. Only a few more to go until we reach the bottom.

"You will never accept another job within five miles of this location, and if you live within that vicinity, you will move immediately."

"That's bullshit—"

I pull his head back and slam it into the metal again. This time, I hear the crack of cartilage as his nose breaks, and he wails in pain.

"What's bullshit is that you still haven't apologized to my wife," I snarl, rubbing his broken nose into the wall. Snot and blood bubble out, and he starts sobbing.

I don't give a flying fuck. He still needs to apologize.

Releasing him, I let him fall to his knees. The elevator comes to a stop and the doors pull open behind us.

Someone gasps outside, but I don't care.

"Apologize." Travis slowly tries to stand, but I set my foot across his back to keep him in place. "On your knees."

Once I remove my foot from his spine, he drags his body around, smearing his own piss into his clothes. Sniveling and pathetic, he tries to lift his head to look at Valentina.

I grab the top of his skull and force his head down. "Apologize *now*, kneeled at her feet, like the fucking trash you are."

Travis apologizes profusely, keeping his eyes locked on my wife's sandaled feet, and I let him go. He scurries away as fast as he can, taking the majority of the piss-and-blood stench with him.

Valentina steps out of the elevator, and I follow her, wiping off any remaining grime on my hands onto a handkerchief. I toss the scrap of cloth into a trash can we pass.

She rushes toward the restrooms, and I follow close behind. When she reaches the alcove, she whirls on me, her face flushed and a fire burning bright in her eyes. "What the fuck was that?"

I tilt my head and admire her beauty. "He deserved much worse."

"You broke his nose!"

"Would you have rather I killed him?"

"Of course not!" She grimaces and paces the little space she has to roam. "He was just a kid. You could have let him go."

"I did let him go." My eyebrows pinch together. "And he was hardly a child. Valentina. Please." I hold out my hand for her to take. "Enough. It's over. Let's return upstairs."

She whirls on me, eyes wide like she's in shock I'd even suggest such a thing. "Return to the party? Are you insane?"

I can feel my patience thinning. First, I have to deal with a scumbag, and now, my wife thinks I'm insane for making sure he paid for his crimes.

"Don't cross me, Valentina."

She glares at me. "Or what? You gonna break my nose too?"

I close the distance between us in two long strides, so fast that she recoils against the wall. Slamming my palm against the stone, I lock her in place beneath me. "I made him apologize to you," I growl, my anger lashing at me like a whip. "I let that little perv go instead of kicking his teeth in like he deserved, yet you taunt me like *I'm* the villain."

"You *are* the villain," she shrieks, battering her fists against my chest. "You've always been the villain. You, my dad, everyone in this fucking place! I didn't see it before, but I see it clear as day now. It's no wonder my mother tried to leave. It's no wonder she got fucking killed for it—"

My eyes narrow as Valentina continues to rant. Not once has she mentioned her mother's death being murder before.

Did she come to that conclusion on her own, or did someone plant the idea in her head?

My thoughts immediately swing to Mikhail. He should learn to keep his mouth shut.

No one actually knows what happened to Maeve. The official story is that she got sick, but to disappear in one day? I'd suspected foul play, but Tolkotsky never said anything, and I knew better than to ask.

The rumors have always been about how Maeve had a secret lover and ran away, or that she got kidnapped by a rival family, or that she died giving birth to a second child. Each rumor was more ridiculous than the last.

But Tolkotsky never looked for Maeve after she disappeared. I'd suspected it was his pride that kept him from action. He didn't want to seem weak, pining after a woman who got away from him, either through death or abandonment.

Of course, there were rumors that he'd killed her, but as his right-hand man, I never saw or heard anything.

Maeve's disappearance got swept under the rug quickly.

Valentina's disappearance, however, enraged him. He took it out on everyone within striking distance, and the reverberations of his rage trickled down into every layer of the Bratva. We spent years looking for Valentina, until finally, Tolkotsky surrendered to his own illness and died.

I never gave up the search, but I didn't order my men to continue theirs. They had spent enough time searching for ghosts of the past.

I grasp Valentina's chin and tilt her head up to gaze into her eyes. Tears shine in the corners, like raindrops about to fall. "How do you know what happened to your mother?"

Her lip trembles, and she jerks her head to tell me *no.*

"Valentina." I press my thumb against her pretty pink lips. "Tell me."

I wait as she gathers herself. With each second that passes, I brush my fingertip against her bottom lip, unable to stop myself. I used to steal kisses from those lips. Chaste, little kisses, like the delicate flutter of a butterfly's wings.

I stole a much better kiss from her the other night. The memory lingers close enough that I can still taste her on my mouth.

Valentina takes a shaky breath. "She tried to leave." One of the tears falls, rolling down her cheek. "I found a letter she wrote to my father. Or, well, it found me." Her face scrunches and more tears fall. "I don't *know*, Andrei." Her voice cracks. "The letter said she was leaving and taking me with her, but then she disappeared before she could ever come get me. I came here to ask my father what *really* happened. He *has* to know something." She chokes on a sob. "*Had* to."

Another sob wracks her body, and the pieces of my heart ache with every broken sound she makes. I shouldn't care so much after everything she's put me through, but *fuck*. My muscles tense as I war with my emotions.

I want to wring Tolkotsky's neck for dying before Valentina got answers, but the bastard's death was long overdue. I'll never regret watching his life snuff out breath by breath on his sickbed.

Part of me wants to kiss away Valentina's pain, but the other part wants to watch her suffer. She deserves some misery after leaving me and the Bratva behind.

I hold my breath as I watch her crumble.

"And now," she murmurs, "now I'm stuck here." She wipes her tear-stained cheek. "I'm not supposed to be here, Andrei!"

That's ridiculous, and if she were thinking straight, she'd know that. A flare of righteousness flickers inside my heart.

"Your place is with me."

She laughs, but nothing about that statement is funny.

There's a question I've always wanted to ask. I've run circles in my head about it since the day Valentina left. Came up with every answer imaginable, even things as far-fetched as alien abduction.

Because why, after everything we planned for our future, all the promises we made to each other, the whispered secrets we told when no one was watching, why did Valentina leave?

She senses the question before I can form the words. With a shake of her head, she laughs again, the sound bitter and sharp, echoing in the tiny alcove we've found ourselves in. "Tell me, Andrei. Why did I leave?"

I swallow hard. The truth settles like a weight in my chest.

"Your mother wanted to leave." I shut my eyes. I can picture Maeve, radiant in the golden summer sun, her smile perfect, as always. "She wanted *you* to leave."

Valentina made a decision based upon her mother's wishes, not her own.

But *someone* planted that seed. *Someone* gave Valentina that letter.

I open my eyes and stare at my bride. No longer blushing, but just as beautiful. "You left because it was your mother's dying wish." I crowd Valentina against the wall, pressing my body against hers. She's trembling, but pressure and weight helps calm the nervous system. I envelop her beneath me, and she fights it. She fights *hard*, struggling against me. Thrashing. Kicking her feet.

I cup Valentina's face and admire my beautiful, stubborn woman until she calms down. Her heart rate falls back to normal, and she breathes deeper.

"You left, not because you wanted to, but because you felt like you had to."

She stares back at me, her eyes wide and lips parted like she's hanging on my every word.

As much as I've been lying to myself about what I want from Valentina, she's been lying to herself too.

"You're scared to want to be here. You're scared of enjoying this. Of wanting me." My lips curve into a smile. I can handle fear. I instill fear in others every day.

Breaking a few fears should be easy.

"You're right, Valentina. I am a villain."

There's no sugarcoating it. The mafia is a dark world. Not everyone survives it, and those who do are turned into something more befitting nightmares than daydreams.

But Valentina was born for this life.

I press our foreheads together and take a deep breath, exhaling slowly. Within moments, Valentina's breaths match mine in depth and rhythm as she continues to calm down.

"I can't love a villain," Valentina murmurs softly. Her fingers wrap around the collar of my shirt. "You're cruel and violent and evil. All of you are."

Her mention of my brothers makes me smile. Mikhail's already rubbed off on her, *maybe literally*, and Ezra's always been a favorite of hers. In time, I've no doubt she'll love all three of us, villainous hearts and all.

"Sometimes, we don't have a choice in who we love." I don't mean that in an *I will make you love me* way, either. Sometimes, the heart wants what it wants, despite what makes the most sense. Despite how fucked up our desires are.

I thread our fingers together and hold Valentina's hand against the wall, over her head. I kiss her forehead, then her temple, the swell of her cheek, the remnants of tears clinging to her skin. With a sigh, I brush my nose against hers, aching to kiss more of her.

But I want her to *give* it to me. Willingly. I want her to *submit* not just to me, but to her own desires.

"Andrei." She whispers my name like a prayer, and I groan against her lips. She presses them to mine gently, hesitantly, and it's reminiscent of our past. She was always so shy about loving me, and now I realize part of that hesitation came from fear.

Fear of what she is and who she will *become.*

I capture her lips in a *real* kiss, demanding more than I've ever received from her. I devour her mouth, forcing my lips over hers again and again, relentless in my pursuit of more. She whimpers, and I swallow the sound greedily. I take her bottom lip between mine and *suck,* groaning as she writhes against me. Her nails scratch the base of my neck as she deepens the kiss and tastes me with her tongue.

She's just as greedy as I am.

Releasing her hand, I reach around and grab her ass, pulling her hips tighter against mine and grinding against her stomach.

She moans, *loudly,* and my hand travels lower to the back of her thigh. I start to lift it over my hip when someone rudely interrupts us, clearing their throat from behind me.

I pay them no mind and hook my wife's calf around my hip, thrusting my length against her molten core.

Valentina chokes on her moan and starts smacking my shoulder in quick, repetitive bursts. "Get off. *Get off!*"

"That's the plan," I grumble, relenting, despite how shitty it feels to release her. I press one final, heated kiss to her lips before grabbing her hand and turning to see who the fuck interrupted us.

Mikhail stands there in his usual suit and tie, a Cheshire grin making him look even more sinister than usual.

Murder crosses my mind as he chuckles, but there's no mistaking the deep thread of desire in his voice. I can't blame him, but if he wants to join in, he could have waited a single fucking minute.

Valentina's face burns crimson as she straightens her dress back over her hips. "Mikhail! What are you doing here?" She looks positively scandalized, but her swollen lips only make her look that much more fuckable.

I'm sure Mikhail thinks the same.

He reluctantly turns his gaze from Valentina to me, and I immediately get the sense that something's wrong. His smile falls in an instant, and he taps his cell phone in his hand. "We've got messages from Ezra. You're gonna want to look at them."

"This couldn't wait?" I run a hand through my hair. It must be bad if Mikhail interrupted his day to come find me.

Mikhail taps his phone again. "Let's get in the car. I'll fill you in on the way."

Valentina hesitates near the elevator. "We're leaving? What about the party?"

I smile at her. I thought she didn't want to go back up. "Party's over, darling." I kiss the top of her head. "But don't worry, I'll throw you a better one soon."

At our wedding. *Very* soon.

We follow Mikhail to the SUV, and all three of us slide into the back seat, with Valentina taking the middle. Our driver takes off as Valentina's attempting to buckle her seat-belt, and Mikhail and I both put a hand on one shoulder to steady her.

"You haven't been checking your phone."

It's not an accusation, but I frown at Mikhail all the same. "I've been a bit preoccupied."

He grins, hooking his finger on one of Valentina's curls and twirling it. "So, I see. Tell me, *malyshka*, how does all that power taste? I bet it got your panties all wet, didn't it?" He licks his lips and Valentina smacks him, blushing furiously as he laughs.

While Mikhail keeps Valentina distracted, I run through the message chain my brothers left me. Videos of an empty workplace. A staged home. A *baited* apartment, with dozens of pictures of *my wife* set up in some sort of shrine.

I understand the obsession, but she's *mine.*

As we travel across the city and I sift through possibilities in my head, one thing about what Valentina told me earlier bothers me.

I interrupt whatever the fuck Mikhail's saying to ask her a question. "Valentina." I stare her down, hoping to catch a lie if she dares tell one. "The letter from your mother. Where did you find it?"

Her eyebrows pinch together. "It showed up in my dressing room. I was given a lot of cards that day, and it was tucked in with them. It looked different than the rest, so I opened it first."

I remember the influx of wedding gifts and private messages meant for only the bride or only the groom before the ceremony began. Well-wishes and words of wisdom, or the like. At least, that's what they were *supposed* to be.

Someone planted the letter in Valentina's things.

Someone sabotaged our wedding and silently encouraged Valentina to leave.

I squeeze Valentina's knee in thanks and speed-dial Ezra. He picks up on the first ring.

"Where is Katya?"

Ezra's voice is tight with fatigue. "Katya is not here. I cannot find her, nor can I find that *suka.*"

"Keep looking. Put your men on it. You sound like shit."

He curses at me before hanging up.

Valentina's watching me, a frown etched on her worried face. "What's wrong? Is my grandmother okay?"

"For now." I drum my fingertips against the armrest. I don't want to worry her before I have any concrete evidence. But if I find out that Katya is the reason Valentina left, *and* that she's been keeping my wife hidden from me all these years?

I'll pull the bitch apart, piece by piece, until there's nothing left but blood and bone.

Valentina doesn't have to know her grandmother is a traitorous bitch. It might be better for her to think that she has *some* redeemable blood relatives.

After all, the reality that we're *all* villains might be a weight she's not able to carry just yet.

Not until she's sitting on a throne of gold, wearing our bloodied Bratva crown one hundred percent by choice.

Until then, I'll carry the weight for her.

It's the least a king can do for his queen.

CHAPTER 14

VALENTINA

ALL THREE MEN become very busy, very fast.

Andrei paces back and forth in his office, on the phone more often than not, and spends the rest of his time sitting in meetings in the dining room and yelling at people in Russian. I can hear him all the way down the hall, no matter where in the house he is, and as much as I want to ask him what's wrong, part of me doesn't want to know.

There are guards posted around every corner, and I know that's no accident. Security detail has *tripled* since I first arrived.

I worry my bottom lip between my teeth as I think of my grandmother. Andrei said she was okay, but only *for now*. Is someone coming after her? Who would hurt a little old lady?

Andrei would, my inner voice reminds me, thinking back to his veiled threat during our first dinner together.

Well, he didn't *say* he would hurt her, but he implied it. And if that's how Andrei a man who actually knows her, handles her, I don't want to imagine what a stranger might do.

I know she's tougher than she looks, but still. She smokes a pipe and laughs at the same soap operas every week. Surely, *she* can't be viewed as a threat.

With no answers and no burly Russian men to pester with questions, I busy myself by rereading books in the library I'd long forgotten about, or chatting with whichever staff is available for small talk. I know I'm meant to run the house, but it practically runs itself. I think the kitchen staff humors me by letting me choose one of the entrees for dinner each night, and the gardeners are so focused on their tasks that they forget I'm standing there half the time.

After five years of working a normal job, it's strange not to have one to occupy my time. I find myself growing restless. It would be one thing to be on vacation and know I'm meant to relax, but there's a thread of tension pulled tight throughout the house, making relaxation impossible. I can't even sketch; my hands shake whenever I try to hold a pencil.

To top it off, ever since Mikhail's mysterious news, I'm having trouble sleeping.

Judging by the dark circles permanently etched under Ezra's eyes, I'm guessing he's struggling too. We run into each other on late-night rendezvous in the kitchen. He takes swigs of clear vodka and smokes a cigarette by the open window while I make us both sandwiches.

We don't talk, but at least he accepts the roast beef and swiss and humors me by taking a few bites.

Mikhail is nowhere to be found, and without a cell phone to message him or a carrier pigeon waiting on standby, I'm out of luck, as far as figuring out what *he's* up to.

On day four of my newfound alone time, I wander the house until I find myself standing in front of the morgue's shining, silver door.

The day I infiltrated the estate, I found Ezra napping next door to the corpses.

A shiver runs down my spine. Why he would choose *that*

bedroom over all the others is a mystery I'm not sure I want to solve.

With a sigh, I push open the door to the morgue. If I'm lucky, I can catch him in bed again. He'll be so sleepy that he'll tell me all the boys' secrets and admit what the hell they're all up to when they're too busy to so much as say *hello* to the girl they've kidnapped and held hostage—

My shoe slides across the waxed floor as I slip on something wet. With a shriek, I catch myself on a silver table before I can bust my ass. Metal instruments clatter noisily as I hoist myself up and check what the hell I just stepped in.

Bright red spots—*no, splatters*—paint the room like confetti. Streaks of it congregate in the middle of the room, with footprints and, *oh god*, handprints smattered all around.

It's like someone forgot to tell the sorority to bring jello for the wrestling match, and someone had the bright idea to improvise with . . . blood.

Blood wrestling. *Wonderful.*

"You should not be here." Ezra scowls at me from the other side of the room, a cigarette dangling from his lips, a hose in one hand and a mop in the other. Judging by the room's current condition, I'd say he's shit at cleaning.

Levity seems appropriate for this situation. "Your clean-up crew on vacation?" I ask, hoping it sounds as much like a joke as it does in my head.

Ezra doesn't laugh. His eyes screw shut, and a heavy sigh falls past his pinched lips. He pulls the cigarette from his mouth and flicks it into a bin nearby. "They are busy with other task."

Oh.

He really *does* have a clean-up crew for shit like this.

I'm not a fan of blood. I know, as a woman, I'm supposed to be okay with blood since I see it almost every month. But that's a load of bullshit, because this blood isn't *mine.*

My stomach churns as the metallic scent hits my nose.

Ezra sighs again and drops the mop to reach into his pocket. Grabbing something tiny, he tosses it in my direction, and I snatch it from the air before it smashes me in the face.

It's a sachet of herbs, smelling distinctly of peppermint and lavender.

I stare at the tiny pouch as Ezra starts hosing the place down in earnest. Water washes away most of the grime, but patches of gore remain in stubborn pockets. I'd never noticed the distinct drain in the middle of the floor, or the tinier ones located in the four corners of the room, but I *definitely* notice them now.

"What . . ." I swallow my nerves and take a hit of the sachet, holding it to my nose and breathing in deep. "What, um, happened?"

Ezra grunts and nudges me to the side so he can hose down the three-foot smear I made from the door. Flecks of blood coat his inked skin, and I find myself following the trail of red down his muscular arms to his large, calloused hands.

He's always been a sturdy man. Broad-shouldered and strong as an ox. More than once, he kept me safe from anyone who tried to get too close or make advances on me at galas, glaring at them and ordering them to back away *or else.*

I didn't think much of it back then, but I imagine this scarlet display is the aftermath of whatever *or else* meant.

I try not to take Ezra's deflection personally as I pick up his discarded mop and follow him around with it, scrubbing the more tenacious stains as he hoses around me. It takes a while, but after a little elbow grease and bleach, the room looks much better than when I first walked in.

Ezra stares at me as I hang the mop up to dry and rinse out a bucket of soap and bleach. I pretend not to notice him as I *double* rinse and start scrubbing my arms.

Yuck.

He makes a strangled sound in the back of his throat, and I look up to find him stiff as a board, jaw clenched, eyes narrowed.

"What?"

He's a man of few words, but he jerks his head to the side and starts heading toward the single door in that direction. The one that leads to his bedroom.

"Come, *lisichka*."

I'm on my feet in two seconds flat, following the mountain of a man into his dark domain. The lights are off, but the curtains rustle as a chilly breeze blows fresh air into the room. Sunlight streams through the darkness, much the same way it did when I first walked in here, and I get my first real glimpse of the place.

There's not much here. A bed. A dresser. A desk laden with a long-barreled gun scattered into its many parts. A laundry basket kicked over near the wall.

Not a single piece of decor in sight. A room made for function, not fashion.

He takes me to a bathroom that's cramped for two people, but we manage to stand side by side at the sink, both of us scrubbing our hands and arms with abrasive, antibacterial soap.

Aside from our midnight snack meets, I haven't spent any time with Ezra since my arrival. He's stalked me around the grounds, sure, but that ended after the Mayor's party. Maybe even before then, if I think about it.

This is the most domestic activity we've ever shared, and it's almost sweet . . . if you forget about all the blood and gore we just mopped up.

I take a moment to consider all three of the men in my life. Mikhail, aloof on the surface but soft underneath. Ezra, a little emo and rough around the edges, but loyal to the bone.

Andrei, tough as nails in business and just as demanding as a lover . . . or so I imagine.

Briefly, I wonder what any one of them would be like as lovers. Would they compliment each other like knives from the same set, or are they as different as they come? I bite my bottom lip and sneak a peek at Ezra, wondering once again what his body would feel like against mine. It feels wrong to crave another man's touch when I'm engaged to Andrei, but I've always wondered . . . and now that I've spent my fair share of evenings rubbing one out in the library, the den, on the back porch, I've imagined *quite* the number of naughty scenarios where any one of them walked in on me masturbating.

After the other night when Mikhail found me knuckle-deep in the library, I have an idea what *he* might do. But the others are still a mystery.

None of them have asked me about that night. Mikhail must have kept the picture he took of me a secret and saved it in his spank bank for private use.

Ezra's eyes narrow in the mirror's reflection as he watches me. "What is it? You are smiling."

Shit.

"Nothing!" I scrub the bar of soap up my arms and redouble my efforts at being clean.

Clean thoughts. Clean body. Nothing can break my concentration.

Ezra's jaw tics in frustration. "You are bad liar, Valentina Baranova."

I scoff aloud and toss a return glare in his direction. "Because everyone's *so* virtuous around here. *Please.* It's nothing, Ezra." The soap bar slips from my strangle-hold and pops against Ezra's hard chest before *thudding* into the porcelain sink.

"It is *something.*" He pulls his black T-shirt over his head and tosses it to the floor. A wave of day-old cologne washes over me, and I choke on how *good* it smells.

"You have been spending time with other men." With a flick of his wrist, Ezra turns on the shower and kicks off his boots. "You have been *thinking* of other men."

It's one thing for Andrei to get under my skin. That's his MO. But Ezra's energy is oddly charged for a man so quiet, and I find myself wanting to fight.

My heart races. Did Mikhail show Ezra and Andrei the photo after all?

I try to keep my voice steady. "I haven't been thinking of anyone I'm not supposed to. Andrei's my fiancé, and Mikhail is . . ."

Well, I'm not sure what to call him.

"A friend," I decide quickly. "There's been no one else, so you don't know what you're talking about."

I can't believe I'm admitting to any of this in the first place, but I won't stand for false accusations.

Ezra's jaw clenches and his dark eyes smolder. "Get in the shower."

A thrill runs down my spine at the deep rumble in his voice, but I take a step back to get some distance and bump against the door. "I . . . really shouldn't."

If Andrei finds me naked in another man's shower, he might *really* choke me to death.

"You are dirty." Ezra points to his neck as his eyes travel down my body. One by one, he points to various locations on his body to indicate spots on mine, and one glance in the mirror proves him right. In my efforts to scrub my arms and avoid Ezra's heavy aura, I forgot about the rest of my body.

Apparently, I was standing in the splash zone while we cleaned up the morgue.

"Ew ew *ew*." Shucking my clothes, which are *also* stained red, I shove past Ezra to claim the shower for myself.

I can handle Andrei's anger when it comes. What I *can't* handle is being covered in gore.

Once safely tucked inside the shower, I pull the door shut and quickly drop my panties and bra so that all of me gets clean.

The door opens behind me and, *ohmyAdonis, he's naked.*

With a cry, I hold one hand over my hoo-ha and try to cover my girls with my remaining limbs. "What are you doing? Wait your turn!"

He lifts an eyebrow. "It is my shower." He steps inside and the frosted glass door *whooshes* shut behind him.

If there were any chance of escape, it vanishes the instant the six-foot-four wall of muscle enters the shower. It was cramped to begin with, but now we're bumping elbows and knees as we struggle to avoid the press of cold tile on our butts.

Ezra reaches up and tilts the stream of water so that it falls directly on my back, and I hiss as scorching hot water scalds my skin. "What are you—"

"You have been thinking of other men," he rumbles, continuing his line of thought from before we were both painfully naked and, at least for me, somewhat afraid.

The fear shoots straight to my core, and I clench my thighs together as foolish desire rushes through me. It's like my body mistakes adrenaline as an aphrodisiac. I can't go to haunted houses or watch scary movies. My body betrays me and turns me into a gushing waterfall.

I'm not sure what I fear most right now: Andrei finding me in here with Ezra, or Ezra touching me for the first time.

Would he touch me?

He's never tried before, and unlike Mikhail, who makes his attraction known by toying with me, or Andrei, who boldly declares his intent to fuck me raw, I'm left wondering what goes on in Ezra's head.

Until now.

Now, he's not only talking, but he's naked in the shower with me.

"I fail to see the problem," I retort, glaring up at Ezra's five-o'clock shadow. "So what if I've been thinking about Mikhail and Andrei?"

His eyes flash like silver lightning. "I hear you kissed them." Taking a step closer, he crowds me against the wall, shifting the stream of water's trajectory from my back to his chest as we trade places. Tattoos cover his chest in thick, bold lines, and I decide staring at them is safer than meeting Ezra's eyes. I try to discern the shapes through the water rushing down his pecs and abs, my gaze traveling lower until I recognize a dark happy trail leading me straight to his—

"Oh god," I groan, smacking my palm over my eyes. That is one *thick* cock. Just as thick as the rest of him. Tight, engorged, hard as a rock—

"There is no god here," Ezra rasps, sounding every bit as devilish as his words promise.

He grabs my wrist with one of his large hands, pulling my own from my eyes. Before I have a chance to protest, he's pinning both of my wrists above my head, forcing my breasts up until they're a mere inch from brushing against his chest.

"I have been working night and day," he growls, anger rolling off him in waves hotter than any steam, "*endlessly.* Making people scream. Piecing together words. Uncovering secrets." His body shakes violently, his tired eyes sliding shut. "Yet you kiss *them.* You think of *them.* You touch yourself to thoughts of *them.*"

Fear strikes another chord, and I whimper as slick desire drips down my thighs.

He heard me. Oh god, he heard me fingering myself around the house.

I'm getting my wish. These are the consequences of

baiting testosterone-fueled men with my body. I'll finally find out what happens when they catch me in the act, one by one. First Mikhail, now Ezra, and then for the finale, Andrei—who is the most likely to fuck me for it.

I moan in part despair, part need. My entire body burns beneath Ezra's knowing gaze. He's heard me slide my fingers against my swollen clit, heard my hot breaths coming out as whines and pants, heard me moan Mikhail and Andrei'a names as I tweaked my nipples in the dark.

Ezra makes a strangled sound like he's in pain, and through my closed eyelids, I see shadows shift around me. He releases my wrists. When he speaks, he's farther away.

"I have *always* kept you safe. But you do not think of me. You *never* think of me."

I brave opening my eyes. Ezra's leaning against the other end of the shower, arms crossed, a disgruntled scowl marring his handsome face.

"I have killed for you." He takes a deep breath and his shoulders fall with the weight of his reality. "I have picked the bones of living things clean. I do this to keep you safe. I am ordered to keep you safe."

A hideous twist to his lips makes me flinch. "I am not ordered to *want* you, but I do. I want to kiss you. To hear my name on your breath. To feel your body writhe when I shove my fingers inside you."

A needy whine catches in my throat. I don't want Ezra to think I only want him because I'm a thirsty bitch, but right now, I'm not sure how to make him see otherwise.

I haven't been thinking of him as much as the others, but he's always been off-limits. I didn't think anything had changed.

"Why do you want me?" I ask, biting my lip. "Is it because I'm ... convenient?"

Ezra's eyes narrow. "You are not convenient. You are *in*convenient. You are temptress sent to ruin me."

I lick my lips and push myself off the wall. Curving around the falling water, I close the two feet between us, careful not to bump the girthy appendage standing at attention. "You never told me you wanted me."

Ezra huffs, his eyes guarded. "You are engaged."

True. But Mikhail's already kissed me and made me come on his fingers, and he and I don't have any history. Ezra and I *do*. Why shouldn't Ezra also have my attention?

I think of all three men, and my heart beats faster than ever before. I want them all. It feels greedy to admit that to myself, but nothing about our situation is normal.

They're different from each other. But they rule the city *together*. All three of them.

Why can't their queen claim all three kings for herself?

I tug at Ezra's wrists and unravel his crossed arms. Placing his hands on my hips, I attempt to guide him back into the water.

We're dirty, after all.

"Kiss me, Ezra." The command feels final, and a shiver runs down my spine as I realize . . . I like how it feels to be in charge. All my life, I let others tell me what to do. I agreed to a marriage because it was expected of me. I ran away from home because it's what my mother would have wanted. I stayed away because my grandmother insisted it was safer where we were than where I wanted to be.

No more.

I'm calling the shots, and right now, that means claiming a kiss from the man I've never been allowed to want.

Ezra follows me beneath the water, all hesitation gone from his movements. He pulls me against his naked chest and twines his hand in my hair, grabbing the strands tight enough that it stings. "Yes, *lisichka*."

His mouth descends over mine hungrily, eliciting a powerful moan from somewhere deep within me. As his tongue traces the seam of my lips, he lifts me, shoving me against the shower wall. Ezra's teeth find my throat as I settle my thighs around his waist, and he reaches between us to cup my sex with his hand.

This is what I've been craving.

My back arches as he grinds the heel of his palm against my clit. A jolt of pleasure rushes through me, making me gasp.

"My fingers fit better than yours," Ezra rumbles in my ear, sliding one thick knuckle past my lips. I buck against his hand as the finger *curls* and electricity zings through me.

Faintly, the working part of my brain remembers that Mikhail said something similar in the library, but all thoughts fade as Ezra pumps his finger in and out, working my tight channel as best he can. With a groan, he adds a second, biting my shoulder when he meets resistance.

"Open for me, *lisichka*. *Yes.*" He arches his fingers and captures my heady moan in a bruising kiss. "You will think of Ezra now, yes? *My* thick fingers. When you fuck this wet pussy, it will be *my* name you scream."

My orgasm crests hard and sudden from Ezra's filthy words. A silent scream catches in my throat as my whole body tenses from the force of it. Ezra continues fucking my dripping wet core, drawing out each shockwave of pleasure for as long as possible.

"*Yes,*" he rasps, kissing me hard as he withdraws his fingers. "That was beautiful, *lisichka*. A treasure." He shuts off the water and carries me into the bedroom, gently laying me down on the mattress. We're both soaking wet when he slides up beside me and pulls me against his chest.

"So beautiful," he murmurs with a yawn. "Truly . . . magnificent . . ." His eyes drift close, and his breathing deepens in an instant. A peaceful expression smooths over his face, and I brush wet strands of hair from his eyes. The dark circles I've glimpsed over the past few nights are even darker up close, and my racing heart clenches with worry.

If he's really been working himself to the bone for my sake, I owe him a lot more than I realize.

The breeze from the open window helps cool my steaming skin, but I snuggle up to Ezra to make the warmth last.

If Andrei or Mikhail find me in Ezra's bed, so be it.

A queen never apologizes.

CHAPTER 15

VALENTINA

MY EYES open to a pink sunset streaming through the curtains. Ezra's heavy breathing warms my shoulder as he spoons me, one thick arm banded around my stomach to hold me close.

We didn't have sex, but we could have . . .

We *still* could. My breath catches as nerves flutter in my stomach. I've wanted attention from all three men—and it looks like I'm about to get it.

A deep chuckle rumbles by the foot of the bed, and my elbow jabs Ezra's chest as I jump up in a panic. I forget to cover myself until I'm sitting up, boobs out to say *hello*, staring at Mikhail's smirking face. "Mikhail!" I snag the sheet from underneath Ezra's arm and hold it up over my chest.

"Have a good catnap, *malyshka*?"

Ezra groans and lifts onto his elbows, dark hair tumbling over his eyes. "Go away, Mikhail."

The other man laughs and starts undoing his tie, copper eyes glinting as he stares at me. Slowly, he peels off his navy tie, shrugs out of his coat, and unbuttons the white dress shirt across his shoulders. He reaches for his belt and flashes another grin. "Good thing I don't take orders from *you*."

Ezra grumbles something in Russian and pulls me back into the warmth of his chest, sighing into my hair as he holds me close.

The bed dips behind me, and a third body joins us under the sheets. A warm hand settles over my hip and starts to rub slow, tender caresses over the outside of my thigh. Lips press to my shoulder, featherlight kisses trailing across my back.

This can't be happening. What is *happening?*

One of Ezra's calloused hands tangles in my curls and cups the back of my head. I open my eyes to find his onyx ones enraptured by my face, and then he closes the distance by sweeping me into a deep kiss.

A cry catches in my throat as Ezra holds me in place and captures my bottom lip between his, the groan he makes sending heat straight to my core.

Mikhail's hand smooths over my ass and squeezes. "You've been busy, haven't you, *malyshka*?" He tuts in my ear as his fingers dip lower, teasing the backs of my thighs. "One night in the library wasn't enough, hm? You keep moaning my name all over the house. Have you missed me that much?"

Ezra's tongue slides into my mouth and I can't respond. My mind blanks as he hooks my thigh over his, spreading me open and allowing me to feel the slick heat pooling between my thighs. This time, it's Ezra's hand sliding up the back of my thigh and cupping my ass, and I gasp as I feel a very hot, hard cock grinding against my stomach.

"Mmm," Mikhail breathes, kissing my neck. "Such a naughty bride, letting two men play with her." His fingers ghost over my molten core, and I whimper against Ezra's mouth. He releases my lips the same instant Mikhail slips a finger inside my heat, and they both catch the moan it elicits. Mikhail starts working me slowly, sliding two fingers in and out, groaning into my neck. "She's so *tight*, Ezra. Feel how tight she is."

A second hand joins the first, and a third finger joins the rest. Both men pulse their fingers in and out, taking turns so that, as one retracts, the other takes his place. I'm full in a way my own fingers will *never* make happen, and I toss my head back with a needy whine.

They've been sharing my dirty little secrets with each other. They probably knew all about Mikhail catching me in the library the night it happened, then the day Andrei nearly fucked me outside the mayor's party, I'm sure someone tattled to Ezra. There's no way Ezra could have contacted them about today, though, so Mikhail must have chanced upon—

Mikhail bites my shoulder from behind, making me clench around his fingers. He groans, curling them inside me to hit my G-spot. "*Fuck*, Valentina. I can't wait to feel you wrapped around my cock."

Ezra punctuates the word *cock* with a well-timed thrust of his own, grinding himself against my hip. "Andrei gets her first," he says, his voice heavy with desire. "But that doesn't mean we can't *taste* her."

Both men remove their fingers, and Mikhail wraps an arm around my chest, holding his glistening digits in front of my face. My cheeks flame as he twists his wrist in the fading sunlight, giving us all a glimpse of how wet I am.

"I think we should see if she is sweet," Ezra rumbles, pressing his thumb against my lips. I swipe my tongue against him, and he shoves the entire thing into my mouth. A hint of *me* hits my tongue and I suck, enjoying the way Ezra's eyes roll back. "*Fuck*, brother," he growls, "I think she likes how she tastes." He pulls his thumb from my mouth and cups my jaw, squeezing hard enough that my mouth pops open.

"Suck," Mikhail commands in my ear, holding his fingers to my lips. "Clean your mess from my fingers."

I've never felt more embarrassed, but riding that wave of embarrassment is full-bodied *need*. I accept Mikhail's fingers into my mouth as he slides them past my lips. The taste of my desire explodes on my tongue, and my eyes flutter closed as I lick him clean.

He growls in my ear, murmuring a *fuck, that's hot*, and notching his cock against my ass. He thrusts hard enough that I squeak in surprise at how much the pressure hurts. He's rock hard, an iron rod grinding into my cheeks. As Mikhail pumps his fingers in and out of my mouth, Ezra's lips travel lower. Cupping my breast, Ezra grumbles something in Russian and kisses the tip, lathing my pink bud with his hot, wet tongue, and licking a stripe across the top of my breast. I buck in Mikhail's arms, and he laughs, grinding harder, undeterred in the slightest.

This is *insane*. I'm wedged between two sinfully hot men as they toy with my body in ways I never imaged. I didn't even say I wanted them to touch me, but *fuck*, I don't know how I'll ever want anything else for as long as I live.

I long to kiss Mikhail, so I twist my spine and lock on to the back of his head, pulling his lips to mine in a needy display of affection. I *did* miss the crazy bastard.

He captures my mouth greedily, rivaling Ezra's tenacity with strong strokes of his tongue, his warm palm sliding down my body to tweak the nipple Ezra just abandoned. With a gasp, I arch my back, and the two men work in tandem to turn me onto my back. Once I'm settled, they both sit back to admire the view of my body.

As I flush darker and my pulse races beneath their gaze, I look beyond them to find that not only has someone turned on a lamp, but a third man has entered the room.

Andrei sits in a chair at the end of the bed, watching everything with a passive expression. When our eyes meet, he raises an eyebrow. "Don't stop on my account. She seems to be enjoying herself."

A rush of pleasure settles between my thighs as Andrei stares at my naked body. He's never glimpsed it before, and this feels as deliciously lewd as I always imagined it would. A tiny tendril of fear at his reaction makes me wetter, and his eyes dilate as he settles his gaze on the desire dripping down my exposed slit.

A massive bulge stands like a mountain in his lap, and I lick my lips as I imagine what lies beneath.

He catches my return stare and his smirk morphs into a triumphant grin. "Do you want to see me, *moya zhena*?"

I bite my lip and nod.

Slowly, like he's enjoying the moment, Andrei stands and undoes his belt, pops the button of his slacks, and slides down the zipper. He cups himself, and I see the thick outline through his black boxers as he squeezes. "Is this what you want, Valentina?"

Oh, god. He doesn't actually want me to answer, does he?

He waits, sapphire-blue eyes darkening to deep navy as he strokes himself through his clothes. "Surely, my queen isn't shy, is she?"

I suck my cheeks in. *Oh, she definitely is.*

"I will give you the world," Andrei vows, rolling his shoulders back and hooking his thumbs into the waistband of his boxers. "All you have to do is claim it, Valentina. Take what you want. Be ruthless, darling."

Take what I want. I hold my breath as I stare at *exactly* what I want.

The man in front of me. The men on either side of me. This house. The pieces of my mother hidden within it. This city, with its beachside restaurants and endless secrets to explore.

All of it.

I sit up and shift my weight to my hands and knees, crawling across the bed to reach Andrei. His hips align perfectly with my mouth, and I glance up at him as I voice my deepest, darkest secret.

"I want you." My voice is thick with desire—not just for the man in front of me, but also for the two behind me. Desire for their touch. Their love. Their secrets. Every dark part of them. The moments of light in between. "I want all of you."

Brushing away Andrei's hands, I pull down the last piece of his clothing and his cock springs free, veined and heavy in my palm. I stroke it once, and Andrei's jaw clenches as he watches me touch him. I admire his length, press a tender kiss to the base, and he growls.

I've never felt very powerful. It's hard to, when everyone around you is so decisive and sure of themselves and their actions. If they're right, doesn't that mean that everyone else is wrong?

But as I stare at Andrei's cock in my hand, a wave of confidence settles over me. I can be just as sure and strong as anyone else. I can convince *them* that I'm right with a simple decision to *be* right.

This feels right.

I suck on the tip and flick my tongue against him, and he groans, pulling my hair back from my face and holding it behind my head.

"You have all the power you need, Valentina. Never forget that." His eyes clench shut as I take him into my mouth. Gripping his quivering thigh, I pull him deeper, and he groans when he hits the back of my throat.

I choke and pull off, a single string of saliva keeping us connected.

The bed shifts behind me, and I'm reminded that we're not alone. Hands caress my thighs and back, lips press tender kisses to my shoulders and neck. I don't know whose hands or lips are whose, but their touch spurs me on, and I take Andrei's cock back into my mouth.

"Do you want them to touch you?" Andrei asks, his eyes flicking up from my face to glance at his brothers. "They'll do your bidding, *zhena*. We can all be yours, if you want us to be."

I moan at the thought of having all three men. Is it okay for me to claim them all at the same time? Won't that cause testosterone issues between them?

Andrei's lips curve into a smile and he cups my cheek lovingly. "Don't worry, Valentina. We all want to please you. We don't mind sharing."

I hollow out my cheeks and close my eyes with a heady moan. The men take that as their cue to continue pleasuring me, with one spreading my thighs and lowering my hips over their face and the other hooking their fingers into my drenched pussy. A tongue swipes against my clit, making me jump.

With a forceful hand, one of them flattens their palm on my lower back to hold me down while the one lying beneath me grabs my ass and pulls me harder against their mouth.

My mind glitches as I try to picture them working my body together. Are they avoiding touching each other at all, or are they so focused on me that they don't care about a little skin-on-skin contact?

The thought nearly tips me over the edge, and I swallow more of Andrei's cock greedily, moaning wantonly as ripples of pleasure rock my entire body.

Someone sucks hard on my clit and I cry out, the sound muffled with my full mouth.

Andrei hisses out the word *beautiful* and thrusts, holding my head tight as he rocks into my mouth.

It's all too much. *Too much.* The pressure builds deep in my belly and breaks all at once, sending me tumbling over the edge. Andrei's cock swells against my tongue and he comes just as hard, tossing his head back as his seed pulses hot in my mouth. As I swallow around his cock, he groans, continuing to thrust as I milk him for every last drop.

When he pulls free, he cups my face and brushes his thumb against my cheekbone. "Did that satisfy you, *zhena*?"

There's an ache deep in me that *needs* to be filled, but I'm not sure if I'm ready to go from zero to one hundred with these men. If I let one fill me, the others might soon follow, and we'll quickly move from regular sex territory to something much bigger and more overwhelming.

"Yes." My voice is hoarse and I swallow, wincing from a slight burning at the back of my throat.

Andrei catches the movement and smiles gently. "You did beautifully, Valentina. Didn't she, boys?"

"Perfect," Mikhail purrs in my ear. "Did you like riding Ezra's face, *malyshka*?"

A wave of embarrassment makes me gasp. *Oh god.* I did *what?*

He chuckles that same sinfully velvet cadence he always does and brushes curls off my shoulder to press a kiss there. "Don't worry, he enjoyed it as much as you did."

Ezra grunts from behind me as I sit back on my heels. A strong, tattooed arm wraps around my waist and pulls me back against a naked chest. "You taste delicious, *lisichka*. My new favorite meal," he rumbles, settling my body into his arms.

I stare at Mikhail and Andrei as Ezra holds me, unsure of where we go from here. I'm supposed to marry Andrei, but he just participated in what I think is called a . . . I squint as I count four bodies. *Does this qualify as an orgy?*

Andrei starts getting dressed and asks Mikhail about how his work at the firm is going, and the two engage in what can only be called a business meeting as both start picking apart their clothes and handing each other their respective property. They dress around words like *contract* and *loophole*, and I watch in complete fascination.

This feels normal, after all. I don't know what I was so nervous about.

Ezra's hand rubs up and down my arm, his fingertips playing with mine once he reaches my hand. "You can stay here," he whispers in my ear. "But I cannot promise good sleep. I will be busy in other room."

If he means torturing people for information, I am *so* out of here.

Mikhail's eyes snap in our direction before I can politely decline Ezra's offer. "No, she will *not* be staying here." With a huff, he crosses to Ezra's dresser and pulls out a clean shirt. "She needs actual rest tonight. I'm taking her out in the morning."

My heart leaps at the chance of spending more time with Mikhail. Even though the beach wasn't exactly *fun*, he's honest with me, and he takes me to new places. "Where are we going?"

He grins as he tosses Ezra's shirt to me. "You'll see."

Andrei frowns at Mikhail. "I do not think it wise to take her off the grounds."

"I'll keep her safe," Mikhail says quickly, slapping a hand on Andrei's shoulder. "You can trust me."

"I trust you." Andrei's lips press into a thin line. "I don't trust the *suka*."

"The what?" I slide out of Ezra's grasp, but he pulls me back for a quick kiss. His lips linger over mine. "Do not trust anyone," he says sternly. "No one but us."

Ooookay.

He releases me and I jump up from his bed. An ominous feeling tugs in my gut, but I ignore it and throw on Ezra's shirt and start looking for my pants. They're in the bathroom and still gross, so I rummage through Ezra's dresser until I find a pair of his boxers and pull them on.

All three of my men are talking in Russian by the time I'm more or less dressed. Each one's expression is as serious as the next. I run a hand through my hair and untangle what knots I can. "Care to fill me in?"

"No," Ezra grunts, buckling a new pair of pants over his hips.

Andrei sighs. "You will go with Mikhail tomorrow, and then you will return home. No detours."

"I'll bring her straight home," Mikhail promises. Taking my hand, he starts to pull me out of the room. "Now, as for where you'll be sleeping *tonight*—"

"*Zhena.* You are forgetting something." There's an irritated glint in Andrei's eyes. "Come here."

Nerves skitter down my arms as I look between him and Mikhail. Hesitantly, I pull out of Mikhail's grasp and step toward my fiancé.

He grasps my chin between his fingers and tilts my head up. "I expect a kiss every time you leave." He lowers his lips to mine and claims one. It's different than the panty-melting kiss he gave me before. This one is . . . *soft.* Tender.

When he pulls back, I'm breathless and blushing. My heart flips as he smiles.

"I'll be waiting for your return home tomorrow. Don't stay out too long." He gives Mikhail a pointed look over my shoulder. "If he tries to lure you somewhere else, remind him that his *pakhan* will be very angry about it."

Mikhail laughs, but there's an edge to it, like he recognizes the vague threat for what it is. "Don't worry, *pakhan.* I'll be good." He holds the door open and waits for me to follow him. Once I'm within reach, he grabs my hand and snickers. "It's *Valentina* you'll have to worry about, the sly little minx. She likes our detours." He winks at me.

I flush crimson at the insinuation and smack him in the chest. "Me! You're the ones pushing me up against walls and—"

Mikhail cuts me off with a kiss, making my head spin.

Three men. I've kissed three men today, and they each watched it happen. They participated. They *liked* it.

A pleasant warmth fills my heart. Despite how new this dynamic is, I like it too. I don't have to choose between them.

I can have everything I've ever wanted and more.

Breaking free from the kiss, I resist the urge to hide my face. All three men are watching me, and every single one of them has the same tender look in their eyes.

Something . . . *big* is happening between us. Something different. Something new.

It makes me think that, maybe, villains do get happy endings, after all.

Chapter 16

Valentina

"What are we doing today?" I bounce in my seat as I wait for Mikhail to finish his second cup of coffee. Despite how lively he seems at any hour of the day, apparently mornings are the one exception.

Watching him struggle without a morning caffeine hit makes him feel more normal. I can't help but giggle a little, and the sound helps brighten the shadows lingering in his hazelnut eyes.

"It's good to see you, Valentina." He reaches under the table and squeezes my knee. "Three days is far too long without seeing your face . . . among other things." He licks his lip slowly, like he's savoring his drink.

I smile sweetly at the confession and ignore the salacious parts. "I never took you for a romantic."

He arches an eyebrow, his hand wandering higher up my thigh. "I'm a man full of surprises. Not all of them can be wicked."

I smack his hand away and he snickers.

"*Fine.* If you insist, I'll be good today." He downs the rest of his coffee in one gulp and slams his mug down. "All right, let's get going before Andrei wakes up and changes his mind about our plans. I'm not letting him steal you from me today."

Taking my hand, he leads me out of the kitchen and toward the back of the house. I haven't spent as much time here, so when Mikhail opens the door to a multi-car garage, I'm genuinely surprised to see it.

I always thought we had drivers and a valet, but I guess it makes sense to have a few cars of our own.

Mikhail tosses a set of keys in his hands. "Guess which one is mine, and I'll give you a prize." He winks at me, and as much as I want to be grumpy for him being cheeky, I can't. His devilish smile makes my heart skip when it's all for me.

Sleek cars are lined in a perfect row, each one more eye-catching than the last—from a black SUV to a white convertible, down to a blue sports car. Each one is branded with a high-end logo. It's too bad I don't know shit about cars, or the foreign insignias might impress me. Peering into the tinted windows gives me a glimpse of their interiors if I squint hard enough, each one screaming luxury. The kind where the leather stitching is done in an accent color. There are six cars and two motorcycles in total, and I scan each of them with interest.

Apparently, I'm easily motivated by the promise of a prize.

I run my hand across the hood of the deep blue sports car and raise an eyebrow. "Is this one yours?" I can't picture Ezra in anything other than black, and Andrei seems far too sophisticated to race through the streets in a sports car.

Only one man has the energy for that.

Mikhail's grin is devious as he clicks the fob in his hands and the sports car comes to life. "Guess you know me better than you think." He slides up beside me and wraps an arm around my waist, yanking me against his chest. My eyes widen as flashes of memories from last night come to mind, and a rush of heat settles between my thighs.

"Now for your prize," he murmurs, dipping his head toward mine. My heart melts as he kisses me tenderly, his hands settling on my hips like we've done this a thousand times. He pulls away and hums in the back of his throat, brushing his thumb against my bottom lip. "I could get addicted to that," he murmurs, already leaning in for another.

Our lips meet, and what began as something sweet turns heated within seconds. He steps me backward until I'm pushed against the hood of his car.

"Mmm, *malyshka*, you taste like honey." He sucks my bottom lip into his mouth and bites my soft flesh, groaning deep in his chest. "I can't tell you how sexy you were last night as you sucked on my fingers." His eyes flash like liquid gold, and a slow, malicious smile spreads across his lips. "And on Andrei's cock. I'm getting a little jealous thinking about it."

I feel the outline of his dick pressing against my stomach, and a rush of heat makes me blush.

He wants me to suck him off too?

Here?

Mikhail chuckles and presses a quick kiss to my forehead. "Ah, but it'll have to wait. If I get my hands on you now, we'll never make it out of the garage." He gazes longingly at his car, then back at me, his wicked smile curving even more. "But I suppose there's always fun to be had both in and *out* of the vehicle. No matter where it's parked."

I swallow hard. I've never given road head. Hell, I'm not even that experienced at anything else. Last night was a fluke. I don't know *what* I'm doing, in or out of the bedroom.

The fact that I managed to fool three sexed-up criminals is a miracle.

He lets me go and opens the passenger side door for me.

I jump inside as quickly as possible to avoid looking at him, and as soon as he closes the door, I have two seconds of alone time *not* to think about how his cock would feel down my throat.

Because I bet it would feel pretty damn good.

We're silent as we drive through the city. I don't recognize the streets we're on, and Mikhail starts pointing things out to me, from popular streets to historic establishments. His voice soothes my nerves, and I relax into the soft leather seat.

"You've lived here your whole life?" I ask, glancing at him.

He's a picture of ease, lounging back with one hand on the wheel. "Mm-hmm. My family is Russian-born, but my sister and I are American. We've spent a few summers in Russia, but I'm the only one who's stayed there long-term."

"You have a sister?" I turn my body to face Mikhail. "How did I not know that?" I picture a woman just as striking as Mikhail, with chestnut hair down to her waist and a sinister sparkle in her eye as she lures men to her with a sultry smile.

He chuckles and turns to watch me instead of the road. "I don't think it's come up yet. I told you, I'm full of surprises."

"Not all of them wicked," I parrot back, admiring how the sunlight brings out flecks of gold in his eyes. He really is handsome, but unfortunately for me, I find him even *more* tempting when he's radiating a hint of malice.

"How long is long-term?" I ask, curious as to why he'd need to be in Russia for any length of time. "Isn't a summer long enough to visit relatives?"

Mikhail chuckles softly. "I wasn't exactly visiting in the traditional sense," he says mysteriously. "But to answer your question, long-term is about . . ." He thinks for a moment. "Two years, give or take. Ezra's spent the most time there out of all of us, though."

I avoid the urge to ask what *visiting* entails. Probably something illegal.

It makes sense that Ezra has spent the most time there, seeing as his accent is the thickest. I get the feeling that he doesn't care to change how he speaks, as long as people can understand him.

"Was he born in Russia?"

Mikhail nods. "Yeah, he was."

"What brought him to the States?"

He's silent for a moment. "You should ask him next time you see him."

"You don't know?"

Taking a deep breath, he exhales slowly before responding. "I know everything there is to know about the man, Valentina. Of course, I know what brought him here. But I'm not going to tell you all our secrets; some of them you have to find out on your own."

We pull up to a gray building and park in one of the many empty spots out front. A plaque on the outer wall reads *Harlin Heights Home for Children*, and my forehead creases as Mikhail shuts off the engine. "What are we doing here?" I didn't even know *homes for children* still existed, let alone so close to my home.

"Teaching you something," Mikhail says easily, shutting off the engine and getting out of the car. He comes around the side and opens my door, holding out his hand to help me stand.

The gray stones stack high enough for three floors, certain portions and roughened edges darkened with age and wear. Some of the lower stones have been restored over the years, and a new roof and tended front garden give the place a patch-work feel. Not brand new, but at least taken care of. Children peer out the window at us, one little girl in particular waving excitedly as Mikhail and I approach. They disappear a moment later, the heavy curtain falling closed in their wake.

I don't know what lesson I'm supposed to learn here, but I grow anxious as Mikhail pulls the aged door open and inclines his head. "After you."

I glance between him and the lobby, relenting when Mikhail's expression cools.

"Don't be so nervous," he murmurs, pressing his hand to the small of my back as we pass through the entryway.

Although the structure appears old, the bones are good. Solid wood frames and rafters scream old money, and the deep, dark wooden floors are polished to perfection. It reminds me of the Baranova estate and all the expensive wood paneled through the halls. If I wasn't so unsure about this place, I'd think they were built at the same time.

As I'm looking around and inspecting the architecture, Mikhail approaches the front desk to sign us in.

"Mr. Monrovia! We weren't expecting you today." The receptionist's eyes flick to me, and although her smile is picture perfect, her eye twitches at the edge, like her smile is forced. "This must be Miss Baranova. We've been waiting for you."

"You have?" I try not to let my mouth hang open. "Why?"

Mikhail's smile is somehow more perfect than the receptionist's. "Come now, Valentina. Meet Francesca. She's a vital part of the team here."

"Nice to meet you," I say politely, my own smile not nearly as dazzling.

Francesca's smile remains in place as her eyes travel down my body and she makes her initial assessment. "Likewise, Miss Baranova." She looks back to Mikhail and some of the tension in her shoulders relaxes. I get the feeling that I'm not as welcome as Mikhail.

"We're here for a tour. Is anyone available?" Mikhail pats the wooden countertop. "I'm afraid I don't know the place well enough to show Valentina around."

Francesca bows her head. "Of course. We can get started right away. Let me lock up, so we don't have any visitors."

Mikhail's mahogany eyes stay locked on me as Francesca

steps away to turn the heavy lock on the front door. Once she's returned, she nods toward me, a steely look in her blue eyes. "Welcome, Mistress. You can come any time you like to check on the children. I'm told that both the late Madame and her daughter came here often, though that was before my time."

The hairs on my arms raise like a ghost entered the room. "The Madame?" The title feels eerily familiar. Where have I heard it before?

Francesca's brows pinch together, and she takes a quick glance at Mikhail. "Yes, we often refer to her as simply the Madame, but you may know her as Katya Baranova. Her daughter Maeve also took responsibilities here. They're . . . your predecessors."

I turn a glare on Mikhail, but he's completely at ease, looking nonchalant as he studies a ceramic bust of the orphanage's founder. Francesca uses his feigned interest as motivation to move on from the tension *clearly* emanating solely from me, and she proudly declares that the founder and his wife, *The Madame*, visited up until their deaths.

"She's not dead," I scoff, still annoyed that Mikhail decided to unceremoniously throw family history at me. Two can play at that game. "Katya's very much alive and kicking. Actually, I'm sure she'd *love* to hear that we're visiting today. Don't you think so, Mikhail? Perhaps she can join us?"

I'd love to see my grandmother, truth be told. If I'm not in danger here, and it feels less and less like I'm a prisoner the longer I'm around these men, I don't know why we can't both live in the city again. My father's men aren't a threat any more, now that Andrei's in charge as *pakhan*. Her transgressions against the Bratva, real or otherwise, can be pardoned with a simple flick of Andrei's wrist. Then, she won't be labeled a traitor for leaving and won't be in danger of sudden death or dismemberment.

Besides, if I explain to everyone that it was in my best interest that she left the Bratva with me, I'm sure they would understand . . . or, well, enough of them would for it to matter. And if they don't understand, she can stay at the estate. The place is a fortress; no one can get in or out without the *pakhan's* permission.

Mikhail's air of nonchalance snuffs out in an instant. He turns his icy gaze on me so swiftly that I flinch. A chill runs down my spine at how cold he suddenly looks. "No, love, I don't think she can. Katya is not welcome anywhere within this city, dead or otherwise."

I can't even enjoy the way he uses the word *love*, like we're more than . . . whatever we are now.

Something's *really* wrong, all of a sudden.

"Why not?" I cross my arms defiantly. "She's *my* grandmother. I can invite her in if I want."

Mikhail's icy expression cracks, and flickers of intense anger ignite in his eyes.

Anger that makes no sense.

"You've never even met her!" I don't know if that's true, but she's been with *me* for the past five years, not here in the city. He wouldn't have had a chance to run into her at the local coffee shop or bake sale.

Francesca slowly backs away from us, and I don't blame her.

Mikhail suddenly looks deadly.

He takes deliberate, forceful steps forward, the scowl on his face much more prominent than the grumpy one he hid behind his coffee mug this morning.

"I haven't had the pleasure," he says softly, his voice a low purr that sends shivers down my spine. There's nothing soft about the look in his eye, and I take a step back with each one he advances. "But if I do . . ." His lips curve up in malice.

"Let's just say, she won't be able to pay this place a visit as part of the *living* anymore."

I'm rendered speechless. My mouth opens and shuts repeatedly, a croaking sound stuck in my throat.

What the *fuck*?

Mikhail smooths a hand over his hair, and his demeanor returns to normal, his perfect smile sliding back into place. "You were saying, Francesca?"

The woman keeps her composure better than I do. She turns her attention to various objects in the room, detailing everything in excruciating detail, from the stained-glass window high above that came from Italy as a wedding present to my grandmother, to the age of the building and what it was prior to being refurbished and turned into an orphanage decades ago.

Mikhail sticks to my shadow, far enough away that I can't punch him for being an ass, but close enough that I can feel him hovering. *Staring.*

On the beach, it was unnerving that he stared at me constantly. The more he stares, whether it's across the hall or across the dinner table, makes it less nerve-wracking and more normal. Flattering, even, in the right light.

Now, however, it's insufferable.

I whirl on him and shove both my palms flat against his chest. "Stop it," I hiss, trying to push him away from me. "Stop *staring*. I'm mad at you."

He smirks, looping his index finger through mine. "A touch of anger looks good on you, *malyshka*."

Before I can blow up at him, he pecks my lips and spins me back around to continue the tour.

Francesca is waiting patiently, but her face is pinched like she *really* doesn't want to be here anymore. I can't say I blame her.

I think Mikhail likes to take me on detours that are anything but *fun*.

The tour continues, but I'm paying *much* less attention than before. My thoughts keep swirling back to my grandmother. Is she okay, or is she in danger? Is it only Mikhail that hates her, or do others I know nothing about? Is it because she left without warning five years ago, or for something else?

Ten minutes pass before we stop in front of a row of framed photographs hanging on the wall. They range from black and white, grainy images to clearer ones, bright with color.

"Here, you can see when the home was founded," Francesca tells us, gesturing toward the oldest of the bunch.

A date gleams up from the bottom edge of the frame, the metallic gold shining to perfection. I glance at each frame along the wall, and every single one has a similarly metallic date imprinted along the bottom. Every ten years, it seems they took a new photograph of the orphanage's staff and its children.

How morbid.

I scan the photographs with feigned interest, knowing I won't recognize a single soul photographed within, when all of a sudden, *I do*.

Third photograph from the end. A woman with long, dark hair beams at me as she sits on bright green grass, surrounded by a dozen children and young teenagers. She looks just like me, and my heart seizes at how happy she is.

Mom.

"It's tradition for the *pakhan's* wife to look after this place," Mikhail explains from behind me.

The picture immediately following it looks similar, only this time, my mom has a little girl in her arms—one with hair as dark as hers and eyes a brilliant emerald that even the camera lens couldn't hide.

Me.

"I've been here before," I gasp, pressing my face close enough to the glass that it fogs under my breath. I stare at my younger self, not believing what I'm seeing. "I was young." About five years old, to be exact. It's no wonder I didn't recognize this place.

One young man standing beside my mom catches my eye, his hair as dark as his eyes, his arms crossed and his jaw set, a familiar black-and-gray tattoo curving across his bicep.

"Is that . . ."

There's *no* way it's him. What would Ezra be doing in a home for orphaned kids?

I brush my fingertips over the familiar brooding expression, recognizing it, even though the boy in the picture can't be older than sixteen. My eyes drift to the boy next to him, and another shock jolts my system.

Andrei is here too.

"See something?" Mikhail asks, placing his hand on my hip as he leans over my shoulder. Francesca might be fooled, but I'm not. He's not interested in the photo. He just wants to touch me and worm back into my good graces by playing nice.

"No." I sidestep away from him and move on to the next photo. My mother's still there, along with a younger version of my grandmother, but I'm pointedly missing.

I must have been locked away in my tower, I think bitterly, frowning at my mother's empty arms. I move to the next image and try to find my mother, but this time, she's missing. Instead, two men stand solemnly in the front of a group of stoic children. No one is smiling. But as I squint between the two latest pictures, I see both of my men standing proud.

Teenagers in one.

Men in the other.

After my mother's death, someone had to keep this place

running. Who better than a *pakhan* and his right-hand men, especially if the *pakhan* himself was raised within its walls?

"Why did you bring me here?" I ask, finally looking at Mikhail dead on.

He doesn't shy away from my gaze. It's like he welcomes it, no matter what I'm feeling in the moment. Because right now, I definitely don't feel fond of him after he basically threatened to kill my last living relative.

"You need to know what will be expected of you." He leans against the opposite wall and kicks his feet out. Despite his professional attire, he sure doesn't carry himself like a businessman. "When you marry Andrei and assume all duties of a *pakhan*'s wife, you need to be prepared. Certain things . . ." He purses his lips, like he doesn't like or agree with this next part. "Certain *expectations* will be there."

Well. I have a history of failing to meet very large expectations. And if people remember who I am, they'll remember *that* too.

We're alone in the hallway. Scurrying feet scuff the floors in a nearby room, but as far as our tour guide goes, she disappeared into the woodwork.

It's just me and Mikhail and his *infuriating* gaze.

"Why did you say those things about my grandmother?" I cross my arms over my chest as my anger starts bubbling back up to the surface. "You have no business being so cruel to her."

"I haven't laid a finger on her," Mikhail deflects, holding both hands up in front of his chest.

"But you will. You said so. *She won't be part of the living anymore,*" I recite, more or less remembering the expression he used. "What the hell do you have against my grandmother?"

Is it something Bratva related? Or is he just mad that I spent the last five years with her, instead of here, under Andrei's thumb?

When Mikhail doesn't answer, I get angrier. "Tell me."

He clenches his jaw. "I . . ." For the first time since I met the man, he looks away from me. "I can't."

Betrayal cracks like a whip against my ribs. "You *can't?*"

What happened to all those pretty words he told me on the beach? What happened to *no secrets* between us?

What the hell could be so bad that he can't tell me?

"Not yet," Mikhail clarifies, his voice pitching. The note of desperation sounds odd coming from Mikhail, and I already hate it. "But I *promise* you, Valentina, I don't make pointless threats. You're going to have to trust me on this. Your grandmother is . . ." His expression falters, and he sighs. "Everything will become clear soon. You have to trust me. Trust *us*. We're doing this to protect you."

I fail to see how that's possible.

"Killing my grandmother," I clarify harshly. "That's what you mean. *Killing my grandmother* is somehow supposed to *protect* me."

He looks me straight in the eye and nods. "Yes, *malyshka*. Yes, it is."

Chapter 17

Mikhail

The tension in the car is stifling.

I'd planned to take Valentina for a fun little spin around town to hear her laugh as I take turns too fast, but she's too preoccupied with being mad to even look at me. I bet if I so much as try to burn rubber, she'll yell at me for it.

It's tempting either way, honestly.

We were supposed to stay at the orphanage longer, but Valentina's entire mood shifted the moment I let something slip about her grandmother. It's not *my* fault the woman came up during the tour—and then Valentina just *had* to get offended that Francesca thought the old woman was dead.

Why couldn't she have remained silent and taken the damned tour without comment?

Because then she wouldn't be Valentina, the voice in my head taunts. *She'd be a remnant of the silent wallflower she used to be.*

Not that there's anything wrong with being a wallflower. It's just not who Valentina is anymore.

We have a few hours before we're expected back at the

estate, so I push the brake and slow our speed to cruise through the streets.

Valentina might be mad *now*, but she'll see reason once she realizes her grandmother is the one keeping secrets from her.

Dangerous secrets.

My blood starts to boil as I think of Liam taking pictures of Valentina while she slept. When she was passed out and defenseless, the bastard was *taking fucking pictures* of her. Who knows what else he's done, or if he drugged her drink to get her to pass out in the first place.

Fake boyfriend. Ex-boyfriend. Dead man.

My grip on the steering wheel tightens.

"So, tell me about your boyfriend," I say suddenly, interrupting the horrible silence between us. "What's he like?"

Valentina tenses beside me. "That's none of your business."

She's still mad at me, but I'm the one trying to keep her safe. She doesn't need to defend a fucking *stalker*.

"Actually, it is. If he's going to come after me for tongue-fucking his girl, I need to know what I'm up against—"

Valentina *snarls*, and I fucking love it. "You're not touching me ever again." Her eyes flash like emerald fire, and it takes every ounce of my willpower not to stare.

I slow the car down to a crawl. "Don't be like that, *malyshka*. I can kill your grandmother *and* your boyfriend *and* make you come all in one night." I press my tongue against the inside of my cheek with a smile.

Yeah, that sounds like a *perfect* night.

"You're fucking sick," she seethes, crossing her arms tight and hugging herself. "Just take me home and go fuck off. I'm done with you."

I could let her sit with her anger, thinking she's right in all her fury.

But I won't.

"I assure you, Valentina, I'm not the sick one here."

Her eyes snap to me, and a shiver runs down my spine. If looks could kill, I'd be dead in a heartbeat. I imagine her holding a gun to my head as she gives me one final kiss goodbye. Sitting in my lap. Yes, wearing a little black dress. Rucked up to her hips, with nothing on underneath—

Okay, I'm a *little* demented compared to the average person, I'll admit that.

"You don't know either of them." A beat passes before a look crosses her face. "Unless you *know* something. Mikhail. *Mikhail.*" She snaps her fingers to get my attention. "Look at me."

"Driving," I reply merrily, gesturing toward the road. We're crawling at ten miles per hour, and she throws her hands up in outrage.

"We're not even going anywhere! Will you look at me?"

I flick my gaze toward my girl. Her eyes dance with turmoil as she battles her desires. A thirst for secrets. A need for security. A hunger for intimacy.

All things I can give her, in time.

"Yes, love?"

Her face flushes prettily and her breath catches in her throat.

Fucking breathtaking.

I grin at her and adjust my grip on the steering. "Hold on. We're going for a little joy ride." I gun the gas, and we both jerk back into our seats.

Valentina screams as I take a corner at double the appropriate speed, and I revel in the sound.

We reach our destination in record time, and I circle the block just to spend more time with Valentina. She clings to the leather seat with a death grip, and I reach over to hold her hand.

She tries to pull it from my grasp, but I hold on tight, refusing to let go. Her responding glare makes my heart soar.

I love when her attention's all on me.

As we pull up to the curb and I cut the engine, I have to take a breath to calm down. My heart's racing, and I'm liable to do something reckless if I'm not careful.

Valentina has, surprisingly, cooled off. The adrenaline rush cut through some of her anger, and she's breathing clear and deep now that we've parked and the adrenaline is fading.

I press a kiss to her knuckles. I wish the danger was over, but I have a feeling it's only going to get worse from here. There's no telling when or where Katya's going to appear, and Valentina's stalker is Bratva.

It's no coincidence that they've disappeared together.

I look over at Valentina and take in the freckles dotted across her cheeks and the way her hair curls behind her ears. I've never noticed little details like that about a woman before, usually preferring when there's mascara smeared down their cheeks and a lusty haze in their eye.

I've never had to notice the little details before, when all women looked and acted the same.

Boring. Each and every one. Begging me for love and cars and cock. An endless cycle, repeating round and round and round.

Valentina doesn't beg for anything. She doesn't ask me for diamond jewelry or quick, hard fucks in the middle of the night.

She doesn't ask me for *anything*.

My chest aches as she drops her gaze to her lap.

Well, she's asked for *one* thing.

A sigh passes my lips. Andrei will *kill* me for what I'm about to say, and he'll have every right to it. I've been ordered not to say anything. A *pakhan*'s order. Not a friend's. Not a brother's.

My *pakhan.*

His word is law.

Valentina doesn't realize it, but she's asking me for more than just answers—she's asking for my *life.*

Instead of telling Valentina outright that we suspect her grandmother is more than likely a traitorous, manipulative piece of shit, I choose a safer route.

"What do you know about your grandmother's side of the family?"

Valentina's gaze stays in her lap as she plays with my fingers, likely not realizing what she's doing. Her eyes are unfocused as she pieces through information on the Dolohovs.

It's likely not much.

"She married my grandfather pretty young . . . It was arranged." Valentina's face scrunches as she digs deeper. "I know they're originally from Russia. But I don't think they're very prominent or rich or anything. That's why my grandmother moved here and married a Baranova, I think. My mother mentioned it to me once."

Ah, so Maeve tried to teach Valentina something, after all.

"You're right, the Dolohovs aren't very well known, but that's intentional. They keep a low profile."

"I thought all mafia families tried to stay under the radar."

I smile. "Not all of them."

The Baranovas are actually well-known as a crime family, but their foothold goes so far back that there are few brave enough to challenge them. It's what made Tolkotsky so intimidating and what keeps Andrei in power as the current *pakhan.*

In reality, though, there hasn't been a male with Baranova blood since Valentina's grandfather was in charge. Katya married into the family, as did Tolkotsky, as will Andrei.

The women should really be the ones in charge, if we're

talking about blood rights, but the men like to pretend they're the ones everyone is loyal to.

But we all know that if a civil war broke out here in the city, half the populace would flock to Valentina's side over Andrei's because *she's* the one with Baranova blood running through her veins.

Valentina has always been the most important piece for maintaining power over the Bratva. She's its queen. The queen can move anywhere on the chessboard, and the pawns will all step aside to make room for her. The king is limited to moving one small step at a time. His path is blocked until someone screams *checkmate* and takes him out.

But the queen is the one *really* paving the way for her king's victory. Sometimes, she's even the one who finally takes out the enemy's king.

She's the most powerful, and most important, piece on the board.

The picture of Valentina passed out in Liam's apartment flashes in my mind. Scrawled handwriting on the back left to taunt us . . . or . . .

What if he realizes just how important Valentina is to this city's Bratva?

Dread snakes into my chest and squeezes, slowly stealing the air from my lungs. I lose focus on my surroundings as the pieces snap into place.

Liam isn't obsessed with Valentina because of who she is. He's obsessed with her because of her *name.* Her *blood.*

I thought the root of his obsession was obvious—*of course* someone would fall in love with our woman and stalk her to the ends of the earth. She's stubborn and broken and breath-takingly angry at so many things that have been unfair in her life.

It makes sense that any man would fall for her.

But a Bratva *man knows who a Baranova is.*

And a Bratva man working with *Katya*, former queen of this city, will have connections that any other Russian man would not.

"Mikhail?" Valentina squeezes my hand. "Hey, are you okay? You look pale."

I force air into my lungs.

Valentina's heart will break if I tell her that her ex-boyfriend has been playing her for power. And then her *grandmother* . . .

I can't *wait* to put a bullet in her fucking skull.

"I was just thinking about . . ."

Katya's blood splattered across the floor.

I can't keep the smile off my face, but luckily, Valentina assumes I'm being perverted. She lets go of my hand with a heavy eye roll. "I told you, you're not touching me again."

"I know, *malyshka*. Forgive me. I can't help myself." I stare at her until she blushes and fumbles with her seatbelt to get away from me.

I should feel bad about wanting to kill someone she loves, but I don't.

Even if Valentina never lets me touch her for as long as I live . . .

It'll be worth it to make sure no one ever takes advantage of her again.

CHAPTER 18

———

VALENTINA

As I step out of Mikhail's sports car, I finally take in our surroundings. A large, gray brick house sits two dozen feet away, the walkway to the front door curving across an immaculate green lawn. It's autumn, yet the grass is just as green as in the depths of summer.

"This isn't home." Turning on Mikhail, I glare at him. Annoyance ripples down my arms to my fingertips, and I clench my fists by my sides. "I thought we were going *home.*"

"This *is* home, Valentina." Mikhail is still grinning wide, like he's in on a private joke and trying not to laugh at my expense. "C'mon. I'll prove it to you." He doesn't try to take my hand, and even though I should be grateful he's not pushing my boundaries, my fingers curl in on themselves at the distinct lack of his touch.

I like it when he holds my hand.

We walk up to the front door, and he knocks loudly, foregoing the doorbell. Movement from behind paneled glass catches my eye, and I shrink away from the door. I've never been good with introductions, and without the glamor of a party dress and Andrei's infallible confidence, I grow nervous.

Mikhail glances down at me and gives me the softest little smile. "Welcome home, Valentina."

The door unlocks and swings open to a woman who looks just as gorgeous as Mikhail, with warm, tanned skin, even warmer brown eyes, and hair the exact shade of chestnut brown as Mikhail's. It's done up in a complicated bun that frames her face, and she's dressed in a soft cashmere sweater that I recognize immediately as one of the new garments hanging in my armoire at the estate.

She smiles broadly at Mikhail, nearly matching his own intensity, before realizing that a shorter, less energized person stands beside him. Her hands fly to her face and she *gasps*.

"You're wearing my dress! Oh! Mikhail, she's *beautiful*. I just knew that color would look good on her." She winks at me. "Why didn't you tell me you were coming? I would have prepped snacks." Grabbing both our hands, she pulls us inside and kicks the door shut behind us. "I'm just *dying* to get to know you, Valentina. Mikhail's not so easily impressed, but he's been enamored by you since the moment you arrived. And cryptic about it," she says, jabbing Mikhail in the ribs. "I can hardly get a word out of him about your return to the city! So, tell me everything!"

She leads us to the kitchen, a sprawling expanse of stainless steel and white granite countertops, and pulls a bottle of white wine from an inlay cooler.

As she pops the top and pours us each a glass, I try not to stare. She's *glamorous*, and in a movie star way. Perfect skin. Flawless French manicure. A smile that dazzles.

She hands me a full wineglass, and I nearly drop it. "Um. Thanks." I take a sip and the crisp sweetness that hits my tongue nearly makes me moan.

"Valentina," Mikhail begins excitedly, a little twinkle in his eye as he looks between me and the woman, "meet my sister, Celia. She's designing your wedding dress."

I nearly choke on my drink. Andrei and I have been planning the wedding, but I hadn't realized someone was already working on my dress. I thought I'd have to shop from a catalog or something.

"Oh," Celia chides, smacking her brother's arm. "We can talk business later. Here, let's sit." We follow her into a living space that's masterfully designed, with white upholstery and a glass coffee table. Celia curls her legs beneath her on a large sofa and cradles her wineglass against her chest.

Mikhail clears his throat as we get settled on opposite sides of the table. "I actually need to make a call." He leans down to press a kiss to the top of my head. "We're in no rush, Valentina, so relax."

"What happened to *no detours*?" I raise an eyebrow, and he smiles brilliantly, like he isn't in danger of getting in trouble.

"Leave Andrei to me, *malyshka*. Now, if you'll excuse me." He walks out of the room, and I'm left with only my wine, my nerves, and Mikhail's sister, Celia.

I take another sip of heaven as Celia studies me.

"*Mm-hmm*. I knew from your picture that you were pretty, but you look fabulous in person. I'm so glad that dress suits you. How have you been enjoying your new clothes?"

"How do you know about that?"

Is Mikhail a chatterbox, after all?

She rolls her eyes, and even *that* seems delicate. "I see Mikhail's told me all about you, but he hasn't so much as mentioned me." Even as she shakes her head, she laughs, the sound like silver bells. "Mikhail called me in such a tizzy the other day. Said that you were back at the estate and needing an entire wardrobe for all the fun things you'd be up to in the city. It's rare I get the chance to dress someone up and plan their entire brand, so I had a *ball* picking out everything for you! But you'll have to let me know which pieces you liked most, and which you haven't worn. I might have an eye for what fits, but that doesn't mean they're all your style."

She suddenly smacks the couch pillow by her side. "Oh! Look at me go on." Smiling apologetically, she takes a small breath. "Sorry, I get a bit carried away. I run a boutique here in the city. You just happened to catch me on a day off at home." She tilts her head toward me, like she's about to reveal a secret. "That's rare for anyone in this family. We're usually up to our eyeballs in work." Her gaze flicks toward the room where Mikhail disappeared. "Case in point. Your boyfriend's working right now when he *should* be in here with you."

I set my wineglass down a little too hard and the glass-on-glass screeches. "Oh, he's not—"

Celia waves her hand at me. "*Please.* He's always pestering me about what to get you as a gift. He never puts that kind of thought into anything other than business. Trust me, he's your boyfriend, even if you don't see him as one."

My cheeks warm, and this time, it isn't from the wine. I can't think of what to say.

I'm having an affair with your brother, and you're stuck designing a wedding dress for me to marry his best friend.

But really, is it an affair if all three men are knowingly involved?

Celia nods sympathetically. "It's complicated, I know. These things always are." She reaches across the coffee table and squeezes my knee affectionately. "But don't worry, I'm not judging. In fact, I'm a little jealous."

This time, it's her turn to blush. "I've always wondered what it would be like with two men. You know, in the bedroom." She takes another sip of her wine. "Or, well, outside of it too, really. Or all the time. Do they take turns? Do you go on dates with both of them? What's the sleeping situation like? Mikhail won't tell me, no matter how many times I ask."

I chew on the inside of my cheek as I try to come up with an answer. "We haven't really . . . discussed all of that." I feel my blush deepening as my mind drifts back to the time we *did* spend together. All *four* of us. "It's been happening kind of fast . . . with all three of them."

Celia's eyebrows lift past her bangs. "Whoa. Hold on. *Three* of them? Who's the third guy?"

As she rattles off possible suspects, ranging from the muscled landscaper to the greased-up mechanic, I find myself laughing and joking along with her, coming up with even more ridiculous possibilities. Once we've exhausted our creativity about *who,* we start rattling off steamy scenarios about *where* and *how,* imagining all the ways in which all three of my lovers end up naked in the same room as me.

At first, the jokes feel impersonal, like we're making fun of my budding relationship with three Russian mafiosos, but the longer we talk about it and the more ridiculous the scenarios we fabricate, I realize that this is *bonding.*

I've never had a girlfriend before, and Celia's more than happy to set the bar high for all who come after her.

More wine is shared, and once we've settled that I'm also banging the *hot bodyguard,* we quickly shift into more serious conversation.

Celia empties her wineglass before giving me a long look. "Let me be honest with you, Valentina. My brother . . . can be a hard man to love." She stares into her empty glass for a long moment. "It's not his fault. I don't think he *tries* to be difficult. But it takes a different kind of woman to love a man like him. Like *any* of them. You have to be tough and unyielding, or the lifestyle will break you."

She squeezes my hand and gives me a sad smile. "These men pick *one* woman. That's it. *You're* it for them. So, if you can't handle this life . . ." She trails off with a sigh. "I know you left before. It's all anyone's talked about for five years." Her gaze hardens as she leans back, glances out the room to make sure Mikhail is out of earshot, then returns to me. "My brother is stubborn. He can handle a lot. When our dad died, Mikhail picked up everything like he was meant for the transition. Like it was smooth." She pulls a sour face. "But we both know that when Dad died, he left the company in shambles. He'd been funneling money out of it for weeks to hatch some sort of escape plan."

The story sounds eerily familiar, and I shiver as the memory of the cold wind on the beach rises to the surface. Mikhail's story about the man who was never buried.

I didn't realize that was his *father*.

"When Dad died, Mikhail didn't even give himself time to grieve." She presses her lips together. "This lifestyle might not break my brother, but if you leave like you did before . . ."

A cold sweat breaks out across my lower back.

". . . he won't come out the other side the same man. He won't survive it."

I swallow the lump in my throat as best I can. "Celia, when I left before—"

She holds up her hand. "I don't need your history. I like you, Valentina, and I want to believe you have good intentions, but you backed out before. It's going to take a while to build up my trust, not to mention the trust of the entire city." With a sigh, she flicks her bangs out of her eyes. "You have a hard task ahead of you. I don't envy you for it."

As Celia sips more of her wine, I straighten my posture to look her dead in the eye. "I don't owe you an explanation, but since you're Mikhail's sister, I'll say this." I steel my spine, feeling surer about this than ever before. "I know everyone may think I'm a flake, fine, but they don't know anything about my life, other than the gossip they spread. Yes, I left, but I was a different person five years ago than I am today. I . . ."

I picture my men standing around Ezra's room after our

misadventure in bed together. They all look so relaxed, and after watching them work themselves into an early grave for the past few days, the difference is striking. *They look happy.* My heart soars when each of them smiles at me, holds my hand, or calls me by some little Russian pet name.

Not only that, but I still need answers. My mom's dead and sadly *not* buried, and now my grandmother is apparently public enemy number one. There are too many hidden family secrets I still have to dig up.

If I have any chance at a happily married future, I need to root out past demons and exorcize them, first.

"I'm not leaving," I assure Celia. "I choose them too."

Celia's demeanor brightens instantly. Jumping up from the couch and crossing over to me, she practically falls into my lap as she tries to give me a half-standing, half-crouched hug. "I'm *so* relieved, Valentina. You have no idea." She stands back up, shaking her arms and twisting her body. "Oooh, okay. Shake it off. Let's clear the air here." Waving her arms around to clear the air, whether literally or metaphorically, she exhales and nods. "Better. Now, I know Mikhail spilled the beans about your wedding dress . . ." Her brown eyes sparkle. "Would you like to see it?"

Warmth bubbles in my chest. The last time I looked at wedding gowns was with my mother. We spent hours looking at catalogs and trying on all the different gown designs delivered to the estate. We ate finger sandwiches in bed, both of us buried in the ruffled skirts of our dresses.

It's one of my happiest memories, and I'll treasure those moments with my mother for as long as I live.

My brief time with Celia feels different than the time spent with my mom. My heart aches for what I've lost, but as Celia takes me into her home office and shows me all the different sketches she's drawn, *hope* flows.

Celia's massive sketchbook is as wide as her arm and

covered in fabric swatches pinned to the edges of every page. Penciled designs in creams and whites and golds fill a dozen or more additional pages.

I haven't given much thought to my wedding dress this go around, but Celia has clearly been planning for a while.

"Now, Andrei told me snippets about you, but he's left a lot of the design up to me. I looked at pictures of your previous dress, but if we've got a new Valentina Baranova on our hands, the old one won't do." She takes me through various design features, between the bodice and the skirt and even the possibility of a train. By the end, we're both sitting on the floor as Celia pulls up inspiration pictures on her phone. Luxurious fabrics are scattered in piles all around us, and we spend a long time coordinating around my tastes.

I want something different from before. So much has changed since then, and I want the dress to be a reflection of everything I've overcome.

Celia stares at the ceiling, the end of a pencil propped against her lips. "Tell me how you feel when you think of your life, Valentina. Of Andrei or Mikhail or Ezra. We'll try and capture those emotions with our design."

While we continue working, I catch Mikhail peering into the room from the hallway. When more time passes, and we aren't anywhere near stopping, he brings a second bottle of wine, then some crackers and cheese on a tray. As he sips his own glass, he leans against the doorframe and watches our progress.

"How was work?" I ask him, offering him a slice of gouda on top of a salted cracker.

He pops the cracker combo into his mouth. "We're having some trouble, actually." He's quiet for a few seconds, his forehead creasing in thought. "I thought I'd secured all the properties my father sold years ago, but apparently, there's been a legal snag." He swirls the wine in his glass, a scowl on his lips.

"I've been fighting our competitors for days, but it seems like I've lost." Bitterly, he downs the rest of his glass and snags the open bottle to pour himself another. "Andrei won't be pleased."

"Guess we shouldn't go home, then."

As my words settle over him, Mikhail's expression shifts, a devious smile taking hold. "Guess not."

Excitement snares my heart before I can remind it that we're mad at Mikhail. He catches the look on my face and grins down at me. Setting down his glass, he walks over and holds out both his hands to help me up off the floor. "Truce? At least until Andrei's wrath has passed? I can't have my *pakhan* and my girl both mad at me."

I grasp his hands, and he pulls me up from the floor. "You'll survive."

"Barely," he breathes, stepping into my space, cupping my cheek, and brushing his lips against mine. "A kiss would help."

I roll my eyes and lightly smack his chest. "You're insufferable."

"Only when it comes to you."

"Not true!" Celia interrupts, pushing herself up off the floor. She takes one look at us and smiles at me over Mikhail's shoulder. "You guys hungry? I'm gonna order some takeout. Chinese okay?"

"Sounds perfect," Mikhail replies, but he's entirely focused on me. Once his sister leaves the room to place the order, he walks me back against a loveseat. "What do you say, Valentina?"

My thighs hit the edge, and I nearly tumble over and spill onto the couch.

"Care to give your *real* boyfriend a kiss? This could be our last night before Andrei kills us, after all."

"If he does, it'll be because *you* took us on another detour."

Mikhail laughs without the slightest bit of remorse. "Time with you, Valentina, is worth every lash of the whip."

I curl my fingers in his shirt collar and tug him toward me. I don't condone violence for violence's sake, but there's something about these men being willing to endure pain to spend time with me that gets me going.

A groan rumbles in Mikhail's chest as our lips meet. He's ravenous, lifting me onto my tiptoes before firmly sitting me down on the edge of the couch. Spreading my thighs, he steps into the space and claims more of me, tilting my head back to deepen the kiss and tangle his fingers in my hair.

He nips my bottom lip and swipes the sting with his tongue. "You are my ruin, Valentina Baranova," he murmurs, sighing against my lips. "I come undone for you. Breaking my *pakhan*'s order." He shakes his head. "I've never done that before."

"I have a feeling he'll forgive you." I wrap my arms around Mikhail's neck. "Maybe I can grant you a pardon."

He laughs, the sound full of heart-warming joy. "The day you wield such power is the day I'll do utterly filthy things to you behind Andrei's back." His hand travels up the outside of my thigh, brushing my bare skin underneath my dress. "I've been thinking about our little chase the other day . . ."

My breath hitches as he plays with the waistband of my panties.

"How about we try that again, but with a dirtier outcome?" His fingertips graze my inner thigh, then he pushes my thighs farther apart to brush against my heated core.

I bite my lip, and he groans. "Careful, *malyshka*, or I might dive between your thighs and taste you. It's not fair that you came on Ezra's face and not mine." He presses his thumb harshly against my clit, making me whimper and clutch his shoulders tightly. I can hear my nails scratching against his shirt.

He kisses me harder, and I have to hold on to him for dear life so that I don't fall backward onto the couch. He seems to *love* this, because he groans deep and plunges his tongue into my mouth. Deftly, he slides his hand into my panties and swirls his fingertip around my clit.

I tremble in his arms. *I can't believe we're doing this.* Pleasure rocks through my body with each practiced swirl of his finger, and I can only *pray* that Celia doesn't walk back into her office to find us like this.

I can't make a friend and then lose her, all in one day!

"Mikhail," I gasp, pulling away from him. "Mikhail, we *can't*—"

He growls, and my core clenches in *need.* "You're only making this hotter for me, *malyshka.* Say that again—"

Celia's voice calls out from the other room. "Takeout will be here in fifteen!"

Mikhail's eyes flash dangerously. "Five minutes is all I need."

Oh, no.

Dropping to his knees, he snickers as he slides my panties down my thighs and hooks them around one of my ankles. I try to close my legs, but he forces them open. With an angry glare, he bites my thigh, and I cry out from the pain.

Shame fills my body, and I have to bite my knuckle to keep from making more sounds. I glare down at Mikhail, but it's too late. He buries his face between my thighs and swipes his tongue against my bare lips, groaning as he starts to devour me.

I clench my eyes shut and stop breathing. If I don't breathe, I can't make a sound, and Celia will never know how *filthy* her almost-sister-in-law is.

Mikhail pushes my dress up higher and grabs my ass to hold me still, diving in with such force that my body convulses against his wicked tongue.

"That's it," he rasps, giving my clit a quick suck. "Come all over my face, love. *Fuck.*"

My core clenches as I get even wetter, and he shoves his tongue into my sex for an even deeper taste of me. With one hand lodged firmly between my teeth and the other cupping the back of his head, my hips start to grind against his face as hot pleasure zings up my spine. I moan as the pressure builds deep in my belly.

Mikhail picks up the tempo and lathes my clit in full-bodied licks, sliding two fingers inside my heat the second he makes room for them.

It's all too much, *too much*—

I come with a silent scream, clenching around Mikhail's fingers as he nips my clit and pulls an earth-shattering orgasm from my body.

I'm vaguely aware of him pocketing my panties as he stands and lowers my dress back over my hips. Wiping his mouth on his shirtsleeve, he grins down at me. "Fucking breathtaking, *malyshka.*" A growl rumbles deep in his chest, and he grinds his erection against my thigh. "You come so perfectly on my face. I can't wait for you to come around my cock."

My face flushes scarlet and my core aches. All the heavy petting and tongue-fuckings really make a girl ache for something a little deeper. "When will that be?" I bite my lip as my voice comes out all sexed up, and I try not to notice the wetness dripping down my thighs.

With a wicked grin, Mikhail helps me stand. "Getting impatient, are we? That's *delicious.* You'll be begging for our cocks all at once." His eyes flash like metallic gold. "Think you can handle three? One here"—he shoves his thumb into my mouth, letting me taste my desire—"and here"—he grabs my pussy with his other hand, making me whimper—"and *here.*" His hand drifts farther back, but he merely brushes the edge of my ass. "*Mmm*, we'll find out, won't we, love?"

The doorbell rings and he removes his hands. Helping me straighten my dress, he grins happily as I glare at him. *You know you liked it,* he mouths, snickering as I try to smack his arm. He darts out of reach and steps into a half bath. "I'm going to wash up. I'll meet you out there."

I roll my eyes and step into the bathroom after him. We stand shoulder to shoulder as we both wash our hands. He watches me in the mirror, a smile playing across his lips.

"What?"

Shaking his head, he dries his hands on a towel before stepping outside the small room. "Just thinking about you, *malyshka.* Always thinking about you." He disappears around the corner, and I hear him strike up a conversation with his sister as dinnerware clinks together. They must be setting a table.

I stare at my reflection in the mirror and smack my reddened cheeks. "You're in big trouble, Valentina."

I thought loving *one* man was hard, but that's nothing compared to loving three men all at once. Andrei will definitely be mad about our detour to Celia's house, but maybe I can soften the blow for Mikhail . . .

Eying my body, I adjust my boobs in their cups, so they don't spill over as much, and straighten out my dress, fixing the V-cut so that it aligns perfectly over my cleavage. I've never really thought about using my body as a weapon, or a shield, or much of anything before. But women do it all the time in movies. They seduce a powerful man to steal his pillow-talk secrets or nab his wallet.

Surely, I can seduce my future husband and get a little something out of it.

I suck in my cheeks as I think it through. Desire thrums through my veins in time with my heartbeat.

Though I might not be able to admit it to myself, my body knows.

I don't want to have sex with Andrei just to get Mikhail and me out of trouble . . . I want to have sex with Andrei because *it's him*. I was celibate until I left Harlin Heights, and admittedly, my experience is practically nonexistent. Andrei is probably a sex god compared to me.

Excitement sends tingles down my spine that settle, unsurprisingly, between my thighs. If I can make a sex god fall to his knees, then I doubt there's anything I'm incapable of.

I smile as I step out of the bathroom to join Mikhail and Celia, a spring in my step that wasn't there before.

It turns out that feeling like a sexual badass does wonders for your confidence.

Chapter 19

Valentina

As soon as we all sit down, the doorbell rings again.

Celia exchanges a look with Mikhail before she excuses herself to check the front door. Muffled voices echo down the hall, and Celia's laughter soon follows.

Who could it be? Their mom? A friend? A boyfriend?

The moment Celia rounds the corner with a sly smile on her face and a bottle of red wine in her hands, I know something's up.

Mikhail's expression cools as he studies her. Neither of us has to wait long, because our mystery guest appears from around the corner, a brutal smile of his own sending chills down my spine.

Andrei.

"Mikhail," he greets, walking over to clap his brother on the shoulder. His grip is tight enough that Mikhail struggles to hide a wince. Then he turns to me, and my nerves light on fire.

He's angry, just like he promised he'd be if we disobeyed his orders.

"Andrei's going to join us," Celia informs the room. "He was generous enough to bring an offering. Thank you."

"My pleasure." He pulls out a chair to my right and takes a seat. Leaning toward me, he cups my jaw and pulls me in for a bruising kiss. His mouth lands hard over mine, his grip unyielding. When he finally lets go, he stares directly into my eyes.

Angry, yes, but there's no hiding the flicker of jealousy in his sapphire eyes.

"I've missed you, *zhena.*"

He releases my chin and addresses the group. "I apologize for my intrusion, but I'd been expecting Valentina home by now. I get antsy when she's late." He gives Mikhail a pointed look. "Despite having the fastest car in the city, you still managed to drag today out as long as possible."

Mikhail chuckles, but it's lacking its usual splendor. "What can I say? Valentina's an addictive little minx." He winks, and I want to murder him. "Can't blame me for stealing her away a little longer."

Andrei hums softly. "Perhaps she needs an accessory. A collar? A tattoo?" His eyes travel up and down my body, like he's imagining his name inked on my skin. Snapping his fingers, he reaches inside his jacket pocket. "Ah, I know what we're missing."

A tiny, black velvet jewelry box.

I stare at the little black box, *really* nervous now.

"What do you say, *zhena?*" He pops open the lid, revealing the most gorgeous black diamond ring I've ever seen. The gemstone is cut into a razor-sharp diamond shape, with the top edge crested by a band of square white diamonds in a matching point. Above this, sparkling black and white diamonds form the tip of the crown, the setting cast in a warm rose gold.

Andrei slips my hand into his and presses a kiss to my ring finger. "I'm afraid your mother's ring went missing after she passed. I searched for it everywhere, even for replica photos to have a replacement custom made, but I couldn't find anything." He pulls the ring from its holder with his other hand. "I hope this one reminds you of who you are, Valentina."

And who you belong to, the voice in my head adds.

He slips it onto my finger, and it's a perfect fit. I hold the ring up and twist my wrist in the light. I've never seen anything so *sparkly* before, and I absolutely love it. A little sparkle may be my new favorite accessory.

"Thank you," I breathe, getting choked up. "It's beautiful, Andrei." I poke the sharp tip with my thumb and pull back quickly when it stings. *And dangerous, too.*

Andrei's smile softens as he gazes at me. "A *pakhan*'s wife deserves only the best. I will give you *my* best, as well," he vows suddenly. "You have my word as your husband."

Overwhelming joy fills me to the brim. I know Andrei and I got off to a rocky start when I first returned, but I have no doubt that Andrei means what he says. I've never known him to lie. And now that he knows I want *him*, not just because I was told all my life to marry a powerful man within the Bratva, but because it's *him* . . . things feel different. Things feel *right*.

The world feels and looks more vibrant than ever, and I wish more than anything that my mom could be here to witness this. She always told me that life has a funny way of giving its support, and I know she'd be happy to see my new support system growing more and more each day.

I was so alone when I was an eighteen-year-old *pakhan*'s daughter. I had my mother and fiancé with me, but it wasn't enough.

Now I have three men to love and a new sister, and I'm sure I'll make more friends as I settle down here in the city.

The hope for a warm, full future is overwhelming.

A single tear slips free, and embarrassment quickly floods my system. A pink blush spreads across my cheeks and down my neck. "I don't know why I'm crying." A nervous, embarrassed giggle catches in my chest. "A bride shouldn't cry when her fiancé gives her a ring."

Andrei kisses my cheek, smoothing away the teardrop with his warm lips. "I will kiss away all your tears, *zhena*, every time."

We gaze into each other's eyes, and I long to say so many things I have no hope of articulating. *I still love you. I still want you. I'm hopelessly, addictively enthralled by you.*

A loud *pop* breaks the silence, and both Mikhail and Celia *whoop* loudly as they work in tandem to pour champagne. "I always keep some on hand for special moments like these," Celia says with a wink. Her warm eyes glitter like the diamonds on my ring. "Congrats."

Mikhail hands both me and Andrei overflowing champagne flutes. "Congrats, *malyshka*." Nodding to Andrei, he presses a kiss to the top of my head and returns to his seat on my left. As we start divvying up the takeout, both men's hands wander beneath the table, one on each of my thighs.

I laugh as the men tell stories about each other and their experiences as unruly teenagers. They didn't meet until Andrei officially joined the Bratva at sixteen, but by then, Andrei was already well-versed in Ezra's dark brooding, and the three men formally met.

"On a routine supply run," Mikhail clarifies, taking another sip of champagne.

"Nothing was routine about it." Andrei stabs a piece of chicken with his fork. "The rooster ate one of the diamonds."

"Ezra had to dig that one out, didn't he?"

A wave of longing for the third man missing from our group stirs in my chest. *I wish he were here.*

As though reading my mind, Andrei squeezes my thigh. "Ezra's busy tonight," he murmurs close to my ear, "but he'll be back tomorrow. I would have brought him otherwise."

I nod. "Maybe we can do this again. I like this."

"I'm glad you're enjoying yourself." He smiles, and it takes my breath away.

Has it always felt like this with Andrei? Or is something different this time?

The dinner ends, and everyone pitches in to help with cleanup. Andrei rolls his black sleeves past his elbows, giving me a fresh look at his forearms. Tattoos crawl up both arms, some of them looking similar to Ezra's.

Celia raises an eyebrow as Andrei fills the sink with soap and hot water. "I have a dishwasher," she reminds everyone. "No need to do them by hand."

Andrei pays her little mind. "I find that the best jobs are done with your hands. Dishes included." He plops silverware into the water. "If you don't mind, I'd like to clean them myself."

She looks to her brother for help, but Mikhail shrugs a shoulder. "Can't tell him what to do. Just let him scrub the dishes, Cel."

As Andrei dips his hands into sudsy water and starts scrubbing plates, I join him to towel off the clean ones. Nodding toward his ink, I ask him about them.

"Tattoos tell stories." He hands me a plate to dry. "In our line of work, they show others your accomplishments. If someone doesn't know you by name or reputation, they can read all they need to know on your skin."

"But there aren't any words."

He chuckles. "Each picture is worth at least a hundred words, *zhena,* if not more."

"Ezra's got a lot of tattoos." I start counting them up in my head. "All over his arms. His neck. His back." *Delicious* ink sprawled across almost every square inch of his skin.

Mikhail catches wind of the conversation and appears at

the island in front of us to join in. "Spent a lot of time watching Ezra, *malyshka*? I'm jealous."

I stick my tongue out at him, and he laughs that rich, full-bodied tone that I love. Not his sinister, mocking chuckle, but a *real*, genuine laugh. I laugh with him, and Andrei shakes his head. He's smiling all the same.

"Remember when I told you that Ezra was born in Russia?" Mikhail removes his suit jacket and drapes it over the back of one of the bar chairs. "They start training earlier than we do here. He was enlisted by the time he was twelve."

"Ten," Andrei corrects, handing me another plate to dry. "Ezra showed promise, so they inducted him even earlier. That's why he has so many tattoos. He's accomplished more than we have."

"Not by much," Mikhail feints with a wink.

"By *a lot*."

"I don't understand." I hand Mikhail our stack of plates to put away. "If Ezra is so accomplished, why isn't he *pakhan*?"

"Different kinds of accomplishments, *malyshka*."

"What do you mean?"

Andrei dries his hands on a dishrag and eyes me carefully. "Ezra's good at what he does, and he's well-known for it. People recognize him from a distance."

"They're scared of him." Mikhail snickers from across the room.

I catch Celia leaning on a door jamb, listening to the conversation just as raptly as I am, and I don't feel as bad for not knowing all of this already.

I think back to everything I know about Ezra to put all the pieces together. When we met, I was still a teenager, and he was in his mid-twenties. He didn't have as many tattoos back then, but he was still a muscled guy. The scar over his upper lip was already there, and he always carried a massive gun slung over his back. An AK-something.

The blood on the morgue floor flashes violently in my mind, and I try not to be sick as the smell of iron fills my nose.

I don't think I *want* to know, but I owe it to Ezra to know *enough*.

I swallow any hesitation that remains. "So, he's not *pakhan* because he's got . . . special talents."

Mikhail's mouth pops open to say something no doubt cheeky, but his sister jabs him in the ribs with her elbow.

Andrei crosses his arms over his chest and leans back against the counter. The black dress shirt hugs his shoulders, and one of the buttons over his pecs struggles to hold. "Yes. He has skills that even I don't possess. Not many do. The Russian sects will teach you everything there is to know about the human body . . . and how to break it."

"Into tiny little pieces," Mikhail supplies helpfully. "While someone's still alive."

Ezra's confession in the shower suddenly makes more sense.

I have killed for you. I have picked the bones of living things clean.

A shiver runs down my spine. "Is that what he's doing tonight?"

Celia makes a show of leaving the room, and I don't blame her one bit. Not only does this conversation feel like it's turning to from casual conversation to business, but it's also liable to get graphic.

Andrei's eyes hyper-focus on my face. There's not a trace remaining of the good-natured groom who sat beside me at dinner. All that's left is the *pakhan*, the cruel leader of *our* Russian Bratva.

"No. He's looking for something."

Mikhail scoffs loudly. "Or *someone*."

I gasp as lightning strikes, zinging up my spine. For

Mikhail to respond so strongly, there's only one person Ezra could be looking for.

My grandmother.

"Who is he trying to find?" I ask, stepping into Andrei's personal space and hooking my hands over his hips. Leaning against his chest, I stare up at his handsome face.

I need answers, and if Mikhail won't give them to me because of orders from his *pakhan*, there's only one man who can give me what I need.

We stare at each other for a long, tense moment. Andrei's jaw tics. "What did you tell her, Mikhail?" I expect his voice to snap with anger, but it rumbles like thunder, and somehow, that's even worse. "I suspected you'd take her on a trip, despite my warning, but if you said something you shouldn't have . . ." His entire body tenses beneath mine, his eyes darkening to midnight blue.

He's staring at *me*, and I have no doubt that the only reason he's not breaking Mikhail's fingers right now is because I'm standing in the way.

I lean against his chest and massage the tension over his heart. "He didn't tell me anything." Pressing a kiss to Andrei's throat, I try to reassure him. "He told me he couldn't. That you had ordered him not to."

"That would be correct."

I lean back far enough to hook my hand on the nape of Andrei's neck and pull his head down, forcing his eyes on me instead of my suddenly *pale-as-fuck* boyfriend. "I'm asking *you*, Andrei. No one else."

My heart hammers in my chest as he lifts his hand and brushes his fingertips against my lips. "If I tell you, Valentina, you might hate me. You might try to run away again." His fingers drift to my neck, closing around my throat and squeezing. "Not that you *can*." A shadow crosses his face, and fear strikes my heart as he squeezes tighter. "If a ring isn't enough to bind you to me, I'll tie a pretty little collar around your neck." Slowly, he bends lower, exhaling harshly against my dark curls. "I'll tattoo that perfect skin of yours. Anyone who tries to touch you will know that you're *mine*." His other hand brushes my hair over my shoulder, and he dips lower, kissing the curve where my neck meets my torso. "And if *that* still isn't enough, *moya zhena*, I'll burn a brand onto that perfect fucking ass of yours." His words turn into a snarl that makes me quiver with fear.

But fear always turns into a rush of *need* for me.

I whimper before I can stop myself, and he nips at my exposed collarbone. "Does that get you fucking wet, *zhena?* Picturing my name all over your skin." His tongue presses a hot, wet stripe across my bone. "I'll bury my cock so deep inside you, darling, that you'll reek of my cum for days. I'll fill you up every fucking morning so that *everyone* knows how much of a whore you are for your *muzh*, your *husband*."

Stars dance in my vision as my blood flow restricts, and a needy moan barely manages to pass my lips. *I might come like this, and he hasn't even touched me down there.* Desire drips down my thighs. Without my panties as a buffer, I'm mercilessly drenched and aching to be filled, just like Andrei promises.

So much for seducing *him* for answers. My resolve flickers along with my heartbeat. At this moment, he holds all the power, not me.

He lessens the grip on my throat, and I drag in a greedy lungful of air.

Pressing a kiss to the corner of my lips, he hums softly. "If you try to run, *zhena*, we will hunt you." Another kiss, this one closer to the center. "Ezra will track, Mikhail will chase, and I will punish. How does that sound, hm?"

"*Delicious*," Mikhail murmurs from behind me. He presses his body against mine, and I can feel his iron desire wedged against my ass. "Please run, *malyshka*. I promise, I'll catch you."

My core clenches at the implication, at what might happen *next* after he's caught me.

Andrei's hand snakes up my thigh, under my dress, and ghosts over my naked lips. He smiles, all sharp canines and wickedness, at what he finds. "I think you like that idea very much."

He flicks his gaze to Mikhail. "Tell your sister that we're leaving. I'm taking Valentina home."

Mikhail doesn't argue and disappears from the room in an instant.

Removing his hand from my dress, Andrei holds it up in front of my face. My desire glistens on his fingertips. He smears it across my lips before pulling me in for a kiss, this one much harsher than the last. Dominating. Possessive. *Sinful.*

He tears his mouth away from mine and pushes me a step backward, holding me at a distance as he takes a deep, calming breath. When he opens his eyes, he's put on a mask that hides every pent-up emotion he let me taste seconds ago.

I lick my swollen lips, ready and eager for more.

Andrei holds me at arm's length as he finally answers my question. "Ezra is searching for Katya, Valentina. She and your fake boyfriend are missing."

Cold dread crashes over me.

Missing?

"That doesn't make sense," I say slowly, my thoughts still fogged from Andrei's kiss. "Who would hurt my boss and my grandmother?"

Andrei's eyes flash. "Liam is your boss?"

I realize my mistake and try not to blush. "Um. Yeah. Boss, boyfriend . . ." I try to make it sound nonchalant. "We've, um, kind of been off and on lately?"

Narrowing his eyes, Andrei repeats my phrase. "Off and on."

"Yeah," I croak. "Kind of."

"Explain what that means." His voice is icy, and his grip tightens hard enough to bruise my hip. "*Now.*"

I suck in a breath. "Well, other than my grandmother, he's been my only friend—"

Andrei's jaw clenches.

"—and one thing led to another, and we've been on a few dates. Not a lot!" I'm quick to add. "But a few. And, um, we may have . . . slept together . . . once or twice. But it doesn't mean anything, I swear."

Any relationship I had with Liam died the moment I got swept back into Andrei's, Mikhail's, and Ezra's arms. Hell, probably even before that.

"*Oh*, it means *everything* to me, Valentina."

I recoil and wrench free from his grasp. "It was just a stupid fling. It doesn't matter. I don't want him."

Andrei laughs, cold and cruel. "But he wants *you*, doesn't he? And he's *had* you. *Before* me." With a hiss, he clenches and unclenches his fists. "I'm not fucking happy about that, Valentina. You are *mine.* You've *always* been mine."

"Y-you seem fine sharing with Ezra and Mikhail."

I regret my words the minute they're spoken.

Andrei turns on a dime and bares his teeth in my direction. "They're different. *They're* the exception. *No one else can have you!*" He crosses the short distance to me and grabs my wrist. "We're leaving. *Now.*"

We're out of Celia's house in a flash. I don't even get to say goodbye before the door slams behind us. "What about my grandmother? Andrei, wait—"

He thrusts my back against a black SUV in the driveway and kisses me, consuming all other thoughts with his fire. It catches within me, and I moan as he drags his tongue against mine. He pins my hips beneath his and growls low in his throat.

"I'm done waiting, Valentina. I've wanted every fucking cell in your body, every beautiful inch of your skin, since the moment I first laid eyes on you. *You are mine.* You were promised to *me.*" He kisses me again, all his fury and desire mixing with mine and making me dizzy. When he pulls back, I'm unsteady on my feet and have to cling to him for support.

"I won't wait any longer for what's mine. I *will* have you, *zhena*, right fucking now."

My heart seizes at the promise, at the possessive fury, at the desire threading around us and tying us together. No one has ever wanted me this badly, and I have a feeling that any experience I gained while away won't mean shit when paired against Andrei's.

He exudes confidence and control . . .

Except when it comes to me.

"I drive you crazy, don't I?"

My question catches Andrei off guard, and he simmers down long enough to gift me a small, genuine smile. "I wouldn't want you any other way."

This time, his kiss is slower, more deliberate, and he coaxes more than lust from my body and soul with each press of his lips against mine.

"I love you," I whisper, cupping his cheek. "No matter what's happened before, or what happens next, know that a part of me will always love every dark and twisted part of you."

I've waited five years to tell Andrei that I love him, and the way my confession *breaks* him makes my heart bleed even more for the man.

His mask cracks, a wave of anguish rippling across the surface and revealing the scarred flesh underneath. I catch glimmers of his pain—deep, throbbing aches that *I* inflicted when I broke our promise to each other and left him behind.

His eyes slide shut, and he draws a slow, steady breath. "I've waited *so long* to hear you say that." He grasps my hand and laces our fingers together, gripping tightly. "You've never said it before."

"I never meant it until now." I thought I loved him before, but I realize now that I loved the *idea* of him—who I thought he was. But now, I've seen the darkest parts of his desire and his passion, and I want it all, exactly as is.

I kiss him first this time, hoping to drown out all the hurt and replace it with love.

Love for our sheltered past, love for our crazy, fucked-up present, and love for all the possibilities of our future.

CHAPTER 20

ANDREI

VALENTINA LOVES ME.

For a long time, I wasn't sure. I always knew that *I* loved her, but despite how much I tried to show her the sweeter side of me, she never fully opened up. She blushed, commented politely on my dreams, shared what few she had . . . but not once did she say or show she loved me.

And then, she left.

"Take us home, Marvin," I instruct my driver. "The long way."

"Yes, sir."

Valentina's emerald eyes widen beautifully. She's flushed all down her neck and across her chest, and I want to lick every heated inch of her body.

"In—in the car?" she squeaks.

I cup her cheek and press yet another kiss to her lips, hoping to silence her worries. "I want to spend time with you, Valentina. *Uninterrupted* time." My cell phone is already vibrating in my pocket, either from the business meeting I'm missing or Mikhail furiously texting our group chat with salacious ideas about what I'm going to do to our woman.

Likely both.

"The car is merely part of the journey." I trail my fingertips up the inside of her arm, enjoying the way she shivers under my touch. "I intend to take my time satisfying you, Valentina . . ." An ugly tear in my heart pumps vicious jealousy through my veins. ". . . And erasing every single fucking memory you have of that fucking *mudak.*"

She blinks up at me. "Who, Liam?"

Rage ricochets across my ribcage like shrapnel. "*Yes*, and he's next on my fucking list," I hiss, snapping open the back door of my SUV. "Get in."

Valentina does as she's told, and I take a deep breath before following. I'm not angry with her. I'm angry that, out of anyone she could have slept with, it had to be the bastard who's been lying to her fucking face for years.

That pisses me the fuck off.

I slide into the seat behind my wife and immediately push her onto her back. "You're going to tell me everywhere that *mudak* touched you. Take off your dress."

Her eyes widen again, and I can taste the fear on her. *Good.* I know she gets off on it.

I unbutton my shirt and tear it from my shoulders. "I *said*, take off your dress, Valentina."

"You can't be serious," she breathes, trying to sit up on her elbows. "We're in a moving vehicle—"

A growl reverberates in my chest, and she cuts off with a *squeak.* Crawling on top of her, I straddle her hips and pull her dress up. When I reach her ribs, I slow down, taking one precious inch at a time. The slow but steady revelation of her skin makes my mouth water.

"I don't care where we are. When I want you, I *will* have you." My hands reach her breasts, and I brush my thumbs over them as I continue dragging the garment up her body. "Lift your back, darling, so I can pull this off."

She obliges, and all that's left now is her pesky little bra. Mikhail's been buying all of her clothes, and I have no doubt he picked out this piece too. "Take it off."

I don't want to see anyone else's clothing on her body right now, not even my brother's.

She hesitates, so I take her hand and curve it behind her back. When her bra is finally unclasped and lying on the floor, I pin her arm beneath her. The sound she makes, half-gasp and half-outraged-growl makes me laugh, even as my cock stiffens in my pants.

"Tell me where he touched you," I command, scanning her body. *So many tempting possibilities.* I brush the pad of my thumb against her lips. "Did he start here?"

To my surprise, she shakes her head *no.*

"He, um, started . . ." She tilts her head to the side. "Here." With her one free hand, she points to the side of her neck. "Came up from behind and kissed me here first."

I swallow the rage roaring inside me and lean over my bride to kiss the place she's indicated. I open my mouth and *suck*, marking the spot as *mine.*

"Where else?" I murmur in Valentina's ear.

She guides my hand to her breast and squeezes, arching her back beautifully for me. "Here," she moans breathlessly.

I kiss down her shoulder and chest until I reach her breast. Kneading her gently, I kiss the exposed top and bite, planting a bruise right where I want one. Valentina hisses through her teeth, but I pinch her nipple between my fingers, and her protest quickly turns to throaty *need.*

"And here?" I cup her gently and blow across her pebbled peak. "Did he touch you here?"

"*Yes.*"

As I wrap my lips around the tip, I flick my gaze up at my wife's face. *Lips parted, breaths shallow, eyes hazy with lust.*

Gorgeous.

Licking her once makes her body twitch, but licking her relentlessly makes a needy whine catch in her throat. She tries to spread her legs, but I lock my calves around hers to keep her from moving.

We'll get there. "Patience, *zhena*," I instruct, adding a third bruise to her body, just beneath her breast. "Tell me where to go next."

We move across her entire body, and each mark fans the flames of hate deep within me.

I *hate* the fucking *mudak* with every ounce of my body and soul. He will pay for every single moment he thought about *my* wife, every single lie he ever told her, and every single time he dared touch what's mine.

As much as I like seeing Valentina on her back, I know he touched her ass, too. No one can resist her juicy peach. "Flip over."

I help her onto her knees and spread her thighs as wide as the seat will allow. Dripping wet *desire* assails my senses, and I have to squeeze my aching cock to relieve some of the pressure. "*Zhena*. You are a feast for the eyes." I slide a finger inside her sticky sweet heat, and she arches her back farther, sucking me in. "*Fuck*, you're going to make me come early, baby."

She moans, her voice thick and heady, and I nearly say *fuck it*, whip my dick out, and slam into her.

But that would be selfish. Valentina didn't want to fuck in the car, so I won't give myself the pleasure.

"Will you . . . . .come inside me?" Valentina's breathless question nearly sends me over the edge. I slide a second finger inside her with a groan and start pumping her nice and slow.

"He . . . he never . . ." She moans, and I stop moving until she can finish her thought. "He never came inside me. He wanted to, but I wouldn't let him."

Fuuuuck.

Need roars in my blood at the same time an inferno of loathing pulses through me.

How dare he even try.

I choke on my rage and push it deep, deep down. I'll kill the bastard later.

"Good girl. No one's going to come inside you but me." *Or Ezra or Mikhail, but for tonight, you're all mine.*

Before she can think to ask about the other two, I curl my fingers and bite her plump ass at the same time, and she convulses, clenching around me.

God, if my cock were inside her, she'd milk me for every last drop of my soul.

"Did you just come, *zhena?*"

She mumbles something unintelligible, and I take that as a yes. The engine cuts out and I press a quick, open-mouth kiss to her drenched core, moaning as I get a taste.

I have to pull myself back and force myself to wait.

"Did you come earlier, darling?"

As I help her sit up, she bites her lip and gazes up at me bashfully, like it's some big secret that Mikhail makes her come behind my back.

I brush my hand over her hair and press a kiss to her forehead. "I'm not mad, baby. You deserve to feel good. We're all here to ensure that happens."

We pull her dress back over her body, and I admire the dozen or so bruises I've marked across her skin. It's not enough to replace what that *mudak* did to her, but it's a start.

As she steps out of the car, I snap a quick picture of her bra on the seat, remnants of her desire smeared across the leather beneath it.

> Gonna need a car detail. Someone's a dirty girl.

Mikhail's message bubble pops up immediately. He's

probably jerking off to the fantasy of me fucking our girl right now.

You didn't lick the seat? Wasteful.

I chuckle and shove the phone back into my pocket. I'm not as depraved as *you*, Mikhail. I'll drink straight from the source.

Valentina is waiting by the door to the house, and I join her quickly. We walk inside hand in hand, and although I pay the guards stationed around the house not to care, a few of them break protocol to smile at us.

I rub my thumb over the ring on her left hand, admiring the sharp point.

Beautiful. Deadly. That's who my queen is, or what she will become. I kiss the back of her hand as I lead her to my bedroom.

"When we get inside, I want you on the bed, naked, in thirty seconds or less."

"Is that a challenge, Andrei?"

"That's an order."

She rolls her eyes and pulls her hand from mine to walk ahead of me. "What if I give *you* an order?" Glancing at me over her shoulder, she smiles wide, and my heart clenches tightly in my chest.

I love her.

I always have, but what the past week has shown me is that I love *all* of her, every infuriating, stubborn, shy, insecure piece of her.

She backs up against my door and tries to open it with her hands behind her back, but it's locked. She's trapped herself. I close in on her, capturing her body beneath mine and cupping her jaw. Tilting her head back, I stare into those beautiful green eyes that have captivated me since the moment I first laid eyes on her.

"I love you, Valentina Baranova."

Her eyes well with tears, and she smiles so beautifully that my heart aches. Not with pain or longing for what I've lost, but with what I've found.

"I love you, Andrei Leonov."

I kiss her deeply, knocking her head against the door, and we both laugh at the blunder. "Forgive me, Mrs. Leonov, I'm a little excited."

She reaches between us and grabs my cock over my slacks, no longer the shy, blushing virgin, but instead a mesmerizing temptress promising *more*.

"Open the door, Mr. Leonov, and show your *zhena* how much she means to you."

I snap the lock using a trick Ezra taught me years ago. *Fuck being patient.*

My wife just gave me an order I have every intention of obeying.

Chapter 21

Valentina

We tumble into the room in a blur of limbs and lips, each of us eager to get the other's clothes off. Every place on my body that Andrei can reach through the tug and pull of undressing, he kisses, no matter if it's the back of my arm or the curve of my waist. Once all clothes are off and scattered across the room, he sweeps me into his arms and drops us onto the mattress, cradling my head protectively as I land beneath him.

"*Valentina*," he murmurs, kissing every tender love bite he made on my skin. Each press of his lips is slow, meticulous, reverent.

My breath hitches as he sinks his teeth into the mark on my neck, the zing of pleasure-pain going straight to my clit.

I ache for him in a way I've never ached for anyone or anything before.

"I've waited so long for this. To finally have you in my arms." He exhales heavily as his body settles over mine, warm and strong and perfect.

Wrapped in his embrace, I'm given free roam to explore. My hands drift up the hard planes of his back and across his broad shoulders, feeling parts of him that I've never dared before. His muscles shift beneath my touch, and he moans in my ear.

"You're beautiful, Andrei."

I've always known he was handsome, but the way he tenderly sweeps his tongue down my neck and caresses the curve of my waist can only be described as *beautiful*. His touch awakens every cell in my body, magnified by the way his scent lingers in the air. With every breath I take, I breathe in a part of him.

He chuckles and lifts his head from the new spot he's claiming with his teeth. "I've never been called *beautiful* before."

I sweep my fingers through his soft locks, admiring his high cheekbones and rough jawline. "You are."

He presses a kiss to the inside of my wrist. "I'll treasure the word, *zhena*." Sliding his thigh between mine, he spreads my legs as he aligns our hips, dragging the tip of his cock through my slick folds.

My eyes roll back in my head as he sets a slow, steady pace, teasing my entrance, one thrust after another. Pleasure rolls through my body as he drags against my clit and *lower*, pulling moan after moan from my lips as he slides inside a little more each time he rolls his hips.

"But you're mistaken, *you* are the most beautiful creature in this world"—he grips my shoulder tightly and presses the head of his cock deeper—"and the next."

The stretch burns as he works to fit inside. Slowly, one inch becomes two, then three, until finally—

We moan in unison, Andrei's head tipping back the instant our hips meet. "*Fuck*," he curses, "baby, you're squeezing so *tight*. Breathe for me."

I take a shallow breath as he pulls out. Again, he pushes, holding me steady as he carves out space for himself.

"*Breathe.* That's it. Let me in, baby."

I've been soaking wet for hours, but it's still a fight for Andrei to fit. Sweat beads across his brow as he lowers his body over mine, holding both his arms over my head. He kisses me hard and thrusts, ignoring any resistance that remains. He *takes,* finally claiming my body as his.

My screams are lost in the vicious, wet slap of skin on skin, and the pressure quickly morphs into *pleasure.* Raw, unbridled pleasure that zips straight up my spine.

My moans are deep, emanating from my chest every time Andrei fills me.

"So fucking perfect," he rasps, groaning into my ear. "Your body was made for me, *zhena.* Made to take my cock." He slams into me with enough force that the bed frame bangs against the wall. "I'm gonna fill you up, beautiful." *Bang.* "Such a dirty girl—" *Bang.* "Asking me to come inside you." *Bang.* "To be your *first.*"

I clench around his cock as my pleasure peaks, his words switching to Russian as he drills into me *faster, harder, louder—*

"*Fuck,*" he hisses, burying deep. His cock pulses as he fulfills his promise, coating my insides with his cum. With each twitch of his cock, my pleasure builds until I finally tip over the edge with him.

Eyes shut and nails digging into his back, I lock my legs around him and ride out every wave of pleasure tearing through me. His cock stills inside me, and when he pulls back, he groans.

Something warm leaks out.

"You can take more, can't you, baby?"

Andrei *thrusts,* the glide smoother than before, and grinds his cock.

All rational thought leaves my body as he arches his back

and hits a pressure point I never knew existed. I pant loudly as he repeats the movement, dragging his length against my walls until he hits that spot again. My eyes roll back, and I can't *breathe*.

"Your body begged for my cum." He sits up and grins down at me. "Milked me for every last drop." He grunts, grabbing my hips and slamming me over his length. The pace ramps up, once again brutal, and I claw at the sheets as I try to find purchase. Stability. *Something* to hold on to.

Andrei's grin curves down at the edges. His nails dig harder into my muscle, stinging as my skin breaks and he draws blood. "*He* never deserved this." The headboard rocks against the wall, and a picture frame crashes to the floor. "He never deserved *you*."

I gasp as Andrei's jealousy kicks up, and he snarls, furiously pounding my pussy. "He'll never fucking touch you again. You're *mine*. This body is *mine*. Your heart is *mine*." He grabs my left hand and laces our fingers together. "Your Bratva is *mine*."

The engagement ring digs into my knuckle, a sharp prick of pain that's quickly lost in the wake of everything else assailing my body.

I've never seen Andrei this unhinged. The comments about collars and tattoos spooked me, but I didn't think he was serious. Now, though, staring at a man possessed by jealousy, I'm starting to doubt that he was joking, after all.

He comes with a roar, unleashing his seed as deep as possible. But he's not finished; with one hand holding mine, he uses the other to swirl against my clit.

"*Nonono*," I whine, my body convulsing, despite my verbal protests. I'm bruised all over, and my hips ache from the onslaught they just endured. I *can't* come.

It might break me.

Andrei's eyes narrow. "One isn't enough, *zhena*."

"Yes, it is," I pant, bobbing my head up and down. "I've already come three times today—"

He pinches my clit and my body seizes. It *hurts*. But right behind the ache is a rush of pleasure that carries me through the pain. I moan loudly, and Andrei's expression softens when he hears it. "That's it, baby. One more. Just one more. You're beautiful when you come, *moya zhena*." He lifts my left hand to his lips and kisses my engagement ring. "I want to watch you come undone for me."

All it takes is a few more strokes and I break, tears streaming down my face as the pressure turns blinding. I start to sob, and within seconds, Andrei is cradling me against his chest.

"You did beautifully, baby. I'm so proud of you." He cups my face and kisses me tenderly. "Thank you for giving yourself to me."

Cum drips from my body onto the bedsheets, and a shiver runs down my spine as my body starts to cool. Andrei pulls a blanket over us and continues rubbing my back.

That was a first in many ways. I've never been *fucked* like that before. I've never loved the man doing it. I've never come so much it *hurts*.

I've never let anyone come inside me, either.

"Are you on the pill?" Andrei asks quietly, stroking my shoulder with his thumb.

No.

I used to be, but it screwed with my hormones so badly that I had to stop. I've had painful periods ever since.

I meet Andrei's eyes and shake my head.

He hums softly in the back of his throat.

"Is that . . . okay?" I ask, suddenly nervous. I know we talked about having kids, but that was five years ago. We're different people now.

I'm not sure if I want to have kids anymore. Not after

what my father did to *me*. What Mikhail's father did to *him*. I look deep into Andrei's sapphire eyes, like I can divine the future from within.

Would Andrei make a good father, or would he carry the sins of the past on his shoulders?

"Yes, *zhena*." He presses a kiss to my forehead. "You're perfect just as you are."

The conversation drifts into silence. Fatigue makes my eyelids heavy, and I start fading fast. I'm exhausted, but my soul is satisfied and my thirst sated.

As I start to fall asleep, my mind wanders to the day's events. How full the hours were. First the orphanage, then the death ride in Mikhail's sports car, dinner at Celia's . . .

My heart jumps into my throat.

The wedding. My grandmother.

Sitting up, I comb my mess of curls from my eyes. "Andrei. *Andrei.* Wait, don't fall asleep yet."

He cracks open an eye and exhales. "Ready for another round?" The Russian accent that's missing during the day slurs in his speech, likely brought on by exhaustion. The dark circles under his eyes rival Ezra's, and yet he's *still* trying to satisfy me.

"No, not that." My face flushes, and he smiles crookedly.

"Then it can wait until morning." Snaking an arm around my waist, he pulls me back down between the sheets and wraps his arms around me, cuddling close.

I bite my lip and roll over so that we're facing each other. "Actually, it can't."

My heartbeat thrums loudly as my nerves get the better of me. I need answers about a lot of things, and if the *pakhan* has ordered my boyfriends not to talk, then he'll have to be the one to give me the truth.

Andrei's eyes slide open. "You have my attention."

It's hard for me to talk with him staring. I try to summon

all the anger I held earlier in the day, but it fizzles out the moment I think I've snared it.

I'm too tired for a fight.

Sighing, I squeeze my eyes shut. *Let's start with the easy question.*

"I know you've been handling finding a venue for us . . ."

Andrei hums in acknowledgement.

"But that requires a date. Celia seems convinced the wedding is happening sooner rather than later. I thought we were waiting a few more weeks." The ring feels heavy on my finger. I slide my hand out from under the covers to see it, but the sun's dipped so low that it's impossible to make it out. "Have you moved up the date?"

Andrei holds my hand against his chest. I can feel his steady heartbeat through his ribs. "Something came up, Valentina. I had to push things up."

My heart skips a beat. "How far up?"

Andrei brushes his thumb across my knuckles. "This week. Our wedding is in three days."

All the air leaves my lungs.

"Three days!" I sit up in a panic. *Three days.* "Why didn't you tell me?"

"I didn't want you to panic," Andrei grumbles, already dragging me back down beside him. "*Like this.* Valentina, I promise you, I've got everything handled."

"It's no wonder you three have been working around the clock."

Andrei grunts as his eyes drift closed.

He must be exhausted.

Memories from the past few days flicker behind my eyes. Ezra in the blood-stained morgue. His confession about keeping me safe. Mikhail's threats on my grandmother's life. The way he enjoyed taunting me with her death . . . and Liam's.

Andrei's passion is intense for a man who's never met my ex-slash-boss.

A shiver runs down my spine as the same realization that struck me in Mikhail's car comes crashing back.

They all know something, and they're not telling me what it is. They're keeping me in the dark.

No matter how warm it is in Andrei's bed, or how safe I feel in Mikhail's arms, or how treasured Ezra claims I am, *they're all keeping secrets from me.*

And *that* is unacceptable.

I pull Andrei's arm off me and slide away from him. Dropping my feet over the edge of the bed, I suck in a breath at how cold the air is away from him.

He sighs and reaches for me. "Valentina. You're restless. Tell me what's wrong."

I run my fingers through my hair and tie it into a knot at the base of my neck. How do I ask him what *else* he's been doing, other than wedding planning? Sitting up at the far side of the bed, far enough away that Andrei can't grab me, but close enough that I can drag the edge of the blanket across my shoulders, I locate a bedside lamp and flick it on.

Andrei is wide awake, his expression calm as he studies me.

The cool night air makes me shiver.

This time, he doesn't try to draw me back into him.

"I need to know what's going on." I wrap the blanket tighter around me, sliding some of it off Andrei's body. He doesn't react, keeping perfectly and scarily still.

"We're planning a wedding."

A flare of anger lashes inside my heart. "That's not good enough."

"It's the truth."

"It's a half truth, Andrei Leonov. You owe me the full truth. As your wife, I demand it."

He sits up so suddenly that I flinch. Flipping me onto my

back, he smiles mirthlessly down at me. "You're not my wife yet, Valentina Violetta Baranova," he snaps, using my full name against me the same way I tried to use it against him. "I might call you *zhena*, but make no mistake. Until I vow my heart, body, and soul to you in three days, you can't make demands of me as my *wife*."

I struggle against his hold, but he grips my wrists tight and bundles them over my head.

"You said I had power," I yell, suddenly bitter. "You said you loved me."

A man who loves me wouldn't keep secrets from me.

Andrei's nostrils flare. "I love you more than I love myself, Valentina. More than I love power. More than I love fucking you raw." His eyes scale my body, latching on to each love mark he's made across my skin. "If you want to know something, my beautiful, stubborn woman, *you ask me*. Do not make demands about truths you aren't ready to hear."

"Fucking tell me, then!" I writhe against his grip, bucking my hips and thrashing about. "I need to know! Why do you all hate my grandmother? Why is Ezra torturing people to death? What the hell is so intimidating about Liam?"

"Do *not* say that name in my *fucking* bed," Andrei snarls.

"I wouldn't have to if you'd just—"

He captures my mouth, a rough force of teeth and tongue and *anger*. It rolls off him in waves, choking me from the sheer force of it. When he pulls back, he's breathing hard, his eyes dark pits of violent rage.

"Your ex-boyfriend"—he laughs coldly—"is a fucking joke. If he wasn't, you would have never come back to me. You would have sat on his cock and swallowed his loads like a good fucking girl, as meek as a mouse beneath his boot." He grips my chin, digging his fingers into my cheeks. "But *I* know that you're a *bad* fucking girl. Asking questions. Making demands. Trying to dig up secrets."

Heat lightning flashes behind the window curtain, illuminating Andrei's face. Behind the anger, hidden in the cracks of his mask, is fear. Crippling, intense, *agonizing* terror. His breaths are shallow and shaky as he lashes out with it.

I say his name as best I can from beneath his grasp and latch on to his hands. Gripping them tight, I drag them from my face and throw his body off mine. Tackling him to the bed, I wrap my entire body around him from behind, holding on as tight as I can.

"I'm not going anywhere. Calm down." I dig my body weight into his back, hoping he can't feel how hard my heart is pounding. "I promise, Andrei, no matter what you tell me, I'm not leaving you. You can't say anything that will scare me off."

He's quiet for a long moment, his body stiff as a board as he wrestles with his emotions. Slowly, the tension in his shoulders relaxes, and he draws a deep, staggering breath. With his head thrust into the pillow, he makes a strangled sound and balls his hands into tight fists.

"*Shhhh.* It's okay. I'm here. I'm not going anywhere. *Shhhh.*"

I rake my fingers through his hair in soothing strokes, scratching his scalp at the base of his neck. When his entire body slumps, I feel safe enough to climb off him. He keeps his face buried in the pillow, even as he reaches for my hand.

Grasping it, I lace our fingers together and press a kiss to his knuckles. "I'll be okay, no matter what you tell me, *muzh.*" The Russian word for *husband* is clunky on my tongue, but it gets Andrei to turn his head toward me.

He takes a deep breath and holds it. "Katya sent you the letter, Valentina. The day you left, she had someone plant it in your room."

"That's impossible. She wasn't even at the wedding. She was . . ." I squint, trying to remember *why* she was missing.

"She wasn't there until I walked out. She had a car waiting, and . . ."

She had a car waiting for me.

I always thought she'd just arrived at the venue, but maybe *she was waiting for me to walk out of it.*

"Why would she do that?" I ask, chewing on my bottom lip. "That doesn't make any sense. She bought a house out of the city and let me live with her for years. No one wants their granddaughter living with them for that long."

"Unless she has a motive." Andrei snorts, the color returning to his face. "Let me guess, she introduced you to Liam, too?"

"Well, that's—" I purse my lips. "She has a lot of friends."

"She made friends while living in the city? *Outside* friends? A man less than half her age?" Andrei rolls onto his side and props his head up on his palm. "Think, Valentina. How does that make sense?"

Everything happened so fast after the wedding. Driving out of the city, finding a place to sleep, figuring out how I was going to live with myself. Grandma bought the house almost immediately. The closing date even came faster than expected. Something about *expediting the process for a friend.*

Our real estate agent was actually the owner of the company I ended up working for, and Liam hired me on the spot. I didn't even have a formal interview. At the time, he said I looked like I needed a pick-me-up . . . and then a few months later, he asked me out on a date.

A year later, I was looking out of his sixth-floor apartment window with nothing but a bed sheet wrapped around me.

My grandma couldn't have set that all up on her own, but she *was* overjoyed when I first told her we were dating . . .

My lips curve into a frown. "Okay, so let's say she *did* plan for me to leave the city. She sets me up with a house and a job, and then she encourages me to date my boss. That's a little . . . weird. But it's not criminal."

"She manipulated you." Andrei's eyes narrow, and even though I know he's not mad at *me*, a chill still runs down my spine. "*He* manipulated you." A muscle in Andrei's jaw tics. It looks like there's more he wants to say, but he swallows whatever it is like a bitter pill.

I take a deep breath and close my eyes. The room is spinning, and it's like pins and needles are dancing inside my skull. "And that's enough to kill them?" I ask.

Andrei squeezes my hand. "Yes, *zhena*. Anyone who manipulates you, hurts you, steals you away from me, or threatens your autonomy has a death wish that I'm *happy* to fulfill."

The more I hear any of my men threaten violence upon others, even if it *is* my grandmother, the less it bothers me.

Or maybe it's the mind-blowing orgasms that make everything else seem less dire.

"Even if she did all those things, she didn't mean me any harm. She loves me." The thought that my grandmother would knowingly do anything to hurt me is ridiculous.

"*I* love you," Andrei declares, wrapping an arm around my waist and pulling me into his chest. "I didn't think you'd take this news so well."

I know he's still only telling me half-truths, but we've made progress tonight, and that's what matters most to me.

I kiss the edge of his lips and love the way they tug up in a smile. "I'm learning to adapt. Sink or swim, right?"

Andrei chuckles. "You are strong, *zhena*. Taking my cock so deep . . ."

I smack his shoulder, and he laughs.

"*Fine.* You handled that well. And I'm sorry that I . . ." He trails off, his voice wavering at the end. "I'm sorry that I doubted you. I should have trusted that you wouldn't leave if I told you what really happened with your grandmother."

I brush my hand against his stubbled cheek. "Celia told me that I'd have to earn the city's trust again. It makes sense that I'd have to start with its king."

Andrei mumbles something unintelligible, so I pull the blankets up over us. Before I can elaborate any more, his breathing deepens and the crease in his forehead relaxes.

Sleeping, Andrei looks ten years younger. All the worry and stress of the day melts away, leaving him with nothing but peace.

I doubt he lets *anyone* sleep beside him, and my heart warms at the realization that he trusts me.

Not to leave.

Not to stab him in the back.

Not to murder him in his sleep.

My body aches all over, but the pain dulls as I press one final kiss to Andrei's lips.

I may not have the full truth, but at least for one night, I can pretend nothing else exists outside of this room, this bed, this man, this love.

CHAPTER 22

VALENTINA

I'M PULLED from sleep by Andrei's warm hands on my body as he spoons me. He lifts my leg and tugs it back, draping it over his thigh and bending my other knee toward my chest to spread me open. Fingers delve into my core, stroking gently, drawing out the pleasure tugging up my spine.

I moan when I feel his cock, rock hard, against my ass. He adjusts our angle so that he can glide against my pussy, the tip of him pushing in just enough to tease before it continues the smooth glide between my lips.

Never *inside*, but only *just.*

Andrei takes my hand and guides it between our bodies, making me feel each thrust of his cock as he teases my entrance.

His voice is rough from sleep, the Russian accent strong with the morning light. "Feel what you do to me, *zhena.*"

Slowly, he draws out my orgasm with deft fingers and sexy-as-hell Russian rumbling in my car. I reach behind me and snag his hair, pulling him against my lips for a perfect good morning kiss. Arching my back with a fierce tug on my hips, he drives into my heat and fucks me raw, groaning and panting in my ear.

The second time I come, he joins me, driving his cock *deep*, making me feel each hot pulse of his cum against my walls.

We kiss and caress each other until the sun's well over the horizon, the pinks and yellows in the sky quickly shifting to a clear blue. "I love you," Andrei murmurs against my lips, sighing as he pulls away. "Unfortunately, there's much to do today. Otherwise, I'd happily spend the day with you in bed." He slips from the sheets, and I get a full view of his body as he walks to the bathroom and turns on the shower.

Tattoos curve around his corded thighs and up his spine, each one clear iconography that somehow merges into a flowing piece of art. I haven't the faintest idea what any of the symbols mean, and I wonder if Ezra and Mikhail have some of the same ones inked on their skin.

I take the brief moment alone to run a hand down my face and take stock of my body. Bite marks and bruises paint me like a canvas, the half-moon pricks of blood over my hips completing the picture.

I look like a train wreck. A *well-fucked* train wreck.

If someone has any doubt about who I belong to now, that person is willfully ignorant.

As I admire the dark markings and stretch lazily in bed, happiness fills my chest. I'm *finally* Andrei's. If not in name, then at least in every way that matters.

The wedding is in three days.

I draw a breath and twist the ring on my finger. Being a *pakhan*'s wife means certain things will be expected of me. Parties. Social dinners. Volunteer work. I've trained for the role my entire life, taking etiquette classes and refining my speech and posture, all under the watchful eye of the Baranova matrons and my father, when he thought to oversee my training himself.

Sitting on a golden throne with a smile plastered on my face doesn't feel right, though, not with what Andrei has been telling me over the past few days. If I really have power as his queen, shouldn't I be making decisions for the family? The *entire* family—not just Andrei and me, but the Bratva itself.

I think of Celia and all the other unknown faces within our ranks. They may not be on the front lines, but they're part of our organization by name, at the very least. They'll need protection if anyone tries to stir trouble. The orphans, too. All those poor children stuck in that old house.

I picture Andrei and Ezra as young boys, each one groomed for a life of violence and politics.

Is that the future that awaits all those children?

Are *they* the backbone of the Bratva?

The shower cuts off and Andrei reappears, blanketed in steam. A black towel hangs low on his hips as he rummages in a dresser for something to wear. "You're welcome to the shower and anything in my closet." He flicks his gaze up at me as he drops the towel and saunters over, capturing my lips in a kiss the moment he's close enough. He hums in the back of his throat, a faint smile playing on his lips. "Of course, if you want to stay here all day and come all over my sheets, I won't mind."

My cheeks flush as he kisses me again.

"There's a bath, too, if you need to soak. I can have someone send up painkillers for you."

My heart flips in my chest at his kind consideration. "I'll be alright. Does it look bad?" I lift my arms to check the marks one more time. They look more painful than they are.

Andrei grins. "You look radiant, darling."

His cock starts to swell before my eyes, and I quickly slide away from him. "Oh no, I'm not ready for more. Please put that thing away."

He laughs as he obliges and hides the weapon between his legs behind boxers and black slacks. "If you want to avoid getting fucked by Ezra and Mikhail today, you might want to hide in here. The moment they smell sex on you, they'll be rabid."

A shiver runs down my spine. I'm not sure that's a bad thing.

"Are you sure you're okay sharing?" I ask, biting the inside of my cheek. "You seem very . . . possessive."

His eyes flash silver as he buttons a white dress shirt over his chest. "They're the exception, not the rule. I like seeing you with them. It makes you happy." Licking his lips, he gives me a sinful smirk. "*And* you'll look ravishing with two cocks in your hands while I fuck you into the mattress." His eyes glaze over as he starts imagining dirty fucking fantasies, and I try to ignore the sudden throbbing ache between my thighs.

"Well. Thank you. They *do* make me happy."

Andrei's expression shifts to cold, hard killer in an instant. "Anyone else who touches you, though, will die a slow and painful death."

Liam's face comes to mind, and I wince. He doesn't deserve a death like that just because my fiancé is the jealous type.

Maybe I can find a way to warn him. Get him to move across the country or something.

"Can I have my phone back?" I slide off the edge of the bed and into Andrei's closet. I'm not ready to wash the scent of him from my skin, but a shirt would be nice. "I'd like to invite my grandma to the wedding."

Andrei's shadow crosses over me as he blocks the doorway. "She's not allowed in, Valentina."

I purse my lips as I pull a white turtleneck from a hanger. "She's my *grandmother*, Andrei. My last living relative. I'd like for her to be there." The shirt is warm, which is exactly what I wanted. My boobs fill the middle well enough, but the arms fall past my fingertips. I can hear Andrei exhale harshly behind me.

"*If* she attends, she's not allowed to be alone with you." His voice hits heavy as hammer against steel. "Ezra or Mikhail will be with you the entire time."

A sliver of fear runs down my spine. I look at Andrei over my shoulder. "You won't let them kill her, will you?"

He sighs again and runs a hand down his face, looking more disheveled than he did five minutes ago. My heart aches for stressing him out, but it's not *my* fault that my boyfriends have a murderous hard-on for the woman.

"I want to ask for her blessing," I admit softly, clutching a pair of cotton briefs in my hands. "I know it's silly, but . . . it means a lot to me. My mom—" My voice cracks. "She isn't here to give me hers. My grandmother is all I have left."

Andrei comes up behind me and wraps me in his arms. Kissing my neck, he sighs. "I won't let them kill Katya. I'll see if we can find her for the invite." His embrace tightens. "For you, *zhena*, I will do this."

I turn around in his arms and press my lips to his. "Thank you."

We both finish dressing, and he checks his phone for the first time since last night. His jaw tics and he types a quick message to whoever sent him something unpleasant. Likely one of the boys.

"Is everything okay?"

Andrei smooths his expression before meeting my eyes. "It will be. I have to go. Don't leave the house today, even if Mikhail or Ezra tries to drag you somewhere."

An ominous feeling weighs in my stomach like a river rock settling on the sediment. "Okay."

He kisses me goodbye and flows out of the room like

water, graceful and elegant as he adjusts his shirt cuffs and steps back into the role of *pakhan.*

His absence makes the room feel massive, and I crave company immediately. Ezra's brooding eyes or Mikhail's malicious smile. I run to the bathroom to check my reflection and find that, *dear God*, I'm more of a mess than I thought.

Andrei wasn't lying when he said they'd scent sex all over me. I *look* like sex incarnate, the bruises on my body mapping every place Andrei claimed me last night.

A shiver runs down my spine as I imagine the brand he's left on my heart, the initials *A.L.* spun in a pretty script.

That mark may be invisible to the naked eye, but with every squeeze of my heart as it pumps blood through my veins, I'll know that I'm his.

Forever, irrevocably, *his.*

Chapter 23

Andrei

"When did these arrive?" I dump the contents of the manila envelope on my desk, the scrawled Russian lettering on the front making my skin crawl. *Moya zhena.* The same words that covered the backs of the photographs in Liam West's apartment.

Someone is sending us another message.

Photographs spill from the package and scatter across my desk, a handful of them falling off the edge to the floor. As Ezra grumbles and picks them up, I brush my hand over the stack on top of my desk, laying them flat.

Annoyance ripples under my skin as I examine each and every picture.

Valentina's face looks up at me, or around me, as she unknowingly glances past a camera lens. The images capture her past week in near chronological order, meaning that *someone* has been watching her since she first arrived.

Ezra murmurs a curse under his breath, while Mikhail's eyes glimmer with murderous intent.

We study the images of our woman, each one taken without her knowledge or consent. Without *ours.*

Hooked to my arm at the mayor's party. A security camera still of me pinning her to the wall and ravaging her mouth. Valentina standing in the entryway of the orphanage with Mikhail. Celia's house, this one taken through the dining room window.

My hand wrapped around Valentina's throat.

Fury pulses through me, and I have to take a deep breath to hold it in.

"That mother*fucker*," Mikhail hisses, not caring to hold anything back. "I'm going to peel his fucking fingernails off."

Ezra grunts, but I recognize the dark shadows in his eyes. He's been planning a thousand different ways to murder the *mudak* already. The photos only add fuel to the fire.

"Why haven't we found him?" I drum my fingertips across the top of my desk. "Ezra, you *always* catch people. Tell me what's happening."

Ezra grinds his teeth together. "They will not speak. I only take little piece of tongue, tiny strips of flesh." He exhales harshly. "Then I take bone. They laugh in my face, if they do not piss themselves first."

"So, we've learned nothing?" Mikhail's nostrils flare. "What the hell?" He runs a hand through his hair and starts pacing the room. "I lost those properties, Andrei. All six of them. They fell like fucking dominos, and all our legal team could say was *sorry*. I know we didn't make a mistake when we redrafted those contracts and deeds three years ago. They were airtight."

"Someone changed them," I muse, rubbing a kink in my neck. I slept fitfully as I imagined Valentina being ripped from my arms, but thankfully, she slept like a rock and didn't stir even once.

Seeing her in my bed helped calm my nerves in between bouts of nightmares.

This shit ignites every single one again.

"You *know* I vet my team, Andrei."

"I know. We do thorough checks on everyone." I sigh. An outsider wouldn't be able to turn our ranks against us.

But a Baranova matron *could*.

"We need to keep an eye on the guards." Ezra presses his thumbs to the back of his eyelids.

I've no doubt the man slept like shit. He should at least get a decent night's sleep before the wedding. I'd hate for my best man to look like a hot fucking mess while Valentina and I say our vows.

I draw an unsteady breath as anxiety rattles in my chest. It's not often that it rears its ugly head, but today, it does.

"Where is Valentina?" Ezra asks, pinning me under his heavy stare.

"In my bedroom." My lips curve up in a small smile. Thinking of Valentina lounging on my bed helps ease my high blood pressure.

"Are you sure?"

I reach inside my desk drawer and pull out a CCTV remote, clicking on the monitor. The TV screen overhead lights up and shows every hallway and room in the house.

Valentina is right where I left her, toying with the shower stream before stepping into its heat.

I long to be there with her, enclosed in a curtain of steam, letting the scalding water pour over the knots in my back. Maybe she'd run her dexterous little hands over my muscles and knead out some of the kinks. *Maybe* she'd get down on her knees and pull the tension from my body, one glorious *suck* at a time.

Ezra's expression softens as he watches Valentina scrub her hair. They shared a shower together, and ever since, he's been more apt to relax. I've no doubt it's a fond memory for him.

Mikhail stops pacing to stare at the screen.

All three of us watch our queen scrub herself clean. Part of me hates that she's scrubbing the sex off her skin, but I can sex her right back up the minute I return to her.

We *all* could.

The echo of an idea forms in the back of my mind. Through the fog of anxiety and lust, I draw it forward, pinning it into place as I think through the ramifications.

Bringing Valentina into the fold was only part one of our plan. Part two involves convincing the Bratva that she's here willingly, and what better way than to show her off in public? The mayor's party was one thing, but that catered toward the elite.

We need to remind the entire city that she's *ours*. She stands with us, not against us, and is here for *them*.

A queen among her people.

I let the idea settle in my gut. It's risky to take her out into the open when she has a stalker and we can't find Katya. The woman is a snake slithering around in the shadows, and soon enough, she'll be ready to strike.

"Let's take Valentina out tonight." I study each of my right hand men to gauge their reactions. I can tell immediately that Ezra doesn't like it; his scowl is damn near permanent these days, but Mikhail brightens, like it's the best idea in the world.

"Yes," he purrs, holding a hand under his chin. "Lure the bitch out."

"I do not like it." Ezra's lips press into a line. "We do not know who to trust, *pakhan*. We could be targeted."

"Anyone caught open firing on a *pakhan* and his wife out in the open will be killed on sight. If not by one of us, then by one of our loyal brothers and sisters." I lean back in my chair and let my head fall back. "It's suicide to come after us in public."

"These people are not normal," Ezra grumbles, frustration laced in every word. "They do not break."

"Perhaps they're from Russia?" Mikhail asks, lifting an eyebrow. "Maybe your tactics don't work on them."

Ezra bristles at the insult. "Their bodies have been numbed with drugs. Pain inhibitors."

In other words, *not my fault.*

"Have you tried removing a finger?"

As Mikhail and Ezra discuss torture tactics, I focus in on Valentina. She's still in the shower, steam billowing up and fogging the camera lens. I watch her for an entire minute, then another, and she doesn't move.

Then, the image flickers, just for an instant, and I narrow my gaze. It does it again, and I count the seconds until it happens a third time.

Someone's fucking with my video feed.

"Mikhail. Stand here and watch the cameras. Keep me on speed dial."

My chair scrapes the floor as I jump up and bolt through the door. Both of my men jump into action, recognizing my alarm in an instant.

I leave Mikhail to the camera footage as I race through the halls.

Someone's in my fucking house.

The click of a magazine slotting into a handgun sounds behind me, and knowing Ezra has my back helps keep me focused on Valentina.

I rush to the other end of the house and burst through my bedroom door. "Valentina?" The shower is off and the mirror has lost most of its condensation. The closet is empty, the floor is empty, the *bed* is empty.

"Where is she?" I storm into the hallway, and the guard who's supposed to be posted here is missing.

Ezra is talking in rapid-fire Russian when he clicks his cell phone on speaker.

"Valentina's still in the shower," Mikhail confirms, unassuming in his casual response. "Why?"

"She is not here," Ezra growls, following me down the hallway. *None* of the guards are on post, and when we cross into the kitchen, I skid to a halt as my shoe slides across a puddle of red. An armored bodyguard is oozing blood from a weak spot in his armor, unconscious if not already dead.

Cursing loudly, Ezra hangs up on Mikhail and calls someone else from his team. I'm not sure who; I stop listening as I pour from room to room, scanning everything in sight for a trace of Valentina.

With a roar, I spill into the backyard, startling the one guard actually present. Snarling, I shove him against the brick wall. I don't care that he's armed with an AK and I'm armed with my fists; he wouldn't dare shoot his leader. "Where is Valentina?"

The guard's shock makes him stutter. "Sh-she's right there." His eyes drift toward the rose gardens. "She wanted a moment alone with the Madame."

The Madame.

I snatch the gun from his shoulders, snapping the strap in two.

I promised I wouldn't let Mikhail or Ezra kill Katya.

I never promised anything about killing her myself.

Chapter 24

Valentina

When I step out of the steam cloud and wipe away condensation from the mirror, I feel completely refreshed. I hadn't planned on a shower, but after sitting with a very wet reminder of Andrei between my thighs, it quickly became necessary.

I brush my fingers through my curls and squeeze any remaining water into the sink. It'll take a while for my hair to dry, but since I have no hair product and no plans, I don't mind it.

Still, it wouldn't kill Andrei to have a few more items on his bathroom vanity. I glance at his toothbrush before deciding, *nope*, gotta get my own.

I'm preoccupied with my thoughts as I exit the bathroom and make a beeline for the boxers I laid out on his dresser for myself.

"It's good to see you, *moya ditya.*"

I scream.

My grandmother's face pinches. "Please, Valentina, lower your voice."

"How—how are you *here?*"

Andrei has stated multiple times that they can't find her, yet *here she is*, in his bedroom, sitting on his bed. "I don't understand."

She waves away my concern with a bony hand. "Do you underestimate your grandmother that much?" She scrutinizes my naked body with shrewd eyes, and I quickly cover up with my towel. I hadn't expected company. Faintly, I remember Andrei breaking the door lock in our haste to get inside last night.

Oh. Maybe that wasn't such a good idea.

Katya's eyes narrow. "You look like you've been beaten, *ditya.*"

I drown in embarrassment. *Oh, God.* "It's not like that." I hide behind the closet door as I shrug on clothes. Boxer shorts. White turtleneck. The biggest pair of pants I can find.

Maybe the clothes will swallow me whole and help me disappear.

When no such thing happens, I emerge from my hiding place to face my grandmother. I don't feel very queenly as she purses her lips at the decor in the room, clearly dissatisfied with what she sees.

It's not her room or her house, so I don't know why she finds the need to criticize everything.

"What are you doing here, Grandma?" I pull the sleeves of Andrei's shirt lower and bunch them in my hands. "How did you even get here? We live two states away."

"Am I not allowed to visit my granddaughter when she goes missing?" She stands from the edge of the bead and walks toward me. "When she doesn't answer my calls for *days* and worries me sick?"

Guilt claws at my chest. I should have tried harder to put word out that I was okay. With everything that's been going on, I hadn't even thought about it.

"I'm sorry, I didn't think—"

"You *weren't* thinking, *ditya*. But I'm here now. Everything will be okay." She takes my hand and leads me toward the door. "Come. Let us sit and talk somewhere more appropriate. This room . . . *stinks*."

My face flushes as more embarrassment pours over me. *My grandmother can smell all the sex I had last night. And this morning. She must think I'm a slut.*

Not that she has any right to shame me for having a sex life, but the last thing I want is for my *grandmother* to know about her little girl's bedroom habits.

I tug the collar of Andrei's turtleneck a little higher, grateful for the extra coverage. The only thing better would be a hazmat suit or one of those things astronauts wear into space. With the helmet and everything.

Anything to keep my grandmother's icy gaze from piercing my skin and digging into my heart.

She's not usually like this, but I can't imagine it's easy returning home after five years to find your granddaughter, who you helped save from this place, naked and in bed with the enemy.

I suck in a lungful of air.

Andrei's not my enemy.

The perspective shift gives me whiplash. Only a few days ago, I felt differently. Or at least, I'd convinced myself he was the enemy . . .

We take a shortcut through the house, my grandmother knowing the halls much better than me. I wonder how long she spent here, wandering the halls. What her duties were as the *pakhan*'s wife. If she enjoyed them, or if she felt trapped within these walls.

The crisp autumn air is a welcome change as we step outside. Blinding sunlight makes me cover my eyes, but my grandmother keeps moving, despite the falter in my step. "Come along, *ditya*. We have much to discuss."

What could we possibly have to talk about?

A chill runs down my arms as I hurry along behind her. Maybe my grandmother can tell me why . . . my men want to hurt her.

Why they think she has hurt *me*.

"You love me, don't you, Grandma?" The question comes out timid, and I feel just like I did five years ago. *Small. Weak. Unsure.*

Standing near the wall like an ornament or piece of decor. Something to look pretty, but not to touch or speak to or hear.

I swallow my unease as best I can.

We step across the lawn and into the rose garden, a maze of hedges and flowering bushes of all colors and sizes. I've hated this place since I was little and got lost among the towering hedges and spiked leaves. If you're deep enough in the labyrinth, the sun can't shine its light within, and everything feels dark and twisty.

"Of course, I love you." Her tone is sharp, but she takes my hand between both of hers and pats gently. "You're my granddaughter."

As if it was the stupidest question possible.

We find a quiet nook with three cement benches arched in a circle and a wrought-iron sundial sticking up from the center. I don't know why it's here; the sunlight never reaches it.

Towering pink roses crowd us inside the circular resting place, and my grandmother takes a seat on one of the benches and pats the space beside her. "Sit, Valentina."

I do as I'm told.

Katya surveys the area in silence, and it's only then that I notice movement behind the hedges near us. Guards shift into position, and some of the tension coiling around my spine eases. Andrei has been hellbent on making sure I have an armed escort, so I'm glad they're following orders.

It makes me feel safer to have a piece of Andrei here with me, even if it's just one of his orders.

I break the silence first. "I'm getting married. The wedding is in three days." I brush a strand of damp hair behind my ear, feeling shy all over again. "I'd love for you to come."

My grandmother's sharp eyes turn to me. "I'm surprised at you, Valentina."

My heart sinks. "What do you mean?"

"You walked away from this marriage once. I don't know why you've come crawling back after all I did to keep you safe."

It's a punch to the gut. "I didn't come here to get married—"

"Yet you *are*."

Irritation prickles at my skin. "I love him, Grandma. I know I left before, but I was scared. I'm not scared anymore. I know what I want."

"You *think* you know what you want." She shakes her head. "*Ditya*. You already have a boyfriend, hm? What about Liam? He's been worrying himself sick about you. We both have."

I rear my head back. Is she not listening to a word I'm saying? "Liam's not a part of this."

Her crystalline gaze narrows. "Should you not consider your partner before making the decision to have an affair? You let another man seduce you, Valentina. I understand that the Leonov boy is powerful and handsome to look at, but he's using your name and inheritance to seduce you. Where do you think he got all of this?" She waves her hand through the air, gesturing to the area around us. The gardens. The main house and every building between it and the outer gates. "It was your father's, and it should have passed down to you when he died. Why do you think Leonov wants to marry you? For *love?*"

Shards of razor-sharp ice cut deep into my chest.

"You don't know what you're talking about."

She laughs, and the sound forces the shards to expand past my ribs. I shiver and wrap my arms around my chest.

"I've lived much longer than you, *moya ditya*. I've been the wife of a *pakhan* for over half my life. I think I know a bit more than you do."

Any irritation I have with her shatters. She *is* older than me, and she worked hard to keep me from the life I'm about to walk into willingly. "Liam doesn't matter," I say lamely, holding on to any argument I have left. "We weren't even together when I left. We broke up a month ago."

She scoffs. "You two have been dancing around each other for years. He loves you, Valentina, which is more than I can say for the other one."

The other one. My fiancé. The man I love with all my heart and soul.

Not to mention, Ezra and Mikhail. It's not just Andrei I have now; it's all *three* of them.

"You don't know what you're talking about," I repeat, louder this time. Clenching my fists, I stand from the bench and step in front of her. "I'm not the same little girl I was five years ago, Grandma. I can make my own decisions. And I choose Andrei. Not *the other one,* Andrei Leonov. I choose Mikhail Monrovia and Ezra Reinoff, too, just so we're clear."

The anger in my grandmother's eyes takes the breath from my lungs. *So much anger.*

It reminds me of how I felt when I first arrived. Andrei and I were so *angry* and *hurt.* We still are, I think, but I like to imagine we're letting a little more of each go with each day that passes.

All of my men hold anger in their hearts, and although I understand some of its origins, there's still one seed of anger that I'm not sure about. One particular topic that doesn't make sense to me. "Grandma," I begin, ignoring the way my heartbeat trips over my nerves, "they seem to think you've done something wrong. You've upset them somehow, but I don't know how. Did you do something to the Bratva before I left?" I wring my hands together.

My grandmother's lips press into a thin line. "Don't believe a thing they've told you, Valentina. Everything I've done, I've done for *you*."

"What does that mean?" A tendril of terror brushes against my heart, sending a tremor through me. Has she actually done something wrong? Is their anger against her justified?

I think back to the day I left the city, thinking I was leaving the Bratva and my past behind. No one was angry that day. We were all waiting for the wedding ceremony to begin, most of us eager for the future it would herald. So, with that in mind, it must be something that happened *after* that made my men so angry. Something that would have changed everything . . .

"Grandma," I start again, "do you know anything about a letter my mother wrote before she died?" Andrei mentioned last night that my grandmother is the one who gave it to me, but that can't be true. In the past five years we've lived together, she's had plenty of time to tell me about the letter. The fact that she hasn't brought it up even once must mean that Andrei has it wrong. It couldn't have been her that planted the letter in my dressing room. She wasn't even in the venue yet. She was still outside in her car . . . waiting for me to walk out.

The former matriarch's lips turn down at the edges, cutting into her face deeper than any wrinkle. "Everything I've done has been for you, *ditya*. For *us*."

A crack splinters inside my heart. "What have you done, Grandma?"

A gun cocks behind me, sending a tremor through my

body. I've only heard that sound a handful of times in my life, and it's never a good sign.

"Step away from her, Valentina."

Andrei.

My grandmother ignores him and tightly grasps both my hands in hers. "Come now, Valentina. Let's leave."

Leave?

Andrei echoes my thoughts. "You're not going anywhere," he growls.

The two guards have shifted their position since our arrival, and now they're standing behind my grandmother. Both of them raise their guns.

Not at my grandmother.

But at *my groom.*

"What are you doing?" Panic beats its wings in my chest, fluttering like a caged bird.

No.

"They're following orders," my grandmother proclaims coolly. "Do not worry, *ditya*. They won't hurt you."

I'm not worried about me!

"Turn around, Valentina," Andrei orders, sounding just as calm as my grandmother. "She's right, they won't hurt you."

Slowly, I turn to face my lover. He's holding the barrel of a gun directly at my chest.

"Move, *zhena*."

I don't recognize the man in front of me. There's a precision in his eyes that scares me, a deathly calm that only an experienced killer can possess.

And he's aiming a gun at me.

"I can't," I whisper, fear rooting me in place. "If I move, you'll shoot her."

Ezra appears behind Andrei, his own gun aimed at the guards behind me. The look on his face is just as calm, but a muscle in his jaw tics. He's not looking at me, solely focused on the task at hand—keeping his *pakhan* safe.

My grandmother clicks her tongue against her teeth. "You'd shoot an unarmed old woman?" I hear her stand behind me. "How cowardly. Tolkotsky at least had dignity, like my husband before him. They wouldn't shoot an innocent."

"She's lying," Andrei hisses, his armor cracking. "They'd kill an innocent in a heartbeat. Valentina. Please. *Move.*"

My heart breaks at the hint of desperation in his voice. "You'll kill her."

He growls deep in his chest, frustration rolling off him in waves. "I'm trying to *save* you, dammit! She's a fucking liar, and the sooner you realize that, the better."

My heart jumps to my throat. I can't believe this is happening. "Put the gun down, Andrei."

His glare is solid, unwavering, *deadly.*

I hold my arms up at my sides and try to stay strong in my resolve. I don't want any bloodshed. I don't want anyone to die. "If you want to kill her, you'll have to go through me."

Andrei's expression morphs into fury. "You choose *her* over *me?*"

"I'm not choosing sides. I won't let you kill her."

"That *is* choosing a side," he yells, his anger lashing like a whip against my cheek. A tear rolls down my face before I even realize I'm close to crying.

My grandmother shifts behind me, and I try to hold her back.

"They won't shoot me, Valentina, or my guards will open fire. You're not thinking with your head." She pats my hand and walks out from behind me, not the slightest bit afraid as she moves behind her guards.

Andrei doesn't shoot. Ezra doesn't shoot. Neither of the guards open fire.

"See?" Katya's smile turns smug. "They're too afraid to hurt you, *ditya*. They don't want you to hate them for hurting me."

I'm not sure if that's true. They might want to avoid getting *shot*.

"I'll see you at the wedding," she says with finality. "And to be clear, Valentina . . ." Her eyes cut into me like daggers. "You do *not* have my blessing."

As the former matron of the Baranova Bratva walks away, what hope I had for a happy family, or even just an amicable one, splinters into sharp, jagged pieces. My arms itch, like I've run through a maze of thorns, and I hug them tight around myself. "You didn't even *try*," I whisper, disappointment washing over me like a slow-rising tide. *She didn't even try to like them.*

Two armed guards materialize from the shadows behind the hedges, and what was once a detail of two becomes four. They flank my grandmother on all sides as she rounds a corner in the maze and disappears.

My sorrow rises higher as I turn back to my men and find them glaring at the space Katya had occupied.

Ezra grunts and makes to follow, but a quick *nyet* from his *pakhan* makes him scowl and hold his gun at attention.

"Valentina has made her decision," Andrei says coldly. "We will honor it."

If Ezra disagrees, he doesn't voice it.

My fiancé turns to me, looking truly and wholly pissed off. "You will *never*," he snaps, the small space amplifying his voice to a yell, "*never* stand in front of a loaded gun again. *I forbid it*." He clenches the gun in his hands so tightly that his knuckles turn white.

His rage flicks a switch inside me, and what was once waves of sorrow become waves of pain.

I'm so *tired* of being in pain.

Fuck everyone right now.

A laugh cracks in my chest as something unhinges. "You know what? *Fuck you.*"

Andrei's nostrils flare and a vein in his forehead throbs. "Say that again."

I must have a death wish, because I'm happy to oblige. "Fuck. You." I don't care if it pisses him off. *I'm* pissed off. *I'm* hurt. *I'm* confused. I clench my shaking fists. "And you know what else? *I* forbid *you* from killing my grandmother." Another laugh, this one sounding as bitter as I feel. "There, problem solved."

Andrei's lip curls. "You think this is funny? You think I *want* to kill someone you care about?"

"Could've fooled me, charging in here with a loaded fucking gun like that."

"You disappeared," Andrei grits through clenched teeth, "and when you disappear, I get anxious. A guard is *dead*, Valentina, and you were gone. What was I supposed to do, sit around and pray?" He pops the bullet from the chamber of his gun and shoves the weapon against Ezra's chest. "God hasn't done me a lot of favors, so forgive me if I'm not a fucking pacifist."

I didn't know a guard was dead. We took a shortcut through the house, so I guess we could have missed it . . . And if it's true that someone really *is* dead, Andrei's reaction is a little more justifiable.

Taking a breath, I lower my voice as my anger cools. "If you'd trust me, maybe you wouldn't have to worry so much."

Andrei exhales a breath he's been holding. "I trust you, Valentina. It's everyone else that's the problem."

I have a feeling that he and my grandmother might agree with each other on that point. They might have more in common than they realize. "If you'd just talk to her—"

"No."

"Why not? What has she done that's so bad, you can't even look at her without pointing a fucking gun at her head?"

Andrei shuts his eyes, takes a deep breath, and remains silent.

I have a feeling he's counting down from ten *very* slowly.

"She's been lying to you." He paces behind the bench across from me. "She's been manipulating you, Valentina, if not for your entire life, then at least for the last five years. Open your eyes!" He gestures wildly towards the gap in the hedges my grandmother disappeared through. "She has a fucking guard detail! She's keeping secrets from you, Valentina!"

All his anger does is fuel my own. I draw myself up to my full height. "I guess that's the new favorite thing to do these days, huh? Let's all lie to Valentina and see if she ever figures it out! I bet she won't; she's just a dumb, horny bitch who'll keep silent if we fuck her hard enough. Are three cocks enough to keep her quiet?"

Andrei's eyes flash. "That's not what we think of you, and you know it."

"You say you trust me, but you won't trust me with the truth. The *full* truth, not only the parts you think I can handle." I cross my arms over my chest. "C'mon, Andrei, I can handle it. If I'm going to run this Bratva with you, I need to know all its dirty secrets. *Especially* if they involve me."

He stares at me for a long moment as he makes his decision. Exhaling harshly, he presses the pads of his fingertips to the back of his eyelids. "Take her inside," he instructs Ezra. "Let's show her how *loving* her grandmother has been all these years."

Ezra doesn't move. His eyes dance between me and his *pakhan.* "Are you sure—"

"For fuck's sake, Ezra, do as your told." Andrei storms out

of the hedge maze without a single glance in my direction, leaving me alone with my former bodyguard.

Silence stretches between us. If it weren't for the tension laying thick in the air, this would be just like old times. Me, wandering the estate, while Ezra keeps a watchful eye and ensures I stay out of trouble. Not that I got into much, back in the day.

"What crawled up his ass and died?" I scrunch my nose. Ezra doesn't laugh, and I sigh as my attempt at levity falls flat. "C'mon, Ezra, it can't be that bad. It's my *grandmother.*"

Ezra's eyebrows pinch together. Stress ripples across his face as he fixes a broken strap on one gun and crosses both weapons over his shoulders. "I have vowed to protect you from harm, *lisichka.* This will . . . bring pain. I do not wish for it."

My heart melts at his sweet confession. "I'll be okay. I can handle a little pain."

I'm not sure what to expect, and that makes me nervous, but I won't break. I'm not made of porcelain. "You don't have to keep protecting me, Ezra. You're not my bodyguard anymore."

He shakes his head. "I am always bodyguard, *lisichka.* I am always *yours.*"

Avoiding the guns as best I can, I wrap my arms around his waist and bury my face in his muscled chest. His body is strung tight, and I wonder if he got any sleep last night. "Are you mad at me?" I ask, bracing myself for his anger, too.

I might deserve it after standing in front of a loaded gun.

He pops a bullet from the chamber of each gun before shifting them around to his back. I don't make the task easy by standing in the way, but he doesn't try to move me.

"I am not mad." Tentatively, he brushes a large hand against my waist and cinches his arm around me. "You did what you thought best. You followed heart." He sighs. "Sometimes, heart can make bad decisions."

"Amen to that."

His lips curve into a crooked smile, stretching the scar jutting through his upper lip. "Be careful. The gods do not favor wicked men."

"Good thing I'm not a man."

He hums softly. "You are not man, that is true. They may spare you for being fox." The smallest chuckle rumbles through his chest, and it makes my heart soar. I've never known Ezra to crack a joke. I didn't know he *could*.

He sobers up quickly and cups my cheek in his rough palm. "But we may not be so lucky. You love wicked men, *lisichka*. Things do not always go in our favor."

I have a hard time accepting that. "Are you trying to scare me off?" I wrap my arms around his neck and run my fingers through the jet-black hair at the base of his neck. "Because it won't work."

"Never." He grumbles deep in his chest, sending vibrations through mine. A delicious shiver rolls down my spine, and I lean up on my tiptoes. He helps me close the distance between our lips, and even though my heart hurts, I cling to my wicked man tightly, letting him soothe away the pain one kiss at a time.

CHAPTER 25

VALENTINA

MIKHAIL MEETS us in the hallway before we reach Andrei's office. "What happened? Andrei won't say anything—" His eyes snag on Ezra's hand holding mine, and his lips curve into a grin. He loses his train of thought and takes position on the opposite side as Ezra, linking his arm with mine and taking my hand. Once he laces our fingers together, he lifts our hands to his lips and presses a kiss to our joined knuckles.

I try not to roll my eyes. It's a little over the top, but still kind of cute that he gets jealous over such a little thing as hand-holding.

We walk in silence to Andrei's office. If I were tied up and half naked, this might be reminiscent of when Ezra first dragged me here. Sadly, neither of those things are true. I have a feeling that if I were ass-up on the desk *now*, the outcome would be much more agreeable for all of us.

Andrei stands behind his desk, staring down at photographs organized into neat rows. Some photos are stacked three layers deep, while others remain as singles. He doesn't look up as we stand opposite him.

I decide to break the ice myself. "So, tell me, what's so

damning about my grandmother that you want her buried six feet under?" Mikhail's grip on my hand tightens, while Ezra turns to stone beside me.

Andrei rearranges some of the photographs, delicately picking one up and replacing it with another. "Oh, she won't be buried, Valentina. I'll make sure of that."

Ice rushes through my veins. "You wouldn't."

I'm sure Mikhail has told him all about my breakdown at my father's grave. I hate the bastard for not burying my mother.

If Andrei kills my grandmother *and* refuses to bury her, not only will my heart shatter, but I'll have to pick up a damn shovel and bury her myself.

No one deserves to be disrespected in death like that. It's cruel punishment, especially for someone who has done nothing wrong.

Andrei looks up, a picture of calm as he meets my eyes. "I will. And you'll agree with me, soon enough."

Dread fills my gut. "What do you mean?"

He gestures to the photographs. "Come have a look. Tell me what you see."

I take a step forward, releasing both Ezra and Mikhail's hands. They stay behind, silently watching me join Andrei on the other side of the desk. Once I'm standing beside Andrei, he cinches his arm around my waist to hold me in place. Warmth radiates from his body, but the heat makes me sick to my stomach.

I scan the photographs, starting at the top row and viewing them from left to right, like how you would read a book. It takes me a moment to understand what I'm looking at. Some of the images are blurry, like they were taken in a rush. Others are crystal-clear—one such picture has my face in focus as I smile politely at someone speaking to me. An emerald green dress hugs my skin, with Andrei looped through my arm as we cavort with socialites in a well-lit ballroom.

The mayor's birthday party.

I pick up the photograph. It's not a bad shot. "That guy must have taken this. The photographer, at the party." He shouldn't have been able to save any of the party snapshots after Andrei smashed his camera and ordered his team to confiscate any backups. A shiver runs down my spine.

Andrei nods in confirmation. "Travis Jacobs."

"You broke his nose."

"I wish I'd done more."

There's a bite to Andrei's voice that makes me flinch. "I don't see what's—"

"Keep looking."

I set down the photo from the party and pick up another one. This time, it's a side-shot of Mikhail dragging me away from my father's grave. Someone zoomed in to take this one from a distance; Mikhail and I were completely alone when this happened. The next image in the row is of me walking down the street behind Mikhail, dirt and grass stains on my knees from the moment before. After that, I see a picture taken from behind, my hair in a messy braid, the ocean sunset in the background.

"Have you been following me?" I frown up at Andrei. He's too busy to do it himself, so he must have paid someone. "Why would you—"

"I wouldn't." He presses his lips together tightly. "I don't need to pay anyone for that. I have these two to keep an eye on you." He nods towards Ezra and Mikhail. "They'll do it for free."

"Gladly," Mikhail immediately chimes in. "I'll always watch over you, *malyshka*."

"Then what is—" I lean further over the table to view the photographs in sequence. Andrei has organized them in what appears to be chronological order, from the moment I entered the city up until last night. The final photograph in the lineup is of Andrei and me getting into his SUV before driving home.

I pick up that final photograph, and the one beneath it falls to the floor. Andrei picks it up for me and hands it over, his face a blank mask as I turn the photo face up.

Andrei and I are centered within the frame, lips locked in one hell of a make-out. Andrei has me pinned against the SUV, one of his hands on my hips, the other gripping my throat. Whoever took this made sure to capture our lip-lock—zoomed the camera waaay the hell in, and took the photo at an angle. It's almost like they're looking up at us from below . . .

The flimsy film slips from my fingertips, and it floats down on top of the others like an innocent little piece of paper.

But nothing about these photographs screams innocence.

"Who took these?" I look between all three of my men. None of them look away from me, but none of them answer, either.

Annoyance ripples beneath my skin. Of all the times for them to keep quiet, they have to choose *now.* "I asked you a question." I clench my fists and return each of their scowls with one of my own. "For once, you damn well better answer. Who took these photos?"

If they say my grandmother, I might scream. There's no way in hell she would be crawling behind a bush to sneak photos of me, and I doubt she'd pay someone to do it, either. If she can show up to the estate, flanked by four armed guards, I doubt she'd resort to clandestine operations if she wanted a fucking photo.

No one else knows I'm here, except—

"We have been looking for boyfriend," Ezra grunts, his dark eyes turning pitch black. "*Liam West.*" He spits the name past his lips. "He is fond of you."

I could have told him that. "We were dating before I came

here. We broke up a month ago." I brush a frizzed curl behind my ear. Liam was an okay boyfriend. I don't have much to compare him to, but he did alright where it counted. "But he's harmless. He wouldn't come all the way here just to, I don't know, do whatever *this* is." I gesture to the stacks of photos.

"You are being hunted," Ezra growls, his muscles tightening.

"I think *stalked* is the technical term." Mikhail glares at the photos. "I'm the only one allowed to watch you, *malyshka*, not some *suka*."

"This is ridiculous. Liam wouldn't—he *couldn't*—"

Andrei reaches inside his desk drawer and pulls out a box. Dropping it onto his desk, he pops off the lid and chucks it to the ground. "I wouldn't be so sure, Valentina." He dumps the box's contents onto his desk, covering the neat rows of photographs with dozens of new ones. These aren't nearly as pristine as the first batch; some are curled at the edges, others faded from age and light exposure.

I bite my lip as my heart hammers in my chest. I don't want to know what's on these . . . but I *have* to know.

One by one, I start flipping the photos over. The words *moya zhena* are scrawled across the back of each one, and my stomach churns as I start piecing the collection together.

These pictures were taken years ago. Some of them as long as *five* years ago, when I first left Harlin Heights and started my new life with Grandma. A few of them are newer—I recognize the company holiday party from last year, the day I won *Employee of the Month* and someone insisted I pose for a photo with the commemorative plaque, the night I stayed over at Liam's house—

Wait.

My hand freezes over that particular image. Then, I find another one. And another. A dozen of them scattered throughout the pile, all of me in Liam's apartment in various stages of dress.

I'm naked in one of them, with a throw blanket wrapped around my shoulders as I look out over the cityscape. That was New Years Eve, almost a year ago. The fireworks in the distance give it away.

Liam has been taking pictures of me without my permission. It's one thing to, I don't know, take a cute photo of your girlfriend on your phone, but it's another to have *dozens* of them printed out. I'm not even looking at the camera in half of these. I'm completely unaware that the photo is being taken.

My skin crawls. Not once did he mention the photos, or being a photographer, or anything of the sort.

"Where did you get these?" I stare at the photo from New Years. If I wasn't so horrified, I might want to keep it.

"Ezra found the older ones in Liam's apartment. The new ones you saw first arrived just today, here at our doorstep." Andrei exhales slowly.

My grandmother's voice rings in my head, repeating the same phrases over and over.

He's been worrying himself sick about you.

He loves you, Valentina.

"My grandmother introduced us. She said she liked him. Liked *us* together." I wrap my arms around my chest and hold on tight. If I inhale too deeply, let my ribcage expand, I might feel my bones fall loose through the cracks. "I don't understand." I look up at Andrei's face and hear the words he's said a thousand times now: *moya zhena.*

My wife.

"I'm not married to Liam."

"And you never will be." Andrei grasps my chin and tilts my head further back, spilling my curls across my shoulders.

"But this means that he knows Russian, and he knows who you really are."

I didn't exactly hide my identity while Liam and I were together. I've been using the name Valentina my entire life, including the years I was gone. Grandma insisted I use my surname, too, despite all of our precautions at remaining hidden from my father. At the time, I didn't think much of it.

Now, though, it adds to my confusion.

"My grandmother could have taught him that phrase. Maybe he was going to propose before we broke up."

Mikhail scoffs and waves his hands in front of him, offense radiating from his movements. "*Please*. Tell me you're joking. Did you ever see a ring?" He shakes his head. "Don't answer that. I don't want the mental image."

I roll my eyes at the dramatics. Some things aren't adding up, though. "So, okay, Liam's a creep. But why does that make you want to kill my grandmother? It's not her fault that he's like that."

"You never should have been introduced, Valentina. You should have been *here*, with me. With *us*." Andrei's forehead creases. "Katya sent you that letter, Valentina. She was waiting for you outside the chapel, took you two *fucking* states away, holed you up in some ramshackle house—"

The house wasn't bad, but Andrei's temper is flaring so hot that I don't dare interrupt.

"—set you up with *Liam*, which, by the way, is a fake fucking name." Andrei's jaw tics. "She has kept you from us for years, kept you from your birthright as head of this Bratva, *and* kept you in a relationship with that fucking *mudak*." His eyes burn with hatred so deep that it cuts straight through me.

The urge to defend my grandmother's honor rises. "She's been looking after me." I grab his wrist to remove his hand from my jaw, but he doesn't budge. His grip tightens, but I refuse to react to his anger. "She's been trying to keep me safe."

Mikhail's glare could cut steel. "Is that what she's been telling you?" He slams his palm on the desk, scattering photographs to the floor. "Is a psycho stalker supposed to keep you safe?" Shaking his head, he laughs. "*Malyshka*. She's been lying to you from the beginning. I wouldn't be surprised if she's been lying to you your entire life."

I glare at him. "That's not true."

Ezra takes a stiff step forward and draws a deep breath. "A guard died today, Valentina. Katya wanted to get inside, and she killed good man for it."

"She came for *you*," Mikhail huffs. "She came to steal you away from us. *Again*."

Andrei's thumb smooths over my lips. "She almost succeeded."

With each beat of my heart, a piece of it breaks. I don't know what to believe. Everything my men are saying goes against what I know in my bones, but they sound so *sure*.

The evidence is damning. Could my grandmother really have done all of this? And for *what*?

I shut my eyes and breathe through the pain. Despite all the accusations and chaos from the day, at least one thing is certain. "I wouldn't have gone with her. I won't leave you again." I look between all three of my men, making sure they understand me clearly. "Any of you."

"I know you wouldn't have wanted to," Andrei concedes. "But she wouldn't have given you a choice."

Ezra sets down both of the guns he's been carrying since our stroll through the garden, and a shiver races down my arms.

Would she have ordered those guards to hold a gun to my back so that I would leave with her?

I shake my head. "I don't believe it. She brought the guards solely for protection. I'm sure of it."

Andrei sighs a second time and kisses my forehead. "I know you believe that, *zhena*. I hope, for your sake, that she doesn't prove you wrong."

I lay my head against his chest. Everything feels so *hopeless*. "What do we do now? Liam's still missing. My grandmother is somewhere out there roaming the streets." I take a breath but it turns into a sigh. "I invited her to the wedding. I still want her to attend as a guest, not a prisoner."

Ezra grunts, like he disagrees with the idea.

I turn my frown on him. "Andrei said she could attend."

"I said I'd try to find her, so that you could invite her. Now, you have." Andrei shuts his eyes. "I have a feeling she's going to show up, anyway. We need to be prepared."

"You're not allowed to kill her." I push away from Andrei and look from one man to the next. Known mafia men. Killers. Kings.

But *lovers*, too.

"I forbid it." I cross my arms and lift my chin. "And if any one of you orders someone *else* to kill her, I *will* find out, and I *will* be very fucking angry about it."

"She's learning," Mikhail muses, a smile curving across his lips. "My, my, Andrei, she almost sounds like you."

Andrei's eyes soften as he gazes at me. "Yes, she does."

My heart flutters in my chest, skipping a beat as each of my men wander closer. Mikhail reaches for me across the desk and brushes his knuckles against my cheek, smiling at the blush he conjures. Ezra hovers by my right, his fingertips hooking onto mine as he plays with my hand. Andrei smiles down at me, the pride in his eyes mixing with a tenderness that only a lover can possess.

It's all *so much*. I can feel my emotions rising, and I have to take a breath to keep them from spilling over. I might do something like *cry* and ruin the moment. I clear my throat and snap my fingers twice in front of their faces. "Hey. Focus. I'm serious. No one touches her."

Mikhail sighs dramatically. "Okay, *malyshka*, I won't kill Katya at the wedding. But what about Liam? Can we kill him?" A glimmer enters his eyes. "He is, after all, stealing my MO. *I'm* the only one allowed to take pictures of you." He winks, and my blush deepens.

Damn him.

"I'd rather talk to him, first." I press my finger to Mikhail's lips when he starts to protest. "I'm not saying you can't kill him—" I wince at the thought. "—all I'm saying, is that I want some answers. I need to hear everything from him directly, or I . . . I don't know if I can believe any of this." The idea of Liam stalking me and taking my picture sends a shiver down my spine. It doesn't feel real. "Can we *please* talk to him before any of you do anything rash?"

Andrei looks between Ezra and Mikhail, having some kind of silent brotherhood conversation that only they can hear. Then, he nods. "We'll talk first. But then, no promises. He may sign his own death wish."

"I hope he does." Mikhail rocks back on his heels as he gives me a once-over. "I'd love to see the look on your face when it happens. I bet it'll be *devastating*. You're so beautiful when you're angry—I can't imagine how you look when your heart's breaking."

Sometimes, I forget who I'm dealing with, and then Mikhail goes and says shit like *that*.

Ezra grunts. "We must find him first."

"I actually have an idea about that." Andrei places his hands on my shoulders. "But we'll need your help, darling."

Nerves flutter through my body and settle in my stomach. "Um, what for?"

Mikhail hums a tune. "What does Liam love more than

anything?" He brushes his palm across the back of my neck as he comes around the desk and joins the others. "What's his favorite little hobby, hm?" A photo crinkles beneath his shoe.

Ezra frowns. "I do not like this."

I can't say *I* do, either.

"You want me to lure him out." If it's the only way I'll get answers . . . I have to take it. I need to know the truth.

Andrei nods. "If you're near, he'll appear. He won't be able to resist."

I grasp the front of Andrei's shirt and meet his eyes. The *pakhan's* eyes. His word is law within the Bratva. "You promise you'll let me talk to him first?"

I need his word, or I won't agree to anything.

"I promise." He inclines his head. "You can talk to Liam. But I won't promise anything else. He's been lying to you, too, Valentina." Andrei slides his fingers through my hair and tilts my face towards his, hovering an inch from my lips. "Anyone who lies to my queen will be punished for it." His lips crash against mine, stealing the breath from my lungs. Leaning in, he demands more, deepening the kiss. His heartbeat pounds, steady and sure, beneath my palm.

When he pulls back, he brushes his palm against my cheek. "Do you understand?"

He's not just talking about punishing Liam for lying.

He's talking about punishing my grandmother, too.

"I understand."

But that doesn't mean I'm going to stand by and let it happen.

Chapter 26

Ezra

By the time Andrei is finished coordinating our plans for the evening and the sun has set, Valentina is nervous. She has no reason to be; all three of us will be with her at all times, and I doubt Katya will be up past midnight.

People sleep longer the closer they are to death, and Katya is *very* close to hers.

"*Lisichka*. Stop dancing."

"She's *fidgeting*," Mikhail corrects with a teasing lilt to his voice, smiling crookedly at Valentina. "It's delightful."

"Both of you, shut up." Valentina shifts her weight from foot to foot as we wait for our ride to appear. "I'm allowed to be nervous."

I try not to sigh. The night will be long if she's uncomfortable. "What is wrong?" We've already discussed Katya at length, going over what happened again and again while she picked at a croissant. I don't know that she actually ate anything today, and that means that she's not allowed to drink tonight.

If Valentina gets tipsy, things will become very complicated, very fast, especially if Liam is involved.

He could snatch her up in a heartbeat if we're not careful.

My heart hardens. I will *never* let that happen.

Instead of answering my question, Valentina scowls at her fingernails and starts picking at her cuticles. "I just don't like waiting."

"It is five minutes."

Mikhail chuckles, likely at some perverse thought running through his mind, and Valentina's head snaps in his direction.

If she had fangs, they'd be bared in his direction right now.

It makes Mikhail laugh even harder.

"Come here, *lisichka*," I grumble, holding out my hand. "You do not need worry."

Even though she's grumpy, Valentina slips into my arms and lets me hold her. I stare out at the driveway while she buries her face in my chest.

"What does that mean? *Lisichka?*"

Her pronunciation needs *a lot* of work, but I'm touched that she tries.

"Little fox," I translate, resting my chin on the top of her head. "Because you try to be sneaky."

Breaking into the estate, rummaging around my bedroom, going on unapproved trips with Mikhail, sneaking off with her grandmother . . .

Someone needs to keep a constant eye on her.

She chuffs. "I do not."

Okay, lisichka. Whatever you say.

The limo arrives exactly on schedule, no doubt thanks to Andrei's superior planning. The man insists on scheduling everything to a T so that there is no room for surprises.

I, however, am always on the lookout for surprises.

Valentina turns in my arms as the vehicle pulls around the curb. She's not paying attention until I open the car door for her, and her eyes widen as she realizes what's in front of her.

"A limo?"

We all thought she'd be pleased with a reprieve from the day's unfortunate events, but the shadow that passes over her face tells me she is, in fact, *unpleased*. She stares inside the open door, like she's waiting for something to pop out and snap its jaws around her.

Mikhail's eyes meet mine as he approaches Valentina from behind. He places a hand on her lower back. "I'm not driving, *malyshka*, so the chances of sudden death are minimal."

She should toss him a glare, or smack his chest, or at least *smile* at the joke.

Instead, she turns pale.

Carefully, I slide my arm under Valentina's legs and pick her up. Otherwise, we'll be here all night.

Her body stiffens, but to my surprise, she doesn't protest. As I lower her into the vehicle, I call for Andrei to grab her. He easily pulls her the rest of the way in, and Mikhail and I quickly follow.

Andrei cradles Valentina in his arms and studies her closely, scanning her face before looking back at us.

We all have the same question.

"Valentina, baby, are you okay? Are you hurt?" Andrei brushes a curl behind her ear.

I checked her for injuries as we came up with a plan for luring Liam out of hiding. She was patient with me as I looked her over from head to toe, but all I found were the hickeys Andrei gave her. Not a scratch or a bruise or anything of note, otherwise.

"Do we have to go out?" she asks, biting her lip and giving Andrei the biggest doe-eyes I've ever seen.

Part of me sizzles with jealousy, but if Valentina *did* look at me like that, I'd give her anything she wanted in a heartbeat. I clear my throat and begin counting the freckles dotting her shoulders. I insisted she wear a jacket out tonight, but she didn't seem interested in trying on outfits.

She chose the first little black dress she could find.

Now I realize I should have picked up on her mood earlier in the day. Shame burns in my chest, and I have to take a breath. As I exhale, I push the feeling down and trap it under the lid of a little black box I keep tucked away inside.

The box that never gets opened.

Pandora's box, Mikhail calls it, but I don't care about its name. The first rule any new recruit in the Russian sector learns is that you seal the box up tight . . . and never let anything out.

"The only way we're going to find Liam is if we leave the grounds. I know you don't want us to hurt him, baby, but he's hurt *you*. That can't go unpunished." He cups her cheek and brushes his thumb against her soft skin. He's become so gentle with her. It's the opposite of how he behaved when she first stumbled into his office a week ago.

It's impossible for five years of suffering to have disappeared that quickly. I suspect that Andrei has his own box tucked away, deep inside, too.

Not Mikhail, though. That bastard lets everything out the moment he feels the slightest bit *temperamental*.

Valentina seems to be holding her breath.

It makes me uncomfortable.

Mikhail reaches for her first, sliding into the seat beside Andrei and clasping Valentina's hands in his. He raises them to his lips and presses a kiss to her knuckles. "*Malyshka*. You're safe with us. We won't let anything happen to you."

Andrei nods his agreement. "There's no need to be nervous, darling. No one will touch you tonight but us."

Their words fall on deaf ears. Valentina's breathing shallows, and her eyes glaze over as panic sets in.

I take a deep breath, letting air fill my lungs to capacity. It's been a long time since I've witnessed trauma, but I recognize the signs more than the two *duraks* coddling Valentina like a child.

She doesn't need to be coddled.

"Come here, Valentina," I murmur, my voice rumbling loudly in the small space. Both of my brothers shoot me an irritated look, but Valentina finally stirs in Andrei's arms. She slides from his lap and wanders into mine, wrapping her arms around my neck the moment she's settled. I hold her close, engulfing her in my arms and against my chest. She's not so tiny that she disappears, but I wouldn't mind if I could keep her hidden forever.

"Do you know what makes me difficult to kill?"

She shakes her head softly. Her emerald eyes pull me in, and it takes *effort* to draw in my next breath. Soft like summer moss, green as a field of spring flowers, soothing as the warm sunlight on your back. I could lose myself in this woman.

I dig my fingertips into the tight muscle on her back, and she draws a deeper breath than before.

"I kill *first.*"

She leans into my chest, and her warmth radiates through my body. With rapt attention, she waits for me to continue.

"In Russia, there is tradition. All youths gather inside pit. It is cold. It is dark. There is one fire in the center." I remember the trial vividly. All twelve of us, no older than ten, some as young as seven or eight, with wooden torches wrapped in kerosine-soaked cloth. "The goal is simple. Light your torch. Be last one standing." A cold stone weighs heavy in my chest. "All other flames must go out."

I don't elaborate. I don't need to; Valentina's eyes fill with tears, and she cups my cheek in her tiny palm. "That's horrible."

Yes, it is.

"I survive," I continue, forcing air into my lungs, "because I act *first.* I *kill* first. The world is cruel, *lisichka,* and you must be crueler to survive. Faster. Sharper." I glance at my brothers, each one wearing a scowl on their face. They don't like what I'm telling her.

Too fucking bad.

I hold Valentina closer and breathe in her sweet vanilla scent. "Be brave in face of danger, and you will not die."

She nods, and a rush of pride swells within me.

"It also helps," I amend slowly, feeling Andrei's glare in my direction, "that I am not alone. I have two brothers with me, and now I have little fox." Her lips curve up, and my heart melts a little more. "My *lisichka* is brave, *da?*"

Her hands tighten around the collar of my shirt as she nods.

"Then, I have no fear." My scar stretches over my upper lip as I smile down at my beautiful little fox. "I will even teach you how to handle gun. Then you will be even more dangerous."

Mikhail huffs like he's dissatisfied. "*I* want to teach her how to shoot, you fucking bastard."

Too late. The honor is mine.

"I'm sorry you had to go through that." Valentina's nails scratch the base of my neck, and it feels so heavenly that I lean into her touch. "But I'm glad you're here with me."

She braces her palms on my shoulders and repositions herself, notching her knees on either side of my thighs and sitting up higher. It's rare for us to be on even ground; I always tower over her when we stand side by side.

The change of position knocks something loose in my chest, and my heart pumps harder.

Slowly, she lifts her face toward mine. "I want to be strong like you, Ezra." Her lithe little hands slide up the back of my neck and tangle in my hair. "I want to keep my men safe."

A groan settles in my chest at how warm her love is. How kind. How tender.

It's always been my job to keep her safe. To keep my *pakhan* safe. To keep *all* of my charges safe.

Not once has anyone wanted to save *me*.

"You *are* strong," I assure her, grasping her full hips and locking her in place. "Only a strong woman could claim three men."

She blushes at the compliment, but I couldn't be more serious.

It takes a heart of steel to care about all three of us. To want to keep *all of us* safe. And very soon, once she ascends her throne and claims her birthright, she will be stronger and more powerful than the three of us combined.

She could bring the city to ruin with a simple flick of her wrist. She could save it, too, just as easily. No matter if the danger lies within its borders or outside of them, trying to break in.

"I don't feel very strong," Valentina admits slowly, like she doesn't want to say the words out loud. "I'm nervous about tonight, because—" She takes a quick breath. "I don't want any of you to get hurt. If Liam is really stalking me, like you guys say he is, he'll show up tonight. If you guys go after him, he could hurt you." Her hands form tiny fists. "I won't be able to live with myself if one of you—" She cuts herself off, and I catch the sparkle of tears in her eyes.

Her unspoken words echo in my head. *If one of you dies.* Now that she's starting to care about us, she's scared that we will disappear—that death will take us from her, just like it took her mother.

Cupping her cheek, I regain her attention. Her gorgeous green eyes meet mine, and nothing else matters but her. "The Reaper himself cannot take me from you," I vow solemnly. "*Nothing* will keep me away from you, *lisichka*. No bullet or blade will bring me down." I stroke her cheek as gently as I know how. I've never done this before. This *being gentle* thing.

Until Valentina, all I knew was how to break bodies and stitch them back together again. She's forcing me to learn how to become something else. Something less monstrous and more human.

"You promise?"

I nod. "I promise."

"We all do," Andrei says, sliding across the leather seat to fill the space by Valentina's right side. "We're yours, Valentina. In this life and the next."

"Not that we're going anywhere." Mikhail shoots Andrei an annoyed look. "In fact, I'm planning on outliving both of these bastards, just so I can keep you all to myself."

"*Mikhail.*"

Valentina laughs, some of the tension leaving her shoulders. "You're all ridiculous. I don't know how I put up with three crazy men."

"Crazy about *you.*" It's a dumb line, but it still makes Valentina smile. Mikhail grins like he's won the lottery and brushes his hand along the outside of Valentina's arm, his gaze softening as it lands on her face. He presses a kiss to her shoulder.

I've never seen the bastard like this. It's proof that Valentina has changed something within each of us, even in such a short amount of time.

We'll never, *ever* let her go.

Andrei slides off Valentina's flats, caressing her ankles and slowly working his way up her body. She melts in my arms as my brothers caress her.

But *I'm* the one beneath her. *I'm* the one who was able to talk her down. Pride swells within me. I press my thumb to her perfect lips, eager for a taste. "Kiss me, *lisichka*. Feel how strong we are together."

A fire sparks in her eyes and she smiles, a breathtaking, heartwarming display of confidence that makes me ache for our woman. Her kiss is as confident as her smile, and she bears down on top of me without hesitation.

I feed into her desire, palming her ass to drag her higher over my lap, letting her feel my growing need. She moans as she settles over me, and I hold her down and *thrust*, needing more of that intoxicating sound.

Together, Andrei and Mikhail lift her dress over her hips, and although I can't see what she's wearing, I can feel it beneath my fingers. Something lacy that rides up the full curves of her ass, not doing a damn thing to hide the gifts underneath.

Her hips roll against mine, and those delicate panties are no match for my cock as she drags her hot little snatch over me, wrapping those tight lips over my erection.

The heat of her makes my blood roar in my ears.

"You want a strong cock?" I hiss, rocking her harder against me. I feel how wet her pussy is, how needy her body is for cock. "Take what is yours, *lisichka*."

As she leans back to steady herself in my lap, Mikhail steals her lips in a brutal kiss. She whines, but Mikhail is grinning as he sucks her bottom lip into his mouth.

I hold Valentina down and grind her against my lap, gritting my teeth at how I can nearly fit an inch inside her, even with our clothes on.

Andrei lowers himself to the seat and busies himself with her panties, tearing them off with a sharp snap of his teeth. Then he bites her hip, and she convulses on top of me, dragging me in deeper.

My eyes roll back in my head as she rotates her hips. I can hear the wet smack of her mouth against Mikhail's, feel the heat of her pussy over my cock, and see the new marks Andrei creates across her skin.

A goddess laying claim to mortal men. Making them want her. Making them *need* her.

Mikhail releases Valentina's lips and immediately lowers his mouth to her ear. "I want to watch you *fuck*," he rasps, nipping her earlobe with a moan. "I bet you're ravishing while you ride dick."

She moans, her gaze flicking back to my face, almost like she needs permission.

I lift her dress higher, splaying my hands over her stomach. It's her choice. I'll enjoy whatever she decides, regardless of whether it ends with my cock buried inside her molten core.

Her hips lift and one of my brothers removes her panties. While she holds herself over me, someone undoes my belt, then the button of my jeans, and finally the zipper.

Valentina takes the final step, lowering my boxers until my cock springs free. I grasp her hand and drag my underwear low enough that the waistband catches under my balls.

Our eyes lock as she drags her fingertips along my length and toys with the swollen tip. I grit my teeth as she aligns her entrance and lowers her hips.

Her breath catches as the first inch slides in, and Mikhail grabs her hips to help. Slowly, Valentina and Mikhail work together to impale her on my cock.

Holy fucking shit.

She grips me like a vice, and I twitch inside her, ready to explode. It's been a long time—a *very* long time—and the way Valentina parts her lips and pants as she tries to shimmy her body *lower* makes me want to slam her down *hard*.

But she's the one in control.

I brace my arms over the back of the seat to keep from moving. My nails dig into the leather as I hold on for the ride of my life.

As Valentina starts to move her hips, my brothers murmur words of encouragement.

"You take his cock so well, baby."

"You're creaming all over him, *malyshka*. Mmm. You're gonna make us all come."

I would kill to see my cock sliding in and out of her. "You feel amazing, *lisichka*."

Her eyes flutter closed and she nods.

"Do you feel good, baby?" Andrei asks, and she nods again. "Good. We want to give you all the pleasure you deserve. *Moya prekrasnaya zhena*."

My beautiful wife.

"*Our* woman." Mikhail kisses Valentina's neck, reaching between me and Valentina to press the heel of his hand against her clit. "She deserves to come for such a pretty performance, don't you think, brother?" He grinds against her clit, and her cadence stutters.

I can't take my eyes off her, but *God*, does that make it hard not to come.

"*Do not fucking come, Ezra*," Andrei hisses, glaring at me. "You will not come until she does."

Fuck me.

While Mikhail plays with Valentina's clit, Andrei rubs her tits through her dress, pinching her nipples between his fingers.

She whimpers, desperation making her move faster. Her tits bounce in Andrei's hands, and her ass smacks against my balls, sending shooting pleasure up my spine.

I growl and snatch Valentina's hair, gripping it tight and wrenching her head back. Her gorgeous neck arches and her beautiful eyes widen, her pupils blown wide fucking open with desire. "Come on my cock, Valentina," I demand, bucking up inside her. I snap my hips and piston in and out, my orgasm raging. "Fucking come *right now*." I can't hold it anymore. If she doesn't come soon, I'll—

She *breaks*, screaming as my brothers *slam* her onto my

cock in unison. I spill deep inside her, my cock pulsing as her walls clench around me.

I wrap my arms around her and hold her tight, capturing her lips in a bruising kiss.

Our woman.

She looks astounding between the three of us.

Mikhail chuckles, and I hear him whisper in Valentina's ear.

"I'm next, *malyshka*, and I promise, I'm a fuck you'll never forget."

CHAPTER 27

VALENTINA

WE EXIT the limo one by one. Despite the fogged-up windows, my men emerge looking sharp and sexy as hell. Ezra is wearing full black, his dark hair slicked back, his jaw set and eyes darker than the midnight sky. In addition to his signature smirk, Mikhail is wearing a deep blue button down with a popped collar, the front buttons open wide to display his tanned chest. His eyes glint gold, like the rings across his fingers. A few tattoos peek out along the edges of his deep V, but they don't hold a candle to the ink wrapped around Ezra's chiseled arms. Andrei's vest is threaded with hints of silver, the heather-gray sleeves rolled up past his elbows, matching the tiniest streaks of silver in his hair.

As we walk the short distance between the limo to the club entrance, people openly swoon, ogling my men with not just their eyes, but their cameras. People pull out their cell phones and snap pictures from behind red velvet ropes.

I had no idea we'd be so popular. If Liam doesn't show tonight, he'll be the only person in the city who doesn't know we're here.

Andrei corrals me forward while Ezra crosses his arms and

scowls at the onlookers, making a gaggle of girls giggle and whisper to each other.

It's not often a man like Ezra exists. I understand the appeal.

But it doesn't mean I have to *like* when others notice.

As my steps linger, Mikhail quickly snakes his arm around my waist as he takes my left side, leaving Andrei to grab my right hand. The pair pulls me forward, leaving Ezra behind to glare at everyone on his own.

A smile plays across Andrei's lips as he takes in my appearance from head to toe. In the limo, he may not have been able to see my outfit, but in the glowing club lights, he can see every freckle dotting my shoulders and feel the press of soft fabric against my curves. While he gets an eyeful, Mikhail wolf-whistles and presses a kiss to my temple.

They all look perfect, while I look like a hot fucking mess. I rake my fingers through my curls and try to tamp them down, desperation burning through my veins. Desperation and *embarrassment.*

Mikhail catches me in the act, and his smile cracks, turning cold in an instant. He grips my hip with bruising force, and as soon as we step through double doors and into a lavish lounge, he swings me around in front of him, catching me before I stumble into the shiny black-tiled wall.

"*Malyshka.*"

I wince. There's not an ounce of playfulness in his voice.

"What *exactly* are you doing?"

I fidget beneath his penetrating stare. "Um. I'm—" *trying not to look like the hot mess that followed you in here* "—fixing my hair."

His nostrils flare. "What makes you think it needs fixing?"

My mouth drops. Were we not on the same steamy car ride just now? "It got a little hot in there, Mikhail. My hair frizzes when it's hot." I try to keep my voice to a whisper, my embarrassment at an all time high.

I felt fine attending the mayor's party, but I hadn't had sex minutes before we arrived. Ezra's cum leaks between my thighs, and my face flames hotter.

Mikhail curves his spine, bending the few inches it takes to meet me at eye level. "Valentina. You are *ravishing*. I don't want you spending a single fucking *second* thinking otherwise." His eyes flash dangerously. "It's an insult. You don't want to insult your men, do you?"

One glance over Mikhail's shoulder proves that both of my other men are watching me closely. Even the *front desk chick* is paying rapt attention.

"No."

Mikhail crooks a single finger under my chin and tilts my head up. "No, you don't. *Unless* . . ." He licks his lips slowly, like he's savoring something sweet. "We need to prove how delicious you are in front of all these people? I think it's Andrei's turn for a taste, don't you?"

My face flushes hotter, the scarlet bloom trailing down my neck and across my chest. I'm already being forced to parade around commando while their cum drips down my legs. What *else* could they possibly do to make this night harder for me?

A heated shiver runs down my spine as I imagine lying flat on my back across the bar, Andrei's dick wedged between my thighs while Mikhail feeds his cock into my mouth and Ezra thrusts between my tits.

Yeah, it could get *way* worse.

"I'm okay," I squeak, pretty sure I might faint if my thoughts continue to spiral. "I don't need a demonstration."

Mikhail grins. "When you change your mind . . ." Splaying his palm across my lower back, he pulls me into his chest. My heart jumps as our lips ghost across each other. "I'll be waiting," he promises, flicking his tongue out to taste me.

A pulse of desire thrums straight to my clit, his promise from earlier still ringing in my ears.

I'm next, malyshka.

He takes a step back and gestures for me to move on. Andrei is waiting at the check-in desk.

When I stumble over to him, Andrei catches me in his arms. "Still nervous?" he asks, quirking an eyebrow. He takes my hand and presses a kiss to my knuckles. "I thought you'd left your inhibitions in the car, darling." His eyes smolder like molten sapphires, and I try, desperately, to get a fucking grip and *not* faint.

If these men don't keep it in their pants, I might die from combustion, and that's not a good look for this city's future queen.

The clerk clears her throat. "Mr. Leonov, is this your guest for the evening?"

"She's a VIP. Diamond tier." He gives the clerk a dazzling smile.

She blinks, pink dusting her cheeks as she returns his smile. Hers is a little more *gooey* than his. "Of course." She reaches over the counter toward me. "May I have your hand, Madame Baranova?"

I blink. I'm not used to being called *Madame*, seeing as that's my grandmother's title. But, I guess that's how people will view me now that Andrei and I have gone public and the previous Bratva leaders have all died or gone into hiding.

The only woman left for the title is me.

I give her my best, practiced smile. "How do you know my name—" I check her name tag. "—Kelsey?"

If my men run this place, I need to learn how to be helpful, starting with keeping up with its staff.

Her smile is patience incarnate. "We've been expecting you, Madame. I apologize for not recognizing you at first. Please, I'll need your scan for VIP access."

Hesitantly, I give her my palm, and she places it on top of a cold, white pad. A light flashes, and with that, she has stored my handprint inside their database.

"Thank you." The clerk smiles again. "Stay as long as you'd like. Our Diamond members have unrestricted access to our facilities. We hope you enjoy your visit."

Andrei takes my hand and leads me into the next room. Past a heavy black curtain, the lounge opens into the heart of the club. Most of the room is taken up by a dance floor, but the wall to our right is entirely devoted to the largest bar I've ever seen, its shelves stacked high with liquors of all shapes and sizes and colors. Soft pink light filters across the room, flickering between silhouettes moving across the dance floor.

Andrei's hand in mine helps dull the sense of overwhelm flooding my system.

Heat at my back makes me glance over my shoulder. Ezra's dark eyes lock on to mine, and what remains of my nerves settles in a heartbeat.

Andrei leads us toward the bar. The moment we approach, both Andrei and the bartender exchange nods. A neat row of drinks appears the next instant, each of my men raising their glasses to their lips and downing the clear liquid in an instant.

I eye my own glass warily. "What is it?"

Ezra grunts and slams his glass down. "Drink."

When I hesitate, he palms the bottom of my glass and tilts it back, splashing the liquid over my lips.

Water. Room temperature water.

As it streams down my chest, Mikhail laughs behind us. I toss him a glare and grab his drink, sniffing its contents.

Their drinks burn with alcohol.

As another round of shots arrives, the men grab theirs before I can snatch one away. As they down their seconds, I down mine.

Water. Again.

I glare at Mikhail's shit-eating grin. They're all in on it, the fucking bastards.

"You have not eaten," Ezra says pointedly, catching onto my ire. "You do not drink."

"If anyone needs a little liquid courage tonight, it's me. *I'm* the one confronting my stalker, here." I cross my arms over my chest. "I don't see any of you confronting your demons."

Ezra downs a third shot. "They live within us, *lisichka*. We do not need confrontation."

"We're best friends with ours, actually." Mikhail wraps an arm around my shoulder and turns me towards the dance floor. "Come, let's find out where yours is hiding, hm? It can't be far."

As I stare out at the sea of bodies, my stomach drops. I've never been out dancing. Even before the wedding, the few lessons I had involved long skirts and practiced movements. None of it involved dancing like *this*. Bodies sashay across the hardwood, some in groups, a few as couples, but all of them in sync with the beat. Many people touch each other freely, moving from group to group, swaying their hips and enjoying the moment.

Nerves flutter across my skin. "I think I'm good back here."

"Nonsense." Mikhail tries to drag me away from the bar, but I snag Ezra's arm as an anchor.

My bodyguard doesn't try to save me. "Do not fear. I will be watching entire time."

With a sharp tug, Mikhail pulls me into the heart of the chaos, with only his hand in mine as my guide. He keeps me close as we weave through the crowd toward a darker corner of the room. The music's softer, the air cooler, the atmosphere more intimate. A few couples linger, but most move on as Mikhail and I claim our temporary home.

He lifts my arm high over my head and spins me, his smile bright as I tumble into his arms. "Get cozy, *malyshka*," he murmurs, "because I'm never letting you go."

My heart skips a beat, pumping faster than the music. "I thought that was Andrei's line."

Mikhail's eyes flash even in the shadows. "We're *all* keeping you, Valentina, whether you like it or not. But I have a feeling you *do* like it." His hand slides across my hip, grazing the edge of my dress. Slowly, he lifts his palm beneath the fabric, brushing my heated skin with his fingertips. "I have a feeling you like it *very* much."

His fingers dip between my thighs, a groan catching in his throat at what he finds there.

My body burns as he wraps his arm around me and cages me against his chest, pressing open-mouth kisses to my neck and panting in my ear. "I can't wait to have you, Valentina. Would you let me fuck you right here? Drag you into a corner and drive my cock inside your dripping wet pussy?" He slides a finger inside my heat and *curls,* hitting just the right spot.

My breath hitches as a wave of pleasure ripples through me. "I thought we were looking for my demons," I whimper.

He drags a knuckle against my walls and nips my sensitive skin. "I might have to share mine with you first."

A shadow falls over us, and Mikhail's attention shifts. His lips downturn in a scowl as he pulls his hand from beneath my dress.

"Behave," Ezra's voice rumbles behind me. "We have audience."

"That's part of the fun," Mikhail says cheekily, thrusting his tongue into the pocket of his cheek. "You can watch while I play with her. You know she'll like it."

A rush of desire leaves my core drenched, and more liquid heat slides down my bare thighs.

I might like that, after all.

Ezra grunts and wraps his arms around my chest, dragging me away from my original captive. "Is that what you want, *lisichka?*"

I wouldn't know how to form the words. Saying *yes, daddy, please fuck me* is still mortifying to imagine.

I wish my drinks were filled with something other than water. Maybe then I could lose myself in the moment, no matter where we are.

Ezra catches me staring out at the crowd and lifts his palm to my face, covering my eyes. "Do not look outside. Focus on me. *Feel* me." With his other hand locked on my hip, he starts swaying us to the beat. Warmth radiates through his body into mine, and I lean into him, resting my head on his shoulder. Beneath the thrum of music, his voice rumbles in my ear. Phrases I can't comprehend fall from his lips, the Russian whispers painting my skin with goosebumps.

"What are you saying?" I reach over my head to touch his face.

His arms lock tighter around me as he continues without pause, stubble scratching against my skin as he peppers his words with gentle kisses along my jawline. I don't know how long we remain wrapped in each other's arms, but the moment of peace is *nice.* My soul soothes as I breathe in Ezra's scent and let him envelop me.

If this is a little piece of forever, I won't mind.

Another person joins us, molding their body to mine from the front. I still can't see, but I recognize the Russian rumble of *Andrei's* voice. He laces our fingers together and lifts my hand to place over his shoulder, taking liberties as he spreads the barest of kisses down my wrist and inner arm.

A third pair of hands joins the others, palms grazing the

curves of my waist, hips, and ass, caressing everything they can touch.

Mikhail, undoubtedly.

Teeth dig into my neck and someone's hand travels lower. I try to guess who it is by feel, but another hand reaches between my thighs to cup my core, and all bets are off. My breasts are squeezed, nipples pinched, ass groped, clit teased. The music fades behind three indomitable Russians murmuring secrets into my skin, weaving love and desire into each reverent caress.

With every beat of my heart, I can feel myself falling deeper and deeper in love with these men.

We become a tangle of limbs as someone drags me in for a kiss. Ezra's palm finally uncovers my eyes, but I can't fathom opening them when someone *grinds* a hard cock against my thigh. My moan is swallowed before I'm able to make a sound. Our sultry seduction continues, with me barely able to come up for air.

Everyone can see us.

That singular thought pierces through the fog of lust, and I snap my eyes open. Across the dance floor, standing directly in a beam of soft blue light, is a familiar face.

A very *tense* ex-boyfriend-slash-boss.

"Oh god," I gasp, carefully detangling myself from my men. "*Ohmygod.*"

"Coming already?" Ezra *tsks.* "We are only getting started, *lisichka.* Come back."

"No, not *that!*" I smack his chest as he tries to pull me back in. "*Liam!* He's here!"

Ezra's entire demeanor changes. "Are you sure?"

I'm struck by the thought that none of my men have ever seen Liam before. Slowly, I nod. "Yeah, he's right over there."

Well, he *was.* Now, he's moved. "Nevermind, he's gone."

"Are you sure you saw him?" Andrei slides up behind me and wraps his arms around my waist.

"You need to let her go, or he will not approach."

Andrei growls, then leans down to whisper in my ear. "Go find him, *zhena*, before I change my mind and kill him for so much as *looking at* what's mine."

"We will be right behind you," Ezra rumbles, squeezing my hip and kissing my hair.

Mikhail wedges himself between Ezra and me and stares into my eyes. "Don't forget who you belong to, *malyshka*, or I will *happily* remind you—" He slides his tongue across his teeth before leaning in and claiming my mouth, sucking my bottom lip between his. "—and force him to watch."

Andrei finally releases me from his arms, and I stumble as I walk off the dance floor. By the time I regain my focus and remember the whole reason we're here in the first place, Liam is nowhere to be found.

Where did he go?

I pick the closest option, spilling into a dark hallway with only the glowing red *exit* sign as my guiding light. The door at the end of the hallway opens, and through the orange glow of streetlights, I spot him slipping outside.

My heels click across the floor, louder with each step I take away from the dance floor. As I approach the exit, my heart-beat fills my ears as adrenaline rushes through my veins.

Here we go. Confronting my stalker psycho ex.

What could go wrong?

Chapter 28

Valentina

I bite my lip as my hands hover over the door lock. I've been thinking of Liam less and less with each day that passes, but every time I catch a flicker of jealousy in Andrei's eyes, I remember.

Liam's in danger too.

He might be a creep, but he doesn't deserve to die by dismemberment. I might be the only one who can save him. I need to convince him to leave town and never come back.

I push open the heavy metal door and stumble into the night. The alleyway is small, ending in a brick wall to my left and the busy street on my right.

Movement out of the corner of my eye nearly makes me scream.

"Liam!"

He steps out of the shadows, the flickering streetlight overhead casting him in an eerie glow. The hairs on the back of my neck rise as he slides his gaze up and down my body.

"What are you doing here?" I ask, taking a step closer. "How did you find me?"

He doesn't answer my questions. "I've been looking all over for you, Valentina."

A chill runs down my spine. If he really took all of those photographs, he isn't lying. If it weren't so fucking creepy, it might be kind of endearing that he cares so much.

"Well, you found me." I laugh awkwardly, trying to wrap my hair in a knot at the base of my neck. "I'm sorry I didn't call. Grandma said you were worried."

He closes the distance between us and pulls me into his arms. "When my best girl goes missing, of course I worry." He takes a deep, shuddering breath. "I thought I'd lost—" He stops himself before he can finish his sentence, every muscle in his body tightening. "You smell like cologne." His grip around my waist tightens. "You smell like *them.*"

I swallow as my anxiety doubles. "I know. I, um, I'm kind of involved . . . with them."

"*Involved,*" Liam repeats, a harsh sigh passing his lips. "It's been ten days since you got here, Valentina. *Ten days.* That's not even two weeks!"

"Things—things have been moving kind of fast." I pull back to try and get some distance, but his grip is tight. I barely get enough clearance to look up at his face without cracking my spine in half from leaning back so far.

Liam's lips press into a thin line. "I can see that." His gaze flickers down to my neck, likely to one of the *many* hickeys I've been given, and shame floods my system at the judgment in his eyes.

"Was that your boyfriend? The tall one, with all the muscles."

I swallow the lump in my throat. "Um. Yeah. Kind of. It's —it's complicated." I push against Liam's chest, but I don't actually get anywhere. "Can you let go? I want to talk to you about this, but you're hurting me."

He's always been gentle in the past. Even when we first

made love, he never rushed me into anything. We didn't just fall into bed together; he was *kind*. He took me on dates and made me laugh and bought me flowers.

By the time I ended up in his bed, we'd already known each other for almost a year. He was a sensual lover, taking things slow and sweet.

Not once has he ever held me like like he could break me in two.

My ribs ache as he squeezes. "Hey. That *hurts*."

Liam grits his teeth. "You've hurt *me*, Valentina. Choosing another man. Choosing *multiple* men, when I've been waiting for you to come home." He rests his forehead against mine, his lips twisting into a grimace. "You let them touch you. I saw it. Another man *kissed* you." His lips brush across my cheek. "You let them *all* kiss you."

There's an edge of desperation in his voice that makes my skin crawl.

"What I do with other men is none of your business—"

Liam *snarls*, fisting my hair and tearing my head back. "You *are* my fucking business, Valentina Violetta Baranova. Five years together, and you *still* don't get it. Every breath you take is my fucking business." His hand wraps around my throat. "Say *thank you, Liam, for coming to rescue me*, and maybe I'll let you sleep in bed with me tonight." His cruel smile bleeds into his eyes, showing me who he really is. Who he's kept hidden all these years.

This is not the man I thought I knew. This is someone else. *This can't be happening!*

I claw at Liam's face in a desperate attempt to flee, and he hisses, spinning us around and shoving my back into the wall. My head *cracks* against the bricks, my vision fading. I drag in a breath, only for Liam's mouth to descend over mine and *steal* it.

This kiss is nothing like the ones we've shared in the past.

Every memory shatters as brutality replaces tenderness, leaving nothing but betrayal in his wake.

My men are right. He's been lying to me this entire time about who he is.

Anger pulses through my veins. How *dare* he. I *trusted* him, gave him my *virginity*, thought he wanted me to be *happy.* I claw his face and dig my nails in deep. He screeches and pulls my hand off of him, slicing my engagement ring across his cheek.

With a howl, he finally lets me go. My knees buckle as I gasp for air.

"Fucking *bitch*," he hisses, pulling his fingers away from the wound. Blood glistens on his skin.

Metal *bangs* against brick as the door to the club slams open against the wall. Ezra barrels through, fists clenched and jaw set, locking onto Liam in a heartbeat. "*You.*" He takes deliberate steps forward and grabs Liam's throat before the man has a chance to speak. "You die."

I watch as Ezra lifts Liam three inches off the ground.

This is the moment where I should stop him. I'm supposed to talk to Liam. I'm supposed to get answers for everything that's happened. The photos from his apartment. His appearance in the city. My grandmother's insistence that he misses me. How the fuck they've been in contact since I left, and *why.*

But the part of me that cared for Liam's safety died the moment he betrayed my trust. "Ezra."

My boyfriend's nostrils flare. Liam's tiptoes scrape the asphalt as he struggles to pry Ezra's fingers loose from his windpipe. "Do not tell me not to kill him," my protector rumbles.

Liam's face turns red as he struggles to breathe. I stare at him, and he stares right back. I feel little remorse, despite knowing that I should. This is *Liam*. I've known him for years. I *should* care what happens to him.

But it turns out, he's a bad fucking guy.

Still. If he dies before I get a chance to interrogate him, this will all have been for nothing. And, there are a few things I'd like to say to him, after all. I swallow, wincing from the pain. "I want to talk to him first."

Ezra grumbles something Russian under his breath. He doesn't let Liam go, but he doesn't strangle him to death with one hand, either.

The club door slams open again, and within seconds, both Mikhail and Andrei are by my side.

Andrei blocks my view of Ezra and Liam, gently turning my head toward him and scanning me for injuries. "Are you dizzy? Nauseous? What should I check for, Ezra?"

"We should have gotten here sooner," Mikhail hisses, storming over to Ezra and Liam. "I *told* you that we should have fucking followed her out here. She should have never been left alone with him!" He glares up at a blinking red dot hanging from the wall, and it takes me a moment to realize it's a camera. Mikhail taps his phone screen before shoving it into his pocket. They must have been watching me from the club's security feed.

"I promised her time to talk," Andrei sighs. "And if you came out here with her, she wouldn't have gotten a single word in." He touches my throat gently, caressing a sore spot. "But it's my fault he touched you. We should have been here. I'm sorry, *zhena*."

I shake my head. I wanted time alone with Liam, he's right. "It's okay. I think I got my answers." I swallow through the throbbing pain in my throat. "But there's something I still need to say. Ezra, drop him."

Ezra doesn't follow directions.

I clench my jaw. That just won't do.

"I *said*, drop him, Ezra. I mean it. Let him go." I don't want to pull rank on my men, but I *am* the only Baranova here. Technically, *pakhan* or not, they all work for me. It's the *Baranova* Bratva. *My* Bratva.

Andrei says something in Russian, a harsh phrase I don't know how to translate, and Ezra throws Liam's body into the brick wall. My ex crumples to the ground like a rag doll.

That makes me cringe. I've never seen a person look so . . . lifeless. Liam gasps for air, choking on his own saliva.

Mikhail crouches in front of Liam, a switchblade glinting in the light as he flicks it open and shut over and over again. "You better talk fast, *malyshka*, because my patience is wearing thin."

With Andrei's help, I walk over to Liam. "We need to talk." I place my hand on Mikhail's shoulder and join him in a crouch. "You can't keep following me, Liam. It's not good for either of us."

"He can't follow you if he's dead," Mikhail mutters, flicking his blade.

I expect Liam to flinch, but he's not looking at Mikhail. He's looking at me.

"I had you first." Liam smiles. At first it's a soft lift of his lips, but then it turns wicked as he glances up my dress. "You'll never forget your first, Valentina. I'll always be right here." He taps his temple. "I'll always be with you. Even when they shove their dirty cocks in your mouth, your pussy will get wet remembering *mine* was there first."

Mikhail strikes fast, plunging his knife into Liam's shoulder. "In your fucking dreams, *mudak*."

Liam grunts from the pain, but his eyes wander back up to my face, like he barely noticed the blade going into his flesh.

Mikhail keeps the knife in, gritting his teeth as he holds it in place. "If I pull this sucker out, it's going right back in again. Talk *fast*, or I swear to God—"

I squeeze Mikhail's forearm and cut him off. He's right. I don't have a lot of time before one of my men decides Liam's time is up.

"You shouldn't have touched me, Liam. I don't belong to you anymore. Really, even that's debatable. We weren't very good at staying together in the first place." I crinkle my nose. We were *very* on-again, off-again, despite what Liam may think. I distinctly remember spending many evenings alone while he was off on business trips. I'd asked to go with him, but the answer was always the same.

Not yet. When you're ready.

I never knew what *being ready* meant. Not that any of it matters now. I shake my head. "I'll be honest, Liam, I came out here to try and save you." I gesture around us. "See these men? They really want to kill you. I was going to tell you to run before they could get the chance. I thought that you deserved a better ending than this." Sighing, I shut my eyes. "Now, I'm not so sure. You fucking *hit* me—"

Someone behind me takes a step closer. I'm not sure who, but I know it isn't good news.

"—so now, I'm wondering if I should even bother being nice. I doubt they'd let you go even if I asked." I take a breath of sour, back-alley air. This really is a shitty place to die.

I was going to ask him questions, but now I'm just *tired.* A man about to die might not have truths to give, anyway, so I could be wasting my breath.

"You've followed me all though the city. You've been *spying* on me since I got here. Maybe even before then." My stomach churns at how long I've known him, how long he could have been watching me. Were those really business trips, or was he watching me through the windows the entire time, jerking off behind a bush while I read a book or drew at my desk?

"Tell me why, Liam. Tell me why you did it. Did my

grandmother put you up to it? Or are you obsessed with me?" My head throbs the longer we sit here. I want to get out of this dirty alley and crawl into a soft, clean bed. Take a bath and scrub the past hour from my memory. Curl up between my men and drift away into a deep sleep.

Anything to forget about Liam fucking West.

Liam laughs, the sound crackling in his throat. "You think they can protect you?" He *tsks*, clicking his tongue against his teeth. "Like they were able to protect your mom?"

My world screeches to a halt.

"What did you just say?"

"They can't protect you like I can, Valentina. They're frauds, pretending they have power over this city. It'll all come crumbling down, and you'll see. You'll know that they can't protect you."

He's talking out of his ass. He *has* to be. It's desperation making him say nonsensical things. He's trying to keep my attention. That's all this is.

"Time to say goodnight," Ezra grunts. "Mikhail. Remove knife. Lift him up."

Andrei pulls me into his arms and holds my back flush against his chest. "Watch, Valentina. This is what we do to people who have wronged you."

Mikhail lifts Liam onto his knees, then stands behind him and plants his foot on Liam's spine, using Liam's arms as anchor points as he leans back and pulls them in the opposite direction, as far as they can go . . . then *farther*.

I can't watch. I turn my face away and clench my eyes shut, wishing I could cover my ears, too, when Mikhail starts cackling at Liam's screams.

Andrei hums, grabbing my chin and forcing my head back around to the front. "Keep your eyes open, darling, or you'll miss a very important lesson. Then we'd have to teach it again, and with a much more fragile subject."

Fear grips my heart. He's talking about my grandmother, a frail old woman who can't fight back. Not that Liam is doing much fighting, either.

"You wouldn't." My voice is barely above a whisper.

"I've told you, *zhena*. When someone wrongs you, we punish them." He buries his face in my hair and takes a deep breath. "Even if you think you love her, she doesn't love you. Not in the way you think. I know it's hard to accept, I know it hurts, but the truth fucking hurts, baby. It doesn't care one way or the other if we bleed."

I choke on a tidal wave of emotion. I feel like a little girl pulling petals off of wildflower, muttering to myself as I pick apart my feelings. *I love him. I hate him.* Right now, I'm not sure which is true. If he makes me watch Mikhail break Liam's arms or Ezra beat him to death, I might hate all three of them, and if they do this to my *grandmother*, not only will my heart shatter into a million pieces, but I might strangle them in their sleep.

"You won't touch her." I reach behind me and grasp the back of Andrei's head, scratching his scalp as I grab his hair and *pull*. "Don't you dare touch her like this. I won't forgive you."

Andrei exhales harshly in my ear. "We'll see if you still feel that way when you finally accept the truth about her."

"*Your* truth. Not mine."

"There is only one truth." He presses his cheek against mine and angles our bodies so that we've got a front row seat to the carnage about to unfold. "Now, *watch*. Don't make me tell you again."

Ezra cracks his knuckles. "Hold him still, Mikhail."

I watch in horrified silence as Mikhail pulls tighter, stretching Liam's body until there's nothing more for it to give. I'm waiting for a *snap* of bone when Mikhail finally stops pulling.

"I made promise." Ezra's voice rumbles low. "Promise to rip out teeth. Shall we begin, hm?"

I don't want to see this. *I don't want to see this.* It's one thing to know Liam might die, but it's another to *witness* it.

"Ezra," I croak, "*please.* Stop."

I've changed my mind. No one deserves to be beaten to death in a dirty back alley, not even my crazy stalker ex-boyfriend.

Ezra's shoulders tense. He doesn't turn around as he speaks to me. "This is who I am, *lisichka.* I punish." He adjusts his posture, spreading his legs with one foot set behind the other. He rocks back for a split second, his fist pulling back with his weight, before he lunges forward, his fist pounding against flesh.

Again and again, he punches.

My scream catches in my throat. I've never witnessed violence before. The closest I ever came was with the photographer in the elevator, and that experience doesn't even come close to *this.*

Ezra's breathing remains steady the entire time, like he's trained for this. *Like this is what he does for a living.*

A piece of my heart breaks for him. No one should have to make violence their specialty. Unlike Mikhail, who's damn near cackling with glee, Ezra looks detached. Disassociated.

I want him to stop more than ever.

"This isn't right," I find myself whispering. "Make him stop, Andrei. Please. Don't make Ezra do this." I turn my begging onto my fiancé. If anyone can make Ezra stop, it's his *pakhan.*

Andrei takes a deep breath but makes no move to intervene. "This is who we are, Valentina. This is what we do." His fingertips brush against my throat idly. "We will always protect you, and we will always punish those who have wronged you."

Liam's words echo in my head.

You think they can protect you? Like they were able to protect your mom?

"He knows something." I grab Andrei's hand on my chin. "*Andrei.* He knows something about my mom. Make Ezra stop. Please."

"I gave you time to talk. Now, it's our turn." My men aren't using their words to talk. They're using their fists.

A weight settles over my heart and a sense of calm fills my mind. If they won't listen to me when I ask nicely or beg for them to stop, then *fine.* I'll stop asking. I'll *order* them.

"Ezra Reinoff, Mikhail Monrovia, release him. *Now.*" I dig my nails into Andrei's wrist. "Andrei Leonov, get your *fucking* hands off me." Adrenaline courses through my veins, making my body tremble. I know Andrei can feel it. I also know that he can laugh in my face and hold me down all he wants.

He is physically stronger than me.

But *I* am the heir to this Bratva, not him. His position as *pakhan* is temporary, if I make it so. He may hold the cards now, but the deck is stacked in my favor, not his.

In the end, I will always win. The Bratva will choose *me* over them if I force the issue, and they fucking know it.

Ezra and Mikhail exchange a look before releasing Liam simultaneously, dropping the man to the ground. His face is swollen and bruised, blood gushing down his crooked nose. He groans in pain, and *hate* flows through me.

I hate that the man I gave all of my firsts to is a fucking creep.

I hate that my men think killing someone is just another day in the office, like this is all *normal.*

I hate that this world speaks with violence before words.

It's going to make my job much more difficult. I don't want to rule over a kingdom of blood and lies.

"We're not killing him. Leave him there, and let's go." If

we don't leave now, *someone* will kill Liam, and I have a feeling it's knife-happy Mikhail who will do it for sport.

Ezra and Mikhail turn to face me. Ezra's face is flecked with Liam's blood, his fists covered in streaks of red. Mikhail's smile is sharp at the edges, like he's enjoying my new play at power *immensely*.

Andrei hasn't followed orders, unlike the other two. "You don't want to take him with us?" My fiancé's lips graze the shell of my ear. "Ezra is a master at interrogation. If you want real answers, *zhena*, he can get them for you."

I grab Andrei's hand as it wanders up my waistline and caresses my ribs. Is he . . . feeling me up right now?

Heat rushes between my thighs, and I clench them together. That should *not* turn me on. This is *so* not the time or place to get freaky.

"I told you to release me."

Andrei listens this time, unraveling his arms and taking a step back. He joins Mikhail and Ezra standing in front of me.

Of the three of them, I didn't expect *Andrei* to follow orders. He's made it very clear that I don't give orders, I take them. But maybe it's time I make my own fucking rules and stop following theirs.

I think of my mother and all the lessons she taught me about being a mafia princess. Stay silent. Do as you're told. Be a good girl and a good wife, and you'll be okay.

I hate to say it, but *sorry, Mom*, those rules haven't done me much good lately, and I don't think they did you any favors, either.

I used to think she was perfect.

Now, I wonder if she was just as scared as the rest of us and trying her best to survive.

My heart aches. I'll never be able to ask her about her life or the choices she made. I'll never know what she thinks of me coming back to the Bratva, or of me taking her place as its queen.

But maybe the truth wouldn't help me, after all. Maybe I'm not meant to follow in my mother's footsteps.

"We're not taking Liam home with us, just so you can kill him behind my back." I give Mikhail a pointed look. "We're leaving him here, and you are taking me home. End of discussion." I cross my arms over my chest. "If I have to walk home in these heels, none of you are sleeping inside tonight."

Ezra exhales slowly and is the first to approach me. "You will not walk home." He lifts me into his arms and holds me bridal style. I have half a mind to tell him *no*, because I've no doubt he's covered in blood, and that's *nasty*. But the gesture is so heartfelt that I melt against his chest.

I don't care if my dress gets ruined. Mikhail can buy me another one.

Andrei meets my eyes, his *pakhan* mask firmly in place. "If we leave him here, Valentina, he could go after your grandmother."

I shake my head. "She can handle Liam. I'm not worried about that."

I *am* worried about Andrei making good on his word of punishing Katya, but that's a problem for tomorrow. Tonight, I want to shower, eat, sleep . . . and maaaybe fuck a little of my frustration out. We'll see how the night goes, first, and who earns a spot in *my* bed tonight.

So far, Ezra's winning.

Mikhail picks up his bloodied knife off the ground and wipes it on his pants. "He could come back for you, *malyshka*."

I know that, too.

"I'm betting on it." I nod towards Mikhail's knife. "Will you buy me a knife of my own, babe? Teach me how to use it?" Next time, I won't be caught off guard. Now that I know who Liam really is, I won't let him so much as *touch* me.

Resignation washes over me like an ocean wave blanketing the shore. This violent world has always been *theirs*, but now, it's becoming *mine*.

I wrap my arms around Ezra's neck. Not just theirs, and not just mine.

Ours.

"Gladly," Mikhail responds immediately, folding the knife closed and setting it in my lap. "You hold onto that. Get a feel for its weight and size, and we'll pick an entire set just for you, love."

Warmth fills my chest. I love when he calls me that.

Finally, Andrei nods. "Okay. Let's go home, boys. Queen's orders." He leans in and claims my lips in a tender kiss, not caring in the slightest that he's doing so right in front of Ezra's face. When he pulls back, he glances up at his right hand man.

They have a silent conversation mere inches apart from each other, and then Andrei takes a step back. Ezra cradles the back of my head in his hand, stealing my attention from my fiancé. "*Lisichka.* I am sorry I did not arrive sooner." Slowly, he closes the distance between us and sighs against my lips. The kiss is just as tender as Andrei's, and it takes my breath away.

How can men so violent be this gentle?

"I will make up to you. I promise."

I cup Ezra's cheek. "I know you will."

Mikhail's turn is next. He grabs my face and pulls me away from Ezra's chest. "That was so hot, when you said my name like that." He licks his lips. "I'm gonna make you scream it for me soon." He brushes a strand of hair from my eyes, his lips twitching into a frown when he glances at my cheek. "When you're healed."

I know Liam slapped me, but I didn't think it left a mark.

A growl catches in his throat, but I don't want to hear any more anger or jealousy tonight. I hold my fingers over his lips to silence him. "Kiss me, Mikhail. Make the pain go away."

He grins and does as he's told, kissing me hard, sweeping his tongue past my lips with a groan.

"*Mikhail.*" Andrei sighs. "For fuck's sake."

Chuckling to himself, Mikhail lets me go with a wink. "We'll finish that later."

None of us give Liam a second glance as we return inside the club. All three of my men lead me back across the dance floor to the front entrance. I know people are looking at us—three impossibly handsome men who can't keep their hands off the same woman, a woman they *share*, for even a second. Mikhail keeps a hand wrapped around my ankle, Ezra cradles me against his muscled chest, and Andrei keeps everyone at bay with a single, sharp look in their direction.

I'm blessed. I'm cursed. Maybe it's a bit of both.

But, blessing *or* curse, in the end, it's all the same.

Love radiates off of my men, strong enough that I can feel it pulsing through the air harder than any bass rumbling from the speakers.

It wraps around my heart and fills my soul with peace.

I love Andrei, I know that, but as I cling to Ezra and catch Mikhail staring at me . . . something shifts into place. A feeling. A sense of belonging. I'm not just Andrei's, I'm *theirs*, and all three of them are going to take care of me in their own ways.

As we settle into the limo, I grab each of their hands and pull them to my chest. "I need to tell you guys something." My heart hammers like a drum. This might be a little fucked up after what just happened in the alley, but—

"I love you." I look at Andrei first, then Ezra, then

Mikhail. "I love *all* of you." In different ways. For different things. But it's love, just the same.

Andrei smiles at me from across the cab. "That's beautiful, baby. I love you, too." He doesn't come closer, but I have a feeling he's giving the others room.

Ezra's hand slides into my hair, and his lips brush my ear. He grumbles, sending tingles down my spine. "You honor me, *lisichka*. I will treasure it."

It's not a love confession, but it melts my heart just the same.

As Ezra kisses my neck, Mikhail grins at me. "You love me too, huh? That's hot."

I roll my eyes. *Also* not a love confession, but if he has more to say, he's saving it for later when we're alone. That's okay. Mikhail's love is the one that scares me the most, and I'm not sure I want an audience when he unleashes it.

Taking a deep breath, I settle back into the seat and let my eyes drift closed. "What do we do now?" Everything feels so fucked up. My loved ones hate each other, with no reconciliation in sight. Liam's been beaten, although it was at least partially deserved for how he handled me. I've got a Bratva to run, but I'm not sure where to start.

Andrei is the one who answers me. "We get married, of course."

My eyes fly open. "You can't be serious. You still want to get married? With everything that's going on?"

"I've always wanted to marry you, Valentina. The circumstances surrounding us won't change that." He smiles at me, displaying a confidence that seeps into my bones and secures my own in place.

"Three days, then." I bite my bottom lip and try not to be nervous. In just three days, I'll marry the current *pakhan* of the Bratva and secure my place as not only his wife, but his *queen*.

It's what I've been waiting for my entire life.

Five years ago, I would have accepted the role blindly. But now, I'm not only accepting my fate, I'm choosing it willingly.

Somehow, that feels like a world of difference.

CHAPTER 29

―――――

VALENTINA

THE DAY BEFORE MY WEDDING, I'm jumping around in a sports bra trying to learn self-defense.

After Liam assaulted me outside the club, my men want to make sure I can defend myself.

I want to make sure I'm never put in that situation again.

"You need to bend knees, *lisichka*. Lower center of gravity, or you will fall over with lightest push." Ezra demonstrates, shoving his palm against my chest with so little effort that it's annoying.

I tumble backward into the padded wall. Sweat drips down my back. We've been working on the same maneuver for thirty minutes, and I'm still struggling with the fundamentals. Spread your feet apart. Bend your knees. Use your opponent's momentum against them. Be quick, or be impossible to push around.

With Ezra as my opponent, it all feels useless. He's a mountain, immobile and hard as rock *everywhere*.

I drag in a lungful of air. The training room is in the back wing of the house, down a flight of stairs, and tucked into a corner next to an underground gym. I didn't know we even *had* a gym, let alone a padded room for martial arts or boxing or wrestling or whatever else people do in here.

That bothers me. I should know this house like the back of my hand after spending my entire life here.

I need to pay more attention. I need to learn all there is to know about the Baranova estate and its surrounding territory. Thankfully, I have three masters to teach me everything there is to know about our Bratva.

"We take break," Ezra grunts, helping me to my feet. He's been just as determined as me during our training, even going so far as to wake up at the break of dawn so that we can get started before the rest of the house wakes up.

Between self-defense with Ezra, shooting and stabbing lessons with Mikhail, and wedding planning with Andrei, I haven't had a moment to breathe.

Ezra watches me closely as I drink from a metal water bottle. "You are tense. It is not good for bride to be stressed."

Kind of hard not to be right now.

A sigh passes my lips. Although I know he's right, nothing is ever that easy. "There's so much I don't know, Ezra. I should be better at all this." I vaguely gesture at our surroundings. "I was raised here. I was born to be a part of this life. But I'm not . . ." I take a breath. "I'm not like you. Or Andrei. Or Mikhail. I'm just . . . *me.*"

A woman who doesn't like to watch people get beat within an inch of their lives. My heart bleeds with others' pain. I'm . . . soft, I guess.

All my men can put up a wall around their hearts when they need to.

I'm not sure that I can.

Ezra sits on a wooden bench and spreads his legs apart. With a grunt, he pats his thigh. "Sit."

Once I'm settled, he holds me in place with a hand on my

hip. "We are all made different. We are all *trained* different. You were raised to be princess, *da?*"

I nod. All my life, I've been told to be *pretty* and *pure* and *silent.* It's not exactly conducive to ruling *beside* a *pakhan* . . . more like *underneath* him.

"I was raised to be killer." Ezra's eyes darken as all traces of light extinguish. He draws into himself for a brief moment, likely drowning in memories of his past.

His *violent* past.

Taking his large hand in mine, I trace the tattoos across his knuckles. The bruising from the other night has mostly faded, but I kiss them, anyway. It's hard for me to imagine Ezra, my quiet, brooding bodyguard, as a man trained for bloodshed.

I hope I never have to see him in action.

"We are trained for different things, Valentina." His voice rumbles deep in his chest. "It is okay. I do not want you . . . like me." His head dips low against his chest as he draws a shaky breath. "You are light at end of dark tunnel."

My heart breaks for this man. Gently, I lift his chin so that our eyes meet. There's a cavern of sorrow etched within, a sorrow so deep that it's impenetrable.

He lifts his palm to my cheek and draws me in. "You are beautiful, Valentina Baranova," he whispers against my lips. "Beautiful enough to drive away darkness. I do not want you to change, but if you do . . . I will love every piece of you. As you are, and as you will be."

He holds me in his arms with the gentle touch of a lover, a killer, a bodyguard, everything at once. Everything he is, and everything we will become.

I taste the darkness in his kiss and let it wash over me, just like he can feel my light. He groans into my mouth and lays me down on the mat, eager for more.

As he kisses down my body, murmuring praise in thick, heavy Russian in between each press of his lips, I stretch my arms over my head and grip the legs of the bench. He parts my thighs and settles his weight between them, sitting up on his knees to press the head of his length against my molten core.

As he claims me with a single, hard thrust, then *again,* and *again,* I find myself repeating the same phrase over and over and over, like a prayer on my lips.

I love you, I love you, I love you.

Ezra responds to each one, matching me word for word and stealing my love, one precious heartbeat at a time.

Afternoon shooting practice goes much the same as the self-defense lessons—poorly.

"You need to be faster with loading the clip."

"I'm *trying.* These things are tiny! I have small thumbs!"

Mikhail takes the magazine from me and loads it within seconds, popping each bullet into place with hard presses of his thumb. "Like this. See?"

I *see,* but that doesn't mean I can *do.*

I cross my arms as he tries to hand the pistol back to me. "Shouldn't I get a gun I actually like?"

"Handguns are the most common ones you'll find. You need to learn to shoot one, then we can move on to the fun alternatives." Mikhail grins at me, still holding the gun out for me to take. "Besides, you look badass with one, *malyshka.* It's sexy as hell."

Ezra grunts from the wall behind us. "Stay focused. We do not have much time until rehearsal."

"What's there to rehearse? Andrei stands at the altar, Valentina waltzes down the aisle with me—"

I roll my eyes. He's been trying to convince everyone that he needs to be the one to walk me down the aisle, since my parents are too dead to do it themselves. "I want to walk alone," I remind him, pursing my lips. "I don't need you to hold my hand."

"But I want to," Mikhail whines. "*Someone* needs to be with you. What if you trip?"

Great. Thanks for the vote of confidence.

I snatch the gun from his hands and turn toward the target. In addition to a gym and sparring dojo, we have a shooting range in a separate building from the main house.

A shooting range. Who the hell has one of those?

As I adjust my posture and steady the gun in my hands, I remind myself that, *oh yeah, my boyfriends do.* Apparently, Andrei found the addition necessary for training purposes, and it was built shortly after I left five years ago.

At least his investment is paying off.

I fire off two rounds. The first one hits the target, but nowhere near the center, and the second whizzes past and hits the sandbags at the back.

"You are not good teacher," Ezra grumbles, walking up behind us. "*Move,* Mikhail."

As they argue over who should be teaching me, I raise the weapon and pull the trigger four more times. Three hits, one miss.

"See? She's getting the hang of it." As I set down the gun on the shelf beside me, Mikhail pulls off my protective earmuffs. The smell of gunpowder fills the air, and I scrub at my nose. I'm not particularly *enjoying* these lessons, but I know they have a purpose. I need to be able to protect myself . . . and my men.

With a sigh, Ezra pushes Mikhail aside so that all three of us are crammed into the tiny booth. "Watch." He reloads the gun in seconds and raises it in front of him, firing off three rounds in quick succession.

I have to squint a little and aim before trying to shoot.

Ezra barely looks before pulling the trigger.

All three bullets hit the target in its paper face, three tiny dots signaling that the target is *way* dead. He pushes a button on the wall beside me and the target zips down the line toward us. My shots are pathetic compared to his.

I lower my hands from my ears and try not to get upset. He's been trained to shoot his entire life, whereas I'm only just beginning.

Ezra catches the look on my face and is quick to cup my jaw with his free hand. Pushing my back against Mikhail, he fills the space at my front, surrounding me with his presence. "You do not need perfect aim. You only need to hit target. Most men take damage and fall to ground. Then you run."

It's a relief that I'm not expected to kill anybody . . .

But what if I have to?

Ezra clicks his tongue. "*Valentina.* You will run. You will *not* fight. Do you understand?"

Arms snake around my waist from behind, Mikhail's voice purring in my ear. "I like it when you run. You're very good at it." He presses a kiss to the curve of my neck. "Run and hide, *malyshka*, and we'll come find you."

Ezra nods, agreeing with Mikhail for once. "Leave killing to us. You can maim, but only to slow enemy down or break away. *This* is the purpose of your training."

"Defense, not offense." Mikhail nips at my shoulder. "We don't expect you to get into trouble. I doubt you'll ever *really* need all of this."

And yet, all three of my men insisted I start self-defense lessons the moment we returned home after the club.

Ezra's phone rings, and as he lifts the call to his ear and steps out of the booth, Mikhail's hands wander. "It's so hot watching you shoot a gun," he groans, cupping my breast and kneading. "I'm gonna need to keep one unloaded under the bed. That way, you can point it at me as you take my cock."

He rolls his hips against my ass, grinding a *very stiff rod* between my cheeks. "*God*, I can't wait to fuck you."

We've been playing a dangerous cat-and-mouse game over the past few days. Now that Andrei and Ezra have fucked me more than once, Mikhail keeps trying to catch me.

"What are you waiting for?" I bite my lip as he lifts my shirt over my tits and tweaks my nipple through my bra.

He chuckles deep in the back of his throat, and the sound goes straight to my clit. I shouldn't be so turned on by this, especially not here, but there's something about these men that makes me come undone.

His free hand dips below the waistband of my pants, and he shoves his hand into my panties. My back arches as he brushes his fingers against my lips, avoiding the *very* sensitive nub aching for his touch. With a *hiss*, he pushes the flat of his palm against my pubic bone to hold me still as he grinds his cock harder into my ass.

"I'm waiting," he growls, sinking his teeth into my shoulder so hard that it *stings*, "for tomorrow night. I want to tear your wedding dress off your body and fuck you *hard*. No, *in* the dress," he corrects suddenly, sliding two fingers inside my heat as he says it. With a groan, he pulls my bra down and grabs my breast, squeezing hard. "*Fuck*, I can't get over the thought of you begging for my cum. Wearing white inside *and* out."

Ezra's eyes narrow as he realizes what we're doing right in front of him. He says something in Russian to whoever he's on the phone with and puts the call on speaker. "Say hello to your husband, *lisichka*."

Oh, God.

"Not married yet," Mikhail snickers, shoving his fingers deeper inside me. As he plays with my pussy, the wet, slick sound of his fingers plunging in and out fills the booth.

Ezra wedges the phone in my cleavage, holding the mic close enough to my face that Andrei can hear me pant.

There's a slight ruffle of fabric coming through the speaker. "Valentina. Tell me how your training's going." There's a hard edge to Andrei's voice. "In *explicit* detail."

Ohgod, ohgod, ohgod.

"Um. It's fine."

Ezra leans over and draws me in for a heated kiss, parting my lips with his tongue with a groan.

I know Andrei can hear the wet smack of our kiss. The way I moan into Ezra's mouth as Mikhail *finally* swirls his wet digits over my clit.

"Valentina. *Now.*" Andrei's breath is harsh as a zipper opens.

What is happening—

Ezra releases my mouth only to move lower, taking my nipple between his lips and sucking hard.

"I—*ah*—I hit the target." Another moan, this time because of Ezra's *teeth*. "And, um, Ezra tried to show me how to aim better—" My eyes roll back as he drags my pants below my hips and undoes his own, notching his cock between my thighs and thrusting. The angle isn't right for him to slip inside, but the glide is smooth from how *wet* I am. "He's really good at—*ahh*—aiming."

Another belt comes undone, and all of a sudden, I have *two* cocks wedged between my thighs. Mikhail pushes against my lower back to bend me at the hips for a better angle and thrusts, grunting hot and heavy as he glides between my lips. Not inside, but *right there.*

Ezra's cock grinds against my clit from the front, and I can't stop the sharp cries tearing from my throat. Pleasure rolls through my body with every move my men make. I'm drenched and aching, and I *really* want someone to fuck me already. "A-Andrei," I whimper, "I wish you were h-here." I dig my nails into Ezra's shoulders as he lifts me off the ground and holds me in place between the two of them.

Mikhail grinds against my pussy while Ezra grabs my hips and holds me down, forcing me to take it. He makes quick, shallow thrusts, rubbing the head of his cock against my clit. Pleasure zings up my spine, and I know I won't last much longer.

The phone clatters to the ground.

No one bothers picking it up.

"I can't wait to bury my cock inside you, *malyshka*." Mikhail groans in my ear. "You're *drenching* me. *Fuck*. If I just —" He slides the tip inside and shudders.

Ezra takes over, lightly bouncing me on Mikhail's tip, up and down, in and out. We all moan in unison as I come without warning, my walls squeezing tight, my body trembling in Ezra's arms. Mikhail hisses, his hot seed shooting against my pussy. He rubs it in with his pulsing cock, spreading it all over and between my lips. "So close," he groans, falling back against the wall. "Soon, *malyshka*, soon. I promise."

Tilting my head back, he kisses me deep.

Footsteps pound the concrete floor, and I open my eyes to find Andrei storming toward us. His eyes flash like blue lightning. "*Zhena* . . ." Biting his lip, he fists his cock through his slacks. "Fuck, baby, you look like sin. Your skin's all flushed, and your pussy's dripping."

I can feel my desire sliding down my thighs, Mikhail's cum only making everything worse. *I'm a mess.* A gushing, hot mess.

And I want more.

I hold my hand out for Andrei.

He curses in Russian. Taking another step closer, he blocks the only exit and grabs my face in his hands. "You need a good fuck, don't you, darling?"

"Yes."

Ezra lowers me to the shelf, knocking the box of ammo and the empty gun to the floor. It's not deep enough for me to fit, so I hang off the edge. The wood cuts into my ass, but I don't have time to complain before Ezra lifts my left leg higher, Mikhail doing the same to my right. They bend my knees close to my chest, leaving me spread open for all to see.

Andrei settles between my thighs and my eyes widen at how thick he is. Swollen and ready for me. He smacks his cock against my pussy, and I *whine.*

"Don't forget to breathe, *zhena.*"

He thrusts, sinking into me completely, stretching me wide and bumping my cervix. It *hurts* and steals the air from my lungs.

"Breathe," he commands, sliding out and thrusting harder.

Black spots dance in my vision.

Ezra watches my face, a scowl on his scarred lips. "She cannot take it all at once."

"She can." Andrei leans over and plants his hands on either side of the divider, digging his heels in to bury himself inside me. He thrusts deep, never fully pulling out before snapping his hips again. "She can and she will."

Mikhail hums in the back of his throat, dragging his fingertips across my lips. He parts them and shoves two fingers inside. The same ones that were buried in my cunt minutes ago.

I gag on the intrusion, but it forces air into my lungs.

"Atta girl," Mikhail purrs, removing his fingers and patting my cheek. "You've gotta breathe, *malyshka.* It's no fun if you pass out."

Andrei drags his cock against my walls, and my head lolls back. At least this time I remember to breathe. Short, shallow, *breathy* pants, but at least I won't black out. My pussy clings to his cock, and I whimper as pleasure builds slowly, each pulse of his head against my cervix sending a rush of pleasure-pain through me. I clench around him each time, drawing out a heavy groan from my fiancé's throat.

Mikhail holds his palm over my heart, enjoying its erratic beat. "*Mmm.*" He plucks my nipple with his other hand, chuckling when my pulse jumps at the pulse of pleasure it sends to my clit.

Ezra grips my thigh. "Once you are ready, *lisichka*, Andrei will fuck your pussy while I fuck your ass." He rubs his still-hard cock against my thigh, a muscle in his thick, tattooed neck jumping. "Have you ever played with your ass?"

I meet his eyes and his lips curve into a slow smile. "She has not." Reaching under me, he grabs my ass, dragging my body higher. Andrei's next thrust hits a new spot inside me, and I gasp as white-hot pleasure nearly tips me over the edge.

"Do you want to try it?" Ezra asks, his eyes liquid black. His hand dips between my cheeks, nearing my back entrance. "You're already wet here too."

His fingers are warm, his calloused palm rough against my skin as he kneads my cheek. I love feeling all of their hands on me, and I have a feeling I'll love their cocks even more.

Biting my lip, I nod to give him permission.

Slowly, he rims my asshole with one of his fingers, applying enough pressure that I can *feel* it, but not pushing inside. It sends another wave of pleasure pulsing through me, and I shudder. My pussy clenches at the new, exciting sensation, and Andrei curses under his breath. "*Fuck*, she likes that."

"I knew she would," Mikhail rasps, nipping the top of my breast. "She's a dirty girl for her men."

That makes me even wetter. Andrei starts pumping faster, his balls slapping against my flesh. "I'm gonna come," he growls, "and you better fucking come with me." With a roar, he buries his cock inside me. The force of it pushes me back on Ezra's finger, and I'm *so full.* Ezra rolls his finger inside my ass, and I come with a *scream,* clenching around both my men.

Ezra's cum paints my thigh as he grinds against my leg, with Andrei's seed gushing around his cock as he thrusts lazily, drawing out my shockwaves of pleasure.

"Breathtaking," Andrei groans, lowering his forehead to mine. "You're *breathtaking,* Valentina." He kisses me gently while the others lower my legs to the ground. Andrei helps me land on my feet and holds me steady.

I'm a complete fucking mess. Swollen lips. Mussed hair. My pants—where the hell are my pants?

"You look thoroughly fucked," Mikhail muses, licking his lips. "*Mmm.* A perfect preview of tomorrow night."

Each of my men gives me a quick kiss and helps me redress. Someone picks up the ammo and gun, too, and within a few minutes, it's like nothing happened.

Andrei straightens his tie, and I catch sight of the sweat glistening on his neck. My thighs clench as I have the sudden urge to lick it off. He catches my eyes on him and smiles brilliantly. "We can have round two later, darling. Right now, we're needed for our wedding rehearsal." He holds his hand out for me. "Come. We'll be late if we don't hurry."

The four of us leave the range, smelling of sex and sin. Andrei is the only one wearing a suit, but it does nothing to dampen the hungry look in his eye. If anything, it exacerbates it, and I'm blushing through the entire rehearsal as he stares at me nonstop.

While we're standing at the altar together, he pulls me in for a kiss before the priest has finished giving instructions. "I've been waiting five years for this," he murmurs against my lips. "To make you mine. To *finally* have you." His hand comes around my throat, and he squeezes, a possessive curve to his lips. "No one will take you from me ever again. *No one.*"

He devours my lips, holding me in place with his hand on my neck and his claws snared in my heart.

Any sane woman would run.

This kind of possessiveness isn't normal.

But I'm powerless under the weight of it, drowning every time it appears.

I'm not afraid of it. Of him. Of any of them.

I let them consume me, because I want to be consumed. I want to be devoured. I want to be theirs.

And tomorrow, I will be.

Forever and always, *theirs*.

CHAPTER 30

VALENTINA

STARING at my reflection is surreal. I've tried the dress on half a dozen times now for Celia to make alterations, but seeing it for real, with the lacy veil draped down my back, the golden embroidery woven throughout, the hints of glitter across my cheeks . . .

It's *surreal.*

I look like a princess. Like the one I was promised to become. Only, not like the one I was five years ago. Something bolder. Better.

I suck in a breath and stare at my reflection. The dress is definitely bolder than my last one. The deep V cut accentuates my cleavage, while the cinched waist highlights my hourglass figure. The skirt doesn't flare out until my thighs, meaning that my full hips are on display. It's unapologetically sexy and makes me feel like a goddess.

Celia comes around to my front with the tube of lip stain in her hands. "I'm *telling* you. They won't be able to keep their hands off you. Mikhail's been trying to sneak a peek at your dress for days. When he sees you, he's going to go feral. They *all* will." She dazzles me with the Monrovia signature smile as she applies a final coat of red to my lips. "I'm jealous." Her smile turns a little sad before she catches herself. "But in the *best* way. You have to tell me all about tonight when I see you next. And your *honeymoon!* Where are you going? *Oh! Don't tell me! Let it be a surprise."

I don't actually think there's going to be a honeymoon, but I don't have the heart to tell Celia. Let her dream.

It beats the reality of knowing that we might be having a wedding *and* a funeral.

I pick at my cuticles while we wait for the ceremony to start. My grandmother is here somewhere. I know she is. But what's her plan? Is she going to sit in the front row as my only living relative left? Will she burst into the church and object to the ceremony right as Andrei and I are about to say *I do*? Have my men already found her and tied her up, or *worse*, put a bullet between her eyes and shoved her into a broom closet?

Celia snaps her fingers in front of my face. "Hello? Beautiful bride? You in there?"

I force a smile as Celia comes back into focus. "I'm sorry, were you saying something?"

She gives me a skeptical look. "We have your something borrowed—" She taps the gold bracelet on my wrist that she let me borrow. "Something new—" The teardrop diamond necklace Andrei surprised me with is cool against my neck. "Something old—" The pearl hairpin holding up my French braid was my mother's. "But your something blue. Didn't we have a ribbon or something?"

I glance down at my bare feet. Mikhail tried to get me to wear pale blue heels, but I declined, insisting that my gold pedicure would look best on display. "I was going to wrap a blue ribbon around my ankle, yeah." It's not the most traditional, but it'll give me a little pop of color in the place of shoes. "It's okay if we can't find it. I don't need it."

It's not like I believe in superstition, anyway.

Celia gasps melodramatically. "Of course you do! Something blue is the most important! It wards off evil." She squeezes my hands with her own. "Don't worry, I'll go find something. I'm sure there are *plenty* of people out there who would love to give their *pakhan's* bride something blue to wear. I'll be back in a jiff."

"No, really, it's okay—"

The door clicks shut behind Celia, and she's gone just like that.

I resist the urge to bite my lip and ruin my lipstick. "Well, here we are again, Valentina. Alone on our wedding day." I turn back to the mirror and brush my palm down my bodice, smoothing any imaginary wrinkles. The gold embroidery is beautiful, a finishing touch that Celia insisted on. It curves around my waist like vines, weaving down into the skirt, with touches of gold petals falling like snow around them.

The dress *feels* magical.

I feel magical. Like I'm glowing.

I wish my mom were here to see it.

The longing *aches*, and I brush a stray tear from my eye. Even if she's not here in person, I know she's in every stitch of this dress. Golden roses were one of her favorite things, and I specifically requested they be incorporated into the design in her honor.

As another tear falls, I slip into the bathroom to check the damage. Celia spent an hour on my makeup, insisting that she do it all herself as part of the whole design package, and I'll be damned if I mess it up.

Once I reapply mascara and dry my eyes, I step back into the dressing room. "Celia, are you back yet?"

I'm met with silence, and anxiety creeps up my spine. It has to be time for the ceremony to start. Where did she go?

As I breeze past the mirror, a light flutter of white catches my eye. I turn my head to find a tiny, folded slip of paper sitting on top of a high-back chair. It almost looks like a makeshift throne . . .

. . .and it wasn't there before.

Neither was the stationery.

"Celia?" I take a tentative step toward the note. "Did someone leave this for me?"

I remember the note Mikhail wrote me when he brought me all those clothes. Looking around, I don't see any shoe boxes holding pale blue heels or miscellaneous gifts left behind.

It's just a chair and a note.

As I approach, I catch a glimpse of myself in the mirror. A shiver runs down my spine at how familiar this is.

The last time I opened a letter . . . things did *not* end well.

But the hope that one of my boyfriends has left me a heartfelt message before the ceremony makes me giddy and light. I pick up the paper and flick it open.

Smile, moya zhena.

A light flashes behind me, and I spin around in surprise. "What's going—"

The letter falls from my fingertips.

Liam's smile looks *painful*, the skin around his eyes mottled purple and yellow from healing bruises. His nose, once perfectly straight, has a freshly scarred crook in the middle. *But his eyes.*

Those are the same as they've always been. Intense and unyielding.

And he's looking right at me.

"Liam, you need to leave." My voice shakes, and I clench my fists tight by my sides to keep them steady. I don't have a gun. I don't even have a knife; we ordered a custom set that won't arrive for a few more days. I'm defenseless. *Again.*

It's starting to get old.

"If they catch you here—"

Liam steps toward me, and if it weren't for the bruised and battered look on his face, he'd look every bit a gentleman. Like a husband reaching for his bride. His suit is immaculate, pitch black with golden cufflinks that match my jewelry.

I step back quickly, and his smile twitches. "Valentina, come here. I have a wedding gift for you."

"I'm not accepting gifts, sorry."

He tilts his head to the side, and a shiver runs down my spine. "Not even this?" He unfurls his hand to reveal a pretty blue ribbon, the same one Celia and I were missing. "It's something blue. I saved it just for you."

"Stole it, more likely," I snap, my patience wearing thin. "Look, I know we had our fun in the past, but I'm not interested anymore, okay? I thought you understood that after what happened last time." I grimace at the nasty bruises covering his face. "Please leave before someone sees you."

The ribbon floats to the floor, and he stomps on it as he continues his approach. "Or what? Are your boyfriends going to beat me again?" His expression sours, and I step around the furniture sprinkled around the room to keep some distance between us.

If I can just get to the door—

"*Don't look away from me,*" Liam snarls, and I lunge for the exit. My fingertips snag the handle just as Liam snatches my veil. He *pulls*, tearing the veil from my head and taking some of my hair with it.

I cry out in pain as Liam drags me farther back into the room. My heart pounds as adrenaline courses through my veins.

Remember your lessons, remember all the self-defense!

I claw at Liam's arms, but it's no use. His jacket is too thick to penetrate, and when I reach behind me to, *I don't know*, shove him in front of me, he bites my neck.

I screech in pain and try to smack him in the head, and he laughs as he drops me to the carpet.

"You used to like it when I bit you," he sneers, "or does *he* do it better? Your *fiancé?*"

"Go to hell." I kick at him..

He snags my bare ankle and *yanks*, dragging my ass across the floor toward him. The carpet burns my skin, but I'm too focused on getting the fuck away to care. I grab the first thing I find—Celia's purse—and throw it at Liam.

It bounces off his face, and he growls. "Your bruises have faded, Valentina, but don't worry. I'll give you new ones."

I break a nail on the carpet as he drags me closer. "Fuck you! Get off me!" The chair topples over as I try to grab on to something, and the mirror falls next. Glass shatters like cracking ice, slicing into my skin.

Liam hisses as one of the larger pieces nicks his calf, cutting through his slacks and making him bleed. "*Fuck!* Why do you have to be so difficult!" He snags my hair and pulls me up onto my knees. Something silver flashes through the air in an arc, and a sharp *stab* hits my neck. I try to scream, but no sound comes out. The room starts to spin, and I groan as my muscles go slack.

"That's it," Liam huffs, tossing a syringe out of his hand. "Go to sleep, *moya zhena*. You'll feel better once we're home."

Home. I think of my room at the estate. Andrei's bed. Mikhail's warm arms. Ezra's shower.

Nothing about *home* screams Liam *fucking* West.

The last thing I feel is rage pumping through my heart.

My boyfriends will make Liam bleed for ruining our wedding. And if they don't, *I fucking will.*

CHAPTER 31

VALENTINA

My body rocks back and forth with the ocean tide, rushing out across the shore as the waves spill over, only to be gently pulled back into the surf. An endless, weightless lullaby.

This dance continues for hours, and the longer I'm there, the more painful it becomes.

Sand scratches my skin, burning my knees; shells scrape my palms, making me bleed. The crashing waves fill my head with noise. So much noise, like buzzing static. Like *bees*, pricking my body in anger, *so much anger*, rolling through me in hot waves, thick and heavy and—

I gasp in a breath and moan.

Heavy. My body is so *heavy*.

I try to open my eyes, but I can't. Each beat of my heart brings a new rush of pain to my chest, pounding, pounding, *pounding—*

"You didn't have to maim her."

The voice is familiar. Pinched. Female. Critical. Stern.

"She didn't have to fight so damned hard."

"That's your fault for not securing her sooner. You let her slip through your fingers. *Five years*, I gave you." The woman says something in a harsh Russian dialect, clicking her tongue like a disapproving mother.

Or a disapproving grandmother.

My eyelids flicker as I try to open them. The pain intensifies as I drag in a lungful of air.

"Ah. She's waking up."

Weight by my side makes the floor dip.

A cold hand brushes hair from my face. "*Ditya.* It's time to wake up now. We have much to do and not a lot of time. Come, now."

"The drugs won't wear off that fast."

Katya Baranova snaps back in Russian. It's a word I know well.

Silence.

Her hand strokes my hair, and she makes a soothing sound, almost like a mother would for their sick child. "Come now, Valentina," she repeats gently. "We've a wedding to attend."

A wedding. *My* wedding.

I force my eyes to open through the pain. Everything's fuzzy, and the light is *so bright.* A groan passes my lips, nausea rising like bile in the back of my throat.

My grandmother rubs my back in small, soothing circles. "There, there. It's okay, *ditya.* The danger has passed. You're safe now."

"Is he gone?" My throat's raw and scratchy, and I swallow as best I can.

"Yes, he's gone, *ditya.* He won't be able to lay a finger on you ever again."

Good. I never want to see Liam's face ever again. I'll gouge his fucking eyes out and shove his bleeding dick down his throat.

Rage fuels me. I blink rapidly to clear my vision.

Liam's *fucking* face, bright purple and sickly yellow from

bruises struggling to heal around a freshly-broken nose, is right in front of me.

I scream.

I can't move my arms, or I'd strangle the motherfucker.

"What—is—he—" I gasp for air between each word. "—doing—here?"

Katya sighs and rises from the bed. "He's your *husband*, Valentina. Honestly."

My *what?*

Bile rises fast, and this time, I vomit.

This has *got* to be a fucking nightmare.

Liam rushes to the bathroom for a wet rag and wipes my mouth.

Yeah, definitely a nightmare.

"It's okay," he says gently, "you're coming down from the meds. It'll take a minute. Try to relax. Breathe."

I choke on my anger as he presses a second, damp cloth to my forehead. "Even now, you're still *beautiful*, Valentina." He presses a cool kiss to my forehead. "Don't worry about your dress. We'll have it cleaned."

I force my head to the side, scratching my cheek against the blankets. I'm on a bed, I realize, face down on a *fucking* bed that isn't my own.

My dress is ruined. Slashes have ripped the top layer to near shreds, and blood is splattered across the bottom. My heart breaks, and hot tears fill my eyes.

Not again. Not this time.

Another wedding *ruined.*

Panic helps clear the fog in my mind. "Where are they?" I push myself up onto my elbows, and Liam helps me sit upright.

I hate the bastard, but I'll kill him later. Right now, I need answers.

"Where is Andrei? Ezra? Mikhail?"

Where are my men?

Katya's eyes pierce my heart like daggers of ice. "Gone, Valentina. They're gone, and they're never coming back."

"You're lying," I croak, pins and needles shooting up my arms as I regain feeling in them. I clench my fists hard enough that my nails break the skin. I cling to the pain to keep me awake and alert. "They'd never leave me."

And you couldn't kill them if you tried.

She lifts her chin, and I'm suddenly reminded of all the times I've witnessed the former matron of the Baranova line wield her power.

This is one of them.

"They would if their princess left them first. If you disappeared at the altar, just like you did five years ago." Her green eyes, mirrors of my own, darken dangerously. "Only this time, it will *truly* break them. They'll be too weak to do anything but grieve the loss. For that, I am grateful to you. You've wrapped them around your finger, *ditya,* and that's no easy feat for men like them."

She's underestimating them. "My men are *strong*. They won't give up so easily."

Her eyes narrow. "They will once they understand that you've made a choice. A different choice. A *better* one." She clasps her hands around a metal cane. I don't know that I've ever seen her carry one before, and it's bizarre enough that I go silent.

She takes my silence as acceptance, a smile spreading across her thin lips. "Our lives are going to be so much better now, Valentina. You'll see."

Liam's hand rests on my thigh like a leaden weight, and I scowl at him. "Don't touch me," I hiss, smacking him away.

The look in his eye changes from soft admiration to heated anger in an instant. "Watch your tone, *zhena,* or I might lose my temper."

The word *zhena* became one of my favorites when Andrei said it to me. Now, it sounds vile.

"Go ahead."

I shouldn't egg on a crazy man, but I can't help it. My adrenaline's still pumping, and the bitter taste of fury is really tough to swallow.

He smiles, but it doesn't reach his eyes. "You've gotten mouthier, haven't you? We'll have to work on that."

"Go to hell—"

Pain flashes across my cheek, my head whipping to the side. I clutch my cheek as my rage doubles. Tears fill my eyes, but I'm not upset. I'm *pissed*.

Liam just fucking *hit* me.

With a sigh, he stands from the bed. "You were perfect, Valentina. You just *had* to let them corrupt you, didn't you?" He slides his suit jacket from his shoulders, and I get a glimpse of muscle that wasn't there a few weeks ago. He's been working out, likely feeling inferior since I dumped his ass.

He'll never be as jacked as Ezra, but it's almost cute that he tries.

"She will learn quickly," my grandmother interjects, gripping the tip of her cane tight. "It's in her blood to obey, Donovan. It's your job to remind her of that."

Liam's nostrils flare, but he nods and says *yes* in Russian. I didn't even know he *spoke* Russian.

And who the fuck is Donovan?

"I will go speak with the chaplain. Make sure she is ready by the time the music starts. We cannot have any more delays." My grandmother leaves the room without a second glance in my direction, and I'm left alone with my betrayer.

"You kidnapped me."

He pulls up a chair from a nearby table and sits on it backward, draping his arms across the back. "You should have come with me when I found you at the club. This would have been so much easier then. We wouldn't have to rush things. You know I hate to rush."

I force my legs to work as I swing them over the side of the bed. Standing, I lean against the wall for support as I walk across the room. Anything to get *away* from this man.

His jaw tics as he watches my poor attempt at escape. "Where do you think you're going?"

I don't answer and pick up the pace, the soles of my feet screaming at me with each tender step.

His chair tumbles to the floor as he jumps to his feet and snatches my wrist. I try to pull myself free, but it's no use. I might as well be manacled.

Liam's eyes ripple like storm clouds. "I only wanted you, you know. That was enough for me. I didn't care about the city. Or the crown. Or the money." He laughs, the sound bitter enough that I recoil instinctively.

He doesn't find *that* funny at all.

His grip tightens, pulling a pained whimper from my lips. "But then your *boyfriends*," Liam hisses, "had to make it *personal.*"

I jerk my head away when he tries to touch my cheek. He's not amused, gripping my face tight enough that his fingers dig into my skin, slicing jagged cuts across my cheek. He licks his lips and lowers his mouth to my new wounds, licking them too, tasting my blood on his tongue. A shiver rolls down his spine.

I think I might be sick again.

"Now I'll take *you*," he promises, his words a slow, deliberate rasp, "and then I'll take their city, and their throne, and all their fucking money."

The man is crazy. No one can take on my men and survive. Hell, he nearly got his face smashed in the last time he ran into them. "If you touch me, they're going to hunt you down. They'll tear you to pieces. They'll *kill* you."

My heart sings at the thought, but I'm too far gone to question it. I'm too far gone to care.

"This time, I won't stop them," I vow solemnly. "Not after this. Not after what you've done."

Liam shakes his head, a smile playing on his lips. "Oh, *zhena*, I won't be caught off guard twice. I've learned my lesson." His iron grip on my wrist keeps me locked by his side as he drags me to the door. "It's time you learned yours."

The door opens to a small chapel. I recognize it as one of the venues Andrei listed as a possibility for our wedding. The room is packed just as full as the real church, only this time, I don't recognize as many faces. A few of them, I do, but not enough for them to matter.

"What is this?"

Liam drags me down the aisle as the Wedding March plays, his grin wickedly confident as we make it to the end. "It's our wedding, *zhena*. Now, smile for all our friends and family."

He dips me without warning, and his kiss is *fierce*. I have to cling to his shoulders for fear I might faint, and he takes that as encouragement to swipe his tongue against my lips.

The crowd cheers and claps, and all I want to do is scream.

This is a nightmare. And I'm scared I won't wake up anytime soon.

Chapter 32

Andrei

I can't explain how I know. A sense of foreboding déjà vu washes over me as I stare out at the crowd, all of us awaiting my bride's march down the aisle.

A pang in my gut makes my stomach clench.

Ezra stands still as a stone to my right, Mikhail fidgeting to my left. All three of us await our bride, but something's wrong.

We haven't left her side for long. She insisted, saying that it was bad luck for the grooms to see her before the ceremony. Otherwise, we'd be right there with her in the dressing room.

We can't give her an inch of space, or we'll forget how to *breathe*. She's become our oxygen—essential for life.

Without her, I . . .

"She is late." Ezra's scowl cuts deep.

"She'll be here in a moment." Mikhail breathes easily, his voice lilting on the lie he tells himself.

Anxiety curls in my chest, foreign and unwelcome.

I take the three quick steps off the platform and down the

aisle, ignoring the hushed whispers of the crowd. Mikhail and Ezra flank me, moving just as quickly.

By the time we reach the double doors at the back of the church, Celia's panicked face peeks through the crack between them.

Mikhail stops to question or soothe her, whichever is necessary, but I don't stop moving.

I can't.

The walk to Valentina's dressing room is quick. The hammering of my heart propels me forward in a rush, and I burst through the door with Valentina's name hovering on my lips.

The first thing I see is blood.

Not a lot, but enough to raise the hair on my arms. Crimson drops paint the beige carpet, with some larger patches smeared across.

Like someone injured was *dragged*.

Ezra starts investigating the scene, crouching to check not just the bloodstains, but the debris scattered around the room. Glass mirror shards sprinkle the floor like snow, crunching under our feet.

I pick up Valentina's ripped veil, cursing at the strands of hair tangled with it.

Someone hurt my wife.

That someone is going to die a very painful, very *slow*, death.

Ezra whips out his phone and rattles off orders to his team, a group of enforcers and bodyguards threaded throughout the city. Most of them are here today, but a few are still out. "Find her," he demands, "and if there are any turncoats in our ranks, slit their fucking throats."

He doesn't usually give kill orders too easily. I glance up at him, taking in the stiff set of his shoulders and the way he glares at the blood on the floor.

"Ezra."

Turning his eyes to mine, he releases a held breath. "Yes, *pakhan?*"

Ezra is my oldest friend, my longest one, and a true brother to me. Titles don't always matter when it comes to him. "We will get her back. I promise."

It's not easy for Ezra to love. He's watched love tear apart families and force powerful men to do reckless things. It's a weakness, one so cutting that it makes it impossible for him to do his job as an enforcer.

You can't destroy things you love. You can't feel for your enemies. If you do . . . *you die.*

Knowing him, he's feeling the weight of Valentina's absence just as strongly as I am.

He takes a deep breath. "I should have crushed that *suka's* face beneath my fists."

I shake my head and place my palm on Ezra's shoulder. "No. She wouldn't have forgiven you."

"At least she would be *here.*"

I can't argue with him on that.

Mikhail charges through the door next, his fury written all over his face. "Celia found this." Thrusting a wad of crumpled paper in my hands, he starts pacing around the disheveled room. "That *fucking bastard* was here. I *knew* I shouldn't have let her out of my sight. I just knew it." His shoulders shake as he throws a picture frame across the room. Its glass shatters and frame cracks, crashing to the floor in a mess of broken pieces. Mikhail crumbles with it, crouching low and hanging his head between his knees. He takes deep lungfuls of air.

The slip of paper in my hands is delicate, ripped in multiple places from Mikhail's rough handling. With careful restraint, I pull it open and flatten it across my palm.

Smile, moya zhena.

As fury roars in my veins, Ezra grunts and grabs something

from beneath a shard of glass. He holds up the tiny square to the light, his eyes narrowing at what he finds.

When he holds it out for me, I trade him for the piece of paper.

Both of us curse at the same time.

It's a polaroid picture, taken while Valentina stares at her reflection in the mirror. She looks perfect, golden and glowing and royal.

Caught in the mirror's reflection is the *mudak* who stole her from us. Face purpled with ugly bruises. A triumphant grin pulling across his lips. Stealing a precious moment from our bride and claiming it for himself.

Claiming *her*.

I throw the photo to the ground and lift my foot to grind it beneath my heel. Hesitation hits, and with a frustrated growl, I snatch the picture back up.

We didn't hire a photographer for today. We didn't want to bring more attention to Valentina, in case someone like *Liam* was still lurking about.

I hate that we were right.

I hate that our caution didn't amount to anything.

Now, this is the only picture we have of our bride.

Walking over to Mikhail, I tap his shoulder.

He lifts his head, a painful sound catching in his throat. When he notices the photograph, he snatches it from my fingertips.

"*Malyshka,*" he breathes, shooting back to his feet in an instant. "I will find you."

As the three of us leave the room, my shoe kicks something small out of the way, the tiny glass object *tinking* against the doorframe.

We all notice it at the same time—a tiny syringe.

"Take that to the lab," I order, fierce chills running down

my spine. I have no doubt what they'll find, and it makes me sick to my stomach.

"That bastard's going to pay," Mikhail hisses through clenched teeth, "but more importantly, how the *fuck* did he get inside the chapel?" He whips around the hallway, glaring at every single staff member in sight. Everyone was properly vetted. People who have been loyal to us for years. A few loyal to the family.

Katya.

I rub the back of my neck as shooting pain hits the base of my skull. Anytime I think of Valentina's grandmother, a headache is inevitable.

We've been trying to track her down, *again*, to no avail. I have no doubt that she's involved in Valentina's kidnapping.

"Put the church on lockdown. Be discreet. We don't want there to be a panic."

Ezra jumps into action without question. Mikhail, however, lingers behind. "We need to be out there, Andrei, not chasing our tails in a fucking church."

I glower at him. Now is not the time to push boundaries. "As your *pakhan*, I'm ordering you to lock the fucking building down." I lean closer, our faces inches apart.

Lesser men would flinch.

Mikhail does not.

"Why?" His tone is layered, anguish reverberating beneath the indignation.

I draw as deep a breath as I can. Exhaling slowly, I sweep my gaze around the hall. People are starting to get curious. They're lurking in the corners. Watching from behind curtains. Whispering.

Scheming.

"We have an infestation." Removing my suit jacket and undoing my golden cuff links, I drop my jacket to the ground and slide the trinkets into my pocket. "It's time we remove some of the filth."

Mikhail's frustration quickly morphs into malicious delight. He's likely itching to spill some blood after what happened to our wife.

"No one will leave, *pakhan*. I'll make sure of it."

As he drifts off to help Ezra secure our new captives, I gaze out an old glass window. The outside world is distorted, and my heart seizes in my chest.

Nothing is right without my Valentina.

A woman screams from the chapel room, and people start pulling on the doors. They're already locked. No one's getting out until we've interrogated every single soul in this building.

We're getting our wife back.

I don't care how many sacrifices it takes.

She is ours.

The world will learn, or it will *burn*.

As I relocate to a balcony overlooking the wedding guests below, I gesture wide, catching the eyes of a few scared sheep below. *Rats* linger among them, and it's time to sniff them out.

"Let's begin, shall we?"

Valentina Baranova will ascend her throne in book two, *Reign of Four*. Read on Amazon and Kindle Unlimited.

Have you met Celia Monrovia's men yet?
Rage, Rebel, and Ruin are waiting for you.
(Don't read at work. This prequel is *full* of smut.)

BRUTAL BEAUTY

Three masked men claim my body. I never meant to give them my soul.

I've created the perfect life. Perfect image. Perfect career. Perfect home.

But when a masked man delivers an exclusive invitation to the most sought-after event in the city, I step out of my perfect world and enter theirs.

Rage. Rebel. Ruin. Three brothers who claim my body in front of a room of masked strangers.

My perfection cracks in their hands. They want more than the image I've created for myself - they want all of me.
The imperfections. The pain. The sorrow.

What I thought was one night of fun turns out to be a lifetime deal with three dangerous devils.

My soul is on offer, and they mean to collect no matter the price.

RUSSIAN TERMINOLOGY

Throughout the book, various Russian words and phrases are referenced. Here are their definitions.

Da: *yes*
Durak: *fool*
Pakhan: *leader of the Russian bratva*
Lisichka: *little fox*
Malyshka: *little girl or baby girl*
Moye ditya: *my child*
Moya prekrasnaya zhena: *my beautiful wife*
Moya zhena: *my wife*
Mudak: *Bastard/Asshole*
Muzh: *Husband*
Nyet: *No*
Shlyukha: *whore*
Suka: *bitch*
Vors: *captains*
Zhena: *wife*

Acknowledgments

This book is a work of the heart. I see pieces of Valentina within myself, and her journey of accepting who she is and who she loves resonates with me.

It's not always the life we planned.

It's not always the life our parents wanted for us.

But it's *ours.*

And that, dear reader, is what makes it *special.*

A huge, unending *thank you* goes to my good friend Angel for sticking with me throughout this journey. From first drafts to never-ending edits filled with tears and late nights chugging energy drinks, you've been my cheerleader, and I can't thank you enough.

We made it. Through a first draft, a six month break of not writing a single word, and an entire fucking *rewrite,* you've been here the entire time, cheering me on. Your support means more than I can ever say.

My husband is my forever muse, my rock, and my cock. *Thank you* for letting me spend hours at my laptop hammering out words, when we could have been watching *Buffy* or *Gilded Age* together. Without your support and unending belief in me, I'm not sure I would have the courage to believe in myself.

To my mother, who I hope is not reading this, thank you for reminding me that I can do anything I put my mind to.

And finally, a *monumental* thank you goes to my *Baranova Beta Babes*. Beth, Lou, Fiona, Lauren - all four of you have been a blessing when I needed it most, and your love for Valentina and her men helps me get through my hardest days writing. I can't say thank you enough.

To all my readers, I hope you've loved Ezra, Mikhail, and Andrei as much as I have. They've been a lot of fun to write, and it's only going to get *darker and dirtier* from here. Book two, *Reign of Four*, will finally have more group scenes and declarations of love. (And yes, Mikhail will finally have his turn.)

Stay tuned, babes.

We've got a wild ride ahead.

About the Author

Just a smut-lover listening to angsty love songs on repeat.

Misti Wilds loves watching characters pine after one another from afar--until a tall, dark, brooding alpha male says *fuck this* and claims his woman. But one man isn't enough these days-- Misti's got her hands full when it comes to writing multiple dark and delicious men with violence in their hearts and a declaration of love etched on the barrel of their guns.

Why choose one when you can have them all?

ALSO BY MISTI WILDS

Baranova Bratva:

Rule of Three

Reign of Four

Brutal Beauty

Claimed by Rage

Tempted to Rebel

Bound by Ruin

Broken Vows